THE KING OF RHYE

CRAIG MULHALL

Published in Australia by Sid Harta Books & Print Pty Ltd,
ABN: 34632585293
23 Stirling Crescent, Glen Waverley, Victoria 3150 Australia
Telephone: +61 3 9560 9920, Facsimile: +61 3 9545 1742
E-mail: author@sidharta.com.au

First published in Australia 2022
This edition published 2022

Cover design, typesetting: WorkingType (www.workingtype.com.au)

Mulhall, Craig
The King of Rhye
ISBN: 978-1-925707-73-1
pp512

ABOUT THE AUTHOR

Craig Mulhall is a Medical Oncologist from Queensland, Australia. He is also an active member of the Australian Society of Authors. The lure of writing fairy tales — and a staunch love of classic rock — drew him from his literary shell to pen his debut fantasy epic, 'The King of Rhye'.

Craig's varied publishing history includes the lyrics for two songs, 'A Tale of Rhye' and 'Long Live the King'. These tracks, recorded by French musicians Fat Bottomed Boys, were released on all major music streaming platforms in late 2021, and compliment 'The King of Rhye'.

By way of versatility, Craig has also produced a non-fiction medical treatise on the use of cytokine therapy for advanced cervical cancer, in 2014.

TABLE OF CONTENTS

PART BLACK

For Ebony

Who, with her love, enabled me to realise my dream.

&

For Ziggy

Without whom, I would have realised it faster.

UNNAMED ISLAND
THE EALING SEA
The Immortal Cliffs
PEAKS OF CIBELLIS
PEAKS OF LIGHT
AERGLO
MAGES PASS
WARNOM BORE
NEVERMORE
THE SEVENTH SEA
TWO WAY MIRROR MOUNTAIN
WINTERGARD
EYRIE
FENMARK HAUNTE
THE MELANCHOLY BLUE
VULTAN RANGE
the Greenway
TROUBLE IN THE WEST
TROUBLE IN THE EAST
NURTENAN
HALLS OF POX
BANWAH HAUNTE
BIJOU RIVER
BERTHELOT
Dragonfly Hollow
REED
PETRICHOR
Pass
PSITHUR GROVE
FLAXAE
KASH VALLEY
VERGE
IMPERIAL & WATERS
VIA
SOUR MILK SEA
GRANVENTIDER
SONTENAN
Dentate Coast
N
DUCK HOUSE
DUNES OF SORDD [ARTEGIA]
THE TRIDENT DEEP
THE CLEMENTINE SEA
RHYE
LUC HUDSON

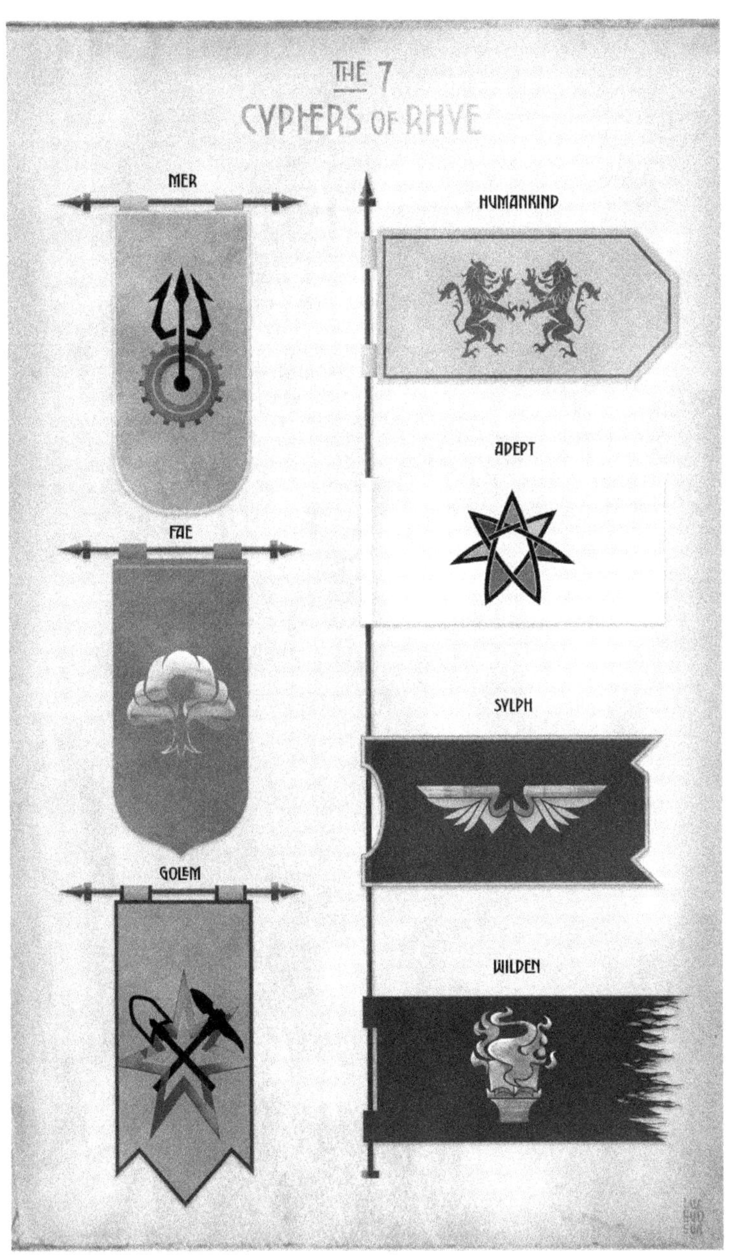
THE 7
CYPHERS OF RHYE
MER
HUMANKIND
ADEPT
FAE
SYLPH
GOLEM
WILDEN

PROLOGUE

AS IT BEGAN

With a name like Ackley James Fahrenheit, my fellows expected me to disappear into the tedious, black-and-white world of science.

Instead, I discovered fairies.

This may sound incredible enough, but the truth of the matter is much more profound. Making my discovery altered the fabric of life as I knew it, changing my perceptions of this strange world forever.

The journey began with fleeing my mind-numbing family and their expectations. I lived in the shadow of my great-great grandfather, that well-known pioneer of thermometry. Wealthy merchants and esteemed physicists followed in his genealogical footsteps, which sounded to me like a family curse.

'Music is my opium,' I told my father, with my travelling bag half packed. To this day, I am unsure which alarmed him more:

my disregard for family tradition, or the inference that I harboured a sinful habit.

I travelled the land, seeking a conservatorium that might have me. Far from finding the world my oyster, I encountered rejection at every turn. At last, penniless but not disillusioned, I fell in with a troupe of musicians. My proficiency at harpsichord and clavichord charmed them, while their promises of unplumbed wealth in the west fuelled my dreams.

As wandering troubadours, we crossed the Prussian frontier, all the way to the French coast. Soon, the white cliffs beckoned. I followed the troupe from one shore to the other.

From village to hamlet we travelled, while our once-bright faces grew long.

We did not find fame and fortune.

They found failure and anonymity.

I found Jenny.

The girl with copper-gold hair and a smile born of sunshine, who drank like a fish and danced like a carousel. She convinced me to drop the hapless vagabonds, declaring that my songs were the stuff of happiness, not fortune.

'Stay with me, Jimmy,' she said, using her pet-name for me. 'Good music and good company shall be all we ever need.'

In Brighton-Upon-Sea, our lives were simple but joyous. For a time, I eked out a humble living as a songwriter, for myself or for travelling minstrels on their way to the court of the Earl. We never had much, Jenny and I, though our hearts were full. Many nights at the hearth were spent with music by firelight.

Then came the winter that took poor Jenny away. She had always been fragile of health, reliant on fresh air and fair weather. This specific season was over foul, bringing with it a treacherous complaint of the chest.

My beloved succumbed, leaving me to continue alone.

My pauper's existence was never quite the same. Having little is somehow more tolerable when you share your meagre things with someone else. Staring at sparse cupboards by yourself is a whole new lesson in despair.

I ceased writing and making music. I could not completely remove myself from the arts that consumed me, though my creative mind grew barren. Instead, I turned to operating a simple shop, where I sold instruments and kept amongst the community I had come to love.

Music — my only remaining link to a world grown cold.

I thought I might spend the rest of my days in that fashion — keeping to myself, not causing a stir, not bothering with the thrill of adventure.

As I discovered, Fate is a capricious maiden.

My existential awakening came courtesy of a deranged old hermit, living in the wreck of a giant, seagoing vessel. A familiar landmark along the shoreline of Brighton-Upon-Sea, it dominated the daily route I took, via the promenade, to my place of business.

The hermit, Khashoggi, once garnered respect in the seaside community, as a young inventor of renown. Nearly fifty years prior, he unveiled to the world his then latest — and now most infamous — creation: an immense craft, which he built for travelling the stars.

Those were days of great derring-do and to-hell-with-the-consequences, long before bureaucracy stepped in and sanitised everything.

Considerable fanfare met the craft's unveiling, with plans announced to journey forth in search of new worlds. That relatively few people knew even how to fly then — let alone pilot a ship among the stars — was an inconsequential detail.

To travel the stars! What a novel, mind-boggling concept. Khashoggi possessed a drive surpassing that of any inventor I had known. He seemed certain of other worlds out there, other places simply waiting for us to reach out and touch them. His manic belief infected those around him, soon taking hold of the entire countryside. Ahead of the mission, circuses, festivals, and lantern-lit parades brought thousands from miles around. A quaint township became a bustling tourist magnet, for many a gay and curious soul.

At long last, the day came. Twenty brave individuals inserted themselves into the untested craft. Unbridled optimism spurred them on, along with a solemn, though misguided, sense of duty.

On a clear, crisp morning back in '39, surrounded by well-wishers, a brass band and every top hat in the city, the roar of engines and the spew of flame marked the passage of the craft up into the sky. The voyage would last one year. Then, the adventurers would return with news of far-flung places for the rest of us to marvel at.

In retrospect, the result was no surprise.

The star-craft did not return. Not after one year, nor after two. Initially, the public responded with shock and mourning for the twenty lost souls. In time, this morphed into malcontent and sinister threats, directed at Khashoggi. At first wide-eyed with incredulity — after all, how could such a spectacular failure be anticipated? — he soon began his long and tragic retreat from public life.

Years later, he re-emerged — raving, confronting passers-by, speaking loudly of some new calamity that faced the earth. Death and damnation laced his tongue, as he rambled about places and people known to nobody. He declared escape to be the only reprieve. To my eye, he only escaped arrest and commitment to the asylum upon the rocky headland. Instead, he banished himself to the dockyards (old and unused) and began constructing a whole new behemoth.

Over time, the framework of an enormous vessel took shape. Observers shook their heads in a 'not-this-again' kind of way, pity etched on their faces. After some months, however, construction suddenly ceased, not to be resumed. Had Khashoggi abandoned his latest endeavour? To the contrary: snooping townsfolk found that he had ensconced himself within the great ship. To all appearances, he did not intend to sail it anywhere. A fortuitous choice, as a sieve would be more seaworthy.

Finding themselves no longer subjected to his fanatical rants, the populace retreated as well, leaving Khashoggi to his steady descent into madness.

Then came the notable day on which Khashoggi imparted the following story to me. I often observed him on my morning commute, a haggard derelict of a man clambering about within the shadows of his ruin. Such a forlorn figure, cast adrift from the world, seeming to fade from it more and more with each passing month. Some days he would not appear at all, neither upon the deck nor through gaping holes in the hull of his creation, leaving me to wonder if he had died. Then, within a day or two, he would appear again, undertaking some erratic industry, which never brought the sea vessel any nearer to completion.

As best I could, I bypassed Khashoggi, hurrying along my way. I became my own kind of recluse, albeit more civilised. No rotting timbers or leaking holes spoiled my roof.

To begin with, he also ignored me. Just another shanty-dweller shuffling past his miserable hulk on the waterfront each day. In any regard, he had no reason to single me out, or care one jot for my existence.

Or perhaps he did.

One day, his wild, staring eyes alighted upon mine as I passed the hull of his wreck. The sheer force behind that gaze startled me, for it belied the wizened frame that carried him around. He straightened to his full height and his bearded jaw worked, as if to utter my damnation.

I continued, with cap pulled low.

The following day, to my horror and dismay, he raised a bony finger to beckon me. He must have recognised me, a regular commuter. I hurried onward to my shop, resolving to take a more circuitous route in future.

Fate or happenstance again intervened — I forgot my resolution. The third day took me along the promenade yet again. Perhaps it was the draw of the sea breeze, or the welcome sight of the ocean on my walk. By some fortune I found myself back in the shadow of Khashoggi's ship.

This time, our interaction sent chills through me. He called out to me ... by name.

'Mr Fahrenheit,' he said. I froze.

'Mr Fahrenheit,' he called again. I knew I had not imagined it. I turned and straight away his unhinged gaze drilled into me.

'I pray ... come aboard.'

The words carried a sense of calm and sobriety that I did not anticipate. Against my better judgement I responded. A few paces brought me to the edge of the crumbling dock.

He tossed a makeshift framework across the void and indicated that I should join him on his vessel. What compelled me to comply is something I question to the present moment. Perhaps the power in his stare, or the sudden parting of clouds I saw in them as he regarded me, stoked my courage, or banished my own sense of reason. Whatever the cause, that day I chose to set my business aside in favour of boarding a vessel that would never sail, to talk with a man that society had discarded.

Ensuring I stayed in daylight upon the visible part of the deck, I spoke with him.

'How do you know me?' I asked.

'How do you know me?' he parroted. Then I recognised his rhetorical question, intended as an answer. 'People talk,' he explained. 'I listen. The world murmurs and these ancient ears flap in the breeze. You work with musical instruments, do you not?'

'I ... I do, yes. Once upon a time, I wanted to be a bard.'

'We are one and the same,' he said. A point of connection. I found myself wanting to speak more with him.

On the surface, his conversation lacked the expected derangement. With a surprisingly firm voice for one so aged and wretched, he asked me about myself. I replied that I, a widower, operated a small business repairing musical instruments. This occupation brought a comfortable return, with the number of troubadours and other performance acts travelling through Brighton-Upon-Sea. I also admitted I knew of his past, having heard stories of his star-craft from the townsfolk.

That remark soured our exchange. For a moment silence ruled him, then his face took on the dark look of a sky filled with thunderheads.

Straight away, I knew my words to be a mistake.

'You know nought of my past,' he scoffed, 'if your greatest knowledge of it runs only to that day!'

'I beg pardon,' I stammered, taken aback by his outburst. 'Perhaps if you explain —'

'Explain! If only I had the time to explain! Yet what is time, but the space between places? I try to explain, but your frivolous ilk heed me not. You bustle about your lives, comfortable in the myth that all you see is all there is. Well, cast a glimpse inside this mind of mine, and see you do not run away in fear.

'Beneath another sun, this dockyard would cease to exist. In its place, a crystal sea I now know only in my dreams. Perhaps it is across the cold vastness of space? Perhaps it only ever dwelled in my slumbering mind? How is it, I know that land's peril so intimately?

'No. No! It is all real, though this petty world has buried the truth beneath a mass of ignorance and pride. Look not on this world and think that you have seen it all. You see nothing but your own doom. Do you hear me?' he cried, grasping my shoulders and giving a shake, with wiry strength made potent by his insanity. On and on went the crazed diatribe, though the thunder began to abate. I could see that he looked through me, to a place in the far distance.

'I hear you,' I replied, hoping the redundant words could placate him.

For a few moments he stood, swaying on his filthy, bare feet. Then, his hundred-yard gaze burned once again into focus. He teetered a few steps towards me, the flesh of his cheeks drawing back from neglected teeth like a rictus grin. 'I know that you can hear me, Fahrenheit,' he said. 'Do you believe in fairies?'

'No … I … I mean, I don't think so, no.'

'You should! Here, I have a fairy tale for you.' His insanity returned, full force. I cast about for means of defence, or escape. The framework he produced to help me on board had vanished. Chastising myself for fearing an ancient and emaciated man, I turned again to face Khashoggi. His expression, while still containing derision, also held something of true plaintiveness. He gestured for me to stay.

I found a sodden, damaged wooden box amongst the ruins. Lowering myself onto it like a seat, I looked up at Khashoggi, preparing to listen. The hermit looked favourably upon this and crouched across from me.

His gaze turned inward as he began to tell his fantastic tale. It was a tale of long-forgotten natural wonders; of terrifying beasts and mystical beings; of eldritch lore and tragic heroes; of a place in which doom and glory danced together in the lap of the ancient gods.

He told me the tale of Rhye.

It started with moonshine, a gilded axe, and a forsaken nut.

PART WHITE

CHAPTER 1

NIGHT'S NOON TIME

'There's nothing quite like some moonshine under the moonshine, am I right?'

Meadow spoke through an impish grin. He gave a jovial laugh and took a swig from the bottle in his fist. Meadow's libertine parents had named him after his place of conception — a popular practice among pixies.

'Hey, save some for me!' said Dique, the pixie to Meadow's left. He took the bottle from Meadow and sipped, while watching a shooting star dash across the cosmos.

In total, four associates sat in a loose huddle on the knoll. Their favoured spot overlooked a silvery glade, into which a growing crowd of shadowy forms filtered. With nefarious intent, the foursome observed the procession of creatures below them.

Meadow and Dique kept eclectic company. Beside them sat an altogether different creature. He appeared as a dragonfly, which indeed he was. Few dragonflies owned names, though this one called himself Herald, in deference to his beloved trumpet, which lay on the grass beside him. Upon meeting the dragonfly, Meadow misheard the name as *Harold* — and the altered moniker stuck.

Harold did not drink. Instead, he stood, stretching his insectile legs, revealing himself as the tallest of the group.

'Midnight is not far off,' observed the dragonfly. His eyes darted about, taking in the new moon, the surrounding forest and the steady stream of creatures entering the space from every direction. 'You might want to show that bottle some mercy.'

'Mercy, schmercy,' said Meadow, grinning. 'We're going to need some fire in the belly for this jaunt, I would say.'

'I'm only suggesting you keep your wits about you.'

Meadow pantomimed the dragonfly's lecture in mocking fashion and grabbed the bottle back from Dique. 'What about you, Mustapha? Need a drink?'

The fourth companion absorbed this exchange in silence, waving the bottle away with a shake of his head. Mustapha sat with long legs drawn up, chin resting on his knees. From beneath a dark curtain of hair, his pensive gaze fell upon the growing assembly.

Mustapha's summons, the previous day, brought the group to this glade, deep in the forest of Petrichor. A grand heist required trustworthy co-conspirators.

He watched as dozens of creatures emerged from the trees, in pairs and small groups. Couples. Families. Making their way to random places within the glade, leaving a vague, circular clearing at the centre. Striving to contain their usual, boisterous natures; stifling the urge to dance or skip their way into the natural arena. Sprinkled amongst the crowd were other races, from within Petrichor and beyond its leafy borders — satyrs, dryads, and emissaries from the Realms of sylphs and humans.

Mustapha sniffed. How many of these convivial creatures truly knew the peril that lurked beyond their quaint neighbourhoods? Would any of them stand a chance against the promised tide of chaos and sickness? They all knew the Song. Did they heed it, or take it for granted?

My head will attract a bounty, for what I am about to do.

It must be done, all the same.

She depends on me.

Finally, Mustapha nudged Meadow and raised a slender finger towards the activity below. 'Look,' he said. Meadow looked.

One figure, entering the glade, stood out from the others. He carried himself with pompousness, strutting through the crowd, giving barely a nod or a tip of the hat. His robes spoke of overwrought splendour and strained to enclose his rotund form. In short, he looked like an overstuffed peacock.

'That's the Mayor, isn't it?' asked Meadow.

'It is, dear,' Mustapha said. 'The Mayor of Petrichor. Funny — for an eminent politician, he has an elegant disregard for the laws of his own Realm.' The foursome watched as the Mayor drew an elaborate pipe from his coat, stuffed it with tobacco and lit it with a snap of his fingers. The Fae Sovereigns outlawed the lighting of fires, with some fantastic punishments on offer.

The Mayor's office oversaw administration of the Forest Realm. This enabled the King and Queen of the Fae Folk to focus their energies on conservation and mystical lore, to protect and nurture all who lived there.

The Mayor's shiftiness made him unpopular.

'Have we bought him?' said Dique, setting aside the bottle.

Mustapha shook his head. 'Not a chance. We'd have a beastly time trying to scrape together enough just to interest him. Even then, he'd likely toss us in a jail tree anyhow. You two might have to neutralise him if he intervenes when things get rowdy.'

Meadow sighed. 'I can't help but think this plan of yours is a little ... complicated. All for what, a blasted nut?'

'Nonsense. The crowd will do much of the hard work for us if this plays out correctly. And no,' Mustapha added, 'I'm not interested in nuts. It's the Apothecary I'm after.'

'You did mention that. What's he got of any interest?'

Mustapha's keen eyes shone as he stared at the swelling crowd below. 'I intend to steal the —'

'Gentlemen! Observe,' Harold interjected with a hiss.

Notables arrived, threading through the hushed night assembly to pick out their own vantage points. First sauntered the Ploughman, a wealthy industrialist. His agricultural empire occupied vast tracts of land just beyond the borders of Petrichor. The Ploughman's farms provided a well-established food bowl for much of civilised Rhye. As a primary producer, this gruff bull of a man threw his considerable weight behind new technology. Needing more efficient ways to manage his enormous crops, the Ploughman turned to building strange contrivances, unlike anything else seen in the land.

The Ploughman's habit of clearing trees to sew corn, sorghum and maize did not bode well with the arbour-loving creatures of Petrichor. To overcome this, he became a high-level sponsor to the Mayor.

Alongside the Ploughman came his son. Both lumbered through the crowd, looking fit to brawl with whoever stood in their way. Ploughman and Mayor exchanged conspiratorial smiles as they took up their positions.

Next, from the opposite side of the clearing, strode a figure for whom the crowds parted: Benjulius, the Archimage, Lord of the Adept.

The coven of Adept lived in a sanctuary called Aerglo, so far away that few Fae had ever been there. The secretive Adept spent their lives in study and contemplation, honing their craft in a variety of Disciplines. A schoolyard poem identified them by the colour of their attire.

THE WEARERS
Brown are Neophytes, apprentices of highest potential.
Gold are Elementals, towards nature and beast deferential.
Green are Apothecaries, brewing elixirs for wellness and health.
Sky Blue are Sorcerers, casting charms for fortune and wealth.
Deep Blue are Astrologers, reading omens in the stars.
Violet are Warlocks, indomitable fighters of wars.
Black were Necromancers, who ... [erased from record and memory]
Scarlet are Mages, many Disciplines conquered with grace.
White is the Archimage, Lord of the Adept, first of his race.

Benjulius carried himself so fluidly, his feet may not have touched the ground. His boots stayed concealed beneath his billowing white cloak. An Apothecary, dressed in robes as verdant as the forest, accompanied him.

Mustapha shifted on his haunches. He still hugged his knees, gazing out from under his dark, shaggy hair, eyes fixed upon the Wearer of Green.

The Adept paused near the edge of the clearing, standing together.

Following behind the Adept came four more figures, representing the four Guilds of Rhye: Defence, Exploration, Construction and Craft. A soldier, a sailor, a tinker, and a tailor walked in unison to a predetermined place by the clearing.

The quartet carried an air that made Harold uneasy. 'Does

anybody else think the Guild representatives look a little stiff?'

'It makes sense that the soldier and sailor would have a military bearing,' Mustapha observed, 'but you're right — they all look cut from the same cloth. We'd best keep an eye on them.'

The procession continued, until the usually quiet glade thrummed with would-be spectators.

All creatures, from their many walks of life, assembled to witness the ceremonial cracking of a chestnut. This event celebrated the commissioning of a new chariot, to carry Titania, Queen of the Fae. No ordinary chestnut sufficed, but the first cultivated from an ancient tree by the shores of the Granventide River. It would be cleaved by a single downstroke with a gilt-edged axe, at the fall of midnight, under the new moon.

'Shall we run through this one last time?' murmured Dique. The allotted hour drew near.

'The Apothecary has what I require,' said Mustapha. 'This whole circus is the distraction I need to get close to him.'

'You're going to pick his pocket?' asked Meadow. 'What's in it?'

'You'll see.'

'I mean ... what's in it for us?'

'You'll see.'

'Is that all you're going to say?'

'It's precious and very valuable. I'll ensure you're compensated for your efforts.' Mustapha unfolded himself, stretched like a languid cat and rose to his feet.

'What if we die?'

'I'm counting on you not to. This is it! Harold, you're up first. You're the tinder to set the whole thing alight.'

Harold executed a brief bow. He gripped his trumpet in tight pincers.

'Meadow and Dique,' Mustapha continued, 'you are running

interference. We all know how much you love a little mayhem — I want to see your best. You should be able to gain help from — ah! There he is. That's our man coming now.' Again, he pointed towards the assembly. Following his finger, the others identified an unassuming human in the crowd.

'You bribed that man to help us?' said Harold, dismayed.

'I did,' Mustapha confirmed, grinning. 'His name is Will. He's very handy and he's just the man for the job.'

At that moment, the man named Will spotted Mustapha and his friends on the knoll and gave a surreptitious half-wave.

'He reminds me of that bloke you brought in on our last great shenanigans,' said Meadow.

'One and the same.'

'How much did you pay him?'

'Never you mind. More importantly, he's motivated. Will is a farmer, you see. He's poor. Still uses horses to drag his wagons to market. He's also likely to lose his livelihood if the Ploughman keeps his monopoly, with all of these "machines" that work his fields. I told Will that we'd be able to save his farm if he helps us.'

'Is that true, Mustapha?'

'I hope so.' Dique shrugged. He stared at the crowd gathered for an imminent spectacle.

'Speaking of people with axes for grinding,' said Harold, 'here come our star attractions.'

As one, the companions turned to see a lithe, athletic pixie, taller even than Harold. He held the look of an outdoorsman, with an assured stride. Across his back, he carried an ornate weapon — a long-handled axe which glinted beneath the moonlight. The sight of this pixie, along with his weapon, drew an anticipatory gasp from the assembly. This was the nutcracker — or, as everyone knew him, the Fairy Feller.

Under his arm, the Feller held *the* chestnut, gourd-sized and golden brown. As the Feller reached the centre of the clearing, he set the chestnut down on a plinth of bare stone. Front row onlookers hemmed him in. None stood too close, except for the ostler from the Oak & Barrel Inn, who hovered nearby and offered up a dumb grin to the Feller.

At last, the Lord and Lady of Petrichor appeared — the Fae Sovereigns, Oberon and Titania. Oberon's antlered crown commanded the crowd's attention, while Titania's ceremonial gown flowed out like dark wine behind her. In her wake followed a squat, old woman with a stern and officious face, which she kept trained on the royal couple.

The arrival of Oberon and Titania yielded reverent cheering and applause.

In the closing moments before midnight, serenity descended on the scene. Hundreds of creatures all stood, or sat, or hovered, in tenterhooks. The Archimage Benjulius positioned himself in a direct line of sight with the Feller, to indicate the exact moment for the stroke. The Feller unslung his weapon. He hefted it, gauging its weight. Onlookers crept a fraction closer.

'This is it, then,' Meadow whispered to his companions. 'It's been a pleasure knowing you.'

'See you at the rendezvous,' Dique said. The two pixies drifted into the crowd.

'Good luck,' offered Harold, raising his trumpet. His focused gaze darted between Benjulius and the Feller.

Mustapha said nothing. He began moving too, though his eyes remained fixed on the Apothecary.

The Archimage glanced at the skies above, then back to the Feller. Recognising the sign, the Feller held the mighty axe poised over his head and waited.

And waited.

Then, many things happened, almost at once.

At the fall of midnight, the Archimage enacted a sharp motion with his hands.

The Feller began his mighty downstroke.

The sudden blare of a horn, dire and clear, tore through the still of the night.

The stroke was wide; it clipped the nut, which ricocheted off the plinth.

There was a thud and a moan, as the ostler took a rogue chestnut to the face.

Voices clamoured, a burble of noise.

'The Feller missed!'

'What was that sound?'

'Danger! Fire! Emergency! Help!'

'The Fairy Feller missed!'

Pandemonium broke. The veneer of civility shattered, with frenetic cries and movement churning through the tranquil forest setting.

The trumpet's cry still faded. Some creatures turned their heads towards the source of the noise and caught sight of the dragonfly on the knoll. Many others thought it signalled an unseen threat and scrambled, climbing over one another to evacuate the glade.

A few spectators were not so readily distracted. Benjulius and his Apothecary stood firm, absorbing the scene. The Mayor glared over the heads of smaller creatures and waved a pudgy hand in Harold's direction. 'There! That creature must be apprehended! Disrupting a regal ceremony!'

The Ploughman and his son needed no encouragement. As Harold made a show of sidling away through the crowd, they waded amongst the sea of panicked pixies towards him. The Mayor followed close behind.

The Fairy Feller attempted to revive the downed ostler. The strange old harridan, who attended Oberon and Titania, ushered the Sovereigns towards the rim of the glade. Still, denizens of Petrichor dashed this way and that. Harold, relishing his role, issued another blast from his trumpet. He had been spotted, leaving little need for discretion. A wailing dirge became, within a few bars, a comical fanfare.

Mustapha grinned widely as he snaked through the evacuees. The crowd grew thin — he needed to make his way closer to the green-clad Apothecary.

At that moment, Meadow and Dique barrelled into view. The pixies flailed about and ran through the crowd, shouting panicked nonsense. Meadow careened headlong into the Archimage himself and somehow made it look like an accident. A gap came between Benjulius and the Apothecary, into which numerous creatures spilled. Mustapha nudged closer and prepared to make his move.

Across the glade, the Ploughman dove towards Harold. He fixed a meaty paw around the dragonfly's leg, as Harold made a late attempt to fly away. All was not lost: Will, the wagoner, appeared at close quarters. He stomped on the Ploughman's wrist, pinning him down. Then came a crushing blow to the industrialist's left temple. The Ploughman bellowed like an elephant. He remained conscious, but let go of Harold, who escaped into the air. The ploughboy leaped to defend his father and Will soon found his hands full.

All around, magnificent confusion reigned.

The pixies managed to corral the Apothecary closer and closer to Mustapha's position. With their help, he could reach out and touch the green cloak. The Apothecary had his head turned — he sought to get back alongside the Archimage.

Mustapha's one opportunity.

In a blink, the deed was done; a brush of cloak, a searching hand and out came a small, polished object. With the practiced hand of a serial thief, Mustapha obtained his prize. For an instant, he exposed it to the moonlight, to be sure of his success. He had it: a glistening stone of deepest vermillion. He wondered not how, or why it came to be within the Apothecary's robe. He knew only that he had to get it away from here, to the woman who sent him for it.

Mustapha stuffed the gem inside his own jacket.

He snatched a glance at his target ... and recoiled.

The Apothecary faced him, glaring. 'No!' cried the Adept. A green-cloaked arm reached out to grab the wily thief.

Mustapha ducked, spun away, and dashed for the tree line.

Bruised and bloodied, the Ploughman and his boy stood, labouring for breath. At their feet lay their victim. The strapping young man proved a bold fighter, though in the end, he lay maimed and still.

'Wasted himself over a dragonfly,' said the ploughboy, unsure whether the stricken wagoner was alive or dead.

'Threw his life away,' agreed the Ploughman. He wiped his bloody nose on a sleeve and cleaned it on the fallen man's shirt. Shaking their heads at the disarray, the two ambled off into the forest.

They spared no thought for the dragonfly, who had gotten away.

Throughout their performance, Meadow and Dique never lost sight of Mustapha. Seeing him secure his prize, they adjusted their erratic course, heading for the gloom of the forest. They stayed close behind him.

The Guild retinue also saw Mustapha at his task. As one, they snapped to attention the moment the thief held his prize. Falling into step together, they swooped upon his exit route, knocking aside pixies and fairies in their path.

Mustapha's eyes were everywhere. Silver moonlight limned the forest of Petrichor, though gnarled tree roots and low branches still made speed hazardous. He fled as fast as he dared, jet black hair streaming behind him. Leaves swirled from the forest floor in his wake.

He caught sight of pursuers on his heels. 'Blast!' he cried. He weaved through the trees, hoping to gain ground, while searching for a place to hide. To the east lay a Fae village. The soft glow of lanterns beckoned from a far-off clearing. Instead, he veered south, keeping to mottled shadows.

The pursuers did not relent. Mustapha wondered at their ability to keep up with him. He risked another glance over his shoulder … and felt the cold chill of fear.

No longer did four Guildsmen tail him.

The four pursuers were transformed, clad in robes of violet. They glided through the thick woodland, narrowing Mustapha's advantage with sickening speed.

Warlocks. The enforcers of the Adept.

Mustapha uttered a cry and hurried onward, gasping. It made sense now. Benjulius and his Apothecary brought a security detail, in disguise … and Mustapha slinked right into it.

Thwarted!

He considered abandoning his prize. A coin-sized gem, perfect and brilliant, nestled within his jacket. A piece of cinnabar. What could the Adept want it for? No matter. His sponsor's cause would trump all.

What would she say, if he lost it? The entire operation, a failure.

He had no chance to hide it. The Warlocks shadowed him.

In wild desperation, he fished the cinnabar from his clothes and swallowed it.

The stone burned Mustapha's throat. He grimaced. Try as they may, the Warlocks would not discover the gem on him.

A small consolation.

Violet robes crowded at his back, reaching with clawed hands.

Then, with an instant to spare, salvation arrived.

A shadow zoomed between the trees, flying at breakneck speed to overtake the Warlocks. A cigar-shaped body, spindly limbs and wings whirring too fast for the eye to follow.

Harold zipped over the top of Mustapha and bobbed to grab him with his rear feet. A second later, he flew up and away.

The Wearers of Violet made no sound as the fugitives escaped beyond the treetops.

Moments later, Meadow and Dique clattered through the trees to the spot where Harold snatched Mustapha into the skies. The signs of his passage stopped here — they had missed seeing his rescue. No sound could be heard, but the calls of night birds.

'We lost them!' puffed Dique. He crouched with hands on his knees.

'Do you think?' said Meadow. 'Did you see the mob following Mustapha though?'

'Warlocks? I can't say I've ever seen a real-life Warlock before.'

'I don't think anyone has. Not lately. Which way do you think they went?'

'We stayed here, waiting for you,' remarked a third voice.

Both pixies spun to face the sound. From out of the darkness emerged a tall form, clad in violet. A hood threw shadow over the Warlock's face.

'You'll be coming with us, back to the Fairy King,' said a chilling voice from behind them. Another Warlock.

Two more appeared, hemming the pixies in from all sides.

'I'll take that mercy now,' mumbled Dique.

Harold's flightpath angled north, back towards the fairy village. From this height, it appeared as a haven of glowing lights, quaint cottages, and interconnected treehouses. The communities of Fae Folk were lively at all hours.

Mustapha whooped with jubilation. 'That's how you hatch a jewel heist!'

'As you and I both know, most of that was unplanned,' said Harold.

'Don't spoil the fun,' laughed the thief.

'What about the others?'

'They were right behind me. They'll find their way to the rendezvous, I'm sure.'

'You're sure?'

'I'm sure.'

Harold still clutched his trumpet, dangling Mustapha hang-glider-style below him.

They soon alighted upon the streets of Flaxae, a village deep within the heart of Petrichor. The streets — clearings between the trunks of nearby trees, with shabby dwellings of clay and bark shingle all about — were busy with late-night revellers. Pixies and satyrs spilled out of numerous ale houses, roaring drinking songs and clashing together horns full of mead and drowseberry wine. None took exceptional notice of a dragonfly and his companion, arriving from out of the indigo sky.

Juniper Juice, a popular drinking establishment, sat nearby. Behind it, a leafy alley served as the team's rendezvous point.

Harold and Mustapha headed for it, anticipating a celebratory mug of ale.

In contrast to the din issuing from Juniper Juice, the alley offered a quiet retreat. Overhanging foliage admitted little moonlight, so the companions edged their way in dim shadow.

Ahead, they saw they were not alone.

'That's not Meadow, or Dique,' said Mustapha.

A short woman stood in the centre of the passage, ten or fifteen paces ahead of them. She wore a cloak about her shoulders and a tall hat — typical pixie attire.

The companions approached warily.

'Who are you?' asked Harold, giving no introductions.

The woman snapped her fingers, setting her hand alight. The fire seemed not to injure her.

The companions could now see her more clearly.

Harold wore a puzzled look, while Mustapha set his mouth in a grim line. The woman looked familiar — the strange harridan, who accompanied Oberon and Titania to watch the Fairy Feller's ultimate failure.

'Who are you,' Harold repeated, 'and how did you get here before us?'

The woman ignored the question, addressing Mustapha instead. 'Did you get it?' she asked in a kindly voice that did not match her wizened appearance.

'I did,' replied Mustapha. He stood, motionless, making no move to come nearer to the woman. His insides churned. He felt a wave of nausea.

The woman smiled. A reassuring smile, the kind grandmothers give, along with a hug and a glass of milk.

'Is someone going to explain what is happening here?' said Harold.

Mustapha turned to him, beads of sweat above his brow. 'I'm sorry. I didn't tell you everything on this one. In case any of us got caught — the less you knew, the better. Do you understand?'

'No. Not really …' Harold began, distracted by the transformation taking place before him.

Ahead in the alleyway, the harridan grew taller. Not only that: she was growing thinner.

And younger.

And more beautiful.

And ever more powerful.

In a few moments, the woman who stood before Harold and Mustapha resembled in no way the woman from the glade. Tall and sinuous, she had lustrous ebony hair that ran in rivulets to her shoulders. Her pixie attire had vanished, in its place an elaborate gown of scarlet and black with delicate gold detail about the bodice.

'I … ah …' mumbled Harold.

Mustapha took a knee. 'My Lady.'

'Stand, Mustapha. You have done very well.'

Mustapha stood, unsteady on his feet. 'Lady Belladonna,' he explained to Harold. 'Consort of Lord Rogar, Lady of the House of Giltenan.'

Harold bowed his head. 'You stole from Lord Oberon for a human?' he exclaimed, out of the corner of his mouth.

Mustapha gave a glum nod, light-headed. His belly felt like a storm-ravaged ocean. Before him, the form of Belladonna drifted in and out of focus.

'My Lady,' Harold said to the shape-shifter, 'forgive me. Much has happened tonight, and I am left short of explanation. I don't know who you are, though you are clearly a being of power. Perhaps you can help us. Do you know of our friends' whereabouts?'

'I do not, though they best have a keen eye and a fleet foot,'

Belladonna replied. 'Many strange and powerful creatures are about in the great forest tonight. Then again, perhaps it is best your friends are apprehended. I am sure your Lord would like a word with them ... and with you, as well.'

Alarm twisted Harold's features. He spun back to Mustapha, who looked pale. His wide pupils stared towards Belladonna, as if through glass.

'You don't want to be here,' said Mustapha to the dragonfly.

Belladonna peered at her charge. 'Mustapha, will you show it to me?'

Mustapha did not respond right away. Rallying his remaining strength, he snarled at Harold. 'Get out of here! This is not your business any longer.'

Harold hovered above the ground, neither leaving, nor staying.

'Mustapha? The cinnabar?' came the sweet lilt of Lady Belladonna. There was a note of insistence in it.

Mustapha's skin was slick. His vision swam. His head dropped to his chest, where he was able to contemplate his belly ... and the precious gem within.

He realised his error.

Too late. His fragile balance shifted. A roar sounded in Mustapha's ears and the ground rose to strike him.

All turned to black.

CHAPTER 2

I HAVE STOLEN

Lub-dup-lub-dup-lub-dup-lub-dup-lub-dup …

His heart pounded like a jungle drum in a tempest.

A violent wind whipped around him — a zephyr, caught in the slipstream.

The land rolled on below, vast and unreachable. A crimson fog enshrouded all, though bursts of wild lightning revealed mountain ranges and yawning chasms. Above the tumult, the thrum of his belaboured pulse roared in his ears.

Lub-dup-lub-dup-lub-dup-lub-dup …

Hot wind thrilled his hair. With sickening speed, he was propelled beyond the peaks, rushing headlong through the gloom. The shadows suggested a forest now. A place he knew. Oberon's Yew flung its ancient branches skyward. Dragonfly Hollow nestled by the bank of the Bijou. His playground of youth. He flew over it, an observer to its wonders and its perils. So near and yet so far.

The forests of Petrichor dissolved. Next, through the swirling mists, he could see figures, but not make them out. Faraway voices reached him — voices he recognised.

You are welcome here, though you do not belong.

Titania ...? Shadows flickered behind impenetrable mist. Her tone suggested both a warm hug and a stately decree. Though the diminutive Queen showed him a kind of love, he never connected with her in a maternal way. 'Mab', as he knew her, made no effort to hide his foster status. Her words echoed, then faded in his mind.

Snuffed like a mote of flame, the Fairy Queen vanished.

I am your mother now. The only one you will ever need.

A different voice this time. Honey on the edge of a knife. Those words were seared into his mind. Baffled him since the day they were uttered. In a primal sense, he did need her, even from the early days. It was a need that only grew as time passed, swelling to fill the recesses of his psyche. She, too, needed him and made no mystery of it. Her need made him feel courageous and just. He revelled in it.

The dryads will know ... they always know. But you must take it and run. My work depends on it. For a Cure.

With these words in his ear he had stolen, time and again, for her. With a song in his heart, he stole for her, because she needed him ... and because her work would save Rhye one day.

The pressure of it made him sweat. A sheen coated him, beading on his skin in those small hours, when he lurked and crept and ran fleet of foot through the night, carrying out her crucial errands without a second thought.

Adrenaline surged within him and still his heart raced.

Lub-dup-lub-dup-lub-dup ...

Of course, the dryads knew. Though they could not catch him, they could still condemn him. Oberon raged; Mab retreated into a shell of bitter disappointment. The illusion of a safe haven, shattered in the face of one risk too many.

For stealing the precious chattels of the Fairy King, Fae Folk were put to death. Yet she — Belladonna — saved his life, pleading for exile. She would be his sponsor.

Her manner persuaded even the staunch Lord Oberon. They left Petrichor together — the thief and his saviour. She continued her work and he stayed beside her, indebted to her.

An incongruous new rhythm cut across the toiling hammer of Mustapha's heartbeat. An insistent knocking that seemed far off. Alongside it, a wailing akin to either torture or passion. Mustapha knew not which.

As he felt neither pleasure nor pain, he shrugged it off, fighting his way out of a nightmare.

The sweat ran, rancid and hot, glistening on his skin. The adrenaline nauseated him. The tempest raged within, a fever soon to break like the crash of thunder.

Below him rushed the unbridled wilderness of a seascape. The roil of granite-coloured waves crested and fell, sending bitter spray up into the air. Mustapha's breakneck flight slowed, and he dropped toward the waves. Try as he may to stay aloft, he descended, feeling the salt spray on his skin. The sea's hungry maw rose to engulf him.

His nerves shouted, with the sudden cold of submersion. Icy shock snatched the breath from him in a torrent of bubbles. Down he went.

He thought it impossible to sink so fast. The sea dragged him down. Though his limbs thrashed, no amount of fight could prevent him from sinking further below the turbulent waves.

Am I awake? Or do I dream still?

Down he spiralled, into darkness and cold. A place with no air. The deepest chasm in the deepest of the Seven Seas would be his tomb. Flashes of silver shone around him — schools of large salmon swam in nonchalant circles, watching his hapless descent in silence.

He shouted. Only a final surge of bubbles ripped from his throat.

Lub-dup ... lub-dup ... lub-dup ...

Below, a light glowed. A pale crescent of sand, far, far from the surface, emerged from the alien darkness. He fell — no, drifted — down towards it.

The sand stirred little beneath the weight of so much water above. Yet there was something else there — something Mustapha did not expect to see, either in his real world or in this dreamlike state.

A man stood upon the sand.

The figure wore only a cloth about his loins. He stood barefoot, surrounded by a strange assortment of great armour plates, made of stone, or perhaps crystal. Amongst the shards lay giant metal fastenings; the whole assembly lay shattered. He held his muscular form with militaristic poise. Lank, auburn hair floated about his visage, buoyed by the vague current at the ocean floor.

His ageless face regarded Mustapha. As Mustapha floated down, the man fixed upon him the fiery eyes of a savage. Like a tractor beam, those eyes drew him close. Mustapha came within arms' reach, though the figure made no move towards him. In a moment, they stood scant inches apart upon the sandy floor, the deep gloom a tremendous cavern all around them.

The figure's eyes blazed with ire, from a place far within him. Mustapha knew that gaze. He saw that carven face almost every day of his life. Still, he did not expect to see it now. Not like this. Rather than race, his heart slowed, almost to a standstill.

Lub-dup ...

The man's lips moved. White teeth flashed. In his mind, Mustapha heard him speak. A voice like lava.

'You! You will help me live forever.' The man gave a cruel, horrible laugh.

What? Who ...? Mustapha could only stare, face taut with shock.

'Do not seek to defy me,' said the molten voice. 'I am the very essence of the land's horror. I am War. I bring with me Death and the inevitable End, for all to witness in their last misery. Do not speak! You are of no consequence. One small gnat like you I would crush beneath my thumb. This I will do, should you not fulfil the task I give you.

'Kill the one you love. Then you will find Death, waiting at the end of the earth.'

As his heart stopped, Mustapha screamed.

The scream awoke him.

The harrowing voice and cryptic words rang in his brain as he threw himself upright, chest heaving for air.

Lub-dup-lub-dup-lub-dup ... lub-dup ... lub-dup ...

Mustapha sat in bed. As the fog lifted, he recognised the bed as his own.

Beneath the sheet, his naked form ran with sweat. He blinked, wiping moisture from his eyes.

The familiar small, tidy annexure greeted him. A soft glow emanated from luminous stones embedded in the walls — an enchanted mineral known throughout the land as *scrallin*.

On a low table beside the bed sat a half-full basin and a poultice. Beside it, a knife with a thin, tapered blade. He recognised this, too, though he did not remember removing it from the hutch of his personal effects at the rear of the annexe.

What do I remember? He eased back the sheet, performing an inventory of limbs and digits. Perspiration dampened his brow and an ache drummed at his temples. The throb of his pulse subsided. His nightmare vision had triggered a spasm of violence in his chest. Ill ease gripped his stomach and he remembered — he swallowed the cinnabar.

All for nothing, he surmised. *Unless I can pass it in a couple of days.*

Mustapha reached for the knife and returned it to a concealed hutch behind his bedhead. Only one other item lay within the space — an elegant, long-barrelled pistol. The sight of the firearm nauseated him, for it spoke of a new Rhye, where blades and sorcery no longer cast the greatest shadows in battle. Outside the Realm of Humankind, few understood the new technology, which brought neither art nor lore. An honourless death of bullets.

He kept the pistol for insurance only.

The annexe could only contain a sleeping pallet, a trunk of clothes, a washbasin — which he now used to rinse away the grime of his fever — and a humble shrine, tucked in one corner. Despite its bare aesthetic, the annexe held greater opulence than any other place Mustapha called 'home' in recent times.

His Lady expected a fastidious living environment. He lived for her approval.

Mustapha shuffled past the shrine, regarding it for a moment. Twelve ornate alabaster figurines, each the size of an adult fist, adorned a makeshift altar. Through blind eyes they stared back at him, challenging him to walk past without acknowledging them. Unlit tapers stood amongst the figures. A ragged mat lay upon the bare stone floor. Finding a thin robe to throw over his shoulders, he passed through a curtained opening, into a much larger room.

Rose-red light suffused the entire space. Here too, luminous scrallin stones fitted, at intervals, into the walls of the chamber. Mustapha saw he was alone. The soft lilt of a stringed instrument reached his ears from somewhere beyond sight, while his nostrils detected the intermingled scents of gardenia, amber and woodsmoke.

Discerning taste appointed every corner. Restraint and extravagance, by equal measure, fought for dominion in the palatial apartment.

A vast bed of carved oak provided a commanding centrepiece. In direct contrast to the rest of the apartment, the bedclothes were tossed about, as though by a cyclone. Fine linen and an embroidered duvet, swirled and bunched like dark ocean waves, lay bundled against a great leather-bound trunk by the foot of the bed.

Other examples of bespoke carpentry furnished the room, in a manner fit for entertaining guests. Table and chairs stood in perfect alignment.

On the wall above the bed, dozens of ornaments stood as decorative soldiers upon a series of shelves. Some were vials and bottles, others were boxes. Many shone or glistened, reflecting the ambient glow of the room. They were all placed in a deliberate way — a display of trophies.

Mustapha knew every item, for he had procured them all.

An imposing wardrobe, a low dresser and a sleek cabinet completed the furnished space. The cabinet contained chalices, goblets and a selection of wine, ardent spirits, and other inebriants of which his Lady was partial. Beyond the cabinet, a small door taunted Mustapha. The forbidden room, the one in which she performed her most important work. The door remained locked in her absence, using a device that defied his attempts to pick it.

Ten paces took him across parquetry to the fourth, outer wall of the apartment. A double door and generous balcony provided a view of the world beyond.

Fresh air. He stepped outside.

Predawn light bathed the scene. The western wall of the House of Giltenan met his gaze. It stretched away from him on either side in a vast semicircle, punctuated by dozens of windows, balustrades, and terraces. The House, a masterwork of stone, suited the benevolent Sovereign of Humankind.

The semicircle contained a courtyard. One of the most beautiful spaces in all Sontenan, the courtyard boasted manicured gardens, aviaries, and a handsome stone mausoleum at the southern end. Inside the mausoleum — and beneath the lush grounds of the courtyard — ninety generations of the Giltenan clan found their eternal rest.

He leaned against the balustrade. What of Harold? The pixies? His friends' unknown plight weighed upon his heart, as heavy as his own predicament.

What of poor, darling Will? The sturdy Sontenean channelled the rage of the downtrodden into his brawling. A gallant display of resistance ... rewarded with a pummelling.

I left him in the dirt!

Nausea gripped Mustapha's insides, a noxious blend of guilt and poison. Somewhere within him, the cinnabar burned. Bilious pain and the urge to vomit came in waves. Steadying himself against the stone, he slowed his breathing and let his eyes drift from the gilded cages at the northern boundary, across the verdant gardens to the squat edifice of the mausoleum.

Something about the scene struck him as unusual. Before his delirious mind could pinpoint it, he detected a new sensation: the fragrance of cinnamon and burnt amber. The scent of rare tobacco, farmed by villagers along the south coast.

Only one woman smelled like that. He turned and stepped inside.

The Lady who sashayed across the apartment towards him bore

no resemblance to the prudish harridan from the Ceremony of the Nut. She now appeared in a form he knew intimately.

'My Lady ...' *Belladonna.*

'Mustapha. We are alone. You may address me informally.'

He sank to one knee, biting back on the name she encouraged in private. 'You've acquired a new skill.'

She smiled, a delicate curve of lips that conveyed her satisfaction. Behind Juniper Juice, before his bewildered eyes, she had transformed from an old hag into a veritable lioness.

She brought a cigarette to her lips for a moment, before exhaling a purple cloud.

'My talents grow!' she said. 'First translocation, now transfiguration. This hobby of sorcery is paying useful dividends. Naturally my dear, I owe much of that to you.' With languid strides, she reached the settee and arranged herself upon it. She gestured, inviting Mustapha to sit beside her.

Mustapha took the proffered place as she continued. 'I know what you're thinking. You wonder why I attended the Ceremony. Why I did not entrust you to bring back the piece of ore without my aid. The answer is simple, devoted one. I move with haste. Your return journey would have been much slower without my assistance.'

For a moment, Mustapha absorbed her words. In truth, a million different thoughts swarmed in his mind. Trying to focus, he visually checked off the trinkets and vials along the shelved wall. 'My Lady ... these spoils suit a different purpose.' Obtaining a small portion of mandrake presented a treacherous challenge. The plants screamed at him — high-pitched whining still rang in his ears. The near-empty jar mocked him. Belladonna must have used most of it to bring them back from Petrichor.

She hushed her charge, with a slender finger to his lips. 'Do not fret. The morsels you have *fetched* ... they are all valuable. None go to waste. As you know, there is talk of hazard and grief that will befall Rhye. But we will be ready with the land's antidote, I assure you. I toil through the hours and days, bringing it to fruition. But I, too, must grow in strength to see the end accomplished. Tell me: What is a potent balm without a lore-wise wielder?'

'You're right, as always,' conceded Mustapha. 'What about the Adept, though? Won't the Archimage have the finest Sorcerers and Apothecaries on the task?'

'The Adept present only a bureaucratic farce!' Belladonna spat, at odds with her typical poise. 'The Mer-Folk, the Sylphs, the Golems — none of them are any better. All they do is talk, bloated by self-importance. Sinotar is the worst of them all. Soon, they will gather here again, for the Council of Rhye ... to talk some more, not to act.

'I am expected to attend, to accompany my Lord.' Her eyes flicked towards the rumpled bed. 'Perhaps I will have you join me ...' Her voice trailed off. She reached across and tousled Mustapha's hair in her fingers. The action sent unwelcome waves of warmth through his scalp, along the nerves and sinews of his lean frame, all the way to his toes. Her sensuality invaded him.

'I feel ill,' he told her.

'You swallowed cinnabar. It is one of the most toxic minerals known ... even contact to the skin can be poisonous.'

Mustapha slumped. He studied Belladonna's face. Usually, her exquisite features revealed little of her thoughts or intentions. As he watched her, a furrow upset their fine composition, though she was more beautiful for it. Genuine concern, perhaps?

The implacable Lady Belladonna. Fearless but never reckless, she carried a stern contempt for the staid traditions of society. Even in the company of Lord Rogar, she presented a hawkish countenance. Still, Mustapha saw the woman behind the veil. His Lady inured him to one dangerous errand after another, granting him a welcoming sanctuary on his return. A warm embrace.

Uneasiness stirred within him. A sense of misalignment.

'I have no idea what the Apothecary was planning with the ore,' said Mustapha.

'Much about the lives and plans of the Adept is impenetrable, but this much I know: Lady Titania likes swift travel, which is one quality the ore can confer. Perhaps the Adept were planning to fuse the cinnabar with her chariot, to augment her gift.'

'That makes sense. Why, then, did you need me to steal it?'

Belladonna sighed. 'The Song of the Prophet,' she replied. 'It speaks not only of a great deluge, but also cataclysmic plague. My Lord confirms word from the fringes of Sontenan — unexplained deaths, disappearing bodies. Evidence of a spreading ill.

'There are cultists abroad' — she glanced across to Mustapha's annexe, to the makeshift shrine within it — 'who choose to blame the wrath of vengeful Gods. Rogar takes a more pragmatic approach, chasing solutions rather than blame. He seeks a way to combat the disease.

'The Adept are notorious meddlers, though they have provided one or two shreds of substance. The Wearers of Green believe that cinnabar will be a key component of the antidote. The other elements are less certain. Rogar searches for answers. In the meantime, I needed your help. I continue to need it.'

Mustapha stared downward at the fine parquetry beneath his bare feet. Rumours a strange malady abounded. Belladonna sought a Cure, in secret.

I swallowed the key to your work!

Another question came to him. 'Isn't it strange — the Adept choose to waste cinnabar on a chariot, rather than commit it to a ward for the land?'

'You are right, Mustapha. A waste. We may learn more when the Council of Rhye meets, in coming days.'

'Coming days! What about this stone burning a hole in my gut? Surely there is a way ...?'

Belladonna shook her head. 'There is no known chelating agent.'

'Then I just have to —'

'No, Mustapha. You will not be able to pass the ore.'

'My Lady?' Mustapha's look was questioning. Fresh perspiration glazed his brow and high cheekbones.

Belladonna set down her goblet. 'The translocation ... it altered the nature of the cinnabar. The mineral now flows in your blood.'

'I ...' No words came. Mustapha's deference to Belladonna forgotten, he leapt from the settee. 'I have to let it out!' He made for his knife.

Poisoned — It must be purged —

'You would bleed yourself to the very last drop?' Belladonna asked. Bemusement danced on her face. 'Prevent your death by hastening it?'

Mustapha halted, halfway to his annexe. Torn between action and inaction. What else could he do? Cinnabar coursed through him.

His shoulders sagged. 'How can I undo this? How long do I have?'

Belladonna's impenetrable mask returned. Mustapha's skin tingled at the intensity of her stare, even below her hooded eyelids.

After an interminable pause, she spoke. 'One thing is certain. You will need to stay close by me whilst this — situation — is resolved. No gallivanting about the land, or you may be too weak to return.'

Mustapha's stomach turned. At that moment, even the lavish proportions of the royal apartment shrunk around him. He retreated towards his own bedchamber.

'I know not how long your toxic blood will sustain you. It might be days, or weeks. It might be longer. Yet there is something you must understand. Within you lies the precious key to my alchemy. You must come when I beckon, for you are now the crucible in which I work.'

Mustapha lurched away from her. Her voice acquired that spellbinding quality — the sweetness of syrup oozing down a well-turned blade. An overwhelming vulnerability consumed him.

Need guidance.

He reached his room. Teetering footsteps brought him to the modest shrine. His eyes ranged over the crudely made figurines, settling on that of a wily creature. The fist-sized effigy wore a grin that seemed to burst forth from his carven features. Beside him, a female wore battle armour and a visage of stern kindness.

Oska, God of Fortune and Lhestra, Goddess of Justice.

Forsaken by both.

Belladonna rose from the settee, hips swaying as she approached the door to her private sanctum. The alchemist's lair.

'I am not to be disturbed.' She tossed the words over her shoulder. Her face held disdain for his desperate fervour. 'I will come for you at the time of the Council.'

'How ...?' he began, the question unformed. The answer was clear: Belladonna already knew.

She knew that bringing him back here would transmogrify the precious ore.

She knew that, with the cinnabar inside him, his fate was in her hands. Did she orchestrate the entire affair? He trembled. The urge to vomit returned.

Mustapha's body folded beneath him. He knelt, crawling before the shrine. With a ragged breath he dedicated his prayer, using the name she gave him for their moments alone.

The name with which she held him in the thrall of her power.

'Mama ...'

He began to pray.

CHAPTER 3

MY FAIRY KING

'My name is Adansonia,' said the hamadryad, in a voice like rustling leaves.

'*Wooden* you prefer I called you "Sonia", for short?' asked Meadow, beaming through the tiny opening, at the tree-nymph above.

'I suppose. I like that. To be clear, though: You will not be charming your way out of here.'

Sonia, like so many forest spirits, spent her life warding the myriad copses and hollows she called home.

The pixies' jailer gave amiable conversation. She related that her beloved sisters were Willow, Olive and Violet. Willow had the distinguished honour of residing in Psithur Grove — the woodland sanctuary of Lord Oberon himself. Sonia hastened to add that the hamadryads were not subservient, having lived in Petrichor since before the time of the Fae Folk. They recognised the Sovereignty of Lord Oberon and Lady Titania out of mutual respect.

Meadow knew about these mysterious, tribal beings through inventive tales from his childhood friends. Fascinated, he relished this first opportunity to meet one. While it lasted, the pixie took his chance to make unexpected small talk. From Sonia, he also learned about her cousins, the dryads — those who had legs and feet of their own and moved through the forest like green-skinned assassins, visiting death on any who upturned the rule of Petrichor.

After a while the discussion waned, until at last Sonia sank into a terse silence.

Dique studied the inside of their prison, as he had done for the past day and a half. With meticulous care, he examined every inch of the floor covered in moss and detritus. Then he inspected the walls of gnarled wood, curving about them like the inside of a giant flagon. Satisfied, he lay on his back upon the packed earth, gazing up at the tiny hole, through which light seeped.

Far too high for a pixie to reach.

'This is a first,' declared Meadow. 'Ever been held captive inside a tree before?'

'Nope.' Dique stared upwards. Maybe, if it rained very heavily, the tree might fill up and they could just *float* their way up to the hole.

The tree, a boab, had a rotund bole and twisted branches reaching skyward, like inverse lightning strikes. Sonia lived as part of the tree, acting as prison guard to any inmates within the hollow of its trunk.

'Nor have I. I mean, there was that one time we made a run for it, after stealing rags from old man Kensington's market stall. Remember that?'

'I wasn't there, actually. That was you and Mustapha.'

Meadow continued, undaunted. 'We hid in a tree. Almost got stuck, too … but that's not the same as being locked up in one, is it?'

Dique ignored the question. Meadow tapped his fist on the rim of a tall, slender opening to the outside world. Somehow — by some ancient tree magic — the hamadryad stretched it open, just long enough for their captors to toss Meadow and Dique inside. The opening then shrank, to barely a handspan in width. No amount of wriggling would allow even the slenderest of pixies through.

'I can see my other boot out there,' said Meadow, peering through the opening. 'Not much else. It's a stone's throw across the glade, then nothing but trees.'

'Funny thing. We're in the middle of Petrichor.'

Meadow frowned. 'If we did escape, do you know which way would get us home? I think north is that way. Maybe you can make a compass with your belt buckle.'

Dique did not answer. He hummed in a low, melodic voice, still staring up at the hole.

Without conscious thought, Meadow's fist drummed along in time with him, thoughts wandering.

Meadow loved Dique like a brother, despite only meeting him a few summers ago. Mustapha had caused their paths to cross — a fateful meeting in the name of mischief and drowseberries.

Petrichor's vast forest network formed the natural playground of Meadow's youth. Like any young pixie, a thirst for exploration and a love for being lost sustained him, providing entertainment for weeks on end. His mother and father only warned him never to cross the Bijou River, for on the northern bank lay Banwah Haunte, where all preconceptions of safety would prove false.

Meadow settled on his favourite hideaway where the bubbling stream of Berthelot broke away from the Bijou. Here, fresh honeycomb could be pilfered straight from the hive and plump, juicy berries begged to be picked and swallowed whole. Dappled sunlight splashed through giant leaves, which stayed green from one Spring right through to the next. All manner of forest creatures came to frolic and drink of the clear, fresh water. Meadow spent many hours aping the role of hunter. He would never be as sure or fleet of foot as the dryads and other forest nymphs, but he loved chasing parcels of fallow deer.

One day, he saw a pterippus come thundering through the trees. A magnificent mare, with taut muscles beneath a hide of ebony gloss. The wings of a giant bird grew from between its mighty shoulder blades — these it kept folded against its muscular form as it galloped. It was extremely rare to see such a beast within the forest — a hidden valley to the west of Petrichor was believed to home the last herds of pterippi in the land.

The huge, winged creature stormed in his direction. A whinny escaped its spittle-covered lips — a strange sound to Meadow's ears unlike that of a common horse. The pterippus looked to evade something in pursuit.

Meadow turned his attention to the assailant. Soon came a hunter, darting through the undergrowth as a fleeting shadow.

It was neither pixie, nor fairy, nor dryad. Too agile to be human. In a thrill of rippling black hair and feline limbs, a strange figure pursued the fantastical horse. The pterippus dodged and cantered through the undergrowth, before launching clear over the stream. With a swoop of broad wings and a *ch-chunk* of hooves upon loam, it achieved the far bank, disappearing behind the green curtain.

The assailant skidded to a deft halt on the near bank, planted hands on hips and issued a bold laugh to the forest sky. 'You win this one, darling creature!' he cried, his voice like a bell above the forest ambience. 'But when we meet again, oho! I will ride.'

Fronds rustled as Meadow emerged from hiding. The strange newcomer spun to face him.

'Perhaps if your boots had wings, you'd have caught him,' offered Meadow.

The stranger laughed again, a sound both welcoming and dark. Bright eyes evaluated Meadow in an instant. He cracked a wide grin — and a hand flew up to cover it. 'An audience, then?'

Meadow stared, entranced. He knew nobody quite like this man. The strangeling resembled a wraith, dressed all in black. He wore a satin tunic, tight to his form but slashed to the waist, revealing a bare chest and sinewed torso. A long sash held up his hunter's leggings, which flowed all the way to his booted feet.

One of the Wilden Folk perhaps, from Banwah Haunte? The wild exuberance suggested as much, though this creature spoke with eloquence. A hunter? Maybe … but unarmed, dressed like a dandy? Unlikely.

The strangeling issued an ornate bow. Reaching out one hand, he dragged Meadow from the undergrowth. 'Well then, let's have it,' he said. 'Mine's Mustapha.'

'M … Meadow.'

'Meadow? In a forest? How deliciously ironic!' That laugh again — boisterous, without a shred of mockery. 'Do you live here?'

'Course I do. I'm a pixie. What's your excuse?'

'I live around these parts, too,' replied Mustapha, jerking a thumb over his shoulder. 'Have done since before I can remember, or close enough.'

'What are you doing then?'

'Trying to catch a winged horse! What did it look like I was doing?'

Meadow baulked. This character, Mustapha, *belonged* on the back of a pitch black pterippus. 'Did you think you'd break it for a mount? Blag your way right into Psithur, perhaps?'

'Oh, no need, dear Meadow. I call that place home!'

Caught for words, again. Meadow understood — this must be what all higher order fairies looked like. He'd never been close enough to Psithur Grove to see one. Now, Meadow smelled opportunity. This fairy oozed self-assurance. It would serve Meadow to keep good company.

He found Mustapha most obliging. A plan for mischief here, a devious wink there and within moments, the pair linked arms, leaving Berthelot stream behind, to chase good times and a little mayhem.

As it transpired, Mustapha did have mischief and mayhem in mind. Most of it involved wheedling free beverages at the Oak & Barrel Inn, or convincing passers-by to sponsor an imaginary expedition to the little-explored far reaches of Rhye. Results were mixed, but it kept the two gadabouts away from honest work.

As summertime wore on, Mustapha suggested adventures with greater stakes. Meadow learned that the strangeling had another associate — a fellow pixie named Dique. Dique knew how to fix almost anything. He proved to be a quiet fellow, who tinkered far more than the average pixie. Mustapha explained that they needed a schemer — and that Dique was a man of solutions.

'Why do we need a schemer? Aren't random, impulsive shenanigans our thing?' Meadow asked.

'Of course, my dear,' Mustapha replied, 'but now, what we need are *trinkets!* A trophy here and there. Trimmings and treats, to add flair to our drab little existence. We must celebrate our greatest exploits! Don't you agree? That's going to need some planning.'

'I guess ... Wait. What do you mean by "trinkets"?'

Dique chimed in. 'Mustapha wants to steal some drowseberries.'

'Drowse ... Those things grow on bushes in the Mayor's garden!'

'Yep. Down by his fence line. Over that same fence is my ma and pa's cheese shop. Are you putting it together yet?'

'So, you're in on this, Dique? What do we want with drowseberries?' asked Meadow.

'Have you never distilled your own drowseberry wine?' grinned Dique, his cheeks already turning rosy.

'No ... because the only place you can get them is that no-good bum-sucker's yard!'

Mustapha flashed a winning smile. 'So ... you're in?'

The first run of drowseberry wine tasted phenomenal. A delicious haze descended on the three and they enjoyed a blissful stupor for the next two days. A second and third expedition took place. After a time, Mustapha declared he would stockpile the berries, for brewing on a rainy day. There were other, greater prizes he had in mind.

Thus did a wild ride begin. Next came a stealth mission for Blackroot, growing on the shores of the Granventide, near the dryads' territory. The root could be ground to a sweet powder, dark as pitch — a true delicacy. After that, a pitcher of bayrne oil from right under the grocer's nose. Then, the swatch of spider-silk from Mr Kensington's stall. The pranksters evolved to a life of petty crime, though their luck with the authorities held.

One fine day, Mustapha vanished. One moment, the three were discussing a foray into Dragonfly Hollow to liberate a mandrake — 'I know just the right bug to help us,' announced Mustapha — the next, he disappeared without trace. The pixies heard no word from him in the weeks that followed. After a long wait, with many hazy afternoons wasted on drowseberry wine, the strangeling faded into memory. To Meadow, his coming and going felt like little more than a thrilling summer vacation.

The wet season arrived. Then, amidst a balmy downpour, Mustapha returned.

He came unannounced — and far from expected — telling a

vivid tale of gypsies, palaces, and adventures abroad. He'd been as far as the City of Via, bringing a kerchief embroidered with the Giltenan crest as proof. Unfinished business brought him back to his old life. 'One last heist,' he pitched, with a tremendous (but mysterious) reward on offer.

The pixies were dubious. Mustapha wore a gaunt look, like one who had seen and heard more than he was divulging. Whispers spoke of new danger abroad; Meadow wondered what troubles Mustapha had stumbled into. In the end, the offer of a new jaunt fired everyone's imagination. It all hinged upon the upcoming Ceremony of the Nut, a grand affair hosting luminaries from across Rhye.

'I'll introduce you to a friend of mine,' said Mustapha, as if this would clinch the deal. 'He certainly knows how to blow his own horn, but I'm sure you'll like him.'

Mustapha spoke true of Harold. The dragonfly did prove likeable, if snooty at times. It mattered not: The whole affair still landed them in a pretty quandary.

On the surface, Meadow continued to bury his concern. 'I'm telling you, it's a major missed opportunity,' he said, without preamble.

Dique's eyes slid from the hole above to his fellow pixie. 'Hm?'

'These dryads. Their names — Willow, Rose, Ash. You don't suppose they could have come up with something better?'

The sound of warping boughs emanated from somewhere beyond their cell. Sonia overheard their chatter and deemed it pertinent to investigate. Her body, being united with the boab, 'grew' from one of the greater branches, overhanging the opening to their cell. A shadow fell and the hamadryad's face appeared at the opening.

Dique sat up. 'What suggestions do you have?'

'Well,' Meadow began, 'a worker dryad could be named Industree. A warrior dryad would be Infantree —'

Dique rolled his eyes. Sonia stared.

'— a Priestess or Shaman would surely be Idolatree —'

'Are you done, Meadow?'

'— not quite. Commoners could be named Peasantree …'

'Do you really think dryads have a commoner class?'

Sonia somehow managed to screw up her leafy features. She remained silent.

'Upper class male dryads can be Gentree.'

'No male dryads, Meadow.'

'Truly?'

'Truly. Dare I ask, then: What name would you give our lovely jailer, Sonia?'

'That's easy,' replied Meadow, throwing a coy look towards the hamadryad. 'Penitentree.'

The boab itself groaned. As Sonia withdrew from the narrow opening, a smirk played about her lips.

A moment later, Meadow went on. 'Do you think Sonia is single?'

'Hold on to your hormones,' said Dique. 'The elder line of forest nymphs doesn't deserve to get tainted by your bitter seed.'

'It would redefine the term "family tree" though, don't you think?'

Dique palmed his forehead. 'Anything but a "root" joke, I suppose.'

Finally, the discussion moved on. 'So … what do you think became of Mustapha?' Meadow asked.

Dique scratched his chin. He no longer studied the hole above them. Rather, he peered out the narrow door of their cell. Meadow knew his friend was contemplating how he might pass a message to someone. This question, however, pulled Dique out of his fanciful planning. The events following the Ceremony could not be overlooked.

Without turning, he said to Meadow, 'Perhaps he was captured by those bogus Warlocks, as well.'

'You didn't buy their act? Me neither. I've no idea what those ghastly things were, other than creepy. Their faces ...!'

'The shamans always taught me that there were no more Warlocks. Not since ...'

'... Not since the Mages' Pass debacle,' completed Meadow.

'Exactly. This turns everything on its head. Imagine, for a moment, those Warlocks were the genuine article. Can we believe anything we were taught at school?'

In truth, Meadow had skipped a lot of school in his younger days, therefore missing much of what had been taught. Even the greenest pixies knew, however, the essential history of the Adept: A monumental conflict exterminated the Warlocks, many, many lifetimes ago.

'Do you think, then, that even one Warlock must have survived?'

Dique shrugged. 'At least one, I figure. To continue their Art.'

'Why would such a revelation be kept under wraps for thousands of years?' Meadow continued. 'Why do we learn about Warlocks in the present tense, while the old Wearers of Black have been half-deleted from schoolbooks? Also — why would the Warlocks choose a forest shindig thrown by Oberon and Titania to reveal themselves — in pursuit of *us*?'

Dique clamped his hands over his ears. 'All your questions are hurting my brain,' he said. 'Look. Until a few years ago, I was a good-for-nothing pixie living in a little town called Reed. I passed my days crafting useless contraptions that nobody ever wanted. Even last week, I was that same pixie, just with a penchant for harmless thievery. Now I'm a wanted man, in the King's prison cell. My friend is missing, or dead ... and we're trying to make sense of Warlock lore. I don't know what all this is about. I just want to go home!'

With those words, creaking sounds once again echoed within the hollow of the tree. Sonia reappeared, wearing an officious look. Her face hovered scant inches from Dique.

'I cannot comply,' she said. She sounded neither harsh nor sympathetic. Her tone only carried an impersonal edge. 'You are to be tried in the court of Lord Oberon. It is he who will decide if you get to see your home again.'

'When? When will he call for us?' said Meadow.

'Soon,' came the simple reply. 'In my root system, I can feel it. Soon.' She withdrew from the entrance. Then, as an afterthought, softened her voice and added: 'In the meantime, your attempts to escape are futile.' More creaking, as her bough straightened, and she disappeared from view.

Neither of the pixies offered a parting shot. Sonia had spoken. Their fate lay in the hands of the Fairy King.

Meadow kicked the dirt and sat down on his haunches. Dique, downcast but resolute, continued to stare out beyond their confinement, into the dense surrounding forest.

As far as anybody knew, the Yew tree at the centre of Petrichor sprouted at the beginning of time. Fairies shared many stories of the tree with their own children; about how it gave the Fairy King his power, or about how its mighty roots held the fabric of the land together. Most Fae Folk held faith in the old Gods, believing that the Yew sprung forth by the hands of Marnis the Creator and Cornavrian, God of Nature.

The majestic Yew stood at the heart of Psithur Grove, the famed seat of Oberon and Titania. The Grove birthed as many legends as the singular tree, known as a place of magic and lore, which few but the very fortunate (or unfortunate) ever beheld. An avenue of willow trees, shimmering silver, gold and green, lead from the untamed forest towards a natural plaza. Within the Grove, a grid of Ficus trees surrounded the towering Yew.

This plaza, beneath the elegant, overreaching branches, served as both palace and court for the Fairy King and his Queen.

A single, forlorn nut sat on the ground between three figures. It exuded no magic.

'Well ... nobody saw that coming,' declared Titania.

Months of meticulous planning — securing the first sacred chestnut, coordinating so many moving parts — all undone in a snap, by the wayward blare of a trumpet and the theft of the Apothecary's gift. Without the cinnabar and a helping of sorcery, the chestnut would be little more than a delectable morsel.

Gone too, were Titania's ambitions for a sleek new chariot, with faster-than-lightning capability. At a time of the land's greatest need, such an asset would have placed her in league with the Sylphs, who flew great distances across Rhye upon powerful wings; perhaps even on par with the Adept, many of whom could move from place to place with thought alone.

'On the contrary, my Mab-nificent Queen,' said Lord Oberon, 'it provided ever the more entertaining spectacle. These Ceremonies are so stuffy and pompous. There's nothing like unbridled chaos and the odd fisticuffs to liven an affair.'

Titania raised an eyebrow. 'I know you are only trying to placate me.'

'Right, as always. After several thousand years together, I am no mystery to you. Can we not make light of events?'

'Three pixies and a satyr were trampled to death.'

'Ah. That is unfortunate,' conceded Oberon. 'I shall declare four days of toasts — one for each.'

'One human also got beaten by those murderous thugs the Mayor calls "neighbours".'

'This, I know. My advisors report that the man's body has already been carted off for burial ... or whatever human peasants do with their dead.'

'Oberon ...'

The Fairy King relented. 'News of the human's death will be conveyed to Lord Rogar,' he said, in a sombre tone. He tugged at his beard. 'It is fortunate Miss Trixel was not already deployed on other business. She and her associates will be swift upon the roads to Via.'

Titania nodded. The force of nature known as Trixel Tate possessed a shrewd propitiousness. As for Halliwell, Dartmoor and Puck ... though they tended towards mischief, they would present at the Council of Rhye with due diligence.

'I still have no chestnut syrup and no chariot,' she lamented — her own attempt to lighten the disastrous mood.

'We shall fashion one for you yet ... shan't we?' said Oberon, turning his head.

He addressed the third member of their meeting: the Fairy Feller. The Feller looked, by turns, beleaguered and baffled; unable to account for his failure at the Ceremony, but also unsure as to whether the Fairy King intended mercy or wrath.

An opportunity for redemption presented itself.

'Ah ... yes! Yes of course, Lord Oberon. A truly splendiferous contrivance will be yours, my Lady. The envy of all the Realm.' He wrung his hands.

'Relax, Feller,' offered Oberon. 'You know this is not your fault. You're the best axeman in Petrichor.'

'Sire — I'm the only axeman in Petrichor.'

'Indeed! And may your axe cleave only chestnuts, lest the next thing it parts be your head from your shoulders!' Oberon gave a jovial snort.

Titania rolled her eyes. Oberon valued the Fairy Feller, as a linchpin of his court. The Feller served as chief ambassador to the wider forest community. Being a pixie of uncommon height, physical prowess and honour, his credentials were iron-clad.

The Fairy Feller could not be blamed for the Ceremony disaster. His head would not roll, on this occasion.

'It was ... *him*, wasn't it?' said the Queen, in a small voice.

'Yes.' Oberon dropped his jocular air.

Titania exhaled. 'I never thought I'd see him again in all the Realm.'

'Yet you're glad you did.'

'Naturally, I am!'

The Feller's eyes darted back and forth between the two Sovereigns, his lips sealed tight.

'The whelp's pluck is hereditary.' Oberon's eyes betrayed deep consternation. His wistful gaze scoured the avenue of willows, as if he sought a distant enigma there.

Titania peered at the Fairy King. 'You miss him, as well.'

'I do, of course. I had to punish him, though it came as a great relief to spare his life.'

'You released him into the clutches of a gypsy, to learn to be an even better thief.'

'Was another path available?' Oberon's beard-tugging grew more insistent.

'You could have nurtured him, Oberon. He needed your love. You know he would never get that from his father. Foster his spirit and he would reward you as a true liege. A man of your court. The son you never had.'

'Pah!' Oberon spat. 'It's not a son I need. What good is an heir, to a man who has already seen a million sunsets?'

'Then what is the youth — Mustapha — to you? It is not another manservant you need; you are already surrounded by those. The Feller here is stalwart and loyal ... when not being spooked by a bugle.' The Feller twitched. 'Trixel Tate is an agent of the highest order. You cannot want for more liveried lieutenants.

'In what light, then, do you view the halfling?'

'Once I unpack that trunk, my Queen, it can never be repacked.'

'Tell me.'

Oberon turned to his Queen. The Fairy Feller, seeing his Lord's expression, froze.

'Two thousand, seven hundred and thirty-nine years ago, my Gods bound me in duty. I pledged my life to their service, carrying out a divine mission here on Rhye. It is my burden and my reverent joy to watch and preserve the Fae Ring.'

The Feller gave an involuntary shudder at the mention of the Ring.

'This I know,' said Titania. 'It has been my honour to stand by your side in this duty.'

Oberon continued. 'Two thousand, seven hundred and thirty-nine months ago, the Seer of Kash Valley told me three things. The first: That a new duty would come to me, at a time when darkness threatened the Ring's power. My choice in that moment would resonate throughout all the land.

'Two thousand, seven hundred and thirty-nine weeks ago, on the same day were born a sylph of unmatched prowess and a human who would ascend beyond her station. This was the second thing the Seer foretold.

'Two thousand, seven hundred and thirty-nine days ago, I banished from this Realm a youth entrusted to me. To do so rent a hole in the fabric of my honour.

'Two thousand, seven hundred and thirty-nine hours ago I felt that hole tear wide. From it poured forth a tide of foreboding: a strained vibration, the mis-strike of a bell. The Ring cried out to me.

'Two thousand, seven hundred and thirty-nine minutes ago, the youth resurfaced, amidst great mayhem at the Ceremony of the Nut.

'Dearest Mab, there can be no mistake. In this very moment, there is a choice to be made, between the life of one youth and life in Rhye as we know it.'

Titania wore a searching look. 'Oberon — what are you saying? Is this —' she scrambled to organise her thoughts. '— You never once mentioned a conversation with the Seer. Most don't even know she exists!'

'She appears to those who need her, whether they know they do or not,' Oberon replied. 'As for me, I've had a few extra years to spend searching ... and the Realm's finest tracker to help me do it. Trixel Tate and I scoured every inch of that wraith-riddled Valley, until we squeezed the humourless Seer from her den ... and saw the thing she was hiding there.'

Titania frowned. 'Could the Gods not provide the answers you seek? Surely Adatar, sympathetic to your cause, could shed light on the future of the Fae Ring?'

'In all my years of prayer — to Marnis, to Cornavrian and yes, to all-seeing Adatar himself — I have never received clearer counsel than I did from the Seer of Kash Valley. My exultant Queen, I fear the Gods and Goddesses have fallen silent. They forsake their people, which is why so many have forgotten them in return. The Seer, on the other hand — she has a name, by the way, it's Lily — she wields the truth, as she once wielded a sword.'

'Then I ask you ... did you find your guidance? What third thing did the Seer say to you? What lay hidden in her den?'

Oberon did not respond. Instead, he turned and gestured with a curt wave to the Fairy Feller. 'I have a new task for you,' he said.

The Feller took a knee. For several minutes, the Fairy King spoke to the Feller in low tones. The Feller registered no emotion, only acknowledgement.

After Oberon finished, the Fairy Feller rose to his feet, hefted his axe, and took his leave of Psithur Grove.

Night came down. The sounds of dusk filled the air, the nightly chorus of song audible from distant Dragonfly Hollow. Will-o'-the-wisps cast their phosphorescence about the dimming forest, while overhead, a waxing moon shone. Silver light limned the forest canopy and blanketed the earth beyond the boab's doorway.

Meadow dozed. Little else remained to be done after devouring a meagre evening meal, brought by a pair of armed dryads. The pixies thought their time had arrived, yet the tree spirits did not usher them from the cell. The pair ate, then returned to their listless reverie.

Dique still stood by the opening. His mind idled. No longer planning an escape, he only stared, registering the glade and the wall of trees beyond.

The figure took him by surprise. Little more than shadow, beyond the moonlit glade, coming towards them. Carrying something. Dique straightened.

The unexpected movement roused Meadow. 'What is it?'

At first, Dique said nothing. He wondered if Sonia was awake. If she ever slept. He waited for the figure to step into the pool of silver glow. When it did, he observed a tall male, approaching them with intent.

Dique caught his breath. 'Well,' he whispered, 'I never thought I'd see *you* here.'

CHAPTER 4

PEERS & PRIVY COUNCILLORS

Lord Rogar Giltenan's formal robes weighed upon his shoulders. Heavy, like the burden of his Sovereignty.

He dismissed his attendants and stood alone in the Royal Chamber. A full-length mirror allowed him to inspect his own attire. He did so in a cursory manner — never one to preen or allow typical regal vanities to dominate his attention.

The Realm before all.

A lordly countenance looked back at him. A stolid eye beneath a timeworn brow. A beard groomed with care, showing premature streaks of grey. Still shy of middle age, the Lord of Humankind bore the pressures of office, as a cliff bears the brunt of endless, crashing waves.

How might it feel, to shrug off my name — if only for a moment?

He cast aside the thought. Freedom from lineage would not serve his people — or the land.

Rogar wore a crimson tunic and surcoat, both embroidered with gold detail. His tunic boasted the family crest: two lions, reared as if in battle, above a crown. As a symbol it was respected, if not revered. The men and women who had worn the crest across the Ages were figures of renown throughout Rhye.

Rogar turned from his reflection and left the Royal Chamber: The Council awaited him.

He strode along a grand corridor towards the famed Atrium, a hallowed space in which history had been forged.

Will be forged. If the rumours and augury were true, then the Sovereigns of Rhye would soon share defining moments.

Elegant, timeless architecture reflected the sound of his advancing bootsteps. He passed beneath trefoil archways and hanging bronze lanterns. In centuries past, the broad passage bustled with countless staff, emissaries, and visitors, undertaking the business of the House. In these uncertain times, many high-ranking House officials were deployed abroad, preparing for the unthinkable. On his way to the Atrium, Rogar found himself alone.

Alone, except for his judgemental ancestors.

At intervals along the passage, portraits of regal clan-folk from ages past gazed down on him. With each passing Giltenan, the oppressive weight of expectation grew. A crisis loomed over Rogar's Sovereignty; he feared the scribes of history were set to record his Sovereignty as a dismal failure.

If anyone survived to write it down.

Walther Giltenan cast a fiery glare down from his place on the wall. Even his warlord's cloak — the hide of a great beast — appeared to bristle, issuing a challenge. The artist captured his image with startling vitality. An expansionist ruler, Walther's abiding legacy remained his famed campaign to extend the northern borders of Sontenan ... at the bitter expense of the sylphic domain beyond. His vivid portrait belied the many centuries since Walther's rule.

We all fear most what we don't know or understand. What is the curse that now faces the land? Is it a disease or some other blight? Is it an invasion, by some foe from across the Seas? Is it a holy war? How can we defend ourselves against an unknown enemy? Walther ... I could use even a fraction of your fearlessness now.

Rogar donned the mantle of Lordship twenty-seven years earlier. Thrust into the Sovereignty with little warning, it still did not sit easily with him. Over time, he earned the fealty of his advisors and the love of the populace — no mean feat, given the rarefied shoes he stepped into. To his fortune, a period of peace followed, throughout the Realm and beyond ... soon to be shattered by a cataclysmic storm, brewing on the horizon.

He reached a curve in the passageway, where the benevolent eyes of Lord Montreux Giltenan looked upon him. Montreux reached an accord with the sylphs, after eighty years of bloody war and the death of his grandfather, Walther. Montreux forged the alliance that bound the two races to this day. Despite his kindness, the regard his portrait gave Rogar seemed even more withering than Walther's.

Pity?

Almost two hundred years since the people of Rhye knew the balm of your wisdom. You offer me your pity ... instead, offer me your advice! I implore you, Montreux. What would you do? How do you forge a treaty with the Gods? How do you parley with fate if that fate is entwined with calamity?

Many more faces passed. Dozens of Lords and Ladies, fondly remembered in the school halls and history classes of Via, mighty capital of Sontenan. Amongst them, the tyrants, conniving or cruel, were remembered for the sake of lessons learned. A handful of names faded in the mustiness of time, passing their Sovereignty with neither fame nor villainy.

Ahead, the hall funnelled into the Atrium. Rogar could hear the voices of those already assembled. One last framed countenance witnessed his approach. He paused for a moment, in reverence and familial love, for an ancestor he regarded with awe: his elder sister.

Lady Maybeth Giltenan. A Sovereign for the Ages, her memory imbued with such grace that Sonteneans — and many others throughout Rhye — continued to mourn her sudden disappearance. Not only a leader, but a mentor and a lover of children, despite never bearing her own. The Lady who, one golden April afternoon, set forth with her retinue for the edge of the Realm ... and never returned home. A long, fruitless search ended with a month of mourning and a solemn memorial feast.

Twenty-seven years later, Rogar missed her still.

You left me, barely a man, to assume the mantle. Why was your flame extinguished so soon?

No wall space remained for Rogar's own portrait. With a grimace, he prepared to enter the Council.

A clamour of voices filled the Atrium. An ornate space greeted the Lord of Humankind — a room with a wide, bowl-shaped floor and a partially domed roof. Overhead, a wide oculus opened to the sky. Gentle, sloping walls, coloured eggshell blue, shimmered with inlaid decorations in lapis lazuli. Giant censers swung from overhead, issuing wisps of fragrant smoke. Tiers of seats lined the bowl; the deepest and innermost tier sat seven places, at a circular table marked with the Heptagram of Rhye. One point of the star indicated each occupant, with five positions already filled. The second tier, above and behind the first, held twenty-one. Three advisors accompanied each Councillor as a retinue.

Rogar cast his gaze about the chamber, taking a mental roll call.

In the first position to Rogar's right hand sat the Wearer of White, Archimage Benjulius. The expediency of the Adept brought Benjulius — and his delegation — from the recent Ceremony of the Nut, in Petrichor. Behind him, unruffled and bedecked in their respective shades, were Sorcerer Faymorgan, Astrologer Mayhampton, and Apothecary Renfelix. While the Astrologer and Sorcerer gave nothing away with their expressions, Renfelix looked dour, as if he had just tasted a bitter herb.

In the second position, Lord Neptune leaned forward against the table, a veritable tsunami surging toward the shore. He sat shirtless, wrapped in brawn, leaving none in doubt as to his dominant might. The custodian of the Seven Seas wore only a look of consternation. Beyond his shoulder perched the undine Salacia, Neptune's consort. Alongside her sat two powerful Mer-men: the Mer-Lord's sons, Fontus and Juturna. The pair spoke to one another in voices too soft to be overheard.

Alongside Neptune sat a warrior in full ceremonial armour, with a mantle of sky blue fastened beneath epaulettes of burnished silver. Like a wolf on the hunt, he glowered at those across from him. Lank, platinum-coloured hair swept down to the collar of his ornate breastplate, while two great, white wings lay folded against his back. Bastian Sinotar — General Prime of the Sylphic race — travelled by air from distant Wintergard. The sylphs, a militant people, garnered respect throughout Rhye as fierce soldiers, both in battle formation and one-on-one combat. Three such soldiers — Vrendari — formed his retinue. Leith Lourden, Dexler Roth, and Roal Cathage wore stolid looks, awaiting the Council's commencement.

Sinotar clenched and unclenched his fists at the table.

In the fourth position, a huge being loomed over his fellow Councillors. Emissary Torr Yosef represented Golemkind, as a proxy for his Sovereign, Torr Enoch. These hulking iron constructs hailed from deep within the Peaks of Light, in the north-west of Rhye. The golems held a unique place in the land, as sentient beings without a soul. This peculiarity wrought the Golems a long history of oppression and slavery, ever since the dawn of their existence. In the present Age, they lived as a proud, industrious race, known for their noble and pious natures. Yosef's retinue — Torr Chabon, Torr Methuselah, and Torr Jasher — crammed themselves onto the seats behind him.

Trixel Tate sat to Yosef's right, dwarfed by the Golem leviathan. As the voice of the Fae Folk, she bore the expectations of Oberon and Titania. The taut creature, bedecked in form-fitting hides and a long overcoat, referred to herself as a "fixie" — the result of interracial dalliance between a fairy and a pixie in Oberon's court, centuries before. Using her razor intellect and natural sense of leadership, Trixel rose to prominence within Psithur Grove. Over Trixel's shoulder sat her entourage of pixies — Halliwell, Dartmoor, and Puck.

Rogar strode to his own seat. Today, he would Chair the Council. His own retinue regarded him with deference as he claimed his place at the Heptagram. Lance Sevenson — Rogar's Principal Advisor and this year's Secretary to the Council — gave him a bolstering tilt of the head. Beside Sevenson sat Rogar's consort: his private confidante, Lady Belladonna. Lastly, at his Lady's behest, came the youth.

Mustapha.

Rogar never knew quite what to think of the fellow. Neither man, nor pixie, nor sylph, nor goblin, nor brownie ... Belladonna brought him with her from somewhere out of the east. She referred to the youth as her manservant, insisting that the day's agenda demanded his attendance.

Rogar knew that the seventh position would remain empty. Lord Ponerog, who had his domain in the dark forest of Banwah Haunte, distanced himself from the Council in recent years. Rumours abroad suggested he ailed with a mysterious disease.

Or perhaps, that he had died already.

Or maybe, that all the Wilden Folk throughout the Haunte had died, too.

Or possibly, that his stronghold had been found, full of gold and precious minerals. The rumours grew ever more fanciful, spread by the Fae Folk, who rarely let facts get in the way of a good story. Of course, none showed the temerity to investigate. Whatever the truth, Lord Ponerog sent neither a proxy, nor an Emissary of any kind.

Just as well — Banwah Haunte seethed with unsavoury beasts.

Lance Sevenson rose in his place. Without needless flourish, he announced: 'One and all, your attention please. The House of Giltenan, the City of Via, and the Realm of Sontenan would like to welcome you to the Council of Rhye.'

The clamour subsided, with expectant shuffling and throat-clearing.

Rogar addressed the room in a sonorous voice that carried with ease.

'Lords and Ladies of Rhye, welcome once more to the House of Giltenan. Twelve years have passed since the City of Via last played host to this Council; each year, the roads and byways of our land grow more treacherous. Your presence is appreciated at this critical time. Observing the form of Councils past, I invite delegates to present an account of their Realms and people.

'Fear is rife in these uncertain days. Let us share our insights and together, strike a light against the darkness. I will open the discussion with an account of my own Realm.

'The finest scholars from across Sontenan gathered in Via,

labouring through these past twelve months. Their task has been to study the Song of the Prophet to an unprecedented depth. Their goal — to shed light on this cataclysm, which lies before us.

'Most beings understand the Song as a portent of natural disaster — overt reference is made to storms and flooding.' Nods around the room. 'As much of Sontenan exists in the sweeping valleys that flank the two rivers, our efforts are focussed in the Sontenean highlands to the south and north. In these regions, great energy and resources are dedicated to carving vast bunkers and seeking natural caverns. We aim to host large populations of refugees, providing shelter and elevation, away from rising waters. Long-term refuge from usual habitats is anticipated.

'The Song's sacred verses also make reference to a plague. While we humans are not imbued with the innate capabilities of the Adept' — with a nod, he acknowledged the robed delegation — 'our houses of healing are committed to providing care in our time of need. We expect sedation and the treatment of infection to be priorities.'

Respectful eyes met with Rogar's as he spoke. Humans did not carry the arcane powers of the Adept, nor the amphibious capabilities of the Mer-Folk, nor the Sylphic power of flight, nor the hulking size and sheer strength of the golems. Resilience and determination connoted Humankind, a linchpin civilisation in the geographic heart of the land.

Behind Lord Rogar, Belladonna sat with adoration in her eyes.

'Between the verses we all know so well,' the Sovereign continued, 'there lies the veiled threat of civil conflict, perhaps even war. Those who hold firm to the old Gods will be looking over their shoulders for the two-legged shade known as Death. I swear before you all, that the armed forces of Humankind will stand against any enemy who bleeds.'

A ripple of unity thrummed across the Atrium floor.

'Now, friends,' said Rogar, 'share word of your Realms.'

The first reply came from the Lord of Mer-Folk, his words like waves crashing against a jagged coast. 'From the shores of Trident Deep to the Artesian Way, all the caverns in between and the northern reaches of Sordd, there are no signs of ill. But in the foothills of lower Sontenan, rumours of trouble abound. Thieves on the road look not just to rob, but to kill. My company buried three dead travellers on our way to Via.'

'Did they stay buried?' enquired Sinotar, without humour.

Neptune grimaced, but did not answer. Instead: 'More compelling news comes from beneath the surface. Many Mer-Folk report unrest — a signal, originating from the sea floor. I have entire schools of my finest deep-divers scouring every trench and abyss for the source of the disturbance.'

'Could it be regular seismic activity?' suggested Benjulius. 'A deep-sea earthquake?'

'It is a possibility,' said Neptune. 'Though the signal is far too rhythmic. Too ... *unnatural*.'

'Have you any fix on the location? A quadrant? A Sea?'

'All advice indicates a source in the depths of Ibex Trench ... in the Ealing Sea.'

The Golem delegation stirred. The turbulent waters of the Ealing Sea railed against the towering Immortal Cliffs, along the north-west coast of Rhye. Within the vault of those Cliffs — the very roots of the Peaks of Light — lay the Warnom Bore. The gargantuan shaft, plunging far beneath the surface of Rhye, homed the Golems.

Rogar turned to Torr Yosef. 'Is it possible these signals come from mining activity within the Bore?'

The Golems, a mute race, communicated with an inner voice that resonated in the minds of those to whom they spoke. The clank and whine of Yosef's telepathic speech came like a thought to those around the table: <*It is indeed possible, Lord Rogar. The mines of Warnom operate at double speed, extracting mineral ore. It has long been our belief that the land's panacea will come from within the earth itself. The Golem race gleaned this from Delvish lore, before the Song of the Prophet was known.*

In recent times, our toil has been great. A sense of urgency clutches our people, as it does your own. However — though it dismays me to say it — we, too, have heard vibrations within the earth, even when our drills sit quiet.>

'Your work must continue with all possible haste,' said the Sorcerer, Faymorgan. 'My Adept remain by your side as this crucial work is done.'

'An alliance, then?' asked Rogar.

Yosef nodded. <*Even now, alchemists from the Bore and Sorcerers from Aerglo strive towards an antidote to the land's ill.*>

Benjulius leaned forward. 'I have directed our most accomplished Sorcerers to the task of working theurgy on the various rare materials as they are brought forth from Warnom. Bismuth and dolomite are the foci of our energies, at present. We believe these minerals can affect a warding charm and be worn as a token against a widespread affliction.

'Cornavrian willing, progress shall come soon.'

'My deep divers will continue to scour the floor of the Ealing Sea,' concluded Neptune. 'We will not assume to have heard only the sounds of your drilling. Complacency is hazard in such uncertain times.'

Satisfied, Rogar continued around the table. 'What of the Sylphic Realm, General Prime?'

'I concur with Neptune, as far as trouble abroad is concerned,' replied Sinotar, in a sleek growl. 'We also encountered signs of brutality in the mountain passes and northern highlands as we journeyed south. It is not the work of brigands, but of foul sorcery.' His hooded gaze lingered on the empty place across from him. He aimed his contempt away from the Adept, who nonetheless shifted in their seats.

'Will you speak of your findings?' pressed Rogar.

'It is not uncommon to find waylaid travellers along the mountain roads, sometimes in pieces. Most people who retain their sanity know not to travel those ways alone. On this journey, we encountered an entire company — a dozen or so. Sylphs. Their wings hacked off, other mortal wounds. A strange smell in the air — sulphur, maybe.

'It was late, with a waning moon. We camped nearby for the night. At first light, we scoured the terrain for a suitable place to raise a cairn. When we returned, all but three of the bodies had vanished ... and those which remained were nearly bare of flesh.'

There were inhalations around the table, though nobody spoke.

Bitterness clouded Sinotar's face. 'We buried the three in haste and did not linger.'

'Spriggans?' offered the Astrologer, Mayhampton.

'Those creatures usually give themselves away with howling, or spoor at the site of a kill. A nitrous stench. It would also take an army of them to overwhelm a company of sylphs.'

'No, this was not the work of spriggans.'

'Do you insinuate that the dead got up and strolled away, then?' asked Neptune with a half-smile.

'I do not. I do suggest that something beyond the scope of blade and blood is at play. Something ... otherworldly. An affliction of sorts, as Benjulius suggests ... or maybe a *plague* of arcane magic.'

The Adept sat in silence, Benjulius in deep contemplation.

'Any word of movement in the eastern Rimhorn?' asked Rogar.

'Aye, there are stirrings in the undergrowth. Some hapless

creatures have begun migrating east, with the intention of setting up camp in the foothills of Two-Way Mirror Mountain. I suspect they believe themselves safe there, as if Fenmark Haunte is a neutral No-Man's Land. They are wrong — that corridor swarms with wights and banshees. They're courting with danger, sitting in the shade of the Mountain ... whether you believe in bedtime stories or not.'

An incensed female voice shattered the decorum of the room. '*The earth will shake from wrath within*!' Heads turned; Trixel Tate stood in her place. In that moment, her presence magnified her diminutive stature. Her quote, from The Song of the Prophet, focused the meandering Council discussion like a lodestone.

'We are not dealing with mere superstition or bedtime stories,' she said. 'Ogres dwell there, behind that wall of luminous rock.'

Sinotar hissed out a sigh. 'If ever there were Ogres — and if they ever lived within that Mountain — they have long since perished from starvation. The refugees may be thankful for that.'

Trixel glared at the Sylphic General Prime. 'My beliefs — the beliefs of many around this table — go hand-in-hand with the augury of the Song. The Ogres are the *wrath within*. They will have their time again upon Rhye, and death will be their dealing: This is our lot, as meted out by the Gods. Doom is prophesied and will be delivered by Valendyne. We must unite and acquit ourselves.'

'And protect those who wander into harm's way!' squeaked Puck, emboldened by Trixel's rhetoric. He stirred a few murmurs of agreement from the nearby undines.

'You may be right, but keep melodrama out of it,' rumbled Sinotar. 'Not all of us put credence in your Gods ... though the words of the Song are to be heeded.' Despite his measured tone and characteristic gruffness, beads of sweat lined the sylph's brow. Muscles bunched at his jaw.

Amongst the Adept, the Golems and the Mer-Folk, there

were solemn nods. Whether devout or blasphemous, faithful or unbelieving, all the creatures of Rhye knew the gravity of the Song. It bound the destinies of all to its grim premonition, while many also clung to its vague inferences of hope.

The Song of the Prophet

Land of Rhye, Light of the World
Born at schism of Night and Day
Praised your bounty and blessed your kin
Mighty Seas at your shores do pray.

A doom it comes, the endless dark
Flood and plague from wretched keep
The earth will shake from wrath within
Beware: The storm brings endless sleep.

A white shroud laid upon the land
Death will stalk while elders wait
The lords of old will crumble hence
The youthful cry but flee too late.

This fateful night, I stand on high
The moon it swells and shows my place.
This Song I give, for songs may save:
Evil purged with hymnal grace.

Water, Fire, Earth and Air
Each one will sing and march with Fate.
But Love is key to kingdom come.
A Cure, a paean, a Song doth wait.

From love estranged does new love grow
Across the Seas, the answer found.
Fly and find and thence return,
To peace and fortune, all around.

O King of Rhye, redeem our land,
With sacred ore, both still and swift;
I know you hear me — take my hand.
The throne awaits, a blessed gift.

Trixel Tate still stood. 'This Council is charged with finding an answer to the Song's augury. All the citizens of Rhye will look to their rulers to light the way forward.'

<*I concur, Miss Tate,*> said Torr Yosef.

'We concur!' squealed the pixie retinue, in true superfluous fashion.

'Any other pontiffs here want to lay down some dogma?' said Sinotar, his voice a cold blade.

The grinding of Torr Yosef's jaw did not require words to accompany it.

'Lord Ponerog may have had something to contribute,' mused the Mer-man, Fontus.

Sinotar thrust an outstretched hand towards the empty seat at the Heptagram. 'Ponerog declares himself: He is not here. There is neither retinue nor Emissary from Banwah Haunte. Nor was there two years ago in Wintergard, or the Council before that in Warnom. With all this discussion of impending calamity, Lord Ponerog is implicit in his absence.'

Again, gasps and susurrations arose from the assembled contingent of humans, sylphs, undines, and other more exotic creatures.

Lord Rogar stayed on the fringe of the discussion. As Sinotar spoke, the Sovereign of Humankind studied his Sylphic counterpart. Something troubled Sinotar ... something other than the talk of religion.

Rogar moved to diffuse tension, seeking lighter ground for conversation. 'Emissary Tate. We value your contribution to Council, though we observe misfortune at the absence of your Lord and Lady. Are there glad tidings from the recent Ceremony of the Nut?'

The sound of rustling garments arose from the Adept.

'Lord Rogar, it is my regret to inform the Council that the Ceremony was aborted at the crucial moment, due to unforeseen circumstances.'

Polite murmurs documented the room's disappointment.

'Pray tell, are the Lord and Lady of Petrichor in good health?'

'Excellent health, my Lord,' Trixel replied. 'The Ceremony was disrupted by anarchists who, by primitive methods, distracted the Fairy Feller and brought the entire Ceremony down in chaos.

'Lord, I speculate that a rogue element works against our efforts to stave off the coming dark. As you know, the Ceremony was heralded as the commissioning of Lady Titania's new chariot. It was also — unbeknownst to many — our bid to brew a unique syrup from the first magic chestnut of the season. In this bid, we have now been thwarted.'

From across the table, Lord Neptune spoke. 'Emissary Tate — will you tell us more about this syrup?'

'Lord, for generations, the fairies and satyrs of Petrichor have sought to create a ward which might protect our sacred forest in times of need — just as the Adept and Golems now act to create for all the land. It has been determined that such a ward can be provided by administering an enchanted liquor to the waters of Bijou and Granventide; and in so doing, cast a line of arcane defence around our Realm.

'The syrup would form the basis of that ward. By the grace of Cornavrian does the first chestnut fall; within it is his essence is his potency. His gift to us would be catalysed by other products of the earth, which were brought to the Ceremony by kinsmen of other Realms, for the purpose of concocting this ward. Our opportunity to create it is now lost. The forest of Petrichor cannot be protected.'

This time, the room responded with genuine dismay. An audible groan issued from somewhere within the human delegation.

The Apothecary, Renfelix, stood and spoke, as if words had been hot coals on his tongue. 'I vouch for Emissary Tate. The Archimage and I were present at the Ceremony. The midnight spell was shattered by the insolent sounding of a horn, clearly meant to incite panic and disorder.

'Within my robes I held a precious piece of rare ore. This was intended as a gift to Lady Titania, an essential component of her ward. It was stolen from me — an act that seemed deliberate, in a sea of reckless panic.'

'Sabotage, then?' asked Lord Rogar. 'Were there witnesses? Any insight as to the perpetrator?'

'Why yes, sire. As happenstance would have it, the perpetrator is amongst us now.'

Silence fell upon the Atrium.

'You accuse one amongst us, Apothecary Renfelix?' probed Rogar.

For a moment, the Wearer of Green wore the triumphant look of a person about to deliver karmic justice. His mouth opened and his robed arm raised, finger pointed. But as he made to stab it in the direction of Lord Rogar himself, a seizure overcame him. Renfelix wavered on his feet. His outstretched arm looked heavy as lead one moment, struck by spastic palsy the next. He grappled with his own coordination. At the same time, his mouth strained to form the shape of his words — he produced only a hoarse retching sound.

The entire Council froze in fascinated horror.

Only his eyes knew their course. Bulging, they stared with burning intensity — not at Rogar, but beyond him. By increments, he wrenched control of his muscles back from an unseen force. His arm steadied. His voice continued to betray him, though he uttered a long, loud moan, like the lowing of cattle.

'Theeeeeeaaaaaarrrrrrrre!'

All faces turned in the direction Renfelix indicated. Rogar found himself looking over his shoulder.

Mustapha.

The strangeling flinched. Rogar frowned. The Council threatened to veer from his control. The theft of a rare mineral usurped all discussion of the land's crisis.

The Sovereign of Humankind held up a hand. 'Everybody, hold.'

Pillow talk from Lady Belladonna secured Mustapha a place in the Human delegation. She gave a whispered assurance that the youth would play a pivotal role. Rogar assumed this meant the sharing of some crucial insight or intelligence, not that he would be defendant in a bizarre accusation.

'Mustapha,' said Rogar, 'can you shed light on the advice of Apothecary Renfelix?'

Mustapha's chalk-white face stared back. Beside him, Belladonna gripped his wrist. 'My Lord, it isn't possible,' he said, colour seeping back into his cheeks. 'The honourable Apothecary says I was there, but now I'm here? I would need to know translocation to arrive so fast! It may be a talent of his, but it is not one of mine —'

'Liar!' shouted Renfelix, reigning in control of his voice.

'I — I honestly don't have it —'

'Liar! Lord Rogar, the whelp lies! I saw him as plain as he is sitting here!'

The audience remained transfixed, if no longer horrified.

Mustapha huffed. 'I swear to you! I do not have it. Search me! Search my belongings! I am a poor orphan with few personal affects, save those that Lady Belladonna allows me to keep in her apartment. It shan't take you long to see — no cinnabar is there.'

For several beats, nobody spoke.

Puzzled glances shot around the room.

Trixel Tate speared the silence. 'I did not hear the Apothecary mention anything about cinnabar.'

Faces of condemnation turned upon Mustapha from around the room. Faces of delegates from almost every Realm, every corner of Rhye. Races unified in their effort to stave off an unknown desecration.

In their midst stood one who worked at sabotage.

'Liar! Traitor!' exclaimed the pixies, Halliwell, Dartmoor and Puck, until Trixel waved them to silence.

Belladonna glared at the Fae Folk. 'Speak no ill of Mustapha. He aids this campaign in ways you do not even recognise. Be still your voices ... or lose them.'

<*There is a crime to answer for,*> said Torr Yosef. <*If what you say is true, then the youth will need to answer for himself, against the law of his people.*>

'He has no people to speak of,' said Trixel. She faced the Lord of Humankind. 'He is an outcast from our Realm and now seeks a foothold in yours, Lord Rogar. It is by the grace of your House that he remains.'

'Enough!' declared Rogar. 'The purpose of this Council is eroded. The Council of Rhye is neither a court of human law, nor a place for one person's integrity to be challenged. It is a place of unity and leadership.

'This Council meets in my home, under my leadership. On this day, you will all listen to *me*.'

The room grew still.

He turned to Mustapha, who sat slumped, behind him.

'Mustapha, an accusation stands against you. Indeed, you will have questions to answer. Until that moment, you are under House arrest. You are removed from this Council.' He gestured to guards standing by the Atrium doors, who raised their hands in a salute of acknowledgement and approached Mustapha in his place.

An uncomfortable quiet settled over the room. People squirmed in their seats, none wanting to be the first to speak. With deliberate slowness, Lord Rogar let his gaze drift across every face. In some he saw glowering anger, in others pure bewilderment. Some faces were blank, in the aftermath of an unanticipated twist. Lady Belladonna, bereft of her young companion, bore an inscrutable look.

A low, guttural sound broke the tense moment. A deep rumble became a stuttering chuckle. Wide-eyed faces turned towards the Sylphic delegation. The sound rose in pitch, swelling until it became a full-bodied laugh: a bitter sound, deep and cold as a midwinter's night.

Strange mirth shone in the eyes of General Prime Bastian Sinotar. He gave a chilling smile as he watched Mustapha be led away.

CHAPTER 5

KILL LIKE KNIVES

In the good times, freedom propelled Mustapha like oxygen. His days in Petrichor, chasing adventure and exploring every gully and grove, brought joy to every fibre of his being.

This new life stifled him.

He found dark humour in the irony of his servitude. It bound his libertine ways to Belladonna's unshakable purpose. In the first instance, he wondered at what cost he had given his freedom away. To ease his disillusionment, he reminded himself that he escaped death in the court of the Fairy King. Such a reprieve demanded a price.

Following his moment of condemnation at the Council, Mustapha's annexe — his own private corner of the world — had never been such a warm, safe place.

He retreated into the annexe as if going back to the womb. He curled up on his pallet, often returning to fitful dreams, sometimes feverish. Food and drink triggered little desire. No Sovereign decree limited him to his room, though in the Council's aftermath, the corridors and grounds of the House swarmed with sentries and Vrendari. His movements would be challenged.

The House still buzzed. Most delegates and their retinues remained — rejuvenating, gathering resources for their respective journeys home. The Adept alone chose to leave immediately, for they could travel by means of their Art.

Belladonna did not reappear for several days. Mustapha knew not where she had gone. She promised to bring help and medicine before she left.

He chose to put his trust in her and wait. What more could he do?

Terror gripped him.

Twice she did return, remaining for only a short while. She brought him an elixir that tasted like drowseberries, but with an odd bitterness. She said it would slow the poisoned blood in his veins. He drank it as he was told, then fell into an intoxicated slumber. When he awoke, she would be gone again.

More time for solitude and thought.

The Council talked at length of a doom to befall Rhye. Mustapha found such an immense subject intangible, being stricken by the more palpable threat to his own life. Carefree bravado gone in a moment, traded for uncertainty and fear.

Will I die here? Will I be alone?

He craved her comfort and wisdom.

Mama. Is this how love is supposed to feel?

He clung to memories in which Belladonna watched over him with overt affection. Together, they left Petrichor and travelled through Sontenan, taking a circuitous route south and south-west of the Forest Realm. Belladonna explained the need to avoid certain foes along more established routes. The route also needed to bypass a challenging river crossing, at the junction of the Granventide and Bijou. Still, on several occasions, spriggans and other devious creatures waylaid them, along dim, misty byroads. Rather than outrun their assailants — for both she and Mustapha were fleet of foot — Belladonna chose to stand against attackers, enacting such a gypsy incantation as would subdue them. In this way, the pair could affect an escape.

By day, they traversed the leagues of greensward and valleys. The countryside bore the goodwill of Cornavrian. Stands of poplars, sighing in a gentle breeze, gave way to orchards and farmland. The villages of Humankind nestled amongst fragrant woodland, connected by rutted roads. Mustapha and Belladonna flitted from one to the next, sometimes stopping to collect provisions, other times passing through. At each sleepy hamlet, Belladonna left Mustapha awed, beguiling the rural folk into parting with items the pair needed for their journey.

They never stayed long in the townships they encountered.

By night, beside a carefully concealed fire, they talked. Belladonna admitted that her way with the townsfolk came from her upbringing amidst a troupe of vagabonds, forever reliant on the goodwill of strangers ... or their naivety. The life of a gypsy, she said, taught her much about the nature (and foibles) of Humankind. She cherished her old life, feeling ever at one with those around her.

A day came when the troupe's fortunes ran dry. One farming community, on the southern shore of the Granventide, knew of their approach and were disinclined to hospitality. Deadly ambush ensued, with gunfire and a clash of blades. Both of Belladonna's parents were killed; she became separated from the troupe. From that day forward, she journeyed alone.

Belladonna did not seek solitude. She never envisaged herself as the lone wolf. The opportunity for a travelling companion — an assistant in her grand venture — she welcomed wholeheartedly.

Mustapha listened to her tale with warmth in his soul. It spoke of family, of belonging and of common purpose — things that he craved, but never truly knew.

Indeed, despite their whimsical wandering, Belladonna's troupe embodied purpose. The Song of the Prophet lived in their hearts. Nomads in body and in spirit, they quested without pause, searching for the meaning behind words long-written, long-remembered. With the death of her parents and the splintering of her 'family', little remained to Belladonna, besides an aching desire to pursue the Song's portent. The hunger grew in her like a flame, until her every action strove towards it.

Passion compelled her.

Mustapha stood on his Lady's balcony. Early evening smouldered. The glow of the setting sun had barely left the sky, though the stars to the east hid behind clustering storm clouds.

Belladonna slept. When she awoke, he intended to press her for word of her travels and activity.

Serenity drifted on a light breeze. Mustapha's position afforded him a view beyond the gardens and the walled boundary of the Giltenan holdings. The House itself stood at the peak of a large hill, on the slope of which sprawled the City of Via. Innumerable avenues and burrows zigzagged within a forest of spires, towers, and steep gables. Scrallin street lanterns and braziers like giant barrels illuminated the network of urban villages, stretching all the way to the distant plain of Sontenan.

Mustapha saw little to draw his attention, amongst the myriad dwellings of Humankind. Without conscious thought, his gaze retracted, a homing beeline, back towards the courtyard below. In time, his eyes once again settled upon the expansive yard, the gilded aviaries, and the mausoleum. Then, he noticed it: the anomaly which failed to register in his addled mind, one previous evening.

The door to the mausoleum, sealed during the lifetime of any ruling Sovereign, yawned wide.

With a furrowed brow, Mustapha backtracked his survey of the courtyard. His pulse quickened.

Did I miss something? Has somebody died?

Strained searching soon yielded reward. Movement caught his eye as a figure emerged from foliage overhanging a gravelled path. The figure moved with a purposeful, unhurried gait, keeping to the edge of shadow. From his build, Mustapha guessed the figure to be that of a man. The hood of a cloak concealed his features. The cloak itself flowed to the ground, at the mysterious night walker's feet. Grime and tatters marked an otherwise magnificent golden garment. A motif of crimson emblazoned the front and, as the stranger progressed, Mustapha identified two lions, with a crown beneath them: the heraldic crest of Giltenan clan.

Far from being an ordinary traveller's cloak, Mustapha recognised it as a ceremonial burial shroud.

A shout of surprise rose in Mustapha's throat. His heart pounded with fury. He rubbed his eyes in disbelief, but the figure did not disappear. Instead, it turned to look straight up at him.

The face of a spectre regarded him.

Impossible! A mask, perhaps? A skull stared at him from beneath the burial cowl. Its bottomless gaze brought the chill of the tomb. Soon, the moment was over — the being continued its passage across the courtyard.

A second figure materialised from the mouth of the mausoleum.

Then a third.

Mustapha's voice seized. He could not wrench it free. At the same time, his mind whirred. The very nature of what he saw challenged him. *This is wrong.*

He reeled on the spot and re-entered the apartment, intent on pursuit.

Never had he dressed in such haste. He brushed past his small shrine, sending the figurines of Onik, Anato, Floe and others clattering to the floor. Trousers, belt, boots and overshirt. In a moment, he reached the recess behind his pallet and grabbed for —

Where is my blade?

Flustered, he dared not stop to think. His long-barrelled handgun still sat in place. Mustapha snatched it up. Checked the chamber. *Loaded.* Slipping it through his belt, he dashed past Belladonna, unmoving in her sleep.

He reached the door and burst out into the dim corridor. Behind him, Mustapha failed to notice that the entrance to Belladonna's alchemic sanctum — for all this time closed to him — was ajar.

Torr Yosef, Golem Emissary, paced through gloomy corridors.

Being a soulless automaton had its benefits. He did not require sleep. He did, however, get lost in his thoughts — a typically human trait.

Some factions in society persisted with the fallacy of golems as witless slaves. Yosef knew this to be an abhorrent lie, fostered by the ignorant. Certainly, in millennia past, the golems acted at the behest of arcane and primitive forces; vulnerable as they were, by lacking a true soul. Golem lore upheld that they were built by Marnis and owed their sentience to him. Ripe for possession, Valendyne usurped the golems for His own means, in a bygone Age. Ancient humans once also held sway over them.

Through the centuries, golems dedicated numerous prayers and songs to their preserved self-dominion.

Still, they endured the sting of prejudice from bigoted folk on the fringe of society. Many, including Yosef, offered entreaties to Lhestra, for the strength to stand and be counted amongst the independent people of Rhye.

Membership of the Council provided a significant boon. An invitation to host the Council within the Warnom Bore followed. The Sovereignty of benevolent Lord Enoch proved a watershed. All were crucial steps towards recognition.

<Has it all come too late? Have we arrived only to see civilisation crash down around us?>

He paced a broad corridor, leading from the guest quarters, down through the Atrium to the galley beyond. Occasional sentries offered him silent nods as he passed their posts.

Seeking to move on from glum political musings, he cast his unique sentience into the night around him.

In return, his senses prickled. He froze.

Other soulless beings were on the move.

<Those are not golems.>

By instinct, he attuned himself with Torr Jasher and Torr Methuselah. They remained in their quarters, 'awake' but inert. They had not left their rooms all evening. Something else lurked. Something sinister. A presence that throbbed in the chill air of the night.

Yosef turned, trying to pinpoint the source of the ill around him, when a fleeting figure careened around a corner and collided with him. With the dull *bong* of flesh striking iron, the figure bounced off him and struck the ground, before scrambling back to its feet.

It was the strangeling, Mustapha. He wielded a gun.

'Torr Yosef!' Mustapha exclaimed. He gathered himself, though his whole body shook. When he continued, a landslide of speech tumbled from him. 'Listen! There is evil afoot. You must believe me, though you will think I've lost my mind. The mausoleum. It's open. There are skeletons ... lots of them! The House is besieged by dead Giltenans!'

Yosef tested his percipience once again. Though his features could not register alarm, in an instant he knew the truth. Mustapha's gibbered warning matched the sense of foreboding the golem held within.

<An attack from the undead?>

The strangeling quivered before him, teeth clenched as he nodded.

Truth could not be denied, no matter how terrible.

Yosef amplified his telepathic voice. Like a psychic shockwave, he shouted out to every mind, awake or asleep, within the House of Giltenan.

<ATTENTION! We are under attack!

The bones of the dead move among us. I repeat — we are under attack!>

Neither of the two sentries at the courtyard portico could sound the alarm bell. Neither of them had a pulse.

The intruders advanced as a wordless tide. A platoon of the dead issued, one by one, from the dank mouth of the mausoleum. They moved without haste as they stole along the borders of shadow. Malevolence radiated from every one of them, a baleful cloak of phosphorescent mist.

The Giltenan dead moved with purpose, clutching the ceremonial knives, swords, and halberds of their burial. Rotted shrouds clung to bare bones. Without hesitation, they approached the House, deathly shadows closing in on their prey.

Two more sentries emerged from within the portico. One uttered a shout, before taking a broadsword to the bowels. The other moved to raise his weapon, only to find he could not, without his sword arm. In moments, both slumped in growing pools of their own blood.

Driven by an unspoken directive, the platoon dispersed. One company continued through the cleared portico. Others fanned out towards the walls of the House and began scaling, angling towards terraces, balconies, and windows.

In the first moment after Yosef's telepathic shout, Trixel Tate's eyes flew open. She realised she was not alone.

In the second moment, she reached for the hunting knife stowed beneath her pillow.

In the third moment, a bare foot lashed out from under her blanket, delivering a savage blow to the dark figure poised at her bedside. The figure, grasping a weapon of its own, clattered to the floor. Trixel became aware of a dire yellow glow and a sulphurous odour.

In the fourth moment, she leapt across the room, landing atop her would-be assailant. Her blade flashed, plunging downward into the glowing socket where an eye should be. Another flash, another strike: The cleaved skull rolled from its owner, releasing a hollow death rattle.

In the fifth moment, Trixel Tate breathed in, then out, assimilating her situation.

She crouched upon the fallen warrior. The creature lacked flesh or sinew. Beneath a tattered red and gold garment, she found only bones — now still.

The malevolent glow dimmed and vanished, though an acrid smell lingered.

Stepping over the corpse, Trixel dressed herself in brisk, well-practised movements. Tunic. Leggings. Boots. Coat. As she made for the doorway, she spied the creature's weapon where it had fallen. She raised it: a large, heavy-bladed knife. Ornate … designed for ceremonies, yet ready to kill or maim with a single blow. The handle sat snug in her palm, the blade the length of her forearm. Embellishment on the pommel caught her eye — the Giltenan crest.

Trixel's lips set in a grim line. She inspected the weapon, then once more regarded its former owner. She slid the knife through the sash at her waist.

A heartbeat later, she was gone from the room.

Lord Rogar's chamber guards entered to find him already roused, a crimson robe about his shoulders. He stood reaching for a claymore, slung above the stone hearth.

The men halted in their tracks. Clad in nightwear though he was, they had never seen their Sovereign readied for battle. He turned; his profile outlined in the glow of dying flame.

'Lord!' exclaimed one. 'The House is beset by wraiths.'

'I know. The golem spoke to me, also.'

'Sire, how —'

'We cannot face them in corridors. Swords are better swung on an open battlefield. Find your Captain. Shepherd our guests to the Praecard. We can form a barricade there and still have room to fight.'

'Sire.' A note of insistence. 'How will we quell such a foe? These are the dead … *your* dead. The Giltenan ancestors have risen.'

Lord Rogar paused. His liegemen saw treason in the act of assaulting the body of royalty, whether alive or dead.

The glint in his eye vanquished the sentries' doubt. The hands that held his weapon knew their task.

'My forebears belong in the vault,' he said. 'Let us put them back there.'

Few remained asleep after the golem's psychic shockwave, though for many, the warning still came too late. Advisors, warriors, and House staff alike were slain in their beds — visited by resurrected death, the *shuffle-clack* of ancient feet and the stealthy hiss of a lethal blade.

Removed from the sanctuary of the sea, the Mer-Folk proved most vulnerable. The sluggish entourage of Lord Neptune struggled to escape the wraiths' onslaught. While the Mer-Lord snatched Salacia from the strike of death, both Fontus and Juturna were murdered. Neptune, vital as an ocean tempest, swept the skeletal enemies from his path. Bones splintered against the dark stone wall.

Still, the creatures advanced.

Neptune thrust Salacia down the corridor as their assailants limped towards them. 'Downstairs!' he bellowed to her. 'Take any of the living with you.'

He longed for the potency of his Trident, locked in the armoury, beyond retrieval.

He turned to see two, then three Giltenan wraiths in his wake. The nearest staggered within arms' reach. He lunged, mashing a mighty fist directly into the skeleton's face. Knuckles crunched against bone and the creature folded to the floor.

'That is for Fontus,' he thundered, 'and this, for Juturna.' His shoulders recoiled and his other fist fell like a breaker against the second foe's temple. The skull caved and it, too, hit the ground.

Neptune did not wait for the third. He surged towards the stairs, following his consort.

An unholy offensive infiltrated the heartland of Humankind. The maze of halls and passages within the House of Giltenan transformed into a web of horror, with advancing death lurking around every corner. Startled shouts and screams, the voices of panic, echoed from all quarters.

Golems and Vrendari worked alongside the soldiers of Lord Rogar to usher frightened civilians along darkened corridors. At every turn a new clash ensued, as skeleton warriors ambushed them from the shadows. With preternatural force, the long-dead Giltenans assailed groups of evacuating humans.

Mustapha became separated from Torr Yosef. The sylph, Roal Cathage, corralled the strangeling towards the stairs. Handsome as a marble bust, Cathage guided him with swift efficiency, before turning to engage with a ghoulish spectre close behind them. Mustapha gripped his pistol in white knuckles. He dared not pull the trigger on a whim; amidst the confusion and hustle, he feared a misfire. The weapon contained a single charge, not to be wasted. He hurried down the stairs.

The living filtered their way down to the Praecard. The vaulted entry hall to the House of Giltenan served to receive guests in grand style, bedecked with ornate thuribles, towering arched windows of stained glass and elegant, carved furniture.

In haste, soldiers flipped long tables and arranged heavy furnishings to form a makeshift barricade. They herded a small, surviving group of Emissaries and House staff behind it for protection. The combat-ready Councillors hemmed them in, creating a defensive line. In their midst, sweeping crimson cloak around him, stood the Sovereign of Humankind. His grim features shone in the glint reflected from his claymore.

'Tonight, I test my own mettle against that of my ancestors,' said Rogar.

On cue, a squadron of skeleton warriors marched forth from the shadows.

'Permission to send your family back to where they came from?' roared Neptune.

'Their welcome has expired. Show them the door.'

The skeletons advanced, as silent as the mausoleum from which they emerged. Rogar unleashed a battle cry, raising his weapon, double-handed.

The nearest of the ghoulish attackers singled him out. With the gnashing bite of claymore against ancient longsword, the fight for the House began.

Fire burned within the hearth. Light and darkness threw macabre shapes upon the walls and columns of the Praecard. Against this flickering backdrop, an existential struggle unfolded. Protected by the brace of fighters, hapless civilians huddled together with terrified cries. They scrambled and ducked, skittering here and there, as sylphs, golems and human soldiers fought the beings from the grave. The night rang out with the furious clash of arms, and the splintering of oak.

The Giltenan dead moved with lethal precision, guided by some fell hand. Their movements, lightning quick, tested the skill of every defender. Leith Lourden and Dexler Roth soon launched an aerial assault, descending on their skeletal foes from above. The golems wrestled several of the fiends at once, resilient against a hail of blows. Trixel Tate fought with astonishing fury, her movements a deadly dance of blades.

Mustapha spun left and right, lest one of Rogar's ancestors cleave him from behind. He dove behind an upturned table just as a brutish fiend, draped in a musty cloak of beast hide, swung a broad axe in a vicious arc towards him.

'Walther!' bellowed the voice of Lord Rogar. 'Though I prayed for your courage, aught did I realise you would visit it upon me! What evil fascination takes hold of you?'

The skeleton did not respond. Instead, the remains of Walther Giltenan lunged at his living clansman, reaching across the Ages in a stoush from the Afterlife.

As the harrowing conflict raged, Mustapha sought to stay alive, above all else. With a start he recalled, with alarm, that Belladonna remained in her apartment.

Could it be, these fiends overlooked her? I have to go back!

He stole between clashing warriors, crawling beneath the wreckage of benches to evade the void-like gaze of the skeletons. The defenders of the House looked to have the upper hand, though as he escaped, he encountered the bodies of numerous fallen. Towards the edge of the carnage, the marble bust of Roal Cathage stared at him from dead eyes.

Mustapha shuddered. Looking up, he saw the fringe of the Praecard. The safety of shadow beckoned, only a short dash away.

He also saw something unexpected. Something that froze his heart.

A figure bounded up the stairs, headed back towards the apartments. A figure cloaked in darkness, swift of foot, bearing eagle wings at its back.

Bastian Sinotar.

Mustapha swallowed a shout. Shrugging off all caution, he dashed for the stairs, scant moments behind the disappearing form of the General Prime.

Why would the General abandon the battle? Thoughts churned, a tumult inside Mustapha's head. Only one reason surfaced: the same one that lead him from the great reception hall.

Sinotar left in search of Belladonna.

Dread gripped him. Hints and insinuations unravelled themselves, falling into place. That hideous laugh; the ire, the rankling disgust on Sinotar's face throughout the Council of Rhye. The General Prime harboured a fierce loathing for another delegate, or so it seemed. Now the truth, in a fleeting instant, was revealed.

A vendetta against my Lady? For what? Has Belladonna's work uncovered a conspiracy? Some dark subterfuge at the hand of Sinotar? A sylphic betrayal? What will he do to her? Does he intend to ...

Electrified by the thought, he bolted up the stairs.

Mustapha's departure from the fray did not go unwitnessed. Several fighters guessed his purpose and followed in pursuit.

The sepulchral upper halls of the House lay deserted. The ringing sounds of combat faded as Mustapha stole ever higher. Floor by floor he climbed, past pools of scrallin light and the artefacts of Human Sovereignty.

Approaching the door to Belladonna's lodgings, Mustapha found it thrown open, just as he had left it. Rose light spilled from within, along with the sounds of disturbance: the crash of an upturned settee and the tinkle of breaking glass.

Mustapha seethed. His face grew hot with rage. On instinct, he resolved to burst into the apartment and blast the sylph away with his gun. Perhaps he would save his Lady. Perhaps, even now, they fought. Could Belladonna best the General Prime? Was her power equal to his might?

A few deep breaths.

One ...

Two ...

No. I need proof of this subterfuge. I must see Bastian Sinotar in the act of treason. Best to use stealth.

Mustapha slunk to the door and peered inside.

Chaos reigned. A tempest upturned the fastidious order of things. Bed clothes and cushions lay scattered across the room. The bed was empty; of Belladonna, no sign remained. All around, the ruinous mess of shattered trinkets covered the parquetry.

Drawing his ornate pistol, Mustapha entered the room.

Immediately, he saw it — the open door to the alchemist's lair. The threshold he had never crossed. The sanctuary he had never beheld. Inside, out of view, a bull raged. Sinotar tore the room apart with wrathful ire. Idols, reliquaries, utensils, a small cauldron: One after another, hurled objects flew from the doorway, across the room.

All her work — all my efforts — destroyed.

Mustapha moved forward. An object struck the floor with a hefty *thunk* at his feet. With a strange compulsion, he bent and retrieved a small, black idol and thrust it in his pocket.

From his vantage within the main apartment, Mustapha could see the General Prime, whirling about in the private sanctum, upturning jars, opening chests, and causing havoc. Looking for something.

The Cure. A Cure for Rhye. Perhaps the antidote to my poison, as well.

Enough.

Mustapha cocked his weapon. In the soft light, it glowed red. A bringer of vengeance. He knew not what happened to his Lady, but Sinotar had to be stopped. He prepared himself for the roar of gunfire.

'Mustapha!'

A screamed warning. A feminine voice — Trixel Tate? — shouting to him from the hall doorway.

Mustapha turned.

Not one, but two figures stood in the entry to Belladonna's apartment. He recognised the elfin form of Trixel. Torr Yosef loomed behind her, almost blocking out the rectangle of scrallin light from the corridor.

Between Mustapha and the two Councillors, stalking Mustapha across the room, came a skeleton. It held an ornamental dirk in its bony fist, the blade a thing of terrible beauty ... pointed at Mustapha's chest.

Trixel Tate crossed the room at a slide, colliding with the fiend's legs from behind. It struck the ground, the dirk skidding beneath a sideboard. In an instant, Yosef advanced and began wrenching the skeleton to splinters of bone.

'Fool! What are you doing back in here?' thundered Bastian Sinotar, bursting from the alchemist's lair. His own sword was now drawn.

Before Mustapha could summon an answer, all were distracted by a new sound from the doorway.

A second skeleton entered the room, scanning the group with sightless eyes.

A third, then a fourth, entered behind it.

'We're trapped!' said Mustapha, uncertain whether the greater evil was the General Prime or the accumulating undead. He edged out onto the balcony as the three fell creatures moved forwards. Trixel and Yosef retreated alongside him.

Sinotar interceded — weapon at the ready — and began to fight all the skeletons at once.

'It's time to get out of here,' said Trixel.

<Down?> came Yosef's question.

Trixel nodded. 'You've got the strangeling,' she said, leaping up and over the balustrade.

The golem grabbed Mustapha, who snatched one last startled look at Bastian Sinotar. The sylph waged a one-man war on his assailants. Without further delay, Yosef leapt over the edge, in pursuit of the fixie.

A four-storey drop brought them to the courtyard.

With feline agility, Trixel landed on her feet and rolled. Yosef crashed to earth beside her, shattering flagstones. He set Mustapha gently upon the ground.

'What is happening?' he said. 'What are they after?'

'My guess is, they're after Lord Rogar,' replied Trixel. 'The only Giltenan left alive.'

<*An ambush of dark sorcery ... just as Sinotar speculated,*> said Yosef.

They landed near the portico, where the macabre attack began. The sentries' corpses still lay in the positions they had fallen.

'I need to go back in!' cried Mustapha, flouncing back towards the door.

<*You must not,*> warned Yosef, reaching out to him.

'There is only danger and death in there,' agreed Trixel. 'This was clearly an ambush set for Sovereigns. The way that creature looked at you, though ... you need to be in a safe place.'

'But ... I don't know anyone outside of the House.'

'Forget the House, Mustapha. We need to leave Via alto—'

Mustapha let out a shriek.

The dead sentries writhed and clambered to their feet. Only now did the three notice the impossible thinness of their arms, the lank droop in their leather armour over emaciated frames. Fleshless grins leered back at them.

Several more of the dead appeared from inside the portico. The fallen defenders — sentries, civilians, and Councillors — now replenished the ranks of Giltenan dead.

'At least one of them is armless ...?' quipped Mustapha, his face pale.

<*Run,*> said Yosef.

'Follow me,' said Trixel. She sprinted away into the night, leaving behind the horrors of the House of Giltenan.

CHAPTER 6

THROUGH STORMY SKIES

Marnis the Creator moulded and set the first humans upon Rhye. He fashioned them as an homage to his own progenitors — Adatar, the Sun, and Anato, the Moon.

The Fae Folk, the Mer Folk and the Delves already inhabited the land in this early Age; elemental spirits, the dryads and undines also dwelled in forests and untamed seas. Many centuries later, the Delves would be the first of the higher beings to disappear, under enigmatic circumstances.

Humans originated in Petrichor, where dryads taught them to hunt. Thus, they too became tribal. They lived a primitive existence, having not yet learned the finer arts of civility. In time, the dryads chased humans out of their domain. The banished tribe moved west from Petrichor in search of their own territory. Roaming the land to its edge, they arrived at the shore of a glittering sea, where a giant crest of land rose to jut over the water, forming an enormous hillside. From the summit of the hill, they claimed all the land they could see as their own. Upon the hill itself, the tribe of humans settled, founding the City of Via.

This settling ushered in the Age of Immortals.

For centuries, Humankind stayed close to the sea and even closer to their Gods. Simple needs were met with humble prayer: To Cornavrian they turned for favourable tides; to Phydeas for bountiful crops and plump vines of drinking grapes; to Augustine to remain hale; to Floe to watch over the coming generation.

The tribe of humans proliferated, venturing away from the hill and the surrounding plain. They searched for more fertile ground and docile game to feed their swelling numbers.

Expansion saw the children of Marnis trace the path of the roaring Granventide River, before fanning out to the north and south. With merciless blades, they swept aside the meek creatures they encountered. In shaded glens the humans met with captivating gnomes and elves.

They slaughtered every last one.

While Anuvin rubbed his hands together at this semblance of conflict, in truth, the humans slowly turned their backs to all the Gods, including him.

The violent advance of Humankind did not go unchecked. The sylphs, the latest creations of Marnis, provided staunch resistance. With their superior military bearing and lofty mountain vantages, the winged warriors pushed back from the northern ranges. Conflict raged, giving birth in blood and fire to the Realm of Nurtenan. In those alpine climes, the struggle for territory continued until the Age of Obelis, with the Sovereignty of Montreux Giltenan.

Eastward expansion bloated Humankind, producing a lust for

blood and territory. The marauding tribe even dared to attempt Petrichor, once a welcome haven. That fateful attempt launched a staggering chain of events, echoing down the corridor of time.

An army of three thousand bellicose men (and women amongst them) marched to the place where the Granventide and Bijou Rivers intersected. Several attempts to erect a bridge failed, the turbulent waters washing construction away in defiance. Such was their greed, the horde attempted a treacherous crossing by swimming, despite the peril. Many, weighed down by armour and arms, disappeared beneath the froth. A stubborn but depleted throng gained the eastern bank. Beyond the point of turning back, the survivors forged onwards into Kash Valley.

Lush, ethereal greenery distinguished the Valley. A silver shroud of mist cloaked gentle slopes. Wild grasses wore dew like diamonds and the perfume of flowers hung light upon the air. The men and women of Via felt their spirits buoyed by the place. For precious days, it rivalled the hill by the sea as a potential new home for their populace.

Like a bright apple with a rotten core, the sanctuary of Kash Valley harboured a dire ill.

Their guard weakened by the wistful lure of the vale, the rogue horde gave little concern to the coven of black-robed beings they found, crouched in a field of white wildflowers. At any rate, the coven numbered little more than twenty. Even after the ordeal at the river, the humans still outnumbered them by one hundred to one.

The creatures gathered around a fire. Smoke spiralled from their centre into the sky. They shared a strange, sing-song language, more akin to a guttural chant than a melodic prayer.

Though the fire crackled in their midst, it cast no glow — it was obsidian black.

A stir of hesitation rippled in the human ranks, though it passed after a heartbeat. Their immense majority gave them bravado. They pressed forward, intent on crossing the field, for the eaves of Petrichor could be seen a few leagues hence. If necessary, they would flatten the mysterious coven as they came.

This error saw many more lose their mortal lives.

As one, the Wearers of Black stood from their hellish fire and set upon the human legion with terrible force. A banshee wail arose from two-dozen throats, as each member of the coven reached into the black malice.

The hapless humans watched in dumb despair as great scythes of fire were hurled at them.

Sheets of flame, the essence of midnight, flew across the interceding ground to sear and envelop the bodies of those invaders who stood nearest. Flesh melted from bone as corpses tumbled to the earth.

The Wearers of Black advanced on the army.

Whether through crazed fear, primal fighting instinct, or a blind belief in superior numbers, the human forces abandoned defence and charged towards the dark coven.

Further bolts of hurled flame cut down swathes of oncoming warriors until, as was inevitable, the two groups fell upon each other. Swords clashed against ebony staves. The black-robed men and women, though soon surrounded, displayed appalling strength and discipline in combat. The humans, still primitive in their battlefield discipline, found themselves outclassed.

The situation soon became critical.

The bodies of the fallen, bereft of flesh, rose from the ground where they had been trampled.

A skeletal army, of scorched and smouldering bones, once more hoisted weapons, dropped in their moment of death. As if animated by an unseen power, the skeletons fell into step and began a new march, hemming in the humans they had recently fought alongside.

A battle raged in the heart of Kash Valley. The undead army grew with every fallen human warrior. Still, the coven fought with wrath and dark magic.

By inches, the tide turned.

As the humans prepared to meet with doom, from out of the east, there came a stout gust; warm, like the breath of the sun. With it came the beating of many great wings and the whinny of horses. In a blinding wave of light and heat, the skeleton army was dashed to the earth, bones crumbled to dust and scattered as motes in the wind.

All those left alive turned, to behold the source of such power.

A herd of fifty pterippi galloped across the sky. On eagle wings they came, borne by the solar wind. Each possessed a glossy coat, ablaze in all the colours of a summer morning: ivory, gold, caramel and more. Upon the foremost horse rode a woman, like a priestess, with a billowing cloak and a head of ash-blonde hair.

The horses descended until hooves touched soil. With a thunderous gallop they bore down on the clashing parties. Above the din came the woman's cry.

'Behold, you feel the Breath of Cornavrian! The gift of the Gods, essence of life on Rhye and the bane of Necromancy! Wearers of Black, I banish you from this sacred vale. Humans, you threaten the peace and balance of the land. Remember this moment, for in mercy you are delivered from Death. Return to your homes and march these sacred paths no longer.'

The humans dropped their weapons and knelt. They recalled the memory of divine power, gone from them for generations. Some wept. The thirst for dominion over Petrichor fled from them.

The Necromancers — for indeed they were the forsaken Adept

— cowed beneath this virtuous onslaught. The pterippi, circling them now, were favoured creations of Marnis; they brought with them the light of Adatar and a gale from the heavens. The priestess herself was no deity, though she commanded the horses. As such, she could only be obeyed.

One by one, the Wearers of Black faded into shadows, becoming darkness, disappearing. They snarled and spat as they departed, having little else with which to rebuke this opposing power.

A lone Necromancer did choose to speak: She was the last of her coven. 'Seer of the Valley, pay heed!' she cried, vicious in her dark beauty. 'You will atone for this incursion. Where there is light, there will always be shade. Where there is life, there is also death. Valendyne endorses it. We are his devoted ones. Rhye is as much our sanctuary as it is yours.

'The time of Valendyne is coming. I pray that your soul is prepared.'

The strange woman still sat astride her winged destrier. The pterippus responded to the Necromancer's words with a snort. As the wind fell low, the woman's cloak fluttered.

She offered her rebuttal. 'You recognise me for a Seer, though you mispronounce the future. The god of the Afterlife will indeed attempt a coup, but it will be blasted from the land, just as I have dismissed your coven. Wary of your movements, I shall remain in this cradle of the land to see the work done.'

'If that is your intent, then perhaps I shall erase you from this place now!' the Necromancer shrieked, enacting a motion such as would summon a burst of power.

The Seer anticipated the move and interceded. Tearing the sash from about her cloak, she made from it an incandescent cord; lengthened, tensile, twirling about the Seer's head. She lashed it at her foe.

With arms bound about her sides, the Adept became impotent, her death-spell muted. The Seer winched her in, close to the side of the pteripus.

'The best plans save room for adaptation,' remarked the Seer. She gave her adversary a chilling glare. 'You would have this place for your dark chapel? Well, now it shall be your sepulchre. Your lot will be to stay as my prisoner. Then, through you, I will always feel the pulse of your evil breed, be they in near lands or far. One by one, they will be slain, until none are left to mar the earth.'

The Necromancer stared up at her captor, with a gaze as ominous as the void. 'Speak your name, Seer,' she hissed, 'so that Valendyne might save you a special corner of his kingdom, in which to rot.'

With unnatural strength, the Seer hauled her quarry upon the rump of the pterippus. Only once her quarry was safely fastened did she grant the Wearer of Black a response.

'I am named Lily, after the pure white flowers you see about you, in this vale I call home.

'Here, I feel the thrum of the world beneath my feet. With my mind I see echoes of the past and peer into the shadows of the future. By the grace of Onik, do I behold his whisperings.

'Many a battle is yet to be fought. Many a life will Death yet consume. At the last will come a song of victory, when Death is vanquished and Valendyne is quieted for all time. The people of Rhye will sing it and rejoice. There, on a glorious new morning, will come the end of darkness.'

~

Mustapha's heart pounded in his mouth.

He stumbled, breathless, through the streets of Via. Overhead, an anaemic light played about the sky. For the first time that evening, he noticed the gathering clouds, stifling the silver beams of Anato.

Only two things guided him as he hurtled along cobbled roadways. The first — the meagre glow of scrallin, emanating here and there from masonry and pavers. It shone a paltry yellow, stuttering, faltering as he passed.

The second — the slight figure who dashed, sure-footed, ahead of him. Her coat flew behind her. She ran as if she knew the streets even better than he, though she had never lived there.

Without words, she urged him on in her fleeting wake.

Torr Yosef lumbered along behind him with heavy, mechanised footfalls. The golem insisted on forming a rear guard. A fortuitous move: Several of their skeletal assailants clawed at them from the shadows, as the trio fled the House of Giltenan. Yosef dispatched them with crushing blows, never falling out of step.

They passed through the outer reaches of the city. The huts and hovels of Via's fringe-dwellers passed them by. Most showed blackened windows.

'I've done a lot of running lately,' panted Mustapha to the fixie, ahead of him.

<Then you must stop giving everyone a reason to pursue,> responded Yosef.

'We aren't yet safe,' said Trixel Tate, the words flying over her shoulder. No exertion strained her voice.

'Those we left behind could have used our help,' pressed Mustapha. 'Is this not cowardice, to think only of our own safety?'

<There remain many formidable warriors, defending the House and its Lord. The Torrs will soon see an end to that fiendish attack.>

'What about your Fae retinue, Trixel?'

'Halli, Dart and Puck know how to dodge trouble. They also know their own way home. You could learn much from them …

except, perhaps, how to find your own way home. Now: Less chat, more running.'

Mustapha frowned at her back. His unbidden companions still overlooked one detail.

'I left my Lady back there.'

<Think not of Lady Belladonna. She is Rogar's charge, and he is true with a sword. May he strike well with it.>

'My goal is to deliver you from danger. Belladonna's immediate fate is not my concern,' said Trixel. She zigged and zagged, sliding down into a deep stormwater drain. Ahead, a low arch rose over the drain, as it passed through the towering outer wall of Via.

'I can't leave her behind. I owe her my life!'

'You owe her no such thing.'

Mustapha huffed in exasperation. Time to divulge all. 'I am poisoned. Toxins course through me. Unless I stay by her side, she cannot succour me.'

Yosef grunted. *<The cinnabar is found, then.>*

Trixel skidded to a halt on the slimy flagstones. Mustapha almost collided with her in his bid to stop. She turned on him in fury.

'How, Mustapha? Tell me: How does she 'succour' you?'

Mustapha blinked. 'Tinctures. Potions. I don't know. She says the poison is still active … that she needs me as some kind of conduit.'

Trixel stared at him. Torr Yosef rumbled something incoherent. It sounded disapproving.

'Listen, Mustapha. I understand your sense of debt to Belladonna. I was there, at your exile. You stole sap from Oberon's Yew and, by some insanity, thought you would get away with it. You could have been put to death. She saved you.

'However, there are still loose threads. Why did you do it? Was it Belladonna for whom you stole? What purpose did she have for the sap?'

Mustapha's mind roiled. His mouth worked, but no words came. Instead, he fumbled inside his clothes. Out came the blackened idol, retrieved from the floor of Belladonna's apartment, where Sinotar threw it.

He gazed at it. The thirteenth alabaster figurine, missing from his set.

A male face gazed back. A face of near perfection, marred by the cruel, upturned corners of his lips and the notable presence of three eyes. The third eye sat in the centre of the figure's forehead. Mustapha knew this eye saw into the future of every living thing. An eye that saw the inevitable End.

The figurine was scorched black, unlike those adorning Mustapha's shrine, coloured the white of ivory.

Valendyne. God of Death and the Afterlife.

'It was for a Cure …' moaned Mustapha.

'Lady Belladonna lied to you,' said Trixel Tate. She and Yosef regarded the figurine, as they might a ball of burnt hair and excrement. 'Whatever she has been up to, her motives aren't as honourable as you think.'

At that moment the third eye shifted, settling on Mustapha.

With a twitch and an involuntary cry, he dropped the cursed idol.

It struck the earth and shattered, the way an alabaster figurine would. The hideous shriek that burst from it startled them all.

The shriek of Lady Belladonna.

From the wracked shards wafted a plume of black smoke. As the plume began to disperse, the terrible sound dissipated. A sulphurous odour hung in the air.

<*We shouldn't linger here,*> urged Yosef.

Mustapha stood anchored to the spot. Trixel grasped his

shoulders and spun him around, shoving him towards the storm water tunnel beneath the city wall.

'As I suspected — it's time to go,' she said.

On hurried feet they left Via behind, with its beleaguered Sovereign still in the grip of battle.

The companions followed the Granventide.

Since the birth of Rhye, the mighty river surged and meandered its way across the centre of the land, like a tortuous belt between the west coast and the east. The devout creatures praised its gentle salinity as the Tears of Marnis. The agnostics — mostly Sontenean — praised it more simply, as a perfect source of irrigation for the crops and orchards of the lowlands.

Under a slate-grey sky, Yosef, Trixel and Mustapha picked a route eastward. Nearby, the Granventide rushed back the way they had come, seeking the Imperial Waters and the open Sea. It writhed, a roil of restless waters, sometimes illuminated by sheet lightning. The occasional rumble of thunder split the heavens, while dank air cast a thick blanket. A storm gathered in wait.

<If a downpour comes, Trixel, I might seize up. You'll have to carry me.>

The golem's unlikely travelling companions did not embrace his attempt at levity.

Mustapha barely spoke. The night's events clung to him. His haunted eyes registered little of the rocky path at his feet, as he tried to reconcile two horrors — visions of the dead reborn and now, the dissolution of his bond with Belladonna.

Mama ...?

The fixie defied prehension in other ways. She led them along a route that only she knew, without the need for guidance. Neither the threatening storm nor eerie shadows distracted her. Her demeanour differed from that of most pixies ... or fairies, for that matter.

Her acerbic voice spliced the gloom.

'Should I carry you, golem? Or should I leave you as a way-marker? Why do you feel compelled to join us?'

If Yosef took any offence at this remark, he did not show it. With a *snap*, his eyes became luminescent. Though he remained at the rear of the group, his towering height enabled him to cast light over the heads of his companions, to better reveal the path ahead.

<I have my uses.>

'If we needed a torch, I'd have brought one.'

<I am as invested as you are, Fae creature. Through Mustapha's actions, your Realm is endangered. The ore he stole came from the Warnom Bore, my home. I am obliged to see that its fate does not lie in devastation. The Adept, too, have a stake in this. Had they not already returned to Aerglo, I imagine Renfelix would be tailing us, as well.

<All is interconnected. For the sake of my people, I know this is where I am meant to be.>

'Fine. Light the way. You'd best not attract every marauder and spriggan in the area.'

<Sensible marauders and spriggans would be finding shelter from such a preternatural sky.>

Trixel's guard softened, making way for curiosity. 'You see this storm as an act against Nature?'

<You know it as well as I, Trixel Tate. The Council spoke of it. The land's peril is near, and the omens materialise. This storm is unseasonal. It brings with it a foul, oppressive air. Consider also: If my vision is true, it brews in the east, over the Forest Realm.

<I see it in the rhythm of your footfalls. You hurry home. Though I understand the pull of familiar places, I counsel a measured flight. Rhye will wait for us until morning, should we seek shelter and replenishment.>

Trixel slowed, then stopped. She regarded Yosef, impassive giant with lantern eyes burning; and Mustapha, pale and fatigued, standing by sheer force of willpower.

'We rest until daylight,' she said.

The trio found shelter readily. Rock outcroppings and overhangs pockmarked the greensward on either side of the Granventide River. A rough-walled cave — serendipitously unoccupied — afforded enough protection to light a small fire. Trixel, ever the creature of wilderness, foraged for roots and mushrooms and slew two hares. The aromas of a late-night repast soon filled their cave.

<Praised be Phydeas, for his Providence,> said Yosef, though he had no need for food. He positioned himself at the cave mouth, intent on watching over his flesh-and-blood companions.

'Praised be Phydeas,' echoed Trixel. Then, to Mustapha, who reclined by the fire: 'Daylight is only a few hours away. Eat a portion, then we will sleep.'

Mustapha accepted a morsel and chewed it. At any given moment, he looked a mere blink away from sleep. Still, the tender game revitalised him. After a few mouthfuls, he rose to an elbow.

'I know what you're thinking. You're thinking this tremendous mess is my fault. I can accept that ... and I'm sorry.'

Trixel crouched beside him, gnawing on the leg of a hare. Bemusement lit her features, chasing away their severity.

'Don't get delusions of grandeur,' she said. 'The Prophet preordained this "tremendous mess". You only made it more interesting.'

Mustapha pondered her words in silence while studying Trixel's face. The fire glow cast a half-light over her, creating the illusion of a being semi-concealed.

A crazy mop of hair hung in great, green fronds over her forehead. From beneath an audacious fringe, bright violet eyes absorbed the world around her, lambent in the dancing firelight. Her inquisitive face bespoke a pixie lineage, though there the genetic throwbacks ended. Her pinched mouth, a disapproving frown, may never have known a drunken giggle. Of her fairy kin, she showed little sign. She had no wings. Her taut body seemed more honed for survival than for flippant leisure.

Mustapha reflected on her strangeness.

'Do you sometimes wish you were pure pixie, or pure fairy?'

'No. Fairies are daft, and pixies are obnoxious,' replied Trixel.

'Wouldn't that make you both, daft and obnoxious?'

'I prefer to think it makes me neither.'

From the cave mouth, Torr Yosef chuckled.

Mustapha tried a different tack. 'Lord Oberon is a fairy.'

'He is unlike any other fairy that has ever walked the land. You ought to know of his superlative nature. He fostered *you*, after all. By the by: Did you just try to catch me out?'

'No,' said Mustapha. 'However, you are fortunate to know your lineage. The Fae — including pixies and fairies — are respected throughout Rhye for their devotion to the land and its creatures.'

Trixel stared into the fire. She shifted her position, kicking off her boots and extending her feet towards the flames. She wriggled her toes.

'You want to know who you are, don't you, strangeling?'

'Doesn't everyone? Until last week when I swallowed this blasted rock, it was all that I truly wanted.'

'It's not what I wanted,' said the fixie. 'I walked away from my parents as soon as I knew how. I was an accident that they didn't know how to handle. Young, irresponsible drunks, the pair of them. That was three hundred and fifty years ago. They're probably dead.

'It makes us both orphans in a way, you and I … though you did not choose that narrative. If it's clarity you seek, I know of somebody who might help you.'

Suspicion darkened Mustapha's face. He peered at Trixel beneath heavy eyelids. 'Are you leading me back to Petrichor?'

Trixel shook her head. 'It wasn't my intention. I think you're a fool, but I don't wish you dead. No, my attention is elsewhere. Much greater forces are at play. We're all caught up in this "tremendous mess", whether we like it or not. I agree with the golem — we're all invested. We just don't know how, yet.

'Enough speculation. Tomorrow, we will reach the confluence of the two rivers. If the skies are not befouled and Cornavrian favours us, we may cross into Kash Valley. There, I hope to find some answers. We must travel with haste ... I sense a presence in our wake. If we are to be efficient on our path, we both need our rest.'

Mustapha did not respond. Sleep engulfed him.

Torr Yosef watched over the pair as the fire quelled to embers.

In the small hours, a squall arose with driving sheets of rain punctuated by the rumbling heavens. Winds wailed like the forsaken creatures of Fenmarck Haunte. By dawn the rain abated, though the swirling gale continued to rip through the trees. The sun did not so much rise, as lurk behind thick clouds.

After demolishing the remains of Trixel's provisions, the three abandoned their cave. Outside, the wind whipped and buffeted them. Relief came when it changed directions and a tailwind aided their progress.

Before midday, the wooded, rock-tumbled terrain ahead of them opened into a wide vista, where wild grasses rippled in the turbulent weather. One league hence, they saw the place where merged the two great rivers of Rhye.

<*Here meet the Milk of Petrichor and the Tears of Marnis,*> observed Yosef.

'So much for a calm river crossing,' said Mustapha. 'Perhaps we're fated to remain in Sontenan.'

'We'll see,' said Trixel, casting a glance at the sky.

Together, they crossed the grassland. Yosef strode first into a new headwind, creating a slipstream in which his smaller companions could proceed. At last, they arrived at a high embankment on the western shore of the Bijou. Not far from where they stood, the two rivers joined. The wide, swift-flowing waters threatened any would-be swimmer with death.

'It's a long walk to the nearest bridge,' said Mustapha. Many spans crossed the Bijou from the fringes of Petrichor, though they were leagues away, where the waters ran timid.

<I may be able to ford it and bear you both across,> suggested Yosef.

'No,' said Trixel. 'The current is powerful. If it is too deep, you'll be swept away … then all of us are lost. I may have a better solution.'

'Oh?' said Mustapha. 'How will the three of us, without a boat, a rope, or a bridge, make it to the far side?'

'There are more than three of us,' answered the fixie. She turned, looked skyward and pointed. 'Since yesterday, we've been followed.'

Mustapha looked to the heavens. Beside him, Yosef did the same and nodded.

High above, against a blanket of cloud, two birds circled in an otherwise empty sky. As the trio watched, the birds continued to bank. Broader, then lower they came. Their silhouettes grew.

Mustapha's stomach clenched.

Those aren't birds …

Against buffeting currents, great, powerful wings beat, keeping the two figures aloft. Though the wind tried to cast them about, they descended steadily. Human forms, with two arms and two legs, supported by gigantic eagle wings.

… They're sylphs.

A gnawing dread gripped Mustapha, an apprehension he could

not suppress. The figures alighted upon the ground, twenty yards from where the companions stood.

To the fore, came the imposing form and scowling visage of Bastian Sinotar. A female sylph followed him. With fluid strides, she drew nearer: Leith Lourden, of the Vrendari retinue. Both remained in light armour, as they had worn during the attack on the House of Giltenan. Weighty ornamental components, displayed during the Council of Rhye, were absent.

Dark blood spattered Sinotar's breastplate and pauldron, originating in a gash by his right temple.

With grim countenances, the sylphic warriors folded their wings and approached the companions on the riverside bluff. Leith's kind features wore the strain of fatigue. Long, platinum tresses, typical of her race, rippled in the wind. Her eyes flicked over the unlikely threesome, settling on Mustapha with a weary smile.

Sinotar also glanced at Mustapha. In contrast to his kinswoman, he did not smile. He regarded each of the three with a perfunctory glare. Then, summoning his most gruff intonation, he addressed them.

'Lord Rogar Giltenan is dead.'

CHAPTER 7

MILK INTO SOUR

Deep in the forbidding bowels of Banwah Haunte, where age-old trees long ago choked out the sunlight, two beings engaged in conversation.

'Welcome, at last, to the Halls of Pox. Your visit is long-awaited.'

'Save the empty platitudes. I did not come to this rancid cave to be social. I came to observe your activities and have you account for your failings.'

'Diplomacy be damned, then?' rasped the accused. 'You threaten me here, in my own stronghold? In my own throne room? I shall have you taken apart, a fleshy morsel for my redcaps.'

'Spare me! I look around this filthy warren and all I see are bags of sepsis, bumbling trolls and vermin. If you are a king, then you are a king of rats.'

'I am Ponerog, Lord of the Wilden-Folk. The eldritch forests of the Haunte are my kingdom. All its creatures are subservient to me.

Since your gypsy double-act rolled into Via, I have amassed much power. You would do well to observe due respect.'

Lord Ponerog lowered his considerable bulk out of his throne and leaned over his reproachful visitor. Bloated by avarice, his habitus daunted most who saw him. A wild mane bristled atop his head and down his back. Wet, pink eyes, set deep in a cruel face, glared at his guest as if he meant to devour her.

Despite being a commanding specimen of her race, she resembled a waif beside Lord Ponerog.

'Amidst all this power, you have also been weak, haven't you?' said Belladonna, unruffled by his display.

'You show gall, naming me weak!' Spittle flew between yellow, slab-like teeth. He leaned close, breathing his latest meal over the woman. 'I killed my own father to sit on this throne. Ha! To know weakness was to know him. I'm baffled by how he managed even to impregnate my hussy of a mother, with such a flaccid prick. Worse, still: In his limp hands, this fortress of mine would have become an insipid house of healing.

'To heal the meek ... it turns my stomach! Is it not through disease and suffering that we grow and become resilient?'

Belladonna eyed Lord Ponerog with distaste. As he spoke, his oversized nose twitched. Dark hairs poked from within it.

'You cannot hide from me,' she replied, with dark intensity. 'You murdered your own father, granted ... but then you seem to have forgotten the art.'

Ponerog baulked. 'I don't know what you mean —'

'You keep her alive. I sense her. I *feel* her. She is here ... isn't she?'

Moving away from Ponerog, Belladonna cast her gaze about the cavernous room. She let her percipience reach through the slime-coated walls around them.

The Halls of Pox — the fortress of the Wilden Lord — existed as a huge, stone bunker in the belly of Banwah Haunte. Without, it resembled a castle, half-swallowed by the ancient forest. Within, it served across the centuries as a laboratory, a fortress of defence and a prison.

In recent decades, the Halls had another name: The *Vater Augustoma*. Lord Vater — Ponerog's father, a devotee of Augustine — sought to provide the crumbling ruin with some redemption from its sordid history. His vision saw the Halls reborn as a place of learning, dedication ... and healing, much to the chagrin of the devious forest denizens living inside.

Destiny would see his plans flounder.

While still in his teens, Ponerog first learned the touch of darkness. A dream here, a thought there; whispered voices, which spoke only to him. They spoke of a coming Age, where a Lord could wield the power of the Gods.

The whispering grew louder. The voices, more insistent. The visions, more alluring. Evil took hold and within him grew the urge to usurp and conquer. With a warped mind came a warped body. At first, he concealed the changes taking place in him, in a bid to keep his father unwary.

Then, in his mid-thirties, he determined to skulk in the shadows no longer. One day, a fantastical, black beast paid him a visit — a beast that came to him with a message ... and a plan.

Ponerog slaughtered his father in cold blood, becoming Lord of the Wilden-Folk. Under his rule, Banwah Haunte flourished stronger than ever, as a haven for the rotten, the outcast, the malignant and the savage.

The forest stronghold received another makeover, this time as a factory, driven by slave labour. Within its twisted, underground vaults, Ponerog harnessed the might and willpower of his subjects, in a push to create something heinous. In doing so, he hoped to finally appease the wicked forces that compelled him.

Belladonna came to witness the fruits of his labours. Beneath their feet, in the deeper Halls, she sensed the bubbling, purulent seep of his creations.

Yet her senses strove upward, away from the stench of industry below. Above the Halls and the cavernous throne room, a crumbling tower rose defiantly amidst the gloom and ancient trees beyond. A tower where she knew the repugnant Lord would retreat when his appetites drove him there.

Belladonna prodded, 'Speak the truth, king of rats. You let her live, didn't you?'

'Who?'

'The April Lady.'

The name gave Lord Ponerog pause. Belladonna uttered the name that mostly humans spoke, in reverent tones, when discussing that fair Sovereign: The Lady who left them, so many years ago.

'You've spent too long amongst your milquetoast human friends,' he said at last.

Belladonna sneered, her eyes glacial. 'You evade the question.'

'The Lady Giltenan's fate is in my hands!'

'The fate of Rhye — and of your Sovereignty — hinges upon her death.'

'She will die when I am good and ready. In the meantime, she is proving herself a valuable resource.'

Belladonna's nose wrinkled. 'How you choose to defile the little bauble is of no interest to me.'

'Oh, but I assure you, it should be. The "little bauble's" life-force is providing an essential catalyst in the production of my Pox.'

For a moment, Belladonna appraised the corpulent Lord. Though repulsed by him, Ponerog harboured talents that suited her grand design. He inherited his father's innate skills with medicine ... but rather than pursue healing, he channelled his energy into toxins.

'Show me,' she said.

Stairs spiralled into the underbelly of the land. Naked flames in wall sconces lit the way through broad passages of stone, tinted green and treacherous with slime. Belladonna hitched the hem of her sweeping, black robes as she descended behind the Wilden Lord.

Redcaps guarded the Halls, stationed in shadowed archways, armed with curved blades or poleaxes. The redcaps remained as cousins to the long-extinct gnomes and dwarves, though they nurtured homicidal leanings. Red eyes glowed like points of fire from angular, deranged faces. Each wore a skull cap stained with blood.

The redcaps bowed low as Lord Ponerog passed. They offered Belladonna derisive jeers, gnashing pointed teeth.

The stair continued, down through the core of the stronghold. From below rose the acrid odour of decay and the echoing clangour of toil. Belladonna also detected a more natural sound: the rush of flowing water.

Ponerog explained without being prompted. 'I am sure a creature of your intellect already knows that these Halls stand near the course of the Bijou. In fact, those waters run a scant half-league from here, marking the edge of the Forested Realms, and the southern limits of Fenmarck Haunte.

'What you may not fathom, is that the Milk of Rhye is a crucial element in the birthing of my Pox. The forest trolls were ever so obliging, carving a channel to redirect the river's flow beneath the foundations of my home.'

On cue, the bellow of great creatures welled up from a place close by. In symphony, the grate and lurch of some tremendous device sounded from an adjacent chamber. Ahead, a high archway of carven stone beckoned. From beyond it issued the sounds of torment and heavy work. The pair stopped at the threshold.

With a flourish, Ponerog ushered Belladonna within. 'Behold,' he announced, 'the genesis of a plague.'

Belladonna gave him a scowl of disdain and entered.

At the roots of Ponerog's stronghold, gargantuan foundations sank into the bedrock of the land. Below the fastness of Banwah Haunte, a huge grotto homed a makeshift river. As Ponerog described, a tributary of the River Bijou flowed through the centre of the vast space.

The shores of the subterranean waterway crawled with activity. Enormous forest trolls, like gnarled old trees, stood chained to a grinding network of machinery crafted from timber, stone and flax rope. With terrible might they heaved and pushed against it, causing water to be drawn from the artificial river. All the while, redcaps used whip-vines to lash at them with glee. The trolls bled dark green sap.

The water they drew, tainted with their ichor, travelled in drums along a conveyor, about which swarmed a host of goblins and imps. They transferred the water from the drums into much larger cauldrons, where all manner of brewing and incantation took place. Noxious liquids from forsaken places, accompanied by chants in a tongue seldom heard, tumbled into the water. Fetid odours, reminiscent of gangrene and disembowelment, met Belladonna's nostrils.

'What is happening there?' she questioned.

Lord Ponerog followed her pointing finger and gave a hideous smile.

At the end of the conveyor, goblins danced in rapturous fervour as they added a final reagent to each cauldron in turn. From the vile mix within, creatures emerged, clambering over the lip of their birthing vat. With rotund bellies and stunted limbs, they waddled like human toddlers, though there any likeness ended. Grotesque, plump and coloured a bilious yellow, the children of sickness reeked of evil. One after another, they climbed from the mixture. Redcaps lead them, stumbling and squelching, towards ready-made cells.

Hundreds of cells pitted the far side of the cave. Each contained hundreds of the ill-born cherubs ... and still they came.

'Those are my Pox!' Ponerog declared, with unhinged malice. 'They are my children — my plague rats — awaiting their time to bring pestilence to the weak.'

Belladonna glowered. Her gaze settled on the final step of the birthing process. 'Contain your gloat,' she said, though the scale of Ponerog's operation did impress her. 'I want you to tell me what *that* is.' She indicated the place where goblins added the final reagent.

'Ah.'

Ponerog reached inside his heavy, furred cloak — or perhaps his grotesque, hirsute folds of skin, it was impossible to be sure — and drew out a crystal vial. A tiny bottle, the size of a human thumb. Within it, a pellucid fluid shone, bright and clear as the crystal that contained it.

'These are tears,' answered Ponerog. 'The tears of the Lady Maybeth Giltenan.'

Belladonna frowned. 'Such clarity ... they are unlike any human tears.'

'She has shown herself to be unlike any other human,' said Ponerog, approaching wistfulness.

'Your covetous fawning disgusts me.'

'Do you behold what I have achieved? The delicate grief of the April Lady — as you name her — provides the catalyst for my greatest undertaking. Her tears transcend the will of the Gods, bringing life to my children.'

Belladonna turned from the scene. Triumph loomed on a desolate horizon. She needed the Wilden Lord to play his part, not stumble at the last step.

She spent many years laying the foundations for her coup de grace. Luring the young and impressionable Ponerog to her cause required agonising patience and guile. The day came when he usurped Lord Vater as the Sovereign of the Haunte. At last, Belladonna knew she might bend him to her will. Indeed, he showed his worth: Turning health into illness — purity into purulence — he vowed to help her achieve her unholy intent.

He needed only one thing: the untainted soul of a human. A soul to sully, to break, from which to wring the essence of misery.

The request dovetailed perfectly with Belladonna's plans ... and she knew the ideal human.

Some political subterfuge, a promised alliance, a hint of gallant romance and a falsified invitation set the scene. Lady Maybeth Giltenan rode forth from Via with her entourage, on a diplomatic mission. She travelled to meet the debonair Lord Vater, patron to a newly established institute of healing, in the depths of the Wilden Realm. It could have been a union unlike any seen before in Rhye.

Instead, tragedy struck, sending shockwaves across Sontenan.

The entire entourage vanished. A fleet-footed Emissary arrived in Via, reporting that the Lady Giltenan never arrived. Rumours also abounded that Lord Vater had fallen ill. Despite commissioning a desperate search for the Sovereign of Humankind, he now lay bedridden. His son, Ponerog, would ably facilitate the mission in his place.

The young Wilden Lord helped a squadron of Vrendari and human soldiers to scour eastern Sontenan and the fringes of the

Haunte, in the region she was last seen. Little more than a few savaged limbs — the remains of a human party, retrieved from a troll den — were ever recovered.

Ponerog conveyed his devastation. The tragic disappearance (and apparent demise) of the ebullient Sovereign, followed soon after by the death of his own father, destroyed him. Weighed down by the despair in his soul, Ponerog drew back from the world.

In the present moment, a fiendish light shone in his eyes.

His loathsome filth aside, Belladonna had to credit him — the Wilden Lord played the role of aggrieved son to perfection. With the virtuous Lord Vater gone, and the Sovereign of Humankind in his psychotic hands, Belladonna's vision for the future coalesced.

Except for one detail. Ponerog had not carried through.

She addressed him.

'For half an Age, I have forged this campaign,' she said. 'It all comes down to what you choose to do next.

'The Fae Ring is bound sevenfold, by ancient power. It must be weakened so that its captive may be freed.

'To accomplish this task, we must dismantle the alliance of Sovereigns. The Lord of Humankind meets his fate as we speak. The Fairy King and his Queen will be next to fall. Enoch shall be overcome by one of the very Gods he fawns to — that much is assured. I savour the deaths of Sinotar and the Archimage the greatest; thus, I leave them for the last.

'You, Lord Ponerog, are my lieutenant. It is through you that victory is assured. Through you can the Ring be dissolved — the rapturous power it binds may then be unfurled. Lady Maybeth is the last of the Giltenans: She must die. Her life force is strong with the memory of Humankind. With her death, ripples of power will flow to Nevermore.'

Ponerog grunted. *Nevermore.* Maps had the place scrawled on them, though nobody alive had been there, except for the Fairy King. A place surrounded by impassable mountains, an unchartable Sea ... and possibly ogres. Belladonna's scheme ranged somewhere between folly and raving madness.

Ponerog resolved to nurture her hubris until it brought her to the brink.

He smiled.

'It shall be done,' he said. 'It does beg the question, while we discuss the dispatch of our enemies — what do you plan to do about the whelp?'

The bilious host of Pox neared completion, ready to be released as a plague upon the land. Beneath the warped spires and ramparts, beneath the roots of Ponerog's home, the slavering creatures of Banwah Haunte toiled without respite. Cauldrons bubbled with the noxious mixtures within. Acrid juices sluiced from cauldron to vat, one set of grasping hands to another, until the abominations emerged.

Trolls dumped the effluvium into the murky offshoot of the Bijou. There it swirled, a slick of liquid despair, as the makeshift river flowed on beyond the cavern.

Foul water found its way through crevices in the bedrock, by way of natural sewers, until it spilled across the leagues into the Sour Milk Sea.

~

THOOM ... THOOM ... THOOM ...

Far across Rhye, looming thunderheads billowed above the waves. The Ealing Sea anticipated the coming tempest with restless chop. Neither gulls nor hawks braved the buffeting winds, instead nestling safe inside the craggy face of the Immortal Cliffs.

As with most of the Seven Seas, the Ealing Sea could be traversed, from the coast to a series of islands, keys, and atolls. Undines and barnacled sailors inhabited some of these, in times of calmer waters. Other islands, barren rock spearing above the waves, supported no life.

THOOM ... THOOM ... THOOM ...

One such upthrust, a day's swift sailing from the coast of Rhye, sat far from the oft-used sailors' routes. It went without a name, for to name it was to consecrate it. Most denizens of Rhye spoke of it only in whispers, reassuring one another that its occupant could not escape.

Wilful prayers so often went awry.

THOOM ... THOOM ... THOOM ...

Time and again came the sound of rock blasting against rock. Unrelenting, the pounding rhythm shook the island's foundations, reverberating into the depths, sending shockwaves a vast distance beneath the surface.

Lord Neptune's deep divers were yet to trace the sound to this small island. Mistaken in their belief that the sound originated on the sea floor, the Mer Folk had their backs turned to the one place a fear of the Gods might have pointed them.

THOOM ... THOOM ... THOOM ...

At the centre of the island, surrounded by natural spires, stood a man encased in a cocoon of quartz. The stone hung about his body in the fashion of enormous plates of armour, fastened to him with enchanted bands and girdles.

Through a fractured faceplate, the man viewed the mainland far away. The Peaks of Light either beckoned or chastised him, depending on the colour of daylight reflecting from their distant slopes.

Over the Peaks, he saw the sky and the storm that broiled there.

A jagged flash burst over the mountains. The weather turned foul, a warning of dark sorcery at work upon the mainland.

Anuvin, God of War, drew strength from the signal. He drank in the vision of bleak thunderclouds, letting his fury and the energy of the storm become one.

He spent almost one thousand years just to gain movement within his quartz gibbet. To raise an arm, one hundred more. The passion of his anger burned, deeper with every passing century, as he stared back across the Ealing Sea to the place of his humiliation.

He staggered back one step — a revelation! — bringing his stone-clad arm down upon the face of stone before him. The mockery of his armour mashed against the edifice. He repeated the movement, the titanic muscles of his chest and shoulders protesting.

THOOM ... THOOM ... THOOM ...

His sinews knew no pain.

His lungs knew no exertion.

His patience knew no limit.

With a single mind, he would endure ... and then, war.

The next impact brought a *crack* as if the island itself split in two. The enormous plate of quartz, fashioned by Marnis, fell from Anuvin's right arm and struck the ground.

The rest would be easier now. He reached for the bindings on his left arm.

For the first time in nearly twenty-eight centuries, Anuvin smiled.

CHAPTER 8

THE EARTH WILL SHAKE

A man strode from the undergrowth. As he moved beyond the tree line into the clearing, moonlight spilled on him. His steps were uneven — he favoured a sprained ankle and hugged crushed ribs. At his side he carried a sack, stained dark about its lower portion. A weighty object sat within it.

'Will?' cried Meadow. His face jostled with Dique's at the opening to their boab prison.

'Will!'

The human recognised the diminutive pair, despite a brief association. A flash of relief broke through his grimace as he approached. Two dryads flanked him, poisoned blades and whip-vines held ready. Their feet made no sound, beside the clumping of his peasant boots. About them, numerous will-o'-the-wisps flickered and darted, luminous gold specks in the silver-blue night.

They halted at the roots of the boab tree.

The boab moaned. Sonia emerged from the lower branches of her home, wary of the foreigner. His escort offered her curt nods.

'You're alive!' exclaimed Dique.

Will threw a fleeting, crooked grin to the pair. 'I had a feeling I'd find two garrulous pixies holed away in here,' he replied. Ignoring his armed chaperones, he addressed Sonia.

'Spirit of the tree: In the good name of Lord Oberon, I urge you to release these pixies at once. The majesty of your forest — your very livelihood — depends on it.'

'It … it does?' pondered Meadow aloud. Dique jabbed him in the ribs with an elbow.

Sonia's eyes narrowed. 'You speak well, for one dressed as a farm boy. Who are you, that I should heed your words in my domain … human? Who are you to invoke the name of our Lord, ancient and noble as Petrichor itself? Speak true … or be killed where you stand.'

Meadow shuddered. The hamadryad seemed hospitable enough towards them. The presence of an outsider to the Realm of Fae Folk revealed an altogether different Sonia.

Will stood, chest out, and spoke in a calm, earnest voice. 'I am a carpenter's son' — the dryads rattled their weapons and pressed forward, for the woodworker's trade was sacrilege to them — 'and, though I risk my life to say it, son of perhaps the finest carpenter and woodturner in Sontenan. I spent my youth in Via, where he made business. I suppose I picked up a phrase or two amidst the crest-wearing people there. At any rate, the day came when I decided I'd sooner grow things from the earth than hack them down.'

Sonia's gaze continued to bore directly into Will's face — searching, scanning for any evidence of subterfuge. Humans scarcely entered Petrichor unbidden. Following the chaos at the Ceremony of the Nut, all intruders endured intense scrutiny.

'These pixies are under arrest for civil disturbance. They are accused of anarchy and will be tried in the Court of the Fairy King and Queen at Psithur Grove. You provide no foundation for their release. Moreover, you appear to *know* them. Justify yourself.'

'We're long-lost half-brothers!' yelped Meadow. All eyes turned to him, filled with either frustration, doubt, or horror.

'I mean ... cousins?'

'Cousins-in-law,' added Dique. 'Thrice removed. Haven't seen Will since dear Daisy Fields got wed to his brother, Alfred, five spring-times ago, bless her.'

Sonia's eyes narrowed further. The dryads stood their ground.

Will shifted on his feet, careful to keep one hand gripping the leather bag, the other empty and in plain sight. Deadly energy crackled at his back. 'I have reason to fear for the Sovereignty of Petrichor,' he said. 'I seek to deliver news to Lord Oberon. The Realm of Fae Folk may be under threat. These pixies hold the evidence necessary to convince him of this danger.'

Nobody moved. Will strained to keep his expression open. Readable.

In the still night, the leaves of the great boab stirred and rustled. An instant later, two of the will-o'-the-wisps peeled away from the group, zig-zagged into the trees and vanished.

Sonia's eyes lowered. 'Empty the bag.'

Meadow and Dique crammed against the hole in Sonia's trunk, holding their collective breath.

Will raised the bag. In a single movement, he upended it. A decapitated head struck the ground with a dull, fleshy *plop*.

The pixies gasped. The dryads bristled. Sonia leaned forwards, her eyes wide.

The Mayor of Petrichor leered up at them. His gaze reached to eternity. Gore seeped and crusted on his blue lips. The fleshy neck ended in a jagged wound — no swift, clean death for him.

'Explain yourself ... *carpenter's son.*'

Venom edged the hamadryad's voice. Regardless of the Mayor's Machiavellian reputation, his severed head in the clutches of an errant human blew diplomatic relations wide open.

'I found the head as I made my way home along the Verge —'

'Home from where?'

'Home from the market square of a nearby village. I earn my living selling produce there. My farm lies against the Verge separating our two Realms.' Encountering no further interruption, Will continued. 'This gruesome find lay in the grass by the windward side of a small copse. I could not find the Mayor's body. The act was recently done — the wound still oozed and carrion birds were yet to feast upon his eyes.'

'Then it lay close to his place of murder,' said Sonia.

'My conclusion, as well. That led to a greater revelation: Near to where I stood, lay the boundaries of the Ploughman's holdings.'

One of the dryad sentries spoke. 'This story is consistent. The human crossed the Verge and entered the fringe of Petrichor from Ploughman land. He was unarmed when we found him.'

Sonia pursed her lips. 'Do you accuse your own kinsman of this killing?'

Will paused. He did not intend to incite conflict between Realms. That, he knew, would come soon enough. 'I accuse no-one. I come to confer grave tidings to Lord Oberon, giving an account of what I have seen. Greater workings are afoot than petty political subterfuge.'

Before Sonia could ask Will what the 'greater workings' were, the arrival of more dryads cut the conversation short. Two, then four, then six of the militant forest spirits materialised, making no sound. Like a slipknot drawing ever tighter, they formed a cordon of warriors that hemmed Will against the boab tree.

An efficient messenger system. He eyed the returning will-o'-the-wisps.

The foremost dryad, a redoubtable creature with vine-like dreadlocks sweeping almost to the ground, acted as spokeswoman. 'The human interloper will be presented at Psithur Grove immediately.' An order, with no hint of invitation. 'He will bring the ... *evidence* with him.'

A second dryad cast a cursory glance at the captive pixies, before addressing Sonia. 'The accused are to attend, as well.'

'We're being taken to Lord Oberon?' gasped Meadow.

'Surely, our merciful Lord is asleep at this hour?' said Dique. 'We can always wait until morning. You know, to be civil —'

A withering glare from the long-haired dryad silenced him. She approached their cell, brandishing a taut length of vine.

Will stooped to collect the head of the Mayor ... and Meadow's stray boot.

Guided by the wisps' darting points of light, the company of warrior spirits, captive pixies and one human wound its way through the blue-black forest. Half a league separated them from Psithur Grove. A circuitous route threaded through stands of ancient elm and beech, across rivulets as dark as flowing shiraz, and past the dens of slumbering beasts, clenched in shadow.

Their captors did not prevent the reunited threesome from talking.

Meadow chose to be blunt. 'We thought you were dead, Will.'

'I'm glad you were wrong,' the wagoner said. 'As it happens, the Ploughman and his heel of a kid left it to chance. All this walking might help straighten the kink in my ankle, at least. How did Mustapha rope you two into this, anyhow?'

'When you're a pixie, mayhem is a professional obligation,' said Dique.

'You must both be fond of him, to follow him into a circus like that.'

'His harebrained schemes don't always make sense, but somewhere in that head of his, it all adds up. We've no clue what he was up to on this jaunt, though. Any ideas?'

Will brushed a low branch from his path, holding it so it did not swat the pixies behind him. Their hands were bound behind their backs. 'Mustapha spoke of a precious ore, destined to embellish Lady Titania's chariot ... but he had other ideas. I lost him there, I'm afraid — something about cures, ancient spell-working and the coming of darkness. If you ask me, Belladonna has him infected with her Song obsession.'

'Don't you believe the Song of the Prophet to be true?' said Meadow, half stumbling over an exposed root at his feet.

'Sure, I do. As a matter of fact, I think great upheaval is on its way, soon. Belladonna seems convinced she can wash it all away with a potion. That part sounds a bit barmy to me.'

'Mustapha adores her,' said Meadow. 'Let's hope it's because she knows what she's doing, not because he's lost his marbles.'

'It's an infatuation,' retorted Dique. He's building her up to be the mother he lost.'

'Is it so wrong to yearn for an absent mother's love?' said Meadow.

'There's no doubt it's love he needs,' said Dique. 'But maybe the place to look for it is in the present, rather than the past.'

Will sniffed, saying nothing. *Pixies are rarely so philosophical.*

The nocturnal march continued.

Without ever faltering — or lowering their trained weapons — the company of dryads led their captives through the looming forest until, up ahead, warm luminescence heralded their arrival in Psithur Grove. Beneath their feet a path appeared, which soon widened, becoming an established roadway of packed earth between the trees. The road curved and sloped down towards a broad, natural depression in the forest floor. They arrived at a hollow, in which the sacred Grove nestled.

The captives stared in wonderment.

Though no more than a few acres in size, Psithur Grove bespoke an opulence beyond comparison in the Fae Realm. At the centre of the Grove stood the ruling majesty of all the trees in Petrichor, Oberon's Yew. High above the canopy it reached, huge limbs pointing in every direction, roots snaking across the packed earth of the hollow's floor. From where the company stood, to the foot of the Yew, ran a wide avenue, swept clear of leaves. Lining the avenue — and spaced evenly throughout the remaining Grove — stood dozens of Ficus trees, like a battalion of forest-born warriors with slender, bone-white trunks.

The entire area glittered with warm light. A mystical glow emanated from many thousands of leaves, giving the impression that the trees themselves were draped in golden stars.

Dique's eyes darted everywhere. The graceful, arcing branches of an enormous willow framed the entrance to the Grove — the embodiment of Sonia's sister. Below her huge, drooping fringe, the hamadryad's face showed. She watched them with a knowing look. Dique reset his gaze forward.

Psithur Grove emanated warmth. The natural splendour made it a festive place, as befitted the womb of Fae culture. A paradoxical chill gripped the captives. Their recent transgression might test the limits of Oberon's good humour.

At the head of the avenue, upon a stage framed by the giant, serpentine roots of Oberon's Yew, stood the Lord and Lady of the Fae Folk.

Oberon's hands cradled his head in anguish.

'Oh no,' groaned Meadow.

The party approached the Sovereign couple with leaden footsteps. Flanking them along the avenue, Oberon's elite dryad guard fixed them with uncompromising stares. They regarded the human with the greatest intensity.

Will strove to maintain a confident air, hefting his satchel as the company came to a halt before the stage.

The Fairy King stood a head taller than most of the Fae Folk, his head reaching Will's shoulder. Legends sang of his anointment by the Gods, conferring superior stature and longevity. The Fae Folk held this as unassailable truth.

The crown upon his head sprouted antlers, resembling those of a stag. Capable of channelling the arcane magic of trees, the crown brought Oberon word from all of Petrichor, as well as from forests the land over.

His ageless face could have belonged to a pixie of twenty-five years, or twenty-five centuries. Most knew his years to be vast, but those who encountered him still caught their breath at his preservation. A beard, tapered and groomed to an absurd point, gave his face length and a certain impishness. His eyes, by comparison, carried an ancient depth.

Upon his form, he wore a voluminous cloak of fern, moss, and mist, which swirled and trailed in his wake. Runes marked its length, the meaning of which had been forgotten by almost all but himself.

A pained expression creased his features.

Beside him, Queen Mab — Titania — exuded rare elegance. Butterfly wings of orange-gold swept back behind her, giving an occasional flutter. Hair of deep magenta, tucked perfectly behind pointed ears, fell to her tiny waist. Her gown, a gift from the forest itself, flowed like wine about her form, ending in tiny rivulets at her feet.

Titania's face, tender and beautiful, bore aeons of care, as though she were a mother to every pixie in the Realm. As with Oberon, her features gave not the barest hint of her years.

Meadow and Dique took a knee before their Lord and Lady. Will placed his bag on the ground and knelt beside the pixies.

The dreadlocked warrior strode forward and offered Oberon and Titania a curt bow. 'Lord, Lady, these are —'

Oberon cut her off with a gesture, while massaging his temples. 'I anticipated one, but there are three of them,' he said. 'You will stand down, chieftess, while I learn their whys and wherefores.'

He turned to Will. 'Human. Stand and account for yourself.'

'My Lord, my Lady,' the wagoner said, rising to his feet. 'I am Will: Sontenean, gourd farmer and ally to the Fae. I come not to sow conflict, but to warn of it. I bring parlous tidings from across the Verge.'

'Speak and be plain,' urged Titania.

'The crux of my matter sits within this bag. I found its contents whilst skirting the Ploughman's holdings.'

Oberon frowned at the bag in disgust. 'It smells worse than troll spoor. What is in it?'

Will straightened himself. 'The head of your Mayor, Lord.'

The Fairy King recoiled by the barest fraction. Recovering in a moment, his eyes flicked towards the dryad chieftess. She gave a simple, confirmatory nod.

Titania skewered Will with a searing look. 'So, you found this head just lying about on human soil and thought it dutiful to bring it back here, as lost property?'

'No, my Lady. Finding this head only begins my tale.'

'We'd better have the rest of it, then.'

Will took a moment to fill his chest and exhale, before

proceeding. All the while, Meadow and Dique remained silent beside him, as still as the trees around them.

'Sire,' said the wagoner, 'though I loathe gossip, I know there is much talk between our Realms of a strange association between the Mayor and the Ploughman. One that may benefit them more than it does either Realm.'

'It is gossip that I, myself, have heard,' said Oberon. 'Continue.'

'Well, Sire, to find one's head on the other's land seemed at odds with the prevailing talk. I considered it prudent to undertake some investigation.'

'How so?'

'He means, he trespassed on Ploughman land to discover some context for this slaying, dear Oberon,' said Titania, now fully engaged in Will's tale.

'Indeed, my Lady,' the human admitted, 'and that is where I made a discovery of grave importance.

'From where I stood by my grisly find, not five hundred yards across the sorghum field, stood an imposing barn — no doubt an outlying storehouse for crop yield or equipment. Seeing no other sign of the Ploughman's industry, I set off toward it.

'Upon reaching the barn, I anticipated the need for stealth, suspecting that his labourers and farmhands would count dozens. On arriving, I found little need for caution — I met no resistance. I gained the barn without meeting another soul.'

Four sets of eyes were glued to Will. Even several dryads struggled to conceal their curiosity.

'What was in the barn, Will?' said Meadow.

'Well, he sure didn't find your absent common sense,' hissed Dique. 'Shut up!'

'Silence, the pair of you,' said Oberon. 'What was in the barn, Will?'

Will stared into the distance, as if he could see beyond the ancient Yew.

'I saw death,' he answered. 'Death ... both past and future.'

'You beheld Death?' cried Oberon. 'It cannot be so. The Two-Legged Death reveals itself to none, but those it will soon consume.'

'Beg pardon, my Lord. I do not speak of that fell creature of sacred lore. I speak of literal death — the bodies of the fallen and a harbinger of much worse to come.

'On the floor of the barn, like neatly stacked kindling, were bodies. Human bodies. Not dozens, but hundreds ... many hundreds. By their dress, they looked to be simple labourers. Perhaps farmers, like me. Though I searched their faces, I knew none of them. How they came to be there, I do not know.'

'Were there signs of conflict?' asked Titania.

'No, my Lady. There were no clues as to how so many met their end. I did perceive that this heinous task must have occupied some weeks. Whilst some of the bodies were whole and appeared simply to sleep, others were skeletal in state.' Will spoke in a monotone. The process of reliving his memory exhausted him.

'In summary: A human of questionable ethics reveals himself to be a mass murderer, by methods yet unknown,' said Lord Oberon. 'Amongst his victims is a bureaucrat — also of questionable ethics — from the Fae side of the Verge.

'Before you birth the question, Titania — I see it on your lips — I did indeed know of the Mayor's dalliance. As to why I would keep such a cretin, a potential traitor to the Realm, so close to the Sovereign Court: The answer is obvious. One keeps friends close, but enemies closer.

'The Mayor's death is hardly mysterious — one may surmise that a shady deal of some kind turned sour. Should we be so disheartened to sacrifice dead wood in a lush forest? I think not.

'What about this matter should stir my passions, farmer?'

'My Lord, within that barn there were not only bodies,' Will explained. 'Such a thing was there as I have never seen, though I do not doubt it is a thing of terror and malice. The Ploughman has undertaken much secretive industry in that place ... and the thing he has wrought looks fit to level a forest.'

Beside Will, the pixies grew still. Oberon's features contorted in a look of wonder and disbelief. The dryads drew nearer, rattling their weapons. From a distance behind them, Willow issued a mournful wail.

'I must know of this forest bane,' said Oberon, through taut jaws. 'Gather your wits and speak of it.'

Will's eyes grew wide as he told of the monstrosity he had seen. 'It is a machine, similar in form to those the Ploughman uses to harvest his vast tracts of land. There, the similarity ends. It is a gargantuan beast, equipped less for sowing fields than for reaping devastation.

'It sits on enormous wheels, like a giant's wagon. The wheels themselves are taller than I — no train of oxen could ever haul this device. Great scythes flank the machine, large enough to cut down a dozen men at one passing. Over the wheels it rises like a fortress, bedecked with turrets and pistons that bristle all over it.

'Then ... there are the guns.'

Psithur Grove could hear a pin drop. Even the Ficus trees seemed to lean in, attempting to absorb Will's tale.

To Oberon, born in the Age of Obelis, the advent of mechanical weapons represented an ungodly twist in the long braid of Rhye's history. The land he knew revered their Gods and respected magic. In this Age, many reserved such reverence for whoever posed the greatest threat.

The monstrosities of Humankind heralded the beginning of the end. Artless, large-scale massacre, blind to the lore of ancient Rhye, threatened to bring war back to the land.

'Describe these guns,' said Lord Oberon, all trace of good humour gone.

Will swallowed. 'They are akin to the hand-borne weapons that have made their way into modern duelling. An ominous, black barrel blasts smoke and fire, with projectiles that part flesh and bone as though they were water. A terrible roar they make, like a wounded beast; and in the wake of that sound, there is only maiming and death. Blade-wielding fighters stand little chance unless armoured, for the reach of a gun's projectile might be limitless.

'My Lord, these guns make me fear for the lives of many, for they are of great size. One barrel alone may have the girth of a birch or an elm ... and I counted no fewer than eight aboard this grim contrivance. Such is its vastness that the ground would tremble as it approached.

'It can be built only for war, and the Realm of Petrichor sits exposed before it. The lives of Fae Folk and the very Sovereignty are at stake, should it prove to be unstoppable.'

'The ground would tremble, you say.' The Fairy King stroked his beard to an even finer point. His antlered crown weighed upon his brow, now knotted in consternation. The import of Will's narrative dawned on him, as it did on all who stood near ... and it was a bleak dawn, devoid of any ray of sunshine.

The dryads stood resolute, the chieftess again their voice. 'We stand alongside all the denizens of Petrichor, Lord. No intruder gains purchase against the living, breathing forest.'

Oberon nodded. 'There is a trial ahead for us. Let us pray that we live and breathe to see the end of it.'

He turned to the pixies. Meadow and Dique long before realised the gravity of Will's news and knelt in stunned silence.

'By all that is sacred, under Adatar the Sun and Anato the Moon.

Who are you, who call yourselves pixies? Speak!'

'Meadow, my Lord. From Flaxae. Ever your liege.'

'… and I am Dique from Reed, Lord Oberon … Lady Titania. Humbled to be in your presence.'

'Humbled? Ever my liege? Your appearance here is testimony to the chaos you would wreak in my kingdom.'

'Oberon …'

'Hush, Titania. These two must know the gravity of their actions. Meadow — Dique — it is my advice that you were present at the Ceremony of the Nut, is that correct?'

'Yes, my Lord,' replied Meadow.

'Did you contrive to interfere with the Ceremony?'

'Not exactly, Lord Oberon,' said Dique. 'Though we were complicit, at the behest of a … a friend.'

Oberon and Titania exchanged a glance.

The Fairy King approached Dique. His movements were deliberate, but not threatening. 'Why do you hesitate, young Dique?'

'We ask for your good mercy, my Lord. A simple heist we were told. It is not his fault either … we believe he was compelled by another. A being of power.'

'He was compelled,' muttered Oberon.

Endless moments passed, in which the Fae sovereigns said nothing more. Oberon searched the pixies' faces, as if the answer to some deceit would be found there. At length he spoke again.

'Meadow. Dique. Witless though you may well be, you have disrupted a sacred ritual of dire importance to the future of our Realm. Within the Ceremony of the Nut and the blow of the Fairy Feller, lay the key to our protection. Long have I studied the Song of the Prophet and toiled towards the realisation of its augury.

'This human, Will — your would-be saviour — tells of a forest bane, an evil that has long been foretold. What you perceived to be an indulgent pomp was, in truth, my effort to cloak us against this bane. Now the effort is wasted. Many lives may be forfeit. Witless or no, your act has cast us into a pall of despair and may be considered one of treason.

'In this Realm, treason is punished with death. Should I add your lives to those innumerable others that may soon fall beneath the wheels of this infernal device? What difference will two more make, if they be justly punished? Is that the action of a great King? I grapple with the answer.'

The pixies knew better than to issue any utterance.

Perdition or penitence. Without the slightest cognisance or realisation, the mischievous plot baked by Mustapha had gone stale, hurling them deep into a drama of much greater magnitude than they could have imagined.

In silence, Dique cursed the day they had decided to pilfer drowseberries.

Lord Oberon continued. 'The hour is very late. I require rest and prayer. Lhestra will hear my plea and guide me to a just course of action. Then will come a song to shackled Anuvin — may his ears not be closed to me. The Fae have had little need for war, yet war has found us.

'Human, if you are a man true to the fading Gods, then stay and pray with me. If you are not, then go and find your own reconciliation, for in coming into Petrichor, you may have also condemned yourself to our fate.

'Warrior spirits,' he said, turning to the dryads, 'take these pixies back to ... back ... to ...'

The sentence fell, incomplete.

Oberon lurched, eyes bulging. His hands flew to his crown, clutching his head, as they had been when the party first entered

Psithur Grove. Unsteady on his feet, the Fairy King swayed, as if struck by a heavy beam.

'Mab,' he uttered, reeling backwards.

'Oberon!' Titania moved to his side. 'Another flare?'

The dryad chieftess came forward, to assist in some way. Titania waved her back.

'My eyes, they burn,' gritted Oberon. He still staggered back, though now with some intent. He drew near to the Yew tree, a towering bastion of strength behind him. He reached it, one hand groping for the mighty trunk, the other holding his head, lest it explode.

Oberon leaned on the Yew, chest heaving, snarling in agony. Some invisible force assaulted him, snatching him from his pronouncement. His knuckles blanched white, pressed against the tree. The contact focused the flood of hurt inside him.

'Tell me what you see!' beseeched Titania.

The Fairy King stared, pupils wide, looking at nobody. He spoke. 'The time, it comes. The storm is near. The earth will shake. It begins with fire ... a black pall will rise and be met by the cloud that brings the doom of the land. In Nevermore, the evil wakes.'

'Oberon, no ...' quailed Titania. 'Never—?'

'Nevermore!' The word came from Oberon in a breathless rush.

The dryads murmured prayers. Meadow and Dique held each other. The entire Grove quivered, stirred by the sinister energy channelled by the Fairy King.

In a searing tone he cried, 'The Fae Ring. *I see it break.*'

A visceral pulse washed through the Grove, emanating outwards from the Yew.

The dryads screamed, as one.

The glittering Ficus trees all winked out.

Psithur Grove fell into darkness.

CHAPTER 9

A WORD IN YOUR EAR

Dead.

The word bored into Mustapha's brain. He trudged along behind the sylphic warriors as the company ventured into the mysterious depths of Kash Valley.

Lord Rogar Giltenan ... dead.

Slain in the night by an ambush of his own long-dead kinsfolk.

Little remained in Via for Mustapha now. No friends, no trust, no safe place. He had only this flight across the land.

The serendipitous arrival of the Vrendari enabled them to gain the far bank of the river. Leith Lourden lifted the petite Trixel with an effortless swoop. In a similar fashion, Bastian Sinotar hoisted Mustapha across. It was a tense moment, in which Mustapha wondered if the General Prime would cast him straight into the turbid froth of the Bijou.

To the strangeling's surprise, he did not. The sylph bore a frosty disposition but showed none of the vitriol he displayed at the Council. In a vice-like grip, he raised Mustapha into the air. Beating immense wings against the wind, Sinotar gained height and soared across the river's span. He set Mustapha upon the eastern bank with unexpected civility.

Conveying Yosef's iron bulk across proved a more perilous undertaking. Leith and Sinotar each hoisted an arm, beneath the golem's shoulders. Lifting him from a dead stop was too difficult: He was almost plunged into the swift current below. Not to be left behind, he strode back a distance and, turning, lumbered towards the cliff edge. Engaging the stout pistons in his legs, he leapt into space, carried aloft on sylphic wings.

Mustapha exhaled, only once the giant creature crashed down on the far shore beside him.

'You'd better prove your worth,' muttered Sinotar to the golem, pushing past into the meadow beyond. Trixel Tate had already bounded off, following her unspoken instincts. Leith beckoned to the others, who fell in behind her. Yosef resumed his role as rear-guard.

The growing company moved with purpose, though Mustapha knew little of what that purpose could be. Trixel said she knew of someone who could help them.

Help us do what? Find an antidote to my poison? Discover who my parents were? Bring back the Sovereign of Humankind?

There was one certainty: This journey inched him back to where he had left his friends — the pixies and Harold — and Wagoner Will.

Mustapha no longer feared the repercussions of being back in the Realm of the Fairy King and his Queen. In a way, he already sensed the sealing of his own fate. The weakness gnawing at his legs, the flutter in his heart, were signs that the blood poison would claim him. No edict of Oberon's could change the course of his life. So, more than anything, he longed to be back in the company of those zany pixies, that resourceful dragonfly and the quietly charming gourd farmer.

The rolling meadow beneath his feet served well to buoy his spirits. Countless blades of verdant grass cushioned his bootsteps. Even beneath an ominous sky, Kash Valley harboured innate resistance, shunning the grim weather that encroached from the east.

Another pair of boots trod the earth beside him. Turning his consciousness outwards, he found his marching companion to be Leith Lourden.

The sylph moved with loping strides, conquering the distance one lissom step at a time. The sylphs' exertions of the past twenty-four hours would have exhausted the average mortal, but Leith shrugged off the leaden veil. Her attentive gaze scanned their surroundings, before returning to the spry figure of the fixie in front of her.

Leith and Sinotar flew from Via to intercept the companions. Mustapha assumed the winged warriors came to halt their progress: an irrational concern, albeit from the instinctive part of his brain.

Instincts can be wrong, I guess. Leith's manner did not threaten him. Sinotar, on the other hand ... It was difficult to tell.

Leith smiled, though her eyes remained on Trixel. 'You've been a wraith, Mustapha,' she said. 'So deep in your own thoughts, not even a golem could dig you out! I sense you've come back to join us.'

Mustapha accepted the remark. He dragged his boots, shoulders rounded, sallow face peering from beneath an unruly mane of hair. To anyone else, he surely resembled the undead.

'It's been a long day. A long week, really. I've lost track of time.'

'I can't argue with you there. The three of you did well to get out of that mess early.'

'By running away, you mean?' Mustapha stared at his boots.

Leith turned to face him, her sunny features like an embrace.

'Forgive me, but you don't appear in any shape for heroics. Self-preservation is often the wisest path.'

'You're right. Torr Yosef and Trixel Tate dragged me out of there. They could have left me behind. Now, we're halfway across Sontenan … on the way to find help. Or so I'm told.'

'Help? That sounds promising!'

'I pray so. I've poisoned myself.'

Even Leith's frown retained a sense of hopefulness. 'The General Prime wondered if you had done yourself some kind of … disservice.'

'Probably rubbing his hands together in glee.'

'Not at all. You are the reason we delayed our return to Wintergard.'

For the first time, Mustapha looked up at the beautiful sylph. 'I find that difficult to believe.'

Leith sighed. 'Something more than poison eats at you. You were at the Council. You are a familiar in the Giltenan Court, are you not? Does the fate of Lord Rogar weigh on you?'

'Out of great respect, yes,' said Mustapha. 'Lord Rogar did not know me well. I lived in the House due to the debt I owed his Lady. She led me to believe I was … more important to her. More than some kind of mule.'

'Lady Belladonna is difficult to contend with. You need bear no shame, admitting an entanglement in her web. To the contrary — it is fortuitous to have you out of it.'

With vehemence, Mustapha shook his head. 'It isn't quite as simple as that. I've been a fool. Oh, what a fool I've been! I sold out my dearest friends.'

Leith blinked, her eyebrows arching.

'Forgive me,' Mustapha continued. 'My life has turned inside out. Lady Belladonna showed me a false love. Blind faith misled me down a treacherous path. I've not only endangered myself, but many others.'

'Love is a potent veil,' said the Vrendari. 'It can be complex. Manipulative. False love will obscure the rational path. Try not to be so self-flagellant.'

Mustapha ruminated. For a while, he attended only to his labouring breath, trying to draw energy from the verdant wonder all around.

The sylph's companionship encouraged him. In a bid to keep the conversation going, he took a leap.

'Who do you love?'

Leith gave a wistful laugh, her face flushing. 'My, my ... it is a day for being candid!'

'It is. I'm not letting you off the hook.'

She shrugged. 'I save my love for my family. That way, when I am freed from deployment and am at last able to see them, they get the best of me.'

Mustapha's mouth twitched. *Family.* 'Don't you have a lover? Are you betrothed?'

'I am wed to my Vrendari vow. I cannot afford to divide my attention between my duties in Sontenan and a fellow sylph in distant Wintergard.'

Mustapha wiped sweat from his brow. The product of the march blended with the slick of fever. 'Couldn't you take a human companion?'

Leith shook her head. 'It is forbidden by Vrendari code. Since the time of Montreux Giltenan, those sylphs who swear an oath of allegiance to Humankind must remain pure of focus. Celibate, unmatched ... without distraction.'

A grimace creased Mustapha's face. 'My heart aches just thinking about it. Do you ever regret your vow?'

Leith looked puzzled. '*Regret* …? I do not know the word.'

Mustapha did not explain. He walked with his gaze fixed in the distance.

Ahead of the party, steep hillsides beckoned them into lush forest, while grasses and wildflowers carpeted the valley floor. The verdure swayed under a gentle breeze. The storm's turbulence did not penetrate this place.

Without a word to the group, Trixel's urgent pace slowed. Soon, she stopped. Sinotar paused beside her. Presently, all five halted in their tracks, absorbing the scene before them.

Kash Valley, famous the land over for its untamed beauty, lay tainted.

The terrain ahead had suffered a blight of misery. With only a brief transition, lush grass gave way to bare, grey earth. In the distance, the spindly trees stood naked. No birdsong filled the air. A forbidding chill gripped the travellers.

Sinotar surveyed the scene in a moment, then turned to Trixel. 'What do you make of it?'

'Desecration,' replied the fixie. The land did not appear as she remembered it.

<*There is a dwelling,*> observed Torr Yosef. The advantage of height, along with telescopic vision, enabled him to pick it out.

Deep in the Valley, where paltry sunlight struggled to penetrate, a wisp of smoke rose like a woeful, lost soul into the air.

<*It is barely a hovel,*> said the golem, <*but a fire lights the hearth within.*>

'Then she lives there still,' breathed Trixel.

'Who?' said two voices in unison.

Mustapha and Bastian Sinotar glanced at one another, each taking the other by surprise.

Trixel advanced towards the wracked earth and ruined Vale

beyond, making a beeline for the wisp of smoke. 'The Seer,' she said, tossing the words over her shoulder.

<Lily of the Valley,> pronounced Yosef. His telepathic speech carried reverence. Galvanised, he followed Trixel. Leith lingered for a moment, until the General Prime gestured her on.

Mustapha found himself alone with Bastian Sinotar.

The sylph's presence dominated him. Though only a head taller, Sinotar exuded steely confidence, forged by a life of combat and command. Rumours persisted that the General Prime's mother gave birth to him in the heat of battle. The wings at his back heightened the aura of grandeur about him. His platinum hair, a mark of his race, served as an adequate crown for his Sovereign head.

Mustapha straightened his own shoulders.

'You survived.' Sinotar's words came as a low growl, without malice.

'I was lucky Trixel and Yosef appeared when they did ... my Lord.'

'I'm not your "Lord"! Find some other way to address me. Now — what possessed you to go scrambling about in the House of Giltenan during a combat situation?'

'I was under House arrest, not room arrest ... sire. I saw the danger coming' — danger, horror, death become life — 'and sought to raise an alarm.'

'Hm.'

'Also, I followed you because ... because I thought you might be going to ...'

'You thought I was going to find and slay Belladonna.'

'I ... yes.'

'You're right. I was. We didn't find her though, did we? What did we find instead?'

Mustapha shuddered, remembering the alabaster figure of Valendyne.

'I'll tell you what we found,' continued Sinotar. 'We found evidence that both you and Lord Rogar were being hoodwinked by a very, very bad person. We found evidence that Belladonna has been dabbling in ancient arts that were best left forgotten.'

'She told me she was studying Sorcery — that she had found some way to save Rhye.'

Sinotar gave a dark grin, baring his teeth. 'All a matter of perspective. She was practising Necromancy. Where do you think all those dead Giltenans came from? Now, there is one more to the tally.' Bitterness laced his words.

'You think Belladonna schemed to kill Lord Rogar?'

'... and we failed to protect him.'

'Why would she do that? As his consort, she already held a position of power.'

'I can only speculate.' The sylph did not do so out loud.

Mustapha stared into space. With Lord Rogar gone, Sontenan would fall into disarray. Perhaps Lance Sevenson could govern as Regent ... provided he survived the ambush.

The death of the human Sovereign carried much greater import: Rogar died without fathering any children. The mighty Giltenan dynasty ended with him.

Mustapha edged towards the burning issues. 'General Prime ... why did you laugh, at the Council?'

Sinotar huffed. 'I suspected Belladonna had big plans for you. Maybe she still has. With you under House arrest, I figured she wouldn't be disappearing any time soon, leaving you unattended. It would be my opportunity to close in on her — an opportunity I intended to relish.

'That opportunity was taken from me. For some reason, she defied expectations.

'The ambush brought everything to a head. Belladonna's absence in the Atrium raised suspicion. I went looking for her, instead finding compelling signs of betrayal. Then, you appeared and almost got yourself killed before Trixel and the golem whisked you off on this holiday.'

'And Rogar ...'

Sinotar grimaced. 'It shouldn't have happened. We had the attack in hand. Rogar knew his way around a sword, but something happened. He was distracted. We all were. A moment's lapse ... he died in an instant.'

Mustapha recalled Leith Lourden's remarks. *I have to know.* 'Why have you followed us here?'

'I'm here because I sense a chain reaction. The attack on the House — Rogar's death — triggered something. You're mixed up in it, I'm certain. By the Breath of Cornavrian, I intend to keep my eye on you.'

Sinotar strode away, tailing the others towards the distant smoke.

Yosef's observations proved correct. As the dwelling materialised, its derelict status became apparent. It consisted of a lean-to made from timber, mud, and thatch, with a hole in the roof, from which arose a white pall. All about lay grey-black mullock, littered with charred and rotting tree stumps.

The tang of sulphur hung in the air. On instinct, the sylphs drew their swords.

A figure emerged from the hovel. An old crone, with a spine like a question mark and rheumy eyes, squinting out from a hessian sack face. Her filthy robe might once have been white. She stood still, leaning on a staff, watching them come.

As the company neared the hovel, Trixel called out. 'Lily! You haven't aged a day.'

The crone flinched. She stared hard at the motley group. Registering some recognition, she stood in place until they arrived.

'What has it been?' continued Trixel. 'Two hundred and thirty years?'

Lily's face roved over them, the wrinkles in her walnut face pulled by the thin, taut line of her mouth. She trembled, horrified to glimpse the future in these five visitors. The golem — a tremendous iron being, who moved like he had a soul, yet had none. The two sylphic warriors — steadfast and battle-ready, rarely seen without their fabled armour. She peered at Sinotar, as if recognising him from dreams.

Next, the strangeling. She considered him the longest. Lithe, yet somehow broken. Long-limbed, built like a whippet. Dark-eyed like a creature of the night, rendered sluggish by an unknown malady. A figure in which doom and destiny announced themselves with equal emphasis. Her look thawed, from implacable terror to general dismay. She settled back on Trixel Tate.

'I see Death, all around ...' she murmured.

'It's good to see you, too,' said Trixel.

The Seer of Kash Valley took a half-step to one side and gestured with an arthritic hand. 'It won't do, to stand too long out here.'

She ushered the travellers into her home.

CHAPTER 10

MY KINGDOM FOR A HORSE

Lily tended her fire with care, to avoid setting part of her makeshift home alight.

Most items within the hovel were arranged by a particular hand. A single carved stool waited by the hearth. Earthenware pots, assembled in a line, sat upon a shelf of stone. A pallet of dried grass abutted one side wall. A threadbare rug covered the rough-swept dirt floor. Hallmarks of a woman who lived in frugality and modesty, taking only her needs from the bounty of Rhye.

Other items lacked congruency. Mustapha could not help but notice the breastplate and faulds, tossed without care in a dim corner. He did not recognise the armour as that of a human or a sylph. *An artefact? A relic from a past feudal Age?* Neglect consumed it, lost to rust and tarnish. In the dust beside the armour lay a sword, likewise uncared for.

A sad end to former glory.

Other oddities joined the accoutrements of war, as departures from the life of an old crone. At the rear of the dwelling, almost out of reach of firelight, lay a serpentine coil of rope and chain. Far from tidily stowed, the coil spilled across the floor. Burst chain links littered the ground nearby.

Lily ignored the unkempt corner. She ushered the group around the fire, where everybody was obliged to sit on the rug. From a pot over the fire, she procured a thin stew, serving bowls to those who required food.

'I imagine you know who we are and why we're here,' rumbled Sinotar. He scrutinised his stew, as if the soup concealed an adversary.

'I need not be a Seer to know why you're here, General Prime,' replied Lily. 'Everybody who visits, does so for the same reason.'

'Everybody? When did you last have visitors?'

Lily nodded in the direction of Trixel Tate. 'Just recently, this Fae came here with her Lord.'

'Just recently?' said Sinotar, continuing to parrot the Seer. 'Two hundred and thirty years ago seems recent to you?'

Lily maintained her deadpan veneer. 'Do I look like a nubile maiden? You're better off asking how your Fae companion still manages to pass for fresh meat.'

The sylph only stared at her.

'Seer, we come seeking your guidance,' said Trixel.

'If it's my guidance you want, I advise you to find shelter and pray. Cataclysm has come to Rhye. The wheels are in motion, and nothing can stop them.

'As for those who have forgotten how to pray: May your eyes be opened before it is too late.'

Sinotar growled. Leith ate from her bowl in silence.

'So ... can Rhye be saved?'

The question came from Mustapha. Heads turned. He hugged his legs, knees beneath his chin, emptied bowl beside him.

At first, Lily did not answer. Ancient, grey eyes looked through the strangeling, as if his biography was written on the wall behind. Her wrinkles multiplied, wizened features arranging themselves in a look of consternation.

She spoke in a dry whisper. 'Rhye needs a King.'

Trixel nodded.

'There are already seven — no, six,' said Mustapha, correcting himself with a glum look. 'Six Sovereigns of Rhye. Will adding another avert this crisis? Is seven a number essential for balance? If so, this issue could be overcome by appointing a Regent in Via.'

The Seer kept her meditative pose, but fixed Mustapha with a pensive stare. He, in return, considered her unassuming appearance. In his travels with Belladonna, he met many gypsies and charlatans. Without exception, they were bedecked and bedazzled with Heptagram imagery, shamanistic bone jewellery and deep blue robes, referencing the Discipline of Astrology. By contrast, Lily went unadorned. She spoke without ostentation. Her visage reflected the burden of a life spent knowing too much.

'The one hope for Rhye is a sole unifying King, who brings to bear the eldritch power of a new Song.'

Her tangential words bore a familiar portent. She referenced the Song of the Prophet, illuminating several faces around the circle.

A sole King, with an answer to the Song of a past Age, would save Rhye.

Torr Yosef joined the discussion. <*A unifying Sovereign in Rhye would be a practice in contradiction. Wars have marred the land for thousands of years, driven by the greed of the dominant races. Now, with peril upon us, hope sits with one of our leaders coming forward as a supreme entity, accepted by all? It is not so much a recipe for peace, as a final bid for disaster. The Golem Race has long held the Gods as the one source of salvation. The Song endorses this.*>

Trixel frowned. 'I disagree with you, Yosef. Fae doctrine upholds that the Gods help those who help themselves. This has been Lord Oberon's catechumenal policy since the forging of the Fae Ring.'

She delivered this comment as a fundamental truth. Many devout beings would recognise the validity of it, for Lord Oberon lived in Rhye during the last visitation of the Pantheon, a conflict known as the Godsryche.

Trixel continued. 'The interracial struggle for supremacy cannot be ignored, though in the past millennium, most races have co-existed in harmony. The Council is an effective forum for joint Sovereignty. In such a moment as this, I submit that the bureaucracies of Rhye could act with cohesion.

'Listening to the Seer now, my chief concern is that the wheels of diplomacy do not turn fast enough. Conducting a vote would take too long to coordinate. I fear that we are out of time to elect one Sovereign for a unified Rhye.'

<*The golem temperament will not brook this notion in any regard,*> said Yosef. <*Too often throughout history have we been enslaved to the will of others. None will now countenance any but another golem as our Sovereign. Torr Enoch has the unflinching support of my people.*> Yosef's mechanical features served only to reinforce his stolid position.

The fire burned low. Lily stoked it as she resumed the thread, giving the impression that she drew her predictions from the fire itself.

'There will be no battle for supremacy between the living Sovereigns,' she said. 'There will be no effort at bureaucratic cohesion. The true King of Rhye will emerge, armed with a new Song as a manifestation of holy power, ordained by the Gods themselves. Such has been my vision for centuries.

'Alas, in recent times, the vision blurred. The arrival of a saviour is not assured. Events yet to unfold may instead lead us down a catastrophic path. I also see, one by one, the destruction and demise of your present Sovereigns, leading to anarchy and chaos. Already, the Lord in Via has met his end. Others will follow in his fall. In darkness, the leaderless Realms will crumble. The power of Sovereignty across the Seven Realms is bonded to the power of the Fae Ring.'

Through this debate, Mustapha watched Bastian Sinotar. In most discussions, the General Prime made his opinion clear, especially if the situation involved matters of faith. This time he said nothing, his signature scowl rearranged into terse introspection. He clamped his tongue, biting down on some inner outburst as he had done at the Council of Rhye. Mustapha wondered if the sylph pondered his own fate, in view of Lily's pronouncement.

Beside him, Leith Lourden sat forward on her haunches, absorbing the exchange with avid scrutiny. 'Do you know then, Seer, the identity of this King?'

'I once thought I did,' said Lily. 'Lord Oberon of the Fae came to me with that same abrupt question. Now, I have cause to doubt myself. In many visions, the King appears to me in scenes of triumph and ecstasy. At other times, the image fades. I see nought but the Two-Legged Death consuming the world.'

'You have seen Death?' asked Leith.

'I have. I do not fool myself: The years catch up to me. My life's journey is very near its end. I do not expect to see the outcome of this crisis by any other means than my dim future vision. The creature of Valendyne stalks me, both in my dreams and in my waking hours.'

To this admission, none had a reply. It was too much for Sinotar. He rose and stormed from the hovel, kicking the dirt as he left.

Night had long since fallen and the hour grew late, though the companions were eager to learn as much from the Seer as they could. Torr Yosef tried a different approach. *<If we know so little of this saviour King, good Seer, is there wisdom you can share about the Song itself?>*

'The lore you seek is laid bare by the words of the Prophet,' said Lily. Her rheumy eyes glistened for a moment. 'Just as a new year replaces the old and the gift of life calls for renewal, it is told that the words of the Song must be replaced with a new covenant — a new promise for the future of Rhye.'

'The land is full of troubadours,' said Mustapha. 'Couldn't a new Song come from the pen of a Fae composer? They write the most magical music.'

Lily gave a wry smile, tinged with sadness. 'The Song must be a gesture of sacrifice. An ode to death and rebirth ... just as it was at the time of the Prophet. It is not so simple as to write a few lines to music.

'Hear me when I say: The doom of Rhye is the rise of Valendyne. To vanquish Death is to see Rhye reborn. The cost of such an epiphany is absolute.'

<You say that the quest for a Song — and the search for the King of Rhye — is a suicide mission,> said Torr Yosef. The mood in the hovel grew dismal.

'Lily,' said Mustapha. 'Tell me ... what became of the Prophet?'

'I get a sense that you already know the answer, strangeling.'

'Say it anyway.'

'It is written that he found a way into Nevermore,' she replied. 'Legend tells that he resolved to voyage the Seventh Sea. From there, all evidence of him runs cold ... he vanished altogether from the land.'

Lub-dup ... lub-dup ... lub-dup ...

Flying again.

The crimson mist still swirled, concealing the anonymous

mountain range. The landscape hurtled by below, thrown into relief by periodic bursts of lightning.

Something very different met him, this time.

Something very wrong.

It rained, though the water struck him from underneath. He soared over the majestic Seas, one after another: the Trident Deep, the Clementine Sea, the Sour Milk Sea. The horror became apparent: All the waters poured upwards, into the great void above.

The reverse deluge battered him as he flew. Below, the Seas, black as midnight, receded from the land. The shoreline fell, down and down, as more and more water poured into the sky. Abyssal depths were laid bare as the Seas turned dry. All around he saw the writhing figures of undines, Mer-Folk, serpents and other beasts, wailing and fighting for life.

Amidst the tumult of misery, Mustapha heard cruel laughter.

A voice like a furnace.

'Blood on your hands! Have you made the sacrifice? Does it torment you? Do you feel the ebb of life's sustenance? Come ... prostrate yourself at my feet. Meet Death ... and make your humiliation final.'

The voice again broke into torrid mirth. Mustapha knew, now. The man with the flowing auburn hair, at the bottom of the Sea, surrounded by the wreckage of his own entrapment.

Anuvin, God of War.

The laugh swelled and grew deep. A terrifying rumble. Soon, it became the titanic bellow of many gargantuan beasts ... enough to shake the mountains.

Mustapha held his hands before his face.

They were on fire.

He exploded forward, colliding with a dark figure crouched beside him. The reverse deluge vanished, and the mist dissipated.

No fire burned.

All around his companions slumbered, sprawled on fresh straw by the dying light in the hearth. He saw Sinotar, back from his sojourn. Trixel Tate by the door of the hovel. Leith Lourden beside her. Torr Yosef, absent, may have been on watch.

In front of him, Lily stared, wide-eyed.

Lily's ancient face, stricken and pallid, hovered scant inches from his own. She looked as if she had beheld a vision not intended for her.

Mustapha baulked. *Did I say something in my sleep? Can she read my mind? Hello — can you read my mind?*

'Who *are* you?' she said.

Mustapha still fought his way through the fog of sleep. Like an encroaching chill, her words settled on him. *Did ... did you, Seer, just ask me who I am?* Sickness rose in him. The weakness of resignation. The receding hope.

'I thought you would be able to tell me that,' he said.

His one remaining wish of the Seer, dashed.

With a sigh, she sat beside him. 'The only past I can look into is my own,' she said. 'For those of you with souls, the future comes to me as a whisper of melody, or the fleeting path of a shooting star. I can read the way ahead. But alas, if you come seeking your heritage ...' She clicked her tongue.

'What do you make of my future, then?' Mustapha squeezed out the question before he became too afraid to ask it.

'Your future is closed to me.'

Mustapha groaned. 'Grant me this one courtesy. Do not shield me from the truth!'

'I speak from a place of honesty, strangeling. For the most part, your future is as unknown to me as your past. There are, however, two certainties.

'The first is that a revelation awaits you in the Forest Realms.

Be it in the Mother Forest or the Realm of the Wilden Folk, your destiny will hinge upon events yet to come, in a place surrounded by the ancient trees.'

Mustapha's parched throat denied his swallow. 'The other?'

'The other certainty is that you — like this wizened Seer before you — will die before the land reaches its final crisis.'

He nodded. *You will die.* Simple and irrefutable.

'So, you do know something,' he murmured. 'In fact, you know the ultimate something, as far as I'm concerned.

'Tell me, though: Will I kill somebody else before I am consumed?'

The mocking countenance and nebulous threats of Anuvin still burned in his mind.

Lily frowned. 'Kill somebody? What a strange question. No, no. That, I cannot see. There is, however, but one piece of advice I can give, if you are to leave a legacy upon Rhye.'

Mustapha had his head in his hands. 'What is that?'

'Whoever he is, bring the old troubadour with you.'

With the arrival of morning, Mustapha's strength dwindled. As the company prepared to depart, he forced down a meagre breakfast. Eating provided a means to an end, nothing more; without energy, he would cease to move. As best he could, he intended to conceal the ravages of poison — and his looming fate — from the others. The waves of nausea, he could suppress. The frailty of his limbs might prove more difficult.

One foot in front of the other.

The sylphs were fastening their travel armour when Yosef's curiosity bested him. Taking a last glance around Lily's home, he addressed her.

<What is the story of the rope and chain? It appears you've housed a prisoner, or at best, an agitated guest.>

With a glimpse at the disarray in the far corner, Lily offered a brief explanation. 'In Ages past, Cornavrian granted me the honour and privilege of tending the divine pterippi.'

<*They are, of course, his prized beasts — gifts to Him from Marnis, if I recall my scripture,*> said Yosef. <*Your boon would be an honour, indeed.*>

The sylphs paused in the doorway absorbing the tale, saying nothing.

'A time came when invaders fell upon Kash Valley. The lesser infiltration consisted of a horde of impolite humans. The greater threat came in the form of a dark coven — Wearers of Black. They intended to harness the power of the living, breathing Valley and reverse it for their own machinations.

'In the name of Cornavrian, I banished them to the Afterlife — back to the lap of their Godhead, Valendyne. There they sleep, to this day … not dead, merely in stasis.'

Mustapha spoke. 'But isn't Valendyne —'

'He is, yes. He has been incarcerated there — within those boughs, inside that trunk — for nearly three thousand years. The Two-Legged Death guards the souls of the departed, in his stead, from that time to this.'

'But that makes you —'

'Old, yes,' said Lily. 'I digress. I banished the Wearers of Black … all of them, except one. One who I could use as a conduit, to find and quell a future uprising.

'I did not allow for the resilience of this one — the last Necromancer. She bided her time, whispering endless incantations: muttering the days, the months, the decades away. The aura of decay seeped from her. You can see it in the land all around this place: Nothing lives. Over time, she grew in power and malevolence, until one day, some years ago …'

Lily indicated the shattered bonds.

'The last Necromancer, a woman,' said Bastian Sinotar, in an even tone. 'In all that time, did you learn her name?'

'I did. I determined that, as we would be sharing an abode for many years to come, I should get to know her. I told her my name. To my surprise, she replied in kind.

'Her name was Belladonna ... the same as the plant with the poisonous black berries.'

Shafts of morning sunlight pushed through the thick blanket of grey-green cloud. The eerie quiet, the absent wildlife, persisted from the previous day. Only a distant rumble disrupted the unnatural stillness.

'It seems like that storm is going to break at last,' said Leith. 'Yosef — need we be worried about your exposure to the rain?'

<My alloy is impervious to all but deep floodwater,> Yosef replied. *<However, I would suggest that the sound you hear is not the storm. I detect vibration beneath my feet — that rumble is terrestrial.>*

The golem carried Mustapha. Within moments of Lily's pronouncement, the strangeling had collapsed. Trixel suggested, at first, he may have been overwhelmed by the condemnation of his former companion. It soon occurred to the group that the throes of illness gripped him. His eyes lolled and his lips trembled.

Mustapha could not stand, much less continue the trek. The golem pledged to carry him. For the time being, the strangeling remained on the verge of consciousness. Nerveless fingers rested over the butt of his only material possession — his ornate pistol. Yosef eyed the weapon — and the whippet who bore it — as he walked.

Lily urged that they were scant hours from Petrichor, with the herbal and mystic remedies of the Fae shamans near at hand. At the edge of Kash Valley they would encounter a hidden pass; the fertile slopes of this region forever the haven for a great herd of pterippi. The company would behold the beasts of Marnis as they departed her homeland for the fringe of the Mother Forest, Petrichor.

A short distance from the Seer's home, the blasted earth gave way to lustrous greensward. Oak and poplar once again remembered their leaves. Giant hills rolled on either side of the vale, funnelling the company toward the shady pass ahead.

Trixel kept pace with Bastian Sinotar, who pressed forward with little regard for the natural splendour about him. A thousand-yard stare cloaked his taciturn face.

'The poison takes hold,' she said to him. 'We can do nought but hope for an antidote. If not the shamans, perhaps the dryads know of a medicinal root to turn the tide.'

'If they do not — or care not — the youth will be lost,' Sinotar replied.

'There was a time I would have turned to the Wilden Folk. Lord Vater knew the secrets of medicine. Do you think, in his place, Lord Ponerog might brook such an intrusion on his demesne?'

Sinotar clenched his jaw. He strained against some thought, to which he gave no voice. Instead, he heaved a shrug.

'I sense the Wilden Realm has become a place of peril. In the same breath, I believe the answers can be sought there. If needed, then Mustapha shall be taken into Banwah Haunte. In the meantime, we go first to Oberon and Titania. They must hear what we have learned, for the greater sake of the land.'

Trixel shot the General Prime a sidelong glance. 'Could it be that you conceal a sensitive side? That you care for the strangeling's future?'

Sinotar growled, ruffling his wings. 'Mustapha has been foolish, but he is an innocent fool. His life has been tossed from one power to the next, beyond his control or understanding. Yet, through his naivety, he gives a good account of himself. He does not deserve to die like this.'

In Yosef's arms, Mustapha drifted in and out of coherence. A smile played about his features; pale lips drawn back from pearlescent teeth. From time to time, he spoke to Yosef in dreamy tones.

'Lead on!' he crowed. 'Take me to the land of serpents and honeybees … dragonflies … oh, and horses! Do you think there will be horses, Torr Yosef? I would so love to see the horses …'

<There shall be horses. A great many of them, if Lily speaks the truth. I would quite like to see them myself. An astonishing tale it would make, for my brethren back at the Bore of Warnom.>

'Ha! They shan't believe you, old chap … whoever heard of a golem meeting a pterippus? Well … you know what? I already have. I met a pterippus, once.'

Eavesdropping, Trixel chimed in. 'Did you truly, Mustapha?'

'My word, I did! Some years ago, deep in Dragonfly Hollow … a magnificent beast … not quite as magnificent as you, dear; or my poor Will, with his brawny arms and mussed-up hair. No, no … but this was still a wondrous creature. Glossy black, like purest midnight. Sleek and powerful … too fast for me to catch, I'm afraid.'

Trixel's brow creased. 'Are you sure?'

'Why yes of course, I'm sure. Difficult to mistake a stallion with giant wings, galloping through the forest …'

'Glossy black?'

'So black it was blue. Such a wicked delight to see …'

'Right.'

<Do you doubt his tale, Trixel? He does seem delirious.>

'If he speaks the truth, he saw something other than a pterippus.

Those creatures are the divine power of the Creator and the essence of Nature, combined. They are born of sunlight, of summer fruits and autumnal leaves. They are all the colours of Adatar. Not one of them is black.'

Mustapha drifted. Trixel chose not to rouse him, only to inform him he had seen a shapeshifter, clad in the black mantle of Death.

At last, the hills enclosed them, tumbling inwards as the company neared the eastern border of Kash Valley. Boulders lay strewn across the terrain. A stretch of woodland thickened, until it threatened to block their path. Beyond nature's curtain, they found a narrow way between sheer faces of rock. The passage became so tight, they were forced to negotiate it in single file. Towering rock choked out much of the light from above. Torr Yosef illuminated the way forward. The oppressive sense of being slowly smothered hastened the company through the gauntlet.

Bursting forth from the claustrophobic pass warranted gasps of fresh air. The landscape spilled wide before them, a great plain rolling away many leagues to the north and south, bounded by the rivers Bijou and Granventide. The perfect home for a majestic herd of pterippi.

The company halted, staring, in throes of surprise and horror.

There were no pterippi.

Not a single creature graced the plain. Torr Yosef, with his enhanced vision, scanned the entire scene from one river to the other, finding no sign of the fabled beasts. He made only a perfunctory search, for a more enthralling vision commanded them, from near away across the plain.

Petrichor burned.

Trixel's home — the place Lily named Mother Forest — lay before them as a vast, green ocean. Within it, billowing smoke spiralled skyward. The glow of fire cut a swathe across the forest, an enormous cleft of destruction, originating in the south. The burning scar evoked abject horror, on the face of the ancient Fae Realm.

Trixel Tate stood speechless, unable to wrench her eyes from the scene. A single, grimy tear streaked her elfin cheek.

Bastian Sinotar swivelled into action. 'It's time we flew,' he said. 'You see the black of that smoke? Do you catch the sulphur on the breeze? This is no natural fire. Petrichor is under attack.' He turned to his subordinate.

'Lourden: We go by air.'

Leith saluted.

'Tate: We could use your help. I'm giving you a lift.'

Trixel remained transfixed.

'Tate!' barked Sinotar.

The fixie jolted, turning red-rimmed eyes towards him. 'Get me in there,' she rasped.

'Yosef?'

<I'll be along, General Prime. I need to find somewhere safe for Mustapha.>

'Be quick about it.' Sinotar's gaze lingered on the limp form in Torr Yosef's arms. Then, he turned away.

Leith leapt into the air. Grabbing Trixel Tate, Sinotar unfurled his mighty wings. With only a few swooping downbeats, he joined Leith.

Yosef tucked Mustapha closer to his chest. Then, on lumbering legs, he stomped towards the verge of Petrichor.

Certain danger awaited beneath its eaves.

CHAPTER 11

DEATH ALL AROUND

In the dark, small hours, the mouth of the stronghold creaked open, sending night creatures scrambling.

The sudden *clank-clank-clank* of the portcullis startled a murder of crows, who alighted from the trees with many a stark cry. In the leafy litter of the forest floor, brownies and hobgoblins skittered to their best hiding places. They knew something malevolent brewed within, but wanted no part of it.

A pale, sickly light shone from the gullet of the keep. Within, the raucous sound of barked orders echoed forth, ruining the tranquil quiet.

A vanguard of redcaps emerged. One hundred pairs of red-hot poker eyes glinted in the night. The fiends marched in tight formation, clad in leather armour and wielding pikes, blades skyward. The *tromp-tromp* of their booted feet matched the cavernous throb of a drum, from the bowels of the keep.

The Pox were unleashed.

Like a thick stream of bile, they vomited forth by the thousand. The cherubs stared forward with sightless eyes; jostling and bouncing off one another, herded through the stygian glade by their redcap guardians. The column grew and grew, until it measured one mile long: innumerable parcels of putrid pestilence, snaking through the little-known byways of Banwah Haunte. An ill yellow glow signalled their passage, serving as both threat and warning.

To touch is to succumb.

Giant forest trolls sounded the drums until every last Pox waddled from its cell, marched up the winding stairs, across the threshold and into the Wilden Realm outside. They owned neither soul nor will. Under the command of their keepers, they would march without rest, until they infiltrated the breadth of the land. Every town, village, and sleepy, unsuspecting hamlet in Sontenan — and much of Nurtenan, too — would suffer a visitation of the Pox.

From an eyrie overlooking the fell procession, Ponerog watched.

Ravenous hunger gnawed at the Wilden Lord. Through the feverish final stages of creating the Pox, he paused little for sleep or sustenance. Thoughts of sweetbreads and sour wine churned in his thoughts, now that he saw his task completed.

Other pangs stirred within him, as well.

He no longer heard the voices of compulsion, pushing him ever onward. With the ceasing of those relentless voices, he hungered for recognition. For worthiness, in the eyes of she who compelled him. This feeling took him by surprise.

Ponerog owed fealty to nobody. He rose to Sovereignty by his own wilful ambition. Neither his philanthropic father, nor his long-forgotten whore mother, would have guessed his vision for the Wilden Realm. He forged victory for himself, in the name of Valendyne … yet the pang of need persisted. It embittered him.

He knew of only one way to sate the hunger: by drowning it out with another primal urge.

Dominion.

He left the window, taking the stair to the high tower.

~

In Sontenan, a juggernaut rose with the sun.

A low rumble shattered the peace of dawn. Soon it swelled, rising higher into a throaty, mechanical roar. The hiss of steam and the pumping of pistons joined the burgeoning sound. Rhye had never heard such a strange cacophony.

The walls and framework of the Ploughman's barn shook, as if swaying in a storm. At any moment, the barn threatened to collapse. Before it could fall to splinters, the vast double doors issued a shuddering groan, then opened wide.

A great plume of soot and debris billowed from within. The clatter of many stamping feet followed and a multitude of pale, spindly shapes appeared.

An army of skeletons emerged from the gloom.

The glow of early dawn shone upon undead bones. A forest of hatchets, scythes, shears, and pitchforks glinted in the pale light — tools repurposed as weapons, clutched in fleshless hands. Without a voice, without a mind, the skeletal army advanced across the sorghum field, driven by the awoken power of the last Necromancer.

One thousand warriors, moving in perfect unison, tramped across the field. Behind them, from a chaos of dust and rattling timbers, erupted the bane of Petrichor. The barn disintegrated in its wake.

The iron titan, all rivets and pistons, glittered with the armaments of war. Grinding treads screamed. It lurched forward, its bulk enough to shake the earth as it passed.

Within an armoured cage, surrounded by levers, pulleys and instrument dials, the Ploughman sat in a gleeful trance. His chance had come to clear the land of those dour dryads, pathetic pixies, and foolish fairies, along with their ridiculous homes amongst the trees. Humankind birthed the future of civilisation. Humans begat industry ... and humans must be fed. The Ploughman's holdings would spread to engulf much of Sontenan — and Petrichor, too — once the Fairy King and his Queen were dispatched.

The Ploughman gave little thought to the thousand lives he sacrificed to gain this footing. The whisper in his ear told him: *This is your destiny.* The farmhands and labourers would find glory in their second death.

Such did the voices promise him, at any rate.

In a straight, unwavering line, the column of skeletons marched towards the forest verge, ahead of the unstoppable juggernaut.

Several leagues hence, the Fae Sovereigns faced their demise, along with their sacred tree.

Petrichor buzzed.

The thrum of myriad warnings flowed along a million synapsing root systems. Alarm spread like pollen through the air, from plant to beast and everything in between. Dragonflies zipped from village to village, spreading the word to everyone with ears.

Danger, the warnings screamed. The directive to all: *fight, or flight.*

Most Fae lead peaceful lives. For fairies and pixies, fighting seldom extended beyond the occasional brawl in the smoky interiors of Juniper Juice, or the Oak & Barrel Inn. These creatures fled for their homes amidst the trees, not recognising the peril.

Dryads secured defensive positions, bracing themselves for the onslaught. Lord Oberon decreed that Petrichor stood in the shadow of its greatest trial, with only two possible resolutions — a saving grace, or doom by fire.

Though Oberon summoned every shred of his mystic potency — though the force of an entire forest lay in wait — none were prepared for the Armageddon that approached.

Will eyed the blade in his hand with doubt. He had been granted a sword from the Fae armoury. Given his human proportions, it counted for little more than a dagger to him.

'Friends ... I think we might be in trouble.'

'I don't call this "trouble",' said Meadow, adjusting an ill-fitting helmet. 'This jostle was foretold by the Prophet, as a sign of the land's doom. This isn't "trouble" — it's "goodbye".'

Dique stood apart from them, swinging a pike. He repeated the same feint-attack combination, over and over. 'Always so melodramatic,' he said. 'You were worried we'd die at the Ceremony of the Nut, yet here we are. We'll get through this stoush, too. I'm sure we've been in tougher scrapes ... I just don't remember when.'

The pixies found themselves drafted into the defence of Psithur Grove, by Lord Oberon. Alongside them stood a fierce contingent of dryads, prepared to give their lives for the Realm. The Fairy King also dispatched a centaine of Fae knights, to form an elite guard for the Grove and the Yew.

The dandy Fae armour provided more ornamentation than functional protection. Regardless of its utility, neither Meadow nor Dique felt at ease within it. The pair remained grateful, at least, that Oberon spared their lives.

He declared that the battle for Petrichor would determine their fate.

Both dedicated a prayer to Oska, God of Fortune. In anticipation of battle, Oberon advised them that a prayer to Anuvin would likely go unanswered.

Will remained in the Grove, explaining that he 'had nowhere better to be.' His determined face concealed much, though he offered the pixies a fortifying grin and a promise: He would stay by their side.

Oberon and Titania joined hands by the base of the majestic Yew, swearing themselves as the final bastion of its defence. The Fairy King still appeared shaken by his ordeal at the tree and his vision of darkness in Nevermore. In his mind, he saw it: the cataclysmic destruction of the Fae Ring. He knew his own Sovereignty — indeed, his own life — depended on the integrity of that artefact, holding the very particles of the enchanted metal together. If his vision became reality ... if the Ring failed ... he dared not contemplate the depths of that despair.

'The Yew at all costs,' he said to Titania.

The juggernaut crashed into the forest verge with mesmerising force.

Ancient trees splintered like tinder, hewn by giant twirling blades at the fore and flanks of the machine. Flocks of birds erupted into the sky with squawks and screeches of alarm as their homes disappeared beneath them. A tremendous cloud of debris sprayed into the air.

Nearby dryads, picketing the verge, leapt away from the path of the deadly blades. Many uttered a mournful last plea to Cornavrian, in a bid to keep the forest intact.

The God of Nature did not intervene. Age-old timbers became chaff before the scythe.

Dryads at the frontline found a new foe to contend with. The skeleton warriors fell upon them dispassionately, wielding makeshift weapons with dextrous skill, honed by tending crops in a recent life.

The forest nymphs struggled. Accustomed to picking off foes from the trees with poisoned bolts, their strategy failed against the new enemy. The skeletons had no flesh to poison, no sinew in which to lodge a barb. The bolts clattered through them, causing no harm.

The dryads adapted swiftly. They regrouped, fighting the skeletons on the forest floor in hand-to-hand combat. With signalling cries, countless reinforcements swarmed from out of the trees.

Though outnumbered, the skeletons cut and thrust with lightning speed and terrible accuracy. They gave relentless offence, being immune to fatigue. As they advanced, they left hundreds of dryads dead or with mortal wounds, behind them. Driving deeper into the forest, their formation fanned out. Many slipped into the dense forest, evading the closing dryad net.

The dryad frontline let them go. Legions of Fae knights, stationed throughout the byways of the Realm, would account for rogue skeletons.

The juggernaut rolled on, demolishing all, on a path to the heart of Petrichor.

With fanatical energy, the Ploughman drove his mechanical behemoth ever deeper through glades and hollows. As he anticipated, the archaic warfare of the forest nymphs held no candle to the might of his contrivance. On the ground, none could approach him, due to the vast reach of those deadly blades — whirring, shearing, felling trees without pause. They threatened to dismember any creature that came near.

Several foolish fairies flew over the top, landing on the superstructure. Dryads joined them, falling upon the giant vehicle from high boughs, overhanging the path of devastation. Flailing with sticks and fists, the assailants dealt no damage to the unstoppable iron beast.

To see the hapless creatures' futile struggle amused him, but the Ploughman wanted more. The insatiable spark inside him needed to see this claustrophobic, nymph-riddled maze of trees destroyed.

The time had come for heavy artillery.

Turning to one side, the Ploughman spoke into a funnel-shaped device. His words travelled to a place deep in the belly of the beast.

'Bring the fire,' he said.

Somewhere below and aft, the ploughboy slavered over an instrument panel of his own. He waited, poised for this very command. His reaching fingers grasped at levers designed to open the floodgates of hell. On the outer shell of the juggernaut, gun barrels lifted like enormous spines, out and away from their housings. A menacing roar escaped every barrel at once.

Will had been mistaken. The weapons did not launch heavy projectiles.

They threw sheets of incinerating flame.

Tongues of fire lashed out across the forest. Scalding serpents blasted forth — the roar of fire, suddenly mingled with the screaming of trees. Within moments, the forest corridor blazed, sending dozens of creatures running for their lives.

Amidst the ancient boughs, the hamadryads could mount no defence. As the flames reached them, they were engulfed and consumed.

The juggernaut rumbled forward, bringer of inexorable destruction. Pushing far into Petrichor, it left only chaos and death behind it.

In Psithur Grove, hysterical wailing rent the air. Dryads rattled their weapons and gnashed their teeth, feeling the torment of their kinsfolk. The voice of conflagration crackled close by. Beyond the canopy, a towering pillar of smoke drifted heavenwards.

Fae knights searched beyond the Grove with restless eyes. Percipience told them that somewhere, just beyond sight, another enemy lurked, using the tumult of fire and carnage as camouflage.

Dique sensed it, too. He stood beneath the foliage of a Ficus tree, hoping the slender trunk could conceal him from a stalking assassin.

'Never thought I'd die defending the Grove,' Meadow said to him, from a place nearby.

'Who says we're dying?' replied Dique, still waving his weapon. It described clumsy arcs in the empty air. *Feint-attack.* 'I haven't seen the Two-Legged Death anywhere around here. Have you?'

Meadow fell silent. Dique saw his friend's sword droop, point aimed to the ground.

Dique, a humble pixie from Reed, saw their predicament in a different light: He stood alongside his Sovereigns at a time of crisis. A foul serendipity landed him there — a very different fate to that which he imagined for himself.

He might have grown old in Reed, had not his father moved the family fromagerie to Flaxae, in a bid to catch the attention of Lord Oberon. The Fairy King had a soft spot for cheese, his father told him.

I sure caught the eye of the Fairy King, alright. He looked at Oberon, standing amidst the great, gnarled roots of the mystical Yew, uttering ancient cantos; the antlers of his crown luminous, steeped in power. An envelope — a ward of sorts — snaked out around the tree and the bounds of the Grove. The Fairy King mounted a last line of defence.

The Mother of Trees. The Womb of Petrichor.

The Yew at all costs.

'Oberon never did get to try any of my father's cheese —'

'Dique!'

Will bellowed the warning, several yards away amidst the Ficus trees. Dique turned towards the human. A simultaneous footfall sounded over his shoulder. On instinct, he twirled the other way.

Without thought, without plan, his hands swung the pike. *Feint-attack* —

His weapon struck another with a jolting crack. Shockwaves ran through the haft to Dique's arms. The pike flew from his grip.

Silent as the grave his assailant came, stalking from the forest depths, leering at him from a bony visage. The skeleton hoisted a shovel with two hands, flipping it to complete a deadly arc.

'Two-Legged ...?'

Dique never completed the fateful name. At that moment, a shape erupted from the forest fringe, hurtling towards the skeleton. The two figures collided with brute force. Bony limbs cartwheeled through the air. In a flurry of blows and a sickening crunch, the ghoulish warrior lay still.

Dique caught a fleeting glimpse of his saviour: General Prime, Bastian Sinotar.

A female sylph appeared by his side. Both had weapons drawn, ready to cut down an army of foes.

A third figure emerged. With a bone-chilling cry, Trixel Tate swore to visit flesh-and-blood vengeance on the enemies of the Mother Forest. Even the dryads quailed at her impassioned display.

Voiceless ghouls filtered from the trees by the dozen, descending on Psithur Grove from all directions. The sacred place became a scene of battle, as living defenders of the Fae clashed with the undead.

Meadow and Dique gave combat in a rush of pure adrenaline.

'Just keep yourselves alive!' Will shouted to them, as the pixies dodged about their ensorcelled foes. Will grappled, kicked, and thrashed at any who came near, achieving a weapon upgrade in the process. A machete clenched in his fist, he set about cleaving skulls with merry abandon.

In the thick of the tumult, Bastian Sinotar fought, a whirlwind of devastation. He hacked and mashed the fell creatures into oblivion, even as they menaced their way into the Grove. Leith Lourden, broadsword shining, commanded the Fae knights on one flank; Trixel Tate, a spinning cynosure, spearheaded the vicious dryads on the other.

'Wherever you hailed from,' panted Will to Leith, 'you sure made a timely entrance!'

'These creatures are a mere distraction,' replied Leith. 'The true foe burns a path to the Yew at this moment. Just as the Fairy King defends the tree, so must we defend the Fairy King ... or all of Petrichor is lost.'

The Fae Sovereigns remained by the foot of the Yew. Both swayed in a kind of trance, communing with the forest itself. Their lips moved together, uttering a prayer in an ancient tongue. The ward pulsed about them, a mist of ardent green.

Beyond the Grove, the relentless approach of the Ploughman could not be ignored. A vast tract of Petrichor burned; an infernal roar swallowed the cries of ten thousand hamadryads. Satyrs bolted from their homes, never to return. The town of Periwinkle lay in the Ploughman's path. He erased the tiny hamlet from the map.

At the helm of the juggernaut, the eyes of the Ploughman showed their whites. With berserk strength, he gripped the controls guiding his megalithic creation.

He held scant regard for the notion of failure when he arrived at the Yew. He knew not what he might do afterwards, or how he might escape the burning forest, evading the teeming Fae who remained within it. His enslaved mind cared naught for details. He heard the inner voice — a sweet dirge in his head, chanting over and over.

The forest must burn.

The Yew must fall.

The Fairy King must die.

In the name of the Black Queen.

'Yes, my Lady,' he murmured, breaking into a frantic laugh.

At last, heralded by the quaking earth, the mighty contrivance burst upon Psithur Grove. At the entrance to the hallowed demesne, the hamadryad Willow fell, thrashed by the brute force of whirling shears.

Within the Grove, conflict waned, the skeletal foes numbering few. Oberon and Titania stood in their fervent trance. As one their eyes rose, round with dread, to meet the towering machine.

The bane of Petrichor loomed over them.

'Fall to! Regroup!' Bastian Sinotar hollered above the din. Trixel and Leith flanked him. A dwindling force of dryads and knights moved into ragged formation.

The Ficus trees, in their precise rows, stood shorter than most of the ancient giants in the surrounding Realm. Mowing them down would be an elementary final hurdle for the Ploughman. Yet the juggernaut slowed, savouring this last leg on its trail of death and destruction. The scythes thrashed with an ominous *woomf-woomf-woomf.*

'The iron beast has a heart that bleeds,' growled Bastian Sinotar. He pointed on high, to the place where the Ploughman sat caged. 'Lourden, with me.'

The Vrendari took to the air, their wings carrying them above the blades. From the air they fell upon the machine, scaling the superstructure to a place where they could approach its maniacal inhabitant. Leith set upon the pilot's iron cockpit with her broadsword, intending to smash the door of the cage from its hinges. The General Prime searched for other weaknesses — seams, welds, any point of leverage — to wrench the human from his seat.

The Ploughman spat at them. 'Your death is certain. The Black Queen comes for your souls.'

Sinotar gave a harsh laugh. 'This is not how I die. I will see you ended, human.'

Leaning over to the mouthpiece, the industrialist spoke to his son. 'Deploy the parahumanoid. Destroy them all.'

A warble of acknowledgement came from the depths of the machine. After a moment, the entire behemoth shuddered, though it continued to advance, splintering Ficus trees row by row. The echoing sounds of clanking gears and the *schtok* of opening bolts issued from within.

Trixel, Will and the Fae Folk watched in horror as the aft segment of the juggernaut dismantled itself, birthing a mechanised giant.

The ploughboy sat harnessed in a humanoid vehicle of iron, a contraption he controlled with his own arms and legs. It stood the height of three men, bristling with pincer arms and weaponry. With juddering steps, he lurched forward, grinning like a fiend at the defenders of the Grove.

Will stood firm, fists clenched, heart pounding. 'I have a score to settle, with or without your tin suit,' he snarled.

The amplified voice of the Ploughman echoed down from his high perch. 'Such fatalist bravado! Step forward and forfeit your life.'

'It's the yokel from the Ceremony,' said the ploughboy, in a rare moment of illumination. 'Seems we didn't kill him properly the first time.'

'Second time is the charm,' said Will, through gritted teeth. He squared up to the parahumanoid.

<*You're going to need my help,*> said a voice like metallurgy inside his head.

Everyone else heard it, too. Heads turned, as a huge golem entered the fray.

'Wonder of wonders,' murmured Will. 'What next?'

'It's high time you showed up,' cried Trixel Tate, as Torr Yosef strode forth, engaging the mechanised ploughboy with a titanic *clang.*

Yosef's arms, like mighty pillars, grappled with the mechanical pincers. Outmatched in size, the golem stood his ground in the contest through sheer resolve.

Dique gaped. The metal mayhem trumped any excitement he had ever known.

'Go on, Will!' Meadow called to the farmer. 'Get around behind him! The ploughboy can't see you unless you're in front!'

Will nodded. He edged around the grappling giants, poised to spring. When his opportunity came, he leapt upon the back of the ploughboy's lurching mechanical suit, tearing at exposed cogs and tubing as he climbed. He drew his blade.

The bane of Petrichor continued its dread crawl, fifteen yards from where Oberon and Titania stood, unflinching beneath the Yew. The Fairy King stared down the monstrosity, as if it could be destroyed by sight alone. All about the Sovereigns stood the forest denizens, in an ever-tightening cordon. In desperation, several dryads screamed blood-curdling battle cries and threw themselves upon merciless blades.

Even as they perished, the Ploughman advanced to his goal.

Dique's jaw still hung open, rapt wonder replaced by numb despair. The blades edged nearer. The wind of their fatal passage wafted across his face. *Woomf-woomf-woomf.* He breathed, letting his eyes drift, absorbing the scene.

Nearby, the ploughboy let loose jets of flame, searing his adversary. Wreathed in fire, the golem pounded away, attempting to bash the metal parahumanoid to scrap.

High above, the juggernaut cast a shade over them. At its peak, the two sylphs continued to tear at the juggernaut's cockpit.

Meadow ... you were right. This is how it ends.

His gaze wandered higher, above the trees and the menacing machine. The storm clouds gathered, intermingling with the black pall of smoke. Dense air cloyed, a foetid soup, almost devoid of life.

Almost ... except for a dark shape.

A dragonfly, followed by more flying shapes.

Winged horses.

Dique grinned. *The product of a dreamer's mind in its final moments.* He tugged at the nearest sleeve, just to be sure.

Trixel Tate.

'Pardon me, Miss. I may just be losing my mind, but ... do you see horses up there?'

Trixel, distracted, still searched for a way to overcome the looming juggernaut. It moved forward through molasses, slowed but not stopped by Oberon's mystical ward. 'They're all gone, young pixie. We came through the Valley. There were no —'

She looked up, anyway ... and saw them.

From out of the west, a herd of fifty pterippi thundered across the sky. A shower of miniature comets, dwarfed against the deathly pall. They shone every colour of the sun, from a glorious summer blaze to a deep vermillion sunset. At their fore, wings an invisible blur, flew the unmistakeable cigar-shaped body of a dragonfly. The forward pincers of the creature clutched an instrument.

'— pterippi,' mouthed Trixel.

Meadow saw them, too. 'Hey, is that ...?'

'Harold!' cried Dique, jubilant. What the dragonfly and his charges might do, he had no idea. It was a welcoming sight, however futile.

The herd drew nearer — galloping, whinnying, following a broad arc in the sky. Soon they circled the Grove, one hundred yards in the air, orbiting in a ring above the Yew and the juggernaut.

The ploughboy swivelled in his robotic suit, to behold the fantastic creatures. It would prove his fatal error. Given an opening, Torr Yosef found purchase on the grille and breastplate at the front of the suit. With a supreme effort, he wrenched it from its hinges. Will, still clinging to the back of the suit, took his chance. His weapon sang as he brought it around from behind his foe: a deadly sucker strike, mashing it into the ploughboy's exposed neck. The parahumanoid jolted and stopped, the pilot lifeless inside it.

The pterippi circled overhead, a halo of natural potency. Within the circle, Harold raised his battered trumpet and blew. The earth-shaking rumble of the juggernaut and the abyssal roar of the burning forest all but drowned out the fanfare, but to the clutch of survivors below, it proclaimed great joy. Harold departed the circle, descending and alighting in the Grove.

Faster the creatures galloped, a stampede without end, churning the sky. They became impossibly fast, a blur of golden splendour.

Far above, the clouds too began to turn, twisted by a vortex.

The winds rose, howling. Sinotar and Leith leapt from the turret of the juggernaut. Unable to fly against sudden turbulence, they were whipped away from the machine and hurled into the trees. Those on the ground anchored themselves.

The heavens opened.

There came from on high a blast of light of such intensity that the enthralled onlookers shielded their eyes. A bolt of hallowed vengeance, like an ethereal lightning strike, plunged to earth from the vortex of cloud, spearing straight through the great circus of pterippi. The bolt touched the earth, sending a shock of sound through the air. All nearby were knocked to the ground.

The mighty blast descended atop the juggernaut. Its superstructure exploded, cracking wide open as the force from above found earth.

The Ploughman simply vanished, obliterated. A fine red mist, perhaps his remnant particles, dissipated in the gale. The juggernaut, ablaze, came to a grinding halt. Whistling scythes slowed, then stopped — scant yards from the Fairy King and his Queen, at the base of the Yew.

Oberon and Titania held fast throughout their ordeal. Now, as one, they collapsed to the ground.

Overhead, the pterippi slowed, visible again as winged horses. Soon the circle broke, the miracle complete. The herd streaked away into the west, with many a whicker of triumph.

Thunder rolled across the firmament. Crooked lightning walked like spiders' legs between the clouds.

The land exhaled. After many days of empty threats, it started to rain.

Bedraggled and drenched, the party of fighters gathered beneath the boughs of the Yew. Trixel Tate, aided by several dryads, tended to the fallen Sovereigns. Meanwhile, old friends and new acquaintances united. Leith marvelled at Meadow's gallant account of his victory over the skeletons. Will joked that Torr Yosef saved him from an honourable death, before offering him sincere gratitude.

All turned towards Harold in anticipation. Before the dragonfly would recount his exploits, he asked: 'Where's Mustapha?'

Torr Yosef started from his place by the ruined rows of Ficus trees. Though his visage would not show it, his telepathy conveyed a need for haste.

<The youth lies within the bole of a stalwart boab, half a league from here. I must go to him — I fear the boab and its sentinel neighbours may have felt the tread of the Ploughman's infernal machine.>

Without waiting to be followed, the golem launched at a dead run into the forest, sweeping Meadow and Dique into his arms as he went. A heartbeat later, Will and Harold followed in his footsteps.

The group crashed headlong through the primordial forest. Rain surged, hammering the canopy leaves, sluicing the faces of those who charged along the forest floor. Far above, the heavens rumbled a declaration. Perhaps it was retribution for the burning forest, or perhaps the deluge of an Age had, at last, arrived. Thunder pealed, while the sky grew as dark as the pall of death over Petrichor.

With a sinking stomach, Will recognised the path taken by Yosef. 'Did you say a boab?' he called after the golem up ahead.

<She vowed to keep him safe,> Yosef replied. He accelerated, stomping through the undergrowth as he went.

Their path away from Psithur Grove, at first lush and untrammelled, gradually became chaotic ruin. With frequency, they stumbled across the fallen trunks of enormous trees, many still burning. Soon, they arrived at a flattened path, twenty yards wide.

Devastation greeted them. Lesser trees, blackened and splintered in death, hissed beneath the rain. Smoke curled skywards from one hundred dwindling spot fires. Yosef picked his way along the ruined corridor, Will and Harold in close pursuit.

'Isn't this where ...?' uttered Meadow.

There might have been a clearing, before the Ploughman's monstrosity carved a way through the heart of it. Ahead, to one side, once stood a proud semicircle of boab trees. Now they lay felled, pushed aside by the juggernaut's passage.

Yosef knew where his footsteps took him. So did Will. So did the pixies. Meadow's heart skipped several beats as he saw the boab, partly crushed, partly intact, amidst the scattered debris of its fellows.

<*This is she,*> said Yosef of the hamadryad, coming to a stop.

'Her name was Sonia,' said Meadow, sobbing. Yosef placed the pixies on the ground.

The face of the hamadryad could be seen. No life shone in her downcast eyes.

Only the golem moved forward. His companions, frozen in place, dreaded what might be revealed within.

Yosef knelt by Sonia's bole and, with greater care than seemed possible, probed the wreckage. None spoke.

<*I see him,*> the golem announced.

Reaching within, Yosef held aloft Mustapha's limp form. The black-clad strangeling was only a dark, sodden wisp in the golem's arms. Moving aside from the hamadryad, Yosef lay Mustapha upon the ground. Not a flicker of consciousness came from the strangeling.

<*He still lives,*> declared Yosef, as several exhaled.

'We need to get him out of here,' said Dique. 'Back to the Grove.'

'What if he's broken something?' countered Meadow. 'He might need a bonesetter. A shaman. We should go to Flaxae. It's nearby.'

'Flaxae lay in the path of the Ploughman's machine,' said Harold. 'All there lies in disarray. I suggest Reed, instead. Perhaps I can fly him.'

A squabble ensued, as the pixies and the dragonfly contested their options in animated fashion. Little regard they gave to their surroundings, until the figure of Will burst apart their huddle, sending all three toppling to the ground.

The human surged past the bewildered Fae Folk, careless for their chatter. Rain and anguish streaked his face. He fell to the muddied earth beside Mustapha.

All were struck silent as the farmer embraced the strangeling and delivered an impassioned kiss to the comatose form of his beloved.

END OF PART WHITE

INTERLUDE

THE LAP OF THE GODS

Before anything else, existed Adatar and Anato.

Light and Darkness.

Sun and Moon.

Day and Night.

Adatar and Anato loved each other. In those earliest of times, they twirled across the cosmos together in what later became known as the Grand Dance. They were the Gods of All: Everything that came to be, came from them.

Stories that describe the origin of the universe are often told. Many of them give a similar account, perhaps because a grain of truth lies amidst the bombast. Creation stories are easier for some to process, than the concept that everything exploded into being from nothing. No living mortal lived to see the Grand Dance; yet, whether right or wrong, Rhye's origin story begins with this most perfect coupling.

The movement of Anato and Adatar brought about the separation of land and sky, the birth of the stars and the Seven Seas. The land itself they called Rhye, which in their tongue meant *a place for gods*. They designed it to be a land of wonder and bounty. The Seas surged with restless energy, a vitality that reflected the passion of the Dance occurring above them.

Before an Age could pass, the celestial union produced Gods, to preside over Rhye. The eldest and most potent of these was Onik. An impetuous offspring, Onik waited for no direction and immediately set about exploring the depths of the universe. Impatient but powerful, his abilities were sufficient to destroy all that Adatar and Anato danced into existence. Fortunately, after only a few cosmic moments, Onik chose his own yoke, by becoming the God of Time.

Next came Cornavrian, God of Nature and the Elements. As his remit, he claimed the fires deep within the earth, the wind, the Seas, and the change of seasons. In this, he worked closely alongside Onik; together, they forged the land of Rhye. They crafted the most verdant greenswards, the most abysmal ocean trenches, and the most dramatic mountain landscapes imaginable. Devoted spirits protected each lush, natural frontier: undines beneath the waves, dryads in the forests and zephyrs to guide the winds.

Above all, the Gods cherished the wondrous garden of Nevermore. Clear streams, overladen fruit trees and fragrant blooms adorned every inch of this magnificent glade. To protect it, they erected jagged peaks all around — an impenetrable wall made from the bedrock of the earth.

Following Cornavrian came the twins — Marnis and Valendyne, representing Creation and Attrition. Onik decreed that there could scarcely be Time without Beginning or End; thus, the twins were welcomed into the celestial family. Marnis, the Creator, dedicated his existence to bringing all new things to origin, while Valendyne ensured a natural process of decay, becoming the warden of departed creatures.

Marnis began creating without delay. In a heady rush of inspiration, he gave rise to all the varied and exotic creatures of land and sea. He barely finished one task when he had moved on to the next, due to a notoriously short attention span and rampant enthusiasm. Still, before long, he stopped to rest. The world swelled with beasts, wild and docile.

The small family of Gods all admired the masterwork that Marnis achieved. The sanctity of life became a thing to be revered.

The Creator's respite did not last: Marnis soon set about designing the higher beings, who would hold dominance over all sentient life. He planned to mould his greatest creations in the likeness of himself, his siblings, and his progenitors. These higher beings would, of course, be immortal ... a decision that would come back to haunt him for all time.

With blithe abandon, he set about his work.

In his own eyes, his first attempts were abominations.

Gigantic, misshapen beings spewed forth from his birthing cauldron. Endowed with godlike strength, they were otherwise brutes, with flailing tree-like limbs and slabs of stone for hands. Eyes of abyssal black (sometimes one, sometimes three or four) stared out from hideous faces. The creatures bellowed, seeming to protest their own existence. A great number of them lurched and thrashed about on the land, finding little to quell their vexation.

Cornavrian spied the creatures that Marnis birthed. 'What do you call those?' he asked.

'Ogres. Something went awry with the mixture. They hold none of our beauty ... their civility leaves much to be desired. I'm quite sure one of them just punched an innocent tree. What will I do?'

'Start over?'

'I will doubtless be trying again,' admitted Marnis. 'But I can't get rid of the Ogres — they are my creations!'

Valendyne, watching from afar, fidgeted in his seat.

Cornavrian rubbed his chin. The Ogres' aggression peaked when Adatar pirouetted towards them, their enormous bodies crashing and thrashing through sunlit woodland and canyon alike.

'They don't appreciate daylight,' observed the God of Nature. 'I have an idea.'

One by one, Cornavrian coaxed the mighty Ogres towards nearby mountains. There he found a cave, which wound down into the dark interior of the earth. He pushed all the Ogres deep inside, then sealed up the cave with a single, massive, highly polished stone. When Adatar's golden rays tried to penetrate the mountainside, they were reflected outwards again.

Marnis exhaled his relief. 'I shall not need to look upon those Ogres again.'

'Ah, but they will keep an eye on your world, its events and all its creations,' replied Cornavrian. 'The stone only reflects light from the outside. The side that faces darkness is transparent. I imagine they're watching us right now.'

'Incredible. You developed this stone with such exquisite properties. It is perfect.'

'I call it scrallin*:* It returns the light tenfold that is reflected upon it but does not obstruct the view in darkness.'

'Most precious. I will model my next creations on your perfect mineral. The Ogres can be forgotten.'

'Do not dismiss them as a mistake, my brother,' Cornavrian warned. 'Even the spurned creation seeks a purpose.'

With this wisdom on board, Marnis returned to his toils. His fertile mind next brought forth the Delves, who were intelligent and masterful — the antithesis of the Ogres. He made them to dwell beneath the surface, in caverns purpose-built to keep watch and protect Rhye from the abominations hidden there. Then came the Fae Folk, to populate the Forest Realms; Mer-Folk, custodians of the Seven Seas; Humans, forthright and ambitious; the Adept, who studied lore and learned the preternatural arts; and last of all, the Sylphs, rulers of the air.

Soon, higher beings ventured across all the domains of Rhye, building lives for themselves. The brothers of Marnis were delighted by what he had wrought ... except for Valendyne, his twin, by this time less than enthralled.

He chose to bite his tongue.

Anato and Adatar saw the works of Marnis and were also impressed. To help the new creatures flourish, Light and Darkness combined once more to bring forth a host of new offspring: Ophynea, Goddess of Love; Lhestra, Goddess of Justice; Phydeas, God of Providence; Augustine, God of Health; Oska, God of Fortune; Floe, Goddess of Children; and Anuvin, God of War. Anuvin, last of all, scoffed at his own birth. His elder sister, Lhestra, recognising his importance, vowed to keep a watchful eye over him.

Onik guided the passage of time onwards. The others worked in unison — or at loggerheads — to ensure that life in Rhye held rewards and tribulations, in equal measure.

Valendyne detested it.

Jealousy consumed him, seeing all that Marnis had done. His twin became the darling of Adatar, who shone down the warmth of his glory on all creation.

He spoke his lament to Anato.

'I long to create, too,' Valendyne confided. 'Marnis has all the fun, all the catharsis. My task is to sit and watch while his wondrous creatures preen and prance about forever. As for lesser beasts, their lives are senseless. They pray to no one, then they die, leaving me to collect their souls and return their decaying bodies to the ground. It is a loathsome task. What is more, I grow tired of carrying the endless burden of insipid souls around with me.'

Anato reflected on this. After a time, she offered the boon of her wisdom to Valendyne. 'Why don't you try to create something for yourself? Marnis will see what you are capable of and hold you in greater esteem.'

This notion filled Valendyne with much enthusiasm. Unbeknownst to his peers, he also created a new race. He gave rise to a people who were deathless, symbolising his loathsome task of carrying a multitude of departed souls in his withering heart. His creations would not die, for they had no soul.

Valendyne knew little of creating new life. He dug in the earth, seeking hardy materials, crude but plentiful. He birthed creations of iron. They were stalwart, but ungainly. They were also massive in form and power, for he wanted to show Marnis — and his brethren — the majesty of his own conceptions.

Valendyne created Golems. Proud of his beings, he paraded them throughout the land, allowing his family to behold them.

The response dismayed him.

Marnis burst into tears of laughter. He rolled from side to side in a fit of hysterics, watching the blank-faced automatons lumbering about. His unbridled mirth was, to Valendyne, tantamount to a slap in the face.

'Nobody outshines me, the Creator!' he chortled. 'Stick to your far corner, Valendyne. Carry the dead. It's what you do best.'

Many other Gods and Goddesses responded with polite, if uncomfortable, laughter.

'Hey,' said Augustine, chewing his lip. 'Sorry to interrupt, but … are we ignoring the fact that these creatures don't have a soul? Do they actually have a life? How will they worship us?'

'Of course, they have a life!' spluttered Valendyne, his temper growing thin at such irreverence. 'They have an *endless* life! I have created beings that will not burden me further with their departed souls, but instead, serve me without end.'

'But ...' mumbled Oska, confused.

Marnis continued to snigger, finding it difficult to compose himself. There were numerous other murmurs of dissent. Only Anuvin remained silent, offering a thoughtful expression, along with a flicker of a smile.

The mockery became too grave an insult for Valendyne. Collecting the Golems, he hid them away in a bore he carved, far beneath the earth. For a time, he sat and watched them as they dug tunnels and made a home for themselves.

Then, he returned to Anato.

'You misread me,' she told him. 'Marnis is the Origin. You are his opposite. Do not aspire to create an approximation of Life. Instead, create Death.'

Valendyne's brow furrowed. Create Death? He returned to his Golems — like canopic jars on legs, bustling about beneath the earth — and he thought.

He sat, pondering Life and Death, for a very long time.

While he was caught in his reverie, Marnis sidled up to him.

'Ah ... Valendyne?'

'What?'

'I ... um ... I might have responded a little harshly earlier. I ... I made something for you.'

Valendyne ground his teeth, fit to burst diamonds. His immense pride took another blow. This added insult to injury — he wanted to flaunt his own mastery of creation, not be humbled by yet another trinket... much less, a gift from his brother.

He resolved to crush Marnis. For now, he still held his tongue, content to bide his time. After all, a gift was a gift.

'I see. What is it?'

Marnis created for Valendyne his own Realm. A place where the souls of dead beasts could reside for eternity, as his subjects.

A place of ethereal beauty met his eyes, ensconced beyond the veil of cloud that forever cloaked the jagged mountain range to the north of Rhye. To enter the sanctuary verged on leaving Rhye behind; truly, it would provide a glorious place of eternal rest for those who resided there.

Valendyne named the place Obelis, the seat of separation between the living and the departed. He mumbled his outward thanks and disappeared into the clouds.

He refused to sit idle.

No longer did the God of Attrition fritter away time in thought and meditation, watching the immortal children of Marnis continue to evade him.

Instead, he moved to reprise his attempt at creation, taking the words of Anato to heart.

Valendyne fashioned Death.

Death would be the bane of Realms, the collector of souls and the agent of Valendyne himself upon Rhye. This agent would not simply retrieve the essence of docile beings and shepherd them with a gentle arm to Obelis, as had been Marnis' intent. Death would wield power sufficient to thresh the souls from higher beings as well, ending their immortal lives, bringing spirits of great esteem to the feet of Valendyne, to be his subjects — or perhaps slaves — forever.

Death became a monstrous being, invisible to all but its intended victim. An agent of purest darkness, stalking the land on two legs, yet able to climb, fly, burrow, and swim to reach any who would hide from it.

These exertions altered Valendyne himself. Once the twin of Marnis, he became something very different — the Creator's opposite. A creature of ashen pallor, cloaked in the shade of darkness.

Valendyne birthed his masterwork, the Two-Legged Death. He placed it upon Rhye ... and waited.

Death did not go unnoticed. Before too long, the entire divine family — as families do — aired their opinions.

'Hey, everyone,' announced Marnis, wearing a perplexed look. 'It looks like Valendyne has created Death. It's killing off all my higher beings. That's not a good idea ... is it?'

Valendyne sat, stony-faced, unrepentant.

Anuvin relished the idea. 'War and Death are a part of Life,' he declared. He immediately slid over and began whispering in Valendyne's ear.

'So are festivals. And harvests. And birthdays!' replied Phydeas, gesticulating with portly arms. 'What use is Providence to those who are dead?' Some eyes rolled. Phydeas excelled at indulgence and short-sightedness.

'Silly fool!' intoned Cornavrian. 'The higher beings of Rhye must learn to cherish their resources and their very lives. How else will the value of Providence be appreciated?'

Lhestra agreed. 'It is just, that all shall die at their allotted time.' Marnis nodded, his face glum. Valendyne remained silent, still listening to the God of War.

The measured tones of disembodied Onik rang out next. 'Unchecked, the races of the world will overpopulate — too many mouths vying for your provision, Phydeas. Times of crisis and natural attrition will occur. From the ashes, fresh life springs anew. This is the legacy of Valendyne and translates to all who walk upon Rhye.

'Death, one way or another, is inevitable.'

Onik's voice resonated as a statement of fact. None could deny his words. As he counted the seconds, minutes, hours, and years, so could he see every possibility, stretching forward in Time. For a moment, everyone simply stared at each other.

'Death has no place loitering near my beloved children!' squeaked Floe, into the awkward silence. Augustine comforted her, a look of consternation belying his calm nature.

Oska, usually boisterous and vocal, grew uneasy. He sensed conflict brewing beneath the family debate. 'Perhaps there is an accord we can reach? Can such a dire outcome be influenced? I propose that all of Marnis' creations shall be mortal, though some will have longer lifespans than others.'

Lhestra shuddered but did not interject. Marnis spoke next, eager to cleanse the bitterness from the air. 'Brothers and sisters, I can see we are a family divided. Perhaps we should seek a verdict from our forebears, to whom we owe our own existence.'

'I'll go ask them,' offered Valendyne, with a wolfish grin.

Anato and Adatar continued their slow Dance across the sky — perpetual motion, ever-undulating waves of golden daylight and silvery darkness. Twin celestial bodies, sharing an intimate orbit since the beginning of the universe.

'See! I created the Two-Legged Death,' he said to them. 'Death will visit every creature, whether high or low born, to drink dry the well of its life at a time determined by the Gods. What do you think?'

Night and Day looked upon Rhye and saw what Valendyne had made.

'My power is unending,' said Adatar. 'The beings who worship me should have forever to bask in my glory. If you give them Death, you will take away those who adore me.'

For the first time since Time itself, Anato gave her lover a withering glare. She turned to Valendyne. 'Every time I spin towards Rhye, the Seas rise to meet me. As I leave them, they recede. It is the natural rhythm of things. Lives shall come and go, like tides.

'You heeded my words, Valendyne. Death is perfection.'

Valendyne smiled, pleased for Anato's approval. But the matter was far from decided. Adatar seethed.

'I am the Sun and the source of life! I will not be betrayed in this way!'

'Love of my life, Valendyne is not talking about mass extinction. New generations will continue to emerge, even as the old fall away. There will always be new beings who grow to adore you, as I do.'

'This is sacrilege!' Adatar blazed furiously. 'You spurn me! You wait for new creatures to be born, so that you can draw them towards your own sallow light!'

Anato stopped still. Never had she heard Adatar speak with such acrimony.

'Then I shall not embarrass your skies with my *sallow light* again,' she said quietly.

From that moment onwards, Day and Night existed separately. Anato and Adatar were seldom seen in the same sky. They remained, however, integral in the fabric of Rhye.

Valendyne strolled back to his brothers and sisters.

As difficult as it might be to surprise a God, he found himself confronted by a huddle of his dumbstruck siblings. Phydeas regained himself first, choosing to avoid tact at all costs.

'Valendyne! You bring nothing but ruin! Now there are half as many hours for harvest. Half as many for trade and craft. What shall our prized beings do, by the light of Anato?'

'Sleep? Regain their energy?' suggested Valendyne, with a callous shrug.

'We shall teach them to mine and use scrallin,' said Cornavrian, trying to salvage the situation. 'It is much more potent and valuable than fire and exists in abundance within the rock of the earth. It will provide the light they need, as well as warmth and security during the hours of Night, until Adatar returns. This — occurrence — can be overcome. It will be overcome.'

'This "occurrence" is a disaster,' spluttered Phydeas. 'If you bring war to this family, the resulting confusion will bring war to the people of Rhye. What do you say, War?'

Anuvin grinned like a fiend but said nothing.

Beside him, Valendyne stood composed. He adjusted his black cloak with a rustle and stepped forward.

'My brethren. My sisters. Cast your eyes towards Rhye. Battles rage between the races of higher beings, as they have done since Marnis created them. They battle over wealth. They battle over land. Some of them battle over whether we even exist.

'Now, regardless of race or creed, all higher beings will devote their eternal afterlives to me. I am not mere Attrition. I am the Eventuality. I am the inevitable End.'

The Pantheon fell silent.

Valendyne's words did not ring hollow. Rhye dwelled in the Age of Obelis: a time of great conflict and change. New Realms were forming, born from the smoke and ruin of war. Ravenous Anuvin orchestrated the rise and fall of many an army, with thousands of souls lost over the drawing of lines on a map. Death entered a rabid frenzy, seizing souls with fervour, sending the dead on a march to the Afterlife. Likewise, the elderly and infirm were stalked by the unseen horror. Soon began a mass exodus of creatures, civilised and wild, from the world.

Marnis poured his energy into matching the losses with new life. Birth to replace Death.

For a time, a new equilibrium existed. Obelis served as a place of eternal respite from the wearying ardour of life. A place where community elders and battlefield champions alike could come closer to the Gods themselves. The passage to the Afterlife became almost as revered as Creation. A new Discipline emerged amongst the Adept, its members devoted to learning the deepest mysteries of Death. They wore black and called themselves Necromancers, vowing to follow the word of Valendyne.

Eventually, Valendyne showed his hand.

One thousand years passed, in the reckoning of those who worshipped Onik and learned how to mark the passage of time. Still, Valendyne did not forget his humiliation at the hands of Marnis. He hid his rage behind a mask of silent ire. Anuvin, for his part, set the stage for battle — not only upon Rhye, but amongst the Gods themselves.

Valendyne prepared to use the life force of the departed to create his own unholy army. He intended to vanquish Marnis ... and whoever else opposed him.

In a cataclysmic burst of arcane power, the souls of countless beings were flushed from Obelis, down the mountain slopes and into the vast host of Golems, long hidden from the eyes of the Gods.

An army of possessed golems marched from the deep well of their interment.

For the peaceful, still-living denizens of Rhye, a period of terror began. The misbegotten warriors of Valendyne commenced an unholy pilgrimage, from the bore beneath the world, back towards Obelis.

Death would not touch them, for they were already beyond the threshold of life.

All along their march, they wrought new death, unleashing still more souls. The Necromancers, in a fever of rapture, saw this as their moment. Seizing up the wayward souls, the Wearers of Black thrust them, haphazard, into the bodies of the departed. In so doing, they created a borrowed army of ghouls to walk alongside the host of Valendyne.

Many of the sentient races of Rhye found themselves ill-equipped to face down such a foe. Some saw it as sacrilege to even make the attempt, presented with the manifest will of Valendyne himself.

Not so the Adept, who alone held powers within divine estimation.

Among their number lived those who developed skill in the offensive arts. In those times, they often roamed the land individually — or in small bands — and were known by their signature Violet garb. Now, they had reason to form a unified body of warriors: To defend the passage back to Obelis, thus protecting the road to the Pantheon.

The assembled squadron called themselves Warlocks.

The Warlocks went forth in a bid to protect the upper reaches of Nurtenan and the sacred mountain road. A seismic clash of powers ensued. In the place later known as Mages Pass, one thousand Wearers of Violet held back multitudes of Golems and the undead for almost a month.

Yet, the will of Valendyne — and his alliance with Anuvin — held overwhelming power. Valendyne appeared, leading Death on a leash of fire. Anuvin came carrying his instrument of dread: The Horn of Agonies. Raising the Horn to his lips, War sounded the dirge of every living soul on that battlefield. The horde surged forward and the Warlock resistance was demolished, every one of them slain.

Thus, did the army of Valendyne arrive at the entrance to Obelis, only a short march from the abode of the Gods. Marnis, horrified by the ill reflection of his creations sent to defeat him, stood anchored by shock. His siblings rallied in his stead, even as the last stand of Warlocks met its end.

Lhestra took the helm, the souls of a thousand Adept screaming out to her for Justice. Cornavrian, Ophynea and Oska flanked her, spearheading their own seraphic armies. In this way did Justice, Nature and Love strive to overcome the evil wrought by Valendyne … with Fortune on their side.

They enacted a swift retribution. Anuvin, rendered impotent, could not turn the tide of battle. A holy deluge swept the vast horde utterly away, leaving only their beleaguered souls to find refuge with the Gods.

The Golems were protected from the scourge by Lhestra, for they had played no conscious part in their creation or enslavement. Marnis adopted them, as one might adopt homeless children, bereft of parental love. In time, they would be granted a vital spark of their own, ultimately repaying the Gods with great devotion.

The renegade deities both managed to withstand the deluge, though both were greatly weakened and cowed. Lhestra condemned both to eternal exile. Marnis, recovering his composure, devised each an ingenious trap, from which they could each fulfil their punishments, but never escape.

For Anuvin, this meant imprisonment upon an island, far beyond the shores of the Ealing Sea. Lhestra locked him in a mockery of his own battle armour, forged of a material so dense that, if he tried to leave the island, he would plunge to the abyss beneath the waves. As a further line of defence, Cornavrian raised a mighty stone edifice along the near shore of Rhye, naming it the Immortal Cliffs.

Valendyne was transferred to the sacred glade of Nevermore, where Cornavrian transformed him into a tree. In a reserve of wondrous beauty, his prison became a thing of hideous contrast: gnarled, withered and black, heavy with pungent fruit and bristling with thorns. There, he would be secluded from nearly all sentient life. His closest neighbours, the Ogres, were themselves fastened deep below his reaching root system, unaware of his presence.

Marnis fashioned a circular Ring to bind the trunk of the God-tree. If Valendyne grew in power — or in size — or made any direct attempt to break the Ring — he would be destroyed by a brace of potent wards.

These wards — fused into the Ring — contained the greatest attributes of all the higher beings on Rhye. Cornavrian scoured all corners of the land, seeking out the essence of its diverse people. The sylphs alone refused to contribute. Brazenly, they chose a secular existence, spurning the Gods and relying on their own resilience. Cornavrian, amongst the wisest and most temperate of the Gods, left the sylphs unpunished, divining that they would one day play a pivotal role in the history of Rhye.

Therefore, to seal the Ring, the Gods used:

The resilience of Humankind;

The discipline of the Mer-Folk;

The potent theurgy of the Adept;

The ingenuity of the Delves; and

The forest law and eldritch power of trees. The Fairy King provided this last contribution. Even at that time, Lord Oberon was King of the Fae Folk, living in the forests that would one day become Petrichor. The power of trees constituted the most crucial element, as it anchored Valendyne within his seal of binding.

Once the Ring was complete, Cornavrian fastened it about Valendyne's trunk. Upon sealing the clasp, a celestial explosion rang out across Rhye. Scripture reported the reaction to have been so loud, it was heard right to the farthest reaches of Sontenan.

With the Ring in place, Lord Oberon would know if any attempt were made to breach it. To recompense him for this role, the Gods conferred on Oberon — and his wife Titania — extreme longevity and vitality.

The Ring itself became known as the Fae Ring.

The Adept, too, were rewarded for their sacrifice. In earlier Ages, they were a nomadic people, having no place to call the seat of their race. The Gods gave them the remains of Obelis, the mountaintop sanctuary separating Rhye from the heavens. The sylphs, already accustomed to the harsh life among the mountains, helped the Adept to construct a great monastery; and below it, to hew a vault within the mountains for their enclave. This place they called Aerglo. The mountain range became dubbed the Peaks of Obelis.

Thereafter, the lush glade of Nevermore, prison of Valendyne, knew no visitors. Stories of the danger within were passed down amongst the peoples of Rhye, through thousands of years. For many, these stories were consigned in time, to myth and legend. Others never stopped praying or believing tales of Gods and volatile magic.

Through all this time, Anato and Adatar never ceased dancing across the sky, bearing witness — each now in solitude — to all that transpired.

PART BLACK

CHAPTER 12

THE SHAPE OF THINGS

Lord Neptune stared out across the slate-grey turmoil of Imperial Waters, through a filter of grief.

The undine, Salacia, stood by his side, an arm about his waist. Cold, granular sand washed over their toes. The waves lapping their ankles at the shoreline slapped them with hostile foreboding.

The pair survived the ordeal at the House of Giltenan, though this came as empty consolation. Tragic losses drained their souls.

Fontus and Juturna. Smote in their beds, with little opportunity to retaliate. Mer-Folk traditionally strove for an honourable demise. As Mer-men of noble bloodline, this travesty would be a blight on their memory.

Neptune gnashed his teeth. He chose to observe the ritual days of mourning in Via. It riled him, as a further affront: True glory came from burial at sea, or interment in the Diluvian Grotto, in Artesia.

The Necromantic spell of the skeletons desecrated those

Mer-men's bodies. In the heat of battle, they were again cut down — a second death — as foes.

Neptune resisted the saltiness of his emotions by contemplating the fate of Lord Rogar. The Sovereign of Humankind fought by his side when a lapse in concentration cost him his life. Killed, in one surreal moment, by one of the greatest of his ancestors.

Walther. The last Giltenan of true warrior ilk, mused the Mer-Lord ... *and that was almost three thousand years ago.*

Rogar did not receive a skeletal reincarnation. Dexler Roth prevented the human from suffering such a fate by beheading him, in a macabre act of mercy.

What an utter fiasco. For a brief moment, Neptune considered the Song of the Prophet.

'*The Lords of old will crumble hence*,' he said.

'Speak plainly, my love?' replied Salacia, looking up at him with eyes of ultramarine.

'Nothing.' Neptune shrugged off his reverie. Speculation would assist little in the coming task.

'I long to return to Artesia, Lord. Will we depart tomorrow?'

'We will,' answered Neptune. Salacia's faithfulness and obeisance were valid attributes. They were also the anchor that weighed her down. But for a stronger intuitive streak, she may have made a fine Sovereign.

'I have no succession plan,' he continued. 'With Fontus and Juturna gone, I must spend time in contemplation and consult with the viziers.'

Salacia held Neptune's bare torso more tightly.

Like her undine kinfolk, Salacia had a humanoid appearance, with amphibious features. Her elongated fingers and toes were webbed, for aquatic mobility. Smooth scales adorned her serpentine trunk. Gills sat behind her ears, which tapered to a delicate point.

As such, undines could be recognised at a glance as different to their Mer-Folk counterparts. Mer-men and women appeared closer in kinship to humans, though physical beauty and natural athleticism blessed each and every one of them. This became an established pretext for their haughtiness.

Differences between the Mer-Folk and the sacred water spirits had also been a long-lived source of contention between the aquatic races. It gave the Mer-Lord a political headache, for his choice of successor could hold consequences for diplomatic stability in Artesia.

The choice would prove more challenging with the deaths of Fontus and Juturna.

'Do you fear an attack, such as befell Lord Rogar?' asked the undine.

Neptune glared out to sea. The Imperial Waters, usually serene, were marred by a threatening chop. His eyes followed the coastline, from the mouth of the Granventide to a tiny settlement in the distant south-west. He recalled that Lady Maybeth would travel there on occasion, to a cottage she built, perched over the water. She called the place something jejune — a name Neptune could not recall — and retreated there when seeking respite and solitude.

The wild oceanfront environs offered little respite now.

'Trouble brews,' he said, after a time. 'If the Song speaks true, my days are numbered. But while the tides still change, I must continue to entreat Cornavrian. I must read the tapestry of the Seven Seas and plan for the future.

'We need to plan ahead, Salacia. If not for next year, then for tomorrow.'

'The ancient ward of the Seven Seas will protect us,' said the undine, with conviction. 'The waters of Trident Deep will offer up an augury to the viziers, for sound counsel in these dark days. Do you pray only for a succession plan?'

Neptune closed his eyes as he spoke, lowering shutters on the uncertainty within. He shook his head. 'No. I also pray they have further unravelled the mystery of the Seventh Sea. Its import continues to elude us. We are yet to chart her distant shore — for all we know, it has none. In some way, the Seventh holds the key to this crisis.

'Following the Council, I also have a dread awareness of this deep-sea anomaly. It concerns me that the finest Mer divers are unable to locate a source for the signal.'

'Perhaps the waters will speak to your Trident, my Lord?'

'A fine suggestion, Salacia. Let us discover what the Seven Seas will tell us today.'

He strode forward, until the shallows reached his flanks. Reaching over his shoulder, he unharnessed the fabled instrument at his back. He carried the standard with him wherever he went, both as powerful weapon and conduit for reading the Seas. Gripping the haft, he held it aloft. Three enormous prongs, crafted of a mysterious organic material, glinted in the wan sunlight.

He dipped the Trident into the Imperial Waters, uttering a simple prayer.

Far in the south of Rhye, a glorious spectacle lay in silent majesty. Locked in an endless dance with the desert winds, ten thousand sand dunes marched towards the Trident Deep.

The Dunes of Sordd were regarded as one of the most beautiful creations realised by Marnis, tempered by the patient hand of Cornavrian. Shimmering sands of every colour stretched for the horizon; a wonder that almost none had seen, for the Dunes' beauty was fatal. Adatar's scorching rays rendered the desert days inhospitable. By night, shanties told that an ancient bane prowled the dunes, hunting and devouring would-be explorers.

In the Age of Obelis, sylphic expeditions attempted to traverse the Dunes of Sordd by air. Several of these vanished without trace. One such party did escape with their lives, reporting a tense conflict with a monster they claimed was a manticore. They told of a beast somewhere between a lion and a dragon, with a distorted human face. Descriptions detailed it as 'endowed with the force of all the elements'; being 'as fierce as conflagration, as swift and turbulent as a gale and as monumental as bedrock.' The manticore displayed an unquenchable rage — perhaps due to intrusion on its territory, or perhaps due to a 'traumatic wound, where once its lethal pronged tail may have been.' Regardless, the sylphic expedition fled from the beast and from the Dunes altogether.

Thereafter, the Dunes of Sordd were considered a place of forbidding danger, devoid of civil habitation.

By stark contrast, deep beneath the many-coloured sands, there thrived a proud and illustrious Realm. A vast, subterranean basin, hewn by the relentless passage of time. In that basin lived numerous aquatic races, who named their home Artesia.

Myriad vaults and dwellings honeycombed the ancient sandstone walls in the depths of Artesia. Within, the dominant civilisations of Mer-Folk and undines carved out a niche existence. They led lives of dauntless dedication, custodians of the Seven Seas of Rhye.

The Mer-Folk, in particular, earned an esteemed reputation as hydraulic engineers. A network of underground caverns connected the various submerged districts of Artesia; these linked to the basin itself through complex airlocks and submersion shafts.

The Artesian Way became known as the premier construction of the Mer-Folk. It yawned like a giant well, rising to the surface at the fringe of the desert, on the southern border of Sontenan. At the mouth of the Way stood a gate, protected by humans and Mer-Folk alike, through which travel and commerce kept both Realms prosperous.

Beyond the worldly disciplines of commerce and engineering, the denizens of Artesia considered themselves deeply spiritual. All observed rites to honour the sacred Seas, upheld by the shrines and ministries of the undines. Undines believed that the fate of Rhye unfurled as a rich tapestry — an allegorical weave constructed by the ever-flowing, ever-changing waters of their Realm.

Throughout history, the Lords of Artesia learned to harness the powers of the aquatic races. The industry of the Mer-Folk helped forge a progressive Sovereignty, while the fervent lore of the undines kept the long line of Mer-Lords anchored in a culture respectful of the Gods.

The iconic Trident represented Artesian Sovereignty. Lore dictated that only the Mer-Lords knew of the relic's true origin, though rife speculation claimed it to be the tail of a manticore.

One detail went unquestioned: The Trident held the power to read the limitless tapestry of the Seven Seas.

The moment Lord Neptune immersed his Trident, all the Seas of Rhye offered him their stories. From the frigid depths of the landlocked Melancholy Blue, to the noble surge of Imperial Waters; even the Seventh Sea whispered a haunting refrain, though this faded the longer Neptune listened. He knew instantly of the taint that seeped into the Sour Milk Sea, from the borrowed waters of the river Bijou. Ghosts of shipwrecked and drowned seafarers called out to him from the Clementine, urging to push his percipience further north.

He did. His whole body grew tense with shock and alarm.

Neptune snatched the Trident, dripping, from the shallows.

On his face showed the awakening of horror.

'My Lord?' Salacia said, touching his arm.

He saw it: the source of the inscrutable signal, which brought consternation to the Council. In a heartbeat, every shred of enigma and doubt disappeared, the hidden danger unmasked. At last, Neptune knew why he could not pinpoint the rhythmic, subaquatic signal before.

'The Rival ... he comes,' said Neptune.

'What do you hear?' Salacia's hand flew to her lips.

From an old Golem verse — *'Rival of all, ally of none'* — the term spoke of none other than Anuvin, God of War.

'Salacia, you must wait here at the shores of Via.' He stepped away from her.

'Lord, speak to me of this ill tiding!' Salacia threw him a beseeching look.

Neptune wrenched free of his consort, anger and apprehension lining his face. 'Anuvin is free of his bonds. The clashing of stone against stone brought sound beneath the surface. The roots of his unnamed prison quaked at his efforts for freedom.

'Now, I can sense him. He is in the water. Unburdened, unshackled, he swims for the shore. I have to prevent his landfall.

'Salacia, you must remain, lest you forfeit your own life. Pray for me. Pray for all who live in the Seas of Rhye.'

He turned his back on her, wading deeper. A moment later he dived, swallowed by the restless waves.

Neptune speared through the Imperial Waters like a subaquatic comet. A tremendous vortex of turbulence churned in his wake, dragging tiny crustaceans along for the ride. The cold ocean rippled about him, recognising his body and parting for him, the way a crowd parts for the passage of a revered nobleman. The ocean currents surged, pushing him along.

The Mer-Lord swam with all his might, holding his Trident out before him. In his racing mind, he sensed the corporeal form of

Anuvin — diving, surfacing, and swimming. The God moved with languid, inexorable strokes across the Ealing Sea.

Locked in a prison of quartz for millennia, Anuvin's physical prowess would be blunted, yet he was still a God.

A diminished God against the mightiest of mortals.

The currents carried Neptune westward and north, leaving the civilised mainland of Rhye. He passed through ocean wilderness dotted with cays, atolls, and volcanic islands; some the playgrounds and cathedrals of undines, while others had never known the footstep of any creature. Neptune hurtled past them all, out beyond the western reaches, where jagged headlands met crashing waves and deep-sea behemoths spent their lives oblivious to all terrestrial concerns.

The water grew colder. Neptune knew he had, at last, entered the Ealing Sea, where glacial ice and melted snow poured down from the Peaks of Light to tumble over the Immortal Cliffs. The presence of War now thrummed in his brain like a headache.

Neptune knew not if this encounter was preordained. He knew of no lore or song that spoke of Anuvin's liberation, let alone any intercession. He wrestled with the idea that he pursued either high blasphemy, or the saving grace of the land, without knowing which.

On his left loomed the dark shelf below the Unnamed Island. As he passed it, he caught a glimpse in the distance of a churning trail on the surface.

Straining to swim ever faster, he closed the gap.

The God and the Mer-Lord met in the water with a tumultuous clash, the slinging of brawny arms and the thrashing of legs. Neptune grappled the mighty torso of Anuvin, finding his sinews as hard as granite.

'Do you assume to slow me down, kingfish?'

The voice of Anuvin came clear through the water, boiling like magma in Neptune's ears.

'War is not welcome in my Realm,' the Mer-Lord replied.

'You make me laugh, mortal.'

'The longer you laugh, the faster you drown.'

Neptune heaved, pulling Anuvin beneath the waves. The pair fought with titanic strength, sinking down towards the limits of sunlight. Swarms of bubbles enshrouded their tangled bodies.

Anuvin's eyes locked on Neptune, his auburn hair a wreath of ire. He lashed out with a huge fist. Neptune ducked aside, bringing his Trident around to counterstrike. The prongs grazed Anuvin's flank, leaving barely a mark.

The God flashed his teeth in a menacing grin. 'Ah, the tail of the desert bane! It shall make a fine victory trinket.'

The water was thrashed to a white spume, as if by a feeding frenzy of sharks. Blow after blow the combatants rained upon each other, sending shockwaves through the ocean. Time and again, Neptune tried to drag Anuvin under. He knew that, if he could drive the God to the ocean floor, he might be able to bury him within a hydrothermal vent.

After what felt like dozens of attempts, the God of War relented, allowing Neptune to dive with him to the distant sea floor. Far below, a chain of vents spewed boiling, sulphurous clouds into the water. At the mouth of an enormous vent, Anuvin resisted the pull of the Mer-Lord.

'I came down here with you to prove a point,' snarled Anuvin. 'You see, I didn't spend thousands of years simply freeing myself from a jacket of quartz. Oh, no! I also learned to hold my breath.

'Another thing: I see you, trying to stuff me inside that vent. Do you expect to end me down here? Fool … this is exactly where I intended to be!'

Anuvin roared with laughter, unleashing a torrent of bubbles.

Neptune lost himself for a moment, wrong-footed by War, who seemed to have read his every move.

'Let me explain, kingfish,' Anuvin sneered, for it is the wont of every egotist to gloat over his own scheme. 'Near to us is the very root of the Immortal Cliffs. Within their ancient rock lie the shafts and tunnels of Warnom Bore. Vast quantities of water also run down within seepage cracks in the bedrock, down to where the great fires burn within the earth. There, the water is heated, giving rise to vents such as these.

'I need only swim through one of these vents to find myself surfacing within the Golem Realm. Heed my words: I have endured much, foolish mortal, so this will be no great test to me.

'Now, give me sport before I crush you.'

For three days and three nights, the underwater battle raged. The pair fought from the whitecaps above to the deepest trench below. Many a time did Neptune feel the tide turn to favour him. Each time, the God of War retaliated with typhoon blows.

At length, the Mer-Lord felt his own gargantuan reserves failing. Seeking a moment's reprieve, he surfaced.

Anuvin followed. Overhead, a new storm split the sky. Torrential rain pummelled the swell, while lightning rent the violet clouds.

'You must desist from this course, lest all of Rhye be lost,' Neptune cried, over the howl of the storm.

Grabbing him by the hair, Anuvin pulled until their faces were almost pressed together. 'War begets war, fool,' he sneered. 'You cannot best me in battle.'

Coiling like a spring, Anuvin delivered a devastating kick to the centre of Neptune's chest.

Pain exploded in the Mer-Lord's body. The breath was expelled from him in a rush of agony. Lights danced behind his eyes. His chest caved in. He began to sink into the gloom, dark mist crowding the edges of his vision.

As Neptune dropped into the void, Anuvin dove and clenched his wrist in a vice-grip. He wrested away the Trident. Holding it above him conjured buoyancy, bringing God and Mer-Lord back to the surface.

'Don't you die just yet, kingfish,' said Anuvin. 'I have a worse fate in mind for you.'

He turned and began swimming away from the Cliffs, dragging Neptune behind him.

CHAPTER 13

WAITING FOR THE SUN

Rain continued to fall, sending rivulets of grimy water down the outside of the glass. Meadow stared out at the dreary world with an absent expression. Few creatures scurried back and forth across the main square of Reed, while his blurred vision showed only two steeds secured out the front of the Oak & Barrel Inn.

He wiped at the inside of the window with his sleeve, grunting when his rain-spattered view of the world did not improve.

Meadow turned back to his companions around the table. Everyone faced unattended bowls of cold soup and neglected hunks of bread. Dique and Will nursed half-empty mugs of ale, whilst Harold sipped from a pot of drowseberry nectar. After initially raising a couple of solemn toasts, they sat, deflated, contemplating a bleak future.

A disconsolate air suffused the entire bar. Few satyrs were present; none brawled or shared bawdy jokes. Two dragonflies buzzed quietly to each other in a far corner. The barman, a lugubrious butterfly named Sammy, polished a spot on the mahogany in endless circles. He looked like he'd rather be anywhere else.

'It's great to have you back, Harold,' said Dique in an earnest voice.

'Your timing is impeccable,' added Will.

'Hardly,' answered the dragonfly. 'Countless lives were lost. Parts of the forest continue to burn. Now, the Fairy King and Queen —'

'Harold. You saved the Yew,' said Dique. I'm sure Lord Oberon would sing your praises. The spirit of Mother Forest is in that tree.'

'He might, were he still here. If every Fae in the Realm prays to Augustine and a mighty Lord can still succumb, what does that tell you? It tells me that the Gods are not listening, even when we do make a stand in their name.' He thumped a fist on the table.

The others heard it in Harold's tone: He blamed himself for the tragedy they all dreaded.

'The Gods did listen, Harold,' said Dique. 'You summoned the pterippi of Marnis. You saw the blast of light they brought from the heavens, did you not? Nothing says, "the Gods are listening" like the full force of Nature incarnate.'

Harold gave a glum nod.

The Voice of Cornavrian had spoken. The Ploughman lived no more. Regardless, the victory felt hollow, for the cost had been immense.

In the aftermath of the attack, the terrible strain of prayer and ward-casting brought both Oberon and Titania to the point of collapse. Despite the swift response and valiant efforts of the Realm's finest shamans, the Sovereigns' life-force began to ebb. Sensing the wane of his power, Oberon ordered the shamans away. He and Titania spent their final hours in private consult with Trixel Tate.

Beneath the blazing red of a forest-fire sunset, with storms churning overhead and the light of the world fading, the Fairy King and his Queen departed Rhye.

Trixel immediately set about coordinating a response to any fires not extinguished by rain. She visited those townships torn apart by the Ploughman's juggernaut. She reassigned several shamans to care for the ailing Mustapha. The grapevine buzzed with word that Oberon and Titania passed their Sovereignty to the fixie, though Trixel did not wear the Fairy King's antlered crown.

'Trixel sure has her work cut out for her,' said Dique.

'Miss Tate is doing alright,' replied Will, a meek attempt at encouragement.

'Doing alright?' cried Meadow, snapping out of his torpor. 'She stepped into the shoes of three-thousand-year-old demigods in the peak of an apocalypse. How can anybody in that situation be "doing alright"?'

'The Fae would do well to get behind her and help her rebuild,' said Harold, 'if that is the task she has been set. Though much about us lies in ruin, Petrichor holds great restorative power. We must unify and recover. Then, when the rain has gone, the sun will shine again on a proud Realm.'

'Well, that's some mighty fine bluster,' retorted Meadow. 'There's something you're not aware of, Harold. Before he died, Oberon foretold the breaking of the Fae Ring. He said, "in Nevermore, the evil wakes." I'd say we have a fair bit more to deal with than the passing of a quick thunderstorm.

'At any rate: What *did* you get up to in all these days, while Dique and I were incarcer—' — he faltered — 'taking involuntary refuge inside a boab?'

Harold looked up from his drink. Three inquisitive faces met him around the table. Will downed the rest of his lager, before motioning to Sammy for another.

'Therein lies a story,' said Harold, a glint in his eye.

As the rain thrummed on the roof of the Oak & Barrel Inn, the group settled in to absorb Harold's tale.

The dragonfly felt he was being wrenched in two as he fled the scene in the alleyway outside Juniper Juice. On the ground below, Mustapha lay crumpled on the ground like discarded parchment. Lady Belladonna stood over him, reciting some kind of spell.

To stay would be walking into a trap, but to leave represented betrayal. In the end, Harold reasoned, he would be no help to Mustapha if he was caught in the same spider's web.

Lady Belladonna certainly gave him spiderly vibes.

There were also Meadow and Dique to consider. Where had they gotten to?

Harold zipped away from Mustapha and Lady Belladonna, threading through the village streets and treehouses of Flaxae. Shortly, he would regain the vast gloom of the forest.

As he flew, he recalled the Warlocks.

At first, he thought the billowing violet robes were an illusion. Yet there they were, as undeniable as the trees of Petrichor. A startling quartet of the warrior Adept, zeroing in on his friend.

The world had not known Warlocks for an Age. They were consigned to the annals of extinction following the Godsryche, the great war which brought the Gods to the surface of Rhye.

Legend told that the events of the Godsryche triggered the Age of Sovereigns. Many chose to believe the Godsryche never happened at all, for it appeared only in stories. Nobody could produce any objective evidence for it; even scholars and historians drew a blank, their records empty for several years following the Sovereignty of Montreux Giltenan and the commissioning of the first Vrendari. Stories of the Godsryche persisted, bolstered by the warnings of the Prophet ... as did remembrances of Warlocks.

To Harold, the entire affair represented a matter of terrible fascination. Dragonflies were known to be avid readers, prone to studying tremendous matters. Such pondering took them well beyond the rustic hum of life in Dragonfly Hollow. Harold oft fancied himself up for a big adventure — one in which he might discover some relic or truth about the Gods and their cataclysmic battle.

Racing around after Mustapha and the pixies, in the depths of Petrichor, did not quite hit the spot.

He pursed his lips. The witless pixies would be fine. They always seemed to turn up after a scrape, bouncing back even sillier for the next one. He worried much more for Mustapha, though he'd likely need Meadow and Dique to help affect a rescue.

Take heart, my friend. You're not alone.

Harold zigzagged through endless trees. To an observer he would appear lost, yet he knew his way. He followed the stars as they winked through the treetops at him from the heavens above.

He prepared to zig left when the unmistakeable sound of nearby voices reached him. Just in time, he spied shadows between the trees ahead — he had only a moment to interrupt his flight and dive headfirst into a bush.

Three dark, corpulent shapes waded through the undergrowth, heading south from the glade where the night's circus had ensued.

Bullish tones and uncouth language gave them away. They were not Warlocks.

'I see straight through your little parlour act, Scaramouch,' came the voice of the Ploughman. 'You need not pretend this is about anything more than my money.'

A second figure responded — Harold recognised the oily tongue of the Mayor. 'Ah, but it is also a sacred parcel of Fae land you wish to plunder, human. A business deal though it may be, there is still the value of moral depravation to be considered.'

'You jest!' snorted the Ploughman. 'You have no morals to be deprived of. Thus, it is a transaction in gold only ... that substance for which you are desperately in need.'

'It is true, the coffers of Psithur Grove are depleted,' said Mayor Scaramouch, 'as are my own pockets. But there is more to the story! A greater scheme takes root beneath the surface, I sense it.

'Oberon spends the Fae reserve like there is no tomorrow. He invests vast resources in an effort to ward the Forest Realm. Few will realise just how it has cost him, to stage that debacle of a Ceremony.'

The third figure — the ploughboy — chimed in. 'Look how well that parade turned out!' he crowed. 'Whole thing got blown apart, by a bloody insect and his trumpet!'

The Ploughman dragged back the reins of negotiation. 'I'll let you in on a little secret,' he said to Scaramouch. 'You're an astute fellow. There *is* a greater scheme taking root ... and I plan to watch it grow until it yields scrumptious, bittersweet fruit.

'A new Age is upon us. It is not, as the Prophet wailed, the end of Rhye, but a new beginning. An Age of Dominion under the true Gods — not those who have forsaken us.

'Valendyne is to be set free, with Anuvin by his side, to reign over all mortals. Under his divine Sovereignty, tribute will be given to those who hold the balance of power and wealth.

'Good Mayor: This is our chance to be front and centre when the music starts. I, for one, intend to be amongst Valendyne's favoured when all of Rhye marches to a new beat. Already, I have forged a union with Lord Ponerog of the Wilden Folk and Lady Belladonna, a human of Rogar Giltenan's court.

'I ask you then, Scaramouch: Will you dance alongside us?'

Harold's eyes were wide as saucers. He swallowed a gasp.

'That's utter nonsense,' said the Mayor, barely containing his own incredulity. 'Give me your gold, Figaro, but you can keep your special brand of claptrap.

'This is my deal. The Fae knight border patrol will be sent on a bogus errand. The Verge will be unattended for one day only, except for the dryads, which are your problem. Do your worst but remember: two hundred acres, not a leafy twig more ... and I had nothing to do with it.'

From his hiding place, Harold saw the silhouetted figures shaking hands.

'You drive a tight bargain,' said the Mayor.

'I drive more than just a bargain,' replied Figaro the Ploughman. 'Say — you may not be invested in the grand undertakings of the land, but I'll wager you've a keen eye for machinations of another kind.

'Would you be interested in viewing my latest agricultural creation? It is a device designed to maximise efficiency, while minimising trauma to arboreal creatures. I call it a "juggernaut". I would be ever so proud to show it to you.'

'A jugger-what?' said Scaramouch with a frown.

'Juggernaut. It's an old human word meaning "to sow with kindness". It isn't far from here to my holdings, just across the Verge. Would you like to see?'

Scaramouch deliberated briefly, before offering a shrug. 'Can't do any harm,' he said.

With a sweeping wave, Figaro gestured along the forest path. Scaramouch took the lead as the three figures continued on their way.

The Mayor did not see the Ploughman gesture to his son as they walked behind him. Harold watched in horror as Figaro used a single finger to draw a line across his own throat.

'Well, that explains much,' said Will. Bottles now cluttered the table.

Sammy the butterfly continued to polish the same spot on the bar. By all appearances, he had forgotten all other aspects of his job.

'It does really top off the episode,' agreed Meadow. 'I mean, the Mayor should have quit while he was ahead. Now, he's sorely missing some capital ...'

'Our resident jester has returned,' muttered Dique, rolling his eyes.

'Quit horsing around,' said Will through a half-grin. 'Harold is yet to tell us the part about the pterippi.'

Harold sat in deep thought for a good long while.

The alliance between Mayor Scaramouch and Figaro the Ploughman was Petrichor's worst-kept secret and did not surprise him. The greater revelation came from the Ploughman's villainous lips: a *coup d'état* threatened the foundations of Rhye — from the farmlands of Sontenan, all the way up to the doorstep of the Gods.

What can a dragonfly do?

With this one sordid exchange, Harold's mission to retrieve his friends from mischief became something utterly profound. In the blue-black of the forest night, he had been handed the secret of an impending catastrophe — a conspiracy of the highest order.

Figaro the Ploughman held devastating plans for Petrichor and had built a contrivance of some kind to carry them out.

Scaramouch the Mayor might be shady ... but he was clueless. Soon, in fact, he could be dead.

Belladonna, on the other hand, now proved wickedly complicit.

I knew it!

Somehow, it all added up to the liberation of Valendyne — the destruction of the Fae Ring in the garden of Nevermore.

Harold knew not how the pieces fit together, but he knew the Ploughman must be stopped.

How? Could it be, this calls for ...? Do I dare?

As a typical, well-read dragonfly, Harold knew the lore of almost every race and creature in the land. In times of desperate need, there was only one place — only one species — he figured he could turn to for help.

His friends would have to wait.

He headed west.

The pterippi — created by Marnis and warded by Cornavrian, as beings of potent natural energy — did not count time by months or years, or even by seasons. Instead, they marked rifts in the firmament. Schisms of power denoted their epochal awareness. As such, little had changed for them since the alliance between sylphs and humans, forged by Montreux Giltenan.

When a single dragonfly appeared amongst them, they first regarded it with detached bemusement. The pterippi had never encountered such a curious creature before. It zipped and darted about, waving frantic arms, behaving for all the world as if it had important news.

The dragonfly wore a fraught expression. It buzzed around them, its mouth moving, forming words. As they did not understand it, it may well have said nothing at all.

The pterippi did understand the whirring vibration of its wings. The dragonfly stirred the air wherever it went, creating tiny zephyrs, here and there, up and down. Near away, the zephyrs cascaded against one another, colliding, creating harmonics in the air. Those harmonics travelled across the vastness of Rhye, ever growing, until far and wide, the whole world trembled with a warning.

The Womb of Rhye — the Forest Realm of Petrichor — was threatened.

The sacred creatures raised their heads from the pasture and shook manes of ivory and gold. Many a whinny arose between them, along with stomping hooves.

Soon, the dragonfly found itself surrounded by a ring of majestic, winged horses, snorting and nodding. In their own way, they said *we hear you.*

Fifty pairs of enormous wings unfurled and began to beat. One by one, they broke into a trot across the greensward on the fringe of Petrichor. A trot became a canter. A canter became a thunderous gallop. One by one, the creatures lifted off into the sky — their first flight since the previous Age. Their noses angled skyward. Up they flew, towards the distant home of the Creator.

The dragonfly followed them. He could do little else.

The Oak & Barrel Inn brimmed with uproarious patrons.

To begin with, Sammy finally dropped his pretence of polishing the bar. He started sweeping the floor, instead. His chore brought him nearer and nearer to the group, until at last he eavesdropped on Harold's tale, unabashed.

The remarkable story also drew the ears of a few nearby patrons, who made no effort to disguise their curiosity. A small collection of pixies, dragonflies and satyrs attracted still more interest from passers-by, out of the window. Soon, a throng of Fae creatures filled the Inn, cramming for position around the table and its occupants.

'So, there we were, zooming higher and higher,' explained Harold. 'All of Rhye spread out below us. My vision became so acute as to make out every wondrous detail and I knew, in that instant, we must be at the roof of the world.'

'Incredible!' piped a random pixie, squished between Will and Meadow. 'Won't you tell us all about it?'

'I shall! Never in your life have you seen anything like it,' replied Harold. 'A genuine journey to heaven and back.

'From the peaks of the heaving Vultan Range to the rolling green Forest Realms below me; from the undines singing atop glittering lilyponds, to the many-coloured dunes of Sordd … not a single corner of Rhye lay hidden, save for the deep caverns below the surface. What a glorious canvas it made, as I rode the slipstream with the pterippi. So much wonder met my eyes that they ached simply to behold it.

'Yet for all the splendour, I could also see danger. I knew what had become of Mustapha, for I could see him, praying for his life, trapped in the thrall of Belladonna in Via. I spied Figaro, committing his workers to an early grave by poison, with no shred of remorse. I saw his infernal machine, ready to roll forth and bring so much wrath and despair to Petrichor.

'Deep in the Greenway, up against the Nurtenean ranges, I saw a lone figure striding boldly. It looked for all the world like the Fairy Feller … but he seemed so far from home, I could not be certain.

'Far away in the west, beyond the shores of the Ealing Sea, I also saw Anuvin, indignant in his bid to escape his prison. I knew, then, the land's woe only began with Petrichor.

'The sacred horses saw the danger as well. Their flight became a dance in the heavens. By intuition, I learned that their dance was a communion with the Gods. The will of Marnis, the strength of Cornavrian and the power of Adatar himself flowed all around and through them. I sensed the warmth of Lhestra's smile and it meant hope.

'Then, their communion was done. Though it seemed to me only moments, it must have been days — when the herd again descended towards Rhye, I beheld new devastation. The juggernaut had already begun its fateful journey. As we dove, my heightened vision left me. I could no longer see Anuvin or know Mustapha's whereabouts. I could only pray that we would arrive in time.

'The rest is as you know it.'

One hundred faces stared, silent.

No creature deigned to break the spell cast over the room. In Harold's words, the tale evolved into an awakening of the spirit. Every soul felt the swell of validation, knowing that the Gods had heard their plea.

A crash and a tinkle broke the moment as the door of the Inn flew open.

Many gasped as a sylph walked in, towering over most of the room's occupants. Streams of raindrops fell from her glistening armour and feathered wings to puddle on the ground by her feet. She scanned the throng, before finding the foursome ensconced at its centre.

'Leith!' exclaimed Meadow. 'You just missed the darnedest story. Harold, would you mind running through that last bit again?'

Leith Lourden smiled. 'Yosef told me I might find you all here.'

'Where is the giant kettle head?' asked Dique.

Leith waded through the Fae patrons, who began to disperse now that story time was over. 'He spends his days aiding the people of Flaxae,' she replied, joining them at the table. 'The township sustained much damage. His size and strength make the work of rebuilding much more efficient. Another day and it should be done.

'I have stayed on to run aerial reconnaissance for Trixel, identifying the last of the fires. This rain is both a blessing and a curse. Forest streams are overflowing now, making some restitution hazardous. At least the Ploughman's inferno is nearly extinguished.'

'What of Sinotar?' asked Harold. 'I heard he sustained an injury during the battle at Psithur Grove.'

'He struck a tree,' the sylph confirmed. 'Minor injuries only. I think his pride took more damage than anything else. He left us yesterday, returning by air to Wintergard. There is much to be done … the General Prime must be home to command the Vrendari.'

Will toyed with an empty bottle, listening to Leith's report. 'Is there word of Mustapha?'

Leith nodded. 'The shamans attend him night and day. Though his condition remains stable, he shows no sign of waking from his coma. There is neither spell nor prayer, neither herb, nor root, which they haven't tried.'

'Then he will need to be borne to Banwah Haunte,' said Will with a grimace, 'even if I have to bear him myself. Mayhap, Lord Ponerog has continued the healing works of his father. It is our last resort.'

Another nod from Leith. 'I thought you might answer so. I'm sure Yosef would be willing to aid you on that quest. It is one of the reasons I sought you out.'

'Let me guess,' said Meadow. 'You also wanted to try the world-famous Oak & Barrel Rhye whiskey? It'll put stars in your eyes and ants in your pants.'

The sylph laughed, a musical sound. 'No, dear Meadow. I have also come to request your attendance in Psithur Grove — all of you. Trixel wants to set aside her duties long enough to thank you all for your aid in saving Petrichor … Oberon's Yew, in particular.'

Murmurs of pleasure arose from the group.

'Lastly,' added Leith, 'it appears that Lord Oberon left something behind. Something he wanted you to have, Harold.'

The following day, the group reunited beneath the hallowed boughs of Oberon's Yew. Raindrops settled like diamonds on its spindle leaves, while in the rest of the Grove, the remaining Ficus trees luxuriated beneath the rejuvenating fall. A rank of Fae knights, alternating with dryad warriors, lined each side of the avenue.

With the arrival of the companions, all the sentries took a knee, in unison.

Beneath the dripping branches of the Yew, sheltered from the rain, stood Trixel Tate. Beside her, the indomitable figure of Torr Yosef.

The fixie's face bore a look of exhaustion, though she appeared calm and collected. When her friends neared her, she managed a warm smile.

Meadow and Dique — recognising the apparent natural successor to the Fairy King and Queen — bowed low in front of Trixel.

'At ease, you twits,' she said. The pixies straightened, feeling sheepish.

'Miss Trixel,' said Dique, 'word all across Petrichor is that you are anointed Fae Sovereign. Is it true?'

Trixel sighed. The events of recent days had trammelled her. 'In all but name, Dique,' she said. 'In their final counsel to me, Oberon and Titania conveyed the deepest lore of my people. They also handed on many responsibilities. Alas — no opportunity arose to formally pass Sovereignty.

'It is just as well. I hold no fondness for titles ... and I would look no good in a crown.'

<*You will lead the Fae well in this time of darkness,*> said Yosef.

The fixie turned to Will. 'Human — I sense your path is already known to me. Your beloved remains in a critical state. The best our Realm has to offer cannot cure his fell poison, to my sorrow.

'Should you choose to search further for an antidote, the prayers of the Fae go with you. You have stood by our people in their time of need, risking your own life and limb.'

Will bowed. 'My Lady, Mustapha and I have known each other

only a short time ... but within fleeting moments has come the connection of a lifetime. I will not be giving up on him here.'

<*You travel to Banwah Haunte?*> asked Yosef.

'I do, for either strife or reward, or both.'

<*Then I offer my help. The Wilden Folk are best known for being unpredictable.*>

'You are welcomed, Torr Yosef.'

Next, Trixel addressed the pixies. 'Meadow and Dique, I absolve you of your charges under the court of the Fairy King. You have acquitted yourselves as pixies of good stature in the defence of your Realm. Go forth as you see fit, with the luck of Oska at your side.'

'Forever humbled, my Lady,' answered Dique.

'Our lives for the good of the Realm,' said Meadow. 'Though we feel bound now to the fate of Mustapha. Where he goes, we go.'

'So be it,' said Will.

Trixel stepped forward, turning to face Harold.

'The final prayer of Oberon and Titania, in the maw of the juggernaut, was for a miracle,' she said to him. 'Harold, when many had given up hope, you delivered that miracle. The tree behind me still stands because of you.

'Oberon recognised that. In his last hours, he wanted to be sure you received this gift.'

As Trixel spoke, a knight stepped from behind the Yew, carrying a peculiar object. He approached Harold and delivered it, executing a deep bow.

Harold studied the item, turning it over in his pincers. A torrent of thoughts flooded his mind. The others craned to get a better look.

A new horn lay in his grasp.

Rather, a very old horn. Ancient, perhaps even an artefact. Exquisite in design and craftsmanship, it eclipsed any instrument

Harold ever dreamed of possessing.

'It's … beautiful,' he managed.

'Lord Oberon claimed it had been in his ownership since the dawn of his Sovereignty,' Trixel explained.

'So … this horn is thousands of years old! I daren't …'

Trixel gave a playful shrug. 'Owner's privilege.'

Several mouths hung open in anticipation as the dragonfly raised the ancient instrument to his lips …

Took a deep breath …

And blew.

A strangulated gasp of nothingness came from the horn.

Not a blare, not a wail, not a peep.

Harold tried again, straining, his face crimson with effort.

The horn remained silent.

Meadow wrinkled his nose. 'What a piece of —'

'No,' said Harold, panting. 'The great Lord Oberon gave me this gift. The Fairy King never did anything without deliberation. Therefore, he meant for this to be passed on.

'There is a secret to activating this horn, I am sure of it. In his name, I will figure it out.'

<It does not look to be of Fae origin,> said Yosef. *<Perhaps the Wilden Folk can enlighten you as to its creator?>*

'It looks like you're coming with us,' grinned Will.

Trixel nodded, then spoke to Leith Lourden. 'These travellers could use a warrior's weapon,' she said.

'If I may be of no further service in Petrichor …?' the sylph replied.

The fixie paused, evaluating Leith. Then, she shook her head. 'The Forest Realm will rise again of its own accord. These companions travel in the direction of your home. Go with them, carrying my lasting gratitude.'

Thus, the group decided their strategy. They would venture together into the Wilden Realm, taking Mustapha with them.

His last hope for a remedy.

Overhead, the skies crackled with a brooding intensity.

CHAPTER 14

STARS OF LOVINGNESS

Through blackest night and sunless day, they walked.

Through howling wind and driving rain, through eerie stillness and bitter chill, they walked.

They traversed swollen streams and misty fens, across lonely plains and through enchanted woods. An inexorable, marching doom.

The Pox walked and did not stop for rest or sustenance, driven ever onward by their redcap slave masters.

Upon leaving the Haunte, the vast horde of Pox fractured, sending masses in various directions. Masses became swarms. Swarms became parcels, each one a bolus of feverish ill, destined for the far reaches of Sontenan and Nurtenan.

They neither suffered nor protested, for they lacked a mind. Nothing more than lambent yellow aliquots of death, they marched with blind purpose across the land. They knew not how or why they existed; only that they must walk, visiting sickness upon the denizens of Rhye.

They approached without a sound, for they knew no words and had no voice.

Into townships and hamlets they crept — viscid, ghostlike, unrelenting. Those who saw them arrive knew them to be malign. Struck by a morbid fascination, most could not turn away from the evil tide.

Others found the insight to reach for weapons — blades, farming implements or sharp tools. Villagers with the fortitude to strike down the vile cherubs discovered they were vulnerable enough. The Pox simply burst when hewn, though this caused acrid spume to gush and spray. The goo corroded weapons at the point of contact.

Any being touched by the Pox became ill within hours. The torment ranged from rigors, nausea, and blistering skin, to paralysis, seizures and an acute dementia.

Settlements soon became choked by plague. Bodies of the dead littered homes and streets.

To flee remained the last recourse.

In straggling groups, survivors fled their homes to cross the countryside with little more than the clothes on their backs. They strove only to keep ahead of the wave of Pox. In the meantime, messengers on horseback rode like the wild winds, bringing news of the creeping death to Via.

Regent Lance Sevenson's moment of reckoning had come.

With an austere hand, he guided the commanders of his human legions and Vrendari. His leadership prioritised defence manoeuvres and the evacuation of civilians. The Sontenean bunkers lay in wait; Sevenson passed orders for the elderly and infirm to be brought first from their homes, unless they planned to die within them. Families and children were urged to travel, under the protection of armed and armoured fighters.

Sevenson prayed for the soul of Lord Rogar. The last of the Giltenan dynasty spent his final months providing for the hour of his peoples' greatest need. The blueprint for salvation was made plain.

If anyone lived to recall it, Rogar's memory would be gilt in glory for all time.

~

With gut-wrenching slowness, the company advanced deep into the dismal embrace of the Wilden Realm. Branches like spindly arms reached out across the path, threatening to snatch them from their way. Flowers of black and green grew from snaking vines, offering a putrid bouquet to the nose. Odd assortments of toadstools watched the intruders' progress from rotting logs, before shrinking from view with a *schlurp*.

'I'm quite sure that mushroom stuck out its tongue at me,' said Dique.

'Obviously not a fun guy,' replied Meadow.

'There's nothing too friendly in this neck of the woods,' agreed Leith Lourden, her blade drawn, at the fore of the group. Harold and the pixies walked behind her. Will and Yosef brought up the rear, bearing Mustapha on a makeshift litter. The strangeling breathed in a shallow rhythm, which occasionally faltered, drawing wary glances from Will. Yosef remained focussed on the path ahead.

'Leith,' asked Dique, 'are you sure of our direction?'

'I have seldom had reason or purpose to visit Banwah Haunte,' replied the sylph, 'though this raven is proving a helpful guide.'

'Raven?'

She pointed ahead with the tip of her sword. 'If I know signs when I see them, that bird is leading us through the Haunte.'

'You mispronounced "luring",' said Harold.

Indeed, the stout, black bird appeared to monitor the company, then fly off ahead, as if encouraging them to follow.

'Strange,' said Dique. 'For the past two days, I've thought we were wandering blind. Now it seems we were being led by that raven the whole time.'

'I thought the same,' agreed Will.

<Harold is right,> said Yosef, studying their avian guide. *<This creature bears a charm of destination. The traveller follows without even realising what they do. We are either being misdirected or lured to a place on the whim of whoever enchanted the raven.>*

'I hope we get led to some fresh food,' grumbled Meadow.

The bounty of Banwah Haunte was unpalatable — or inedible — by most denizens of Rhye. The company brought provisions for a trek of only a few days. Due to their unintentional meandering, it had already dwindled to small, daily rations.

<Your prayers must be as loud as your stomach, Hungry One. Look ahead.>

They walked a twisting path through the forest. Not fifty yards ahead of them, just discernible in the murk, the raven alighted on a bramble bush. Its chosen perch sat at the intersection of the path and a much larger byway through the Haunte.

The bramble bush sagged under the weight of dewberries. At its foot, a wild hog snorted and upturned the earth with its trotters, revealing a cache of truffles. It took no notice of the approaching group.

The pixies exchanged a glance and a nod, drawing their blades.

Day passed as night in the Wilden Realm.

Somewhere far above, the moon must shine, Meadow thought. He wished them back to that moonlit glade, awaiting the stroke of the Fairy Feller.

Through the gloom, he could discern the nearby huddle of sated bodies, slumbering in a hollow by the roadside. Will nestled against Mustapha's litter, one hand outstretched to feel the thready rise and fall of the strangeling's chest. Harold, Dique and Leith completed the loose knot. Harold buzzed peacefully. Dique muttered incoherent sleep-talk. The sylph appeared to have one eye open.

<*They will be safe here,*> said Yosef, ever on watch.

'It's too quiet,' said Meadow, who struggled to find sleep. 'My parents always told me "Don't go near the Haunte", like it bustled with marauders. So far, it's only managed to throw up a half-baked crow and a pig who found us dinner. Was my ma having a lend of me?'

<*Not in the slightest.*> The golem stared down the roadway, as his words rang in Meadow's mind. Ruts and potholes covered the road, with odd puddles of some viscid liquid splashed along its course.

<*The Haunte is a nest of depravity. It has been so for over two thousand years since a troupe of satyrs felt themselves to be above Lord Oberon's rule. They were not. Still, rather than let the matter be resolved with bloodshed, the Fairy King made an unprecedented move, offering the satyrs a gift: all of the Forest Realm north of the Bijou. It came with one stipulation — that the satyrs never again set cloven hoof in Petrichor.*>

'Why, then, have I never heard of these satyrs, who established the Wilden Realm?'

<*Lord Oberon knew they would quickly be usurped, forgotten in the shifting sands of time. He was correct. Satyrs are foolish — wine in the belly, rocks in the head. Within moments of settling their new domain, they were set upon and bested by more devious creatures, who lay in wait for them. In turn, these victors were also challenged. Banwah Haunte became known as a lawless place, rife with violence and corruption. Only*

those hardened to an errant lifestyle may thrive here.

<Numerous Lords have attempted to purge the vile elements of the Wilden Realm. Lord Vater was only the most recent. I fear that he fell victim of circumstance ... Moreover, I fear that Lord Ponerog has only further enabled a festering evil.>

'Sounds like he's some sort of boil to be lanced, if you ask me,' answered Meadow, in a tone of cool defiance. The pixie looked into the middle distance, watching for any shadows that might flit across the darkened road. Though his heavy eyelids suggested a kind of languidness, his lip trembled.

<Always ready with a quip, young Meadow,> said the golem. *<Is there nothing you're afraid of?>*

The pixie's head sank. He studied his boots for a long moment, then looked up at the iron hulk by his side.

'When I was a kid, I was invincible, like most of my fellows,' he replied. 'Then once, not very long ago, I was afraid of how my Lord, the Fairy King, might punish me for treason. How petty it seems now — how trifling it was — to be afraid of that! Now, I'm afraid that my best friend might die. He's got too much living left to do.

'At the same time, I'm afraid of the future. One Realm at a time, our Sovereigns are being overcome. Petrichor was nearly destroyed. Harold says he saw Anuvin on the move. Could that be true?'

<I have no doubt it is. Our fate, so it seems, is in the lap of the gods. As far as we mere denizens are concerned, we are strapped to the great wheel of destiny, with only so much we can do about it. But fear, young pixie, knows no place here.

<You see, there are two kinds of problems in the world. There are problems for which you have a solution — in which case there is no need for fear. Then there are problems for which you have none, whereby there is nought you can do. Your fate is with the gods, so what is there to fear?

<Meadow ... we will either get through this, or we won't.>

Meadow's jaw fell. Shock and hurt flashed across his face. 'Is that your response? Don't you want to stay alive? Do golems even die?'

Yosef turned his expressionless face towards Meadow. The pixie braced himself for more terse proselytising … but it never came. When Yosef's voice sounded again, it whirred with humility. The downshift of gears suggested sadness.

<No … not really. We can "give up" our consciousness. After that, the rust and tarnish set in. We do not know the suffering of death, as you flesh creatures do. I know of grief, though I have never experienced it. I also know, now, that you still prepare yourself … for the deaths of others, and for your own.

<Are you afraid of dying?>

Meadow thought of giant scythes, mere yards away, inching towards him. 'I sure as hell don't want to die,' he said. It wasn't an answer, but it was the truth. 'Why does everything about life have to be so inevitable? Sometimes, I figure it'd be easier if I'd never been —'

Meadow froze.

Beside him, Yosef also stopped still. He saw it, too: a pale shape, emerging from the hollow.

<Do not move, or cry out,> said Yosef, his giant hand steady on Meadow's shoulder.

A wraith appeared from the direction of the sleeping company. It approached the forest road; not where the pixie and the golem sat, but only a dozen yards away. As it stepped onto the road, the near-impenetrable gloom fell from it, and ghostly luminescence revealed a familiar form.

Mustapha.

The strangeling's face resembled a blank canvas, though his eyes were wide. The leaves and low branches parted for him as he passed. Gravel crunched softly beneath his dirty, black boots. No spectre would affect its surroundings in such a way.

Somehow, Meadow contained the urge to hail his friend. *Mustapha ... are you awake? Cured?* The surreal moment bound him like a spell — a spell which refused to be broken. The form of Mustapha moved along the roadway, away from his friends on an unseen tether. Eventually, the night swallowed him.

<It seems our stricken companion is arisen.>

'Come on, get up!' cried Meadow, springing to his feet and heading for the road. 'We have to follow him!'

<On the contrary: We should first rouse the others. There is more here than meets the eye. An enchantment grips Mustapha, enthralling his mind and animating his form. It comes from a power perhaps greater than any of us.

<I will wake our friends. We must confer before we follow him.>

Meadow peered at the silent road, flecked with a strange, malevolent ichor. In the distance, beyond sight, the raven cawed.

Without asking, the pixie knew they had happened upon the way to the throne of the Wilden Lord.

Mustapha knew nought but a whispered threnody in the recesses of his mind.

His borrowed strength came from a veiled place beyond his ken. One footstep at a time, it lured him onwards. White noise banished any conscious thought.

The lodestone of his compulsion could not be denied.

His companions had, without realising, set up their camp a stone's throw from the Halls of Pox. To this edifice, with its crumbling crenelations and foreboding gullet, Mustapha advanced.

He made his way through the colonnade of whispering trees and mottled shadows. The trees bowed towards him as he walked, shrouding him. Ahead loomed the black maw of the Halls, materialising from the gut of the forest like a monster from the deep.

In his trance he halted, contemplating the lair of the Wilden Lord through eyes of glass.

A façade of stone rose before him — cloaked in midnight, dotted with windows. Glances of illumination pierced the gloom. A sickly glow emanated from the portcullis, suggesting an enchanted fire within. Sallow lantern light shone from two tiny windows on high: one in the massive face of the keep, another at a vertiginous balcony, near the pinnacle of a tower.

Mustapha stood, inanimate. Not a flicker arose from his waxen face.

The night grew still. All of Banwah Haunte held its breath. Leaves on trees gave the barest rustle, waiting for the moment to break.

Then she came.

The figure of a lady appeared at the tower balcony. A being of utmost grace and puissance, she emerged as a beacon in human form. All around, the air grew light. She took gliding footsteps upon the balcony, while about her flowed a gown of white gossamer and lace. Hair in grey-gold ripples fell to the curve of her hips. Within her tresses shone a plethora of pinpoint lights — a nest of glittering stars.

The April Lady, Maybeth Giltenan. Abducted and enslaved by the Wilden Lord, transformed in her imprisonment by the will of the Gods.

Mustapha started, with a jolt.

He swept towards the foot of the keep, where black water, a tumble of rocks and the occasional protruding bone filled a shallow moat. In his trance, he ignored the chill water. Gripping the slick, lichenous stone in his bare hands, he began to climb.

High above, the ethereal Lady sang. At first, her melody emerged without words. Her voice carried the weather and warmth of middle age, while her lilting tone recalled the songbirds of fairer woodlands. The weight of mourning subdued the song, though its author continued to illuminate the night.

Hand and foot, the strangeling ascended towards the object of his thrall. Crevices and outcroppings pockmarked the stone wall, just enough for searching fingertips and the toes of boots. The tower rose far above the forest floor, a dizzying climb with the constant threat of a fatal slip.

By some fortune, a natural ledge jutted from the stone beneath the balcony. Scarcely six inches wide, with an edge worn smooth by the passage of the elements. Still, to a creature with the thew of entrancement, it provided a comfortable perch. He found it and clung to the rock, gazing above in mute adoration.

The song of the April Lady became a hymn of loss and restitution. Her face bespoke dignity and sorrow entwined. She sang through a wistful smile, though her eyes were haunted.

As northern winds grow colder
It takes me to that place
I won't see when I'm older
The etchings on your face

Blessed be Ophynea
Her promises were true
Forbidden were those bitter nights
When I lay close to you

The pangs of duty turned me
For Realm a union made
This tower now I call my home
Forever I'm afraid

A pact I keep with Lhestra
The King of Rhye will stand
One eldritch word can liberate
Love yet may save the land.

Deep within him, Mustapha's waning soul stirred. It fought against the crippling, toxic cinnabar. The ghost of emotion welled up inside like a new spring. His heart ached — he longed to call out to her. He tried and failed. His mouth, drier than desert sand, swelled with his dead tongue. He barely rasped.

The April Lady stood poised at the balustrade, only a few feet above him. He might have reached out to her, or otherwise caught her attention; though he was so enraptured, he only crouched and looked on. For a heart-stopping moment, she seemed ready to cast herself from the tower. She did not, but instead pressed her hands upon the stone, as if drawing from it the fortitude of living.

As she stood, bathed in a halo of light, her song fading, a single tear rolled down her cheek. The tear shone like a pearl as it traversed her face, slid down to her delicate jaw …

And fell.

By all that is serendipitous, Mustapha crouched directly below her. The tear spiralled down, a liquid jewel in the air, arriving on Mustapha's face with a gentle *plash*.

At the moment of impact, a preternatural energy crackled through the strangeling. Like a coruscation, vitality flickered along every nerve. From the inside out, an eruption of glacial fire seared through his sinews. A blast of white-hot consciousness exploded in his mind. His hair rippled in the still night air and every muscle snapped, a full-bodied contraction of ecstasy.

With a violent twitch, his fingers slipped from their holds and Mustapha fell backwards from the tower.

Lord Ponerog stormed up the tower stair, bursting through the door into Maybeth Giltenan's chamber. Hideous anguish contorted his murine features. His entire bulk shook. One great paw clenched a gleaming, ornamental knife.

Lady Maybeth Giltenan turned from the balcony, re-entering the prison cell she had called home for twenty-seven years. Sparse furnishings outfitted the tiny cell; the form of Lord Ponerog filled half of the available space.

She faced him with infinite calm.

The Wilden Lord's wet-rimmed eyes burned. Lady Maybeth knew those eyes with a grotesque intimacy. What flashed in them now intrigued her: Instead of pure rage, she saw contorted passion, fuelled by an intense inner torment.

Maybeth looked upon him with pity.

'Lhestra, hear my prayer. The time has come,' she whispered, invoking the Goddess of Justice.

The room became suffused with an astral glow, as the shimmering adornments of Lady Maybeth's hair shone with an otherworldly warmth.

Lord Ponerog strove to ignore the illumination. It caused bile to rise in his throat. Without the dark compulsion of the Black Queen in his mind, his resolve threatened to crumble. The knife in his hand drooped towards his side.

Lady Maybeth still murmured her devotion. She focused inwards.

Preparing.

The outside world shrank from her. The forests of the Haunte dissolved to nothing in her mind. She knew only the white light, the tower, the hulking edifice all around her.

She continued, oblivious to the shadow that loomed over her.

'I'm sorry,' said a guttural voice she did not hear.

She barely registered the sudden, piercing shriek of her mortal tissues, as Lord Ponerog drove his knife deep into her breast, embedding it in her heart.

In a near hollow, the ringing bite of steel on steel disrupted the eerie stillness.

A redcap patrol discovered the company and summoned a brace of reinforcements. The leafy depression soon seethed with combat. Fifty, seventy, one hundred pairs of hot poker eyes bobbed and darted about. The redcaps aimed vicious jabs at the intruders with their pikes.

'Do you think Lord Ponerog welcomes all visitors this way?' asked Will, cutting and thrusting at the filthy Wilden Folk with his machete.

'It does not bode well for a fair encounter,' answered Leith. Her warrior training outclassed that of their foes, though they came in swarms and fought with bestial instinct. 'Meadow, eyes right!'

Meadow turned and parried with his weapon. The redcap snarled; its surprise attack foiled. Meadow countered with a blade to his assailant's windpipe — the snarl became a gurgle and the creature fell dead.

'Born in frivolity ... remade in conflict,' Leith whispered, eyeing the pixies with a bittersweet smile.

Nearby, Torr Yosef carved through waves of attackers. Arms like iron stanchions swept aside multiple redcaps at once, only to meet a flood of replacements. Harold dive-bombed the fiends from above, wielding a stolen halberd to lethal effect.

'How many more?' he yelled, above the noise of barbary. The whole forest writhed.

'It looks like I'm dead on time, if you'll pardon the expression,' said a new voice.

A startled pause quieted the throng of battle. The words rang out above the din like the tolling of a bronze bell, cutting clear across the night. Even the multitude of redcaps whirled around, appraising the newcomer.

A resplendent Mustapha stalked towards them along the roadway. Cleansed in divine fire, taintless white clothed his form, from coat to boots. The long-barrelled pistol he carried, all the way from Via, remained as ever tucked into his sash. His hair, still a lustrous black, parted above a fierce brow. Through a wicked grin his teeth flashed: A warning — or a dare — to any who would assail him.

'What happened to you ...?' mouthed Harold.

'Look — winged boots!' cried Meadow, pointing at Mustapha's feet. The strangeling's boots, swept back at the heel, gave him the appearance of a bird of prey, poised for a mid-air dive.

Dique blinked at the apparition. 'Hey, weren't you wearing black before —'

A primal cry ripped from one hundred throats, drowning out the pixie.

The redcaps surged, as one, to confront the strangeling.

Mustapha stood upon the road — front-footed, assured. With a glint in his eye, he stared them down.

As the bloodthirsty swarm approached, he filled his lungs and opened his vocal chords.

A gale tore through the hollow. Leith planted her sword in the ground for purchase. Yosef stood fast, grabbing the pixies. Harold and Will each hugged a tree.

The brutal squall did not howl, but instead carried a sound like an abbey choir. The swell of voices filled the hollow, while the wind swept every last redcap away. Many were flung into the forks of trees or became impaled in spidery branches. Some were thrown high into the air, never to be seen again.

When the redcaps were scattered from sight, Mustapha relinquished his assault.

His companions relaxed. For several minutes, leaves, branches and other forest debris rained down in a gentle patter. Here and there came the *thump* of a body striking the earth.

'Neat trick,' said Dique, as the group regained their feet. 'Where'd you learn it?'

Mustapha smiled, but did not answer. His eyes stayed locked on Will's.

'You're real, aren't you?' asked the wagoner. He edged forward with tentative steps.

'Come here and find out!' Mustapha replied, with outstretched arms.

This time, the others knew well enough to stand out of the way as human and strangeling collided. Will clenched his eyes tight, squeezing out tears.

'Don't nearly die on me again, please and thank you,' he said.

Leith clapped. 'Never did I expect to see such candour beneath the boughs of Banwah Haunte!'

'Group hug!' cried Meadow, dragging Harold and Dique into a tangled embrace.

Once all five extricated themselves, a sense of gravitas returned.

'Can we go home now?' asked Dique. 'I'd rather like to see my own bed.'

Meadow agreed. 'We solemnly swear to stay out of trouble next time. For now, Mustapha, we've got zillions of questions. What in the name of Marnis just happened to you? Where did this suit come from? When did you learn to sing like that?'

'I … ah …'

'No, wait. Don't answer now. Can we deal with it over a pint of lager?'

'About that ...' Mustapha began.

His friends' faces fell. 'We aren't done yet, are we?' said Harold, fiddling with the shoulder strap securing his strange horn. 'I had a feeling there was more to come.'

Mustapha nodded. 'There is more.' He turned to Leith and Torr Yosef. 'In Kash Valley, Lily told us about the King of Rhye. About how a living Sovereign would not emerge as sole ruler. About how the search would lead to great sacrifice.

'Well ... Lily was wrong. Now I know! I know who the King shall be and how the pieces fit together. I also know where I need to go and what must be done.

'But first ... there is somebody we need to save.'

'You think Lily was wrong? Are you sure?' said Leith.

Before he could answer, a tremendous blast of dazzling white light turned night into day. It arose from a place beyond sight, just down the roadway. Being unaccustomed to such brilliance, everyone shielded their eyes.

<*Are we all ready to run towards some more peril?*> asked Yosef.

The companions had little choice. Mustapha had already spun on his winged heel, heading back towards the Halls of Pox.

Within the tower, an arcane magic burst free of containment. White, molten fury raged, illuminating the high window.

Inside, Maybeth Giltenan — or, the essence of her — stood wreathed in argent fire. In the miserable dark of the Haunte, the light dazzled. As her mortal form faded, a spectre within the blaze, the flames reached out to lick the walls of her prison. The tiny room became as a beacon, over a sea of shadows outside.

Lord Ponerog, numb with shock, stood rooted in place. The fire tentacled toward him. He did not feel the pain of burning; only the warmth of a holy incantation, reaching deeper within him than any mere terrestrial fire could have done.

He knew ardour, at the joyous vision unfolding before his eyes. There followed dismay, humiliation and at last guilt, as the Wilden Lord saw all the sordid moments of his life careening towards this one moment.

The epiphany of the tower did not go unwitnessed.

A third figure appeared, embraced by the white fire; an illusory vision, yet at the same time undeniable. A woman, statuesque, with a face of terrifying authority. She wore plated armour in an ancient style, emblazoned with ornate designs. At her back were slung a shield and sword. She held her hands apart from her body — one to each side, in an attitude of contemplation.

Lhestra, Goddess of Justice.

She weighed the truths of the April Lady and the Wilden Lord, then spoke.

'No confinement shall wither the unbound spirit. The boundless soul cannot be contained.

'Lady Giltenan: through the love of Ophynea did you venture here. Love knows no fetters. May the captive now become the sanctuary and the bastion of divine power. You are the White Queen, Pillar of Rhye and a light in the darkness.'

Since the time of the Lady's ensnarement, Justice watched over Maybeth Giltenan, fortifying her for this moment. The years of oppression now fell like broken shackles.

As Lhestra delivered her decree, the white fire spread, lining the walls of the chamber. Wicks of flame ran through every crevice. The ward reached through the stone, penetrating to the very framework holding the tower erect.

The form of Maybeth Giltenan began to dissipate. She became one with the flames and in turn, became one with the place of her incarceration.

Lord Ponerog knelt, clutching his face, crying silent tears.

The company arrived at the foot of the stronghold to find the upmost tower a luminous white, the blockwork permeated by a lustrous enchantment. The surrounding woods clung to their black mantle, though by increments, the glow of white fire pushed back at the shadows. The rancour of the Haunte receded, little by little, as if in fear.

Will and the pixies gawped, speechless. Leith wore a faint smile. With deliberate hands, she worked a gesture evoked by no sylph since the time of the Godsryche: a gesture of prayer.

Mustapha stepped forward. In a heartbeat, Harold was at his shoulder.

'Ancient wills are locked in battle,' said the strangeling. 'I need to be up there.'

'I'll give you a lift,' said the dragonfly.

Mustapha shook his head. 'I'll race you.' In a blink, he regained the foot of the keep and began to climb for a second time. He could not be stopped — hand over foot, like a being born of treacherous mountain slopes, he rose towards the balcony. The pure white of his mysterious new attire glistened beneath the crackle of flames above.

Harold shrugged, turning to Leith. 'Someone should follow him.'

The sylph nodded.

'We'll … wait here,' said Meadow, still saucer-eyed.

Leith and Harold took to the air, swooping towards the balcony.

Mustapha arrived just ahead of them. With nimble footwork he attained the landing and strode within, heedless of the blaze.

Curlicues of white flame wreathed the doorway. As Harold and Leith approached, they knew that the fire would not harm them; yet from within, a voice howled in agony.

They went inside.

In the heart of the conflagration stood a female figure, clad in armour. At her feet kneeled a beast of a man, piteous in his prostration. From his throat came wordless sobs, a torrent of anguish.

When the trio entered, he lifted his face from the floor. His eyes were red, swollen with passion. Great hands clenched at his clothes, as if tearing them away would assuage his guilt.

Lord Ponerog observed the three and his features grew taut. Upon the sight of Mustapha, he issued a shriek and leapt to his feet, retreating for the door.

Mustapha advanced. All around, the walls, floor and ceiling throbbed with white fire. From a place beyond the material bounds of the chamber, there came the exulted strains of music: the song of the April Lady, an echo from another world.

The Wilden Lord howled once more, then dashed from the room.

The others followed the fleeing figure at a run. Down onto the spiral stair, winding towards the dark innards of the Halls. In places, limned white luminescence showed them where the White Queen's power was driving deeper into the stone ramparts. After a few moments, they found themselves running through dark and forbidding passages, lit only by conventional torchlight.

Ahead of them, Lord Ponerog charged onward, through vaulted room and blackened tunnels. Over his shoulder rang his wailing cries, the sound of a creature beyond hope or reason. Another hall, another spiralled staircase, down into the vile underbelly, to a place that had seen the labour of trolls and the birth of the Pox.

No life stirred in the cavernous room. The entrenched offshoot of the river Bijou churned and bubbled as it flowed from one shadowed extremity to the other. On the bank, several giant forest trolls lay dead. One enormous manacle contained only a tree limb, the floor around it stained with a sap-like ichor. In a sentinel row, the vats of unidentifiable sludge sat dormant, their cursed work complete.

In a fit of grief, the Wilden Lord stumbled into the room. The sight of this place, the setting of such atrocity, drew another howl from him. He moved without pause, out upon a ledge that skirted the voluminous cavern. His three pursuers arrived just behind him.

'Wait,' said Leith, gesturing to the others. They paused at the landing, eyes glued to the Wilden Lord.

Nothing remained for Ponerog, in a world bereft of all but his looming fate. He made his way far out into the room, ledge crumbling behind him. Below, the vats stood with mouths wide.

He looked once again at the three who followed him to his doom. A warrior, an insect and the manifestation of his guilt, come to haunt him. He locked eyes with Mustapha.

'She should have killed you!' he cried, his voice devoid of mockery or triumph. With a final bellow, he leapt from the ledge.

The great vat swallowed him with a *galump* of foul, viscous liquid — the same crucible that spewed forth the Pox, with the tears of the April Lady as catalyst. The noxious potion consumed him in a moment.

He neither struggled, nor resurfaced.

Disease of immense virility enveloped him. He was soon overwhelmed. His skin frothed and melted, burning from a thousand sores. His muscles cramped into a terminal rictus and his organs protested in a bloat of failure. The fluid he inhaled, beckoning a swift end.

At last, his tortured mind winked out. Lord Ponerog was gone.

CHAPTER 15

BLOOD OF MY VEINS

At the fringe of Banwah Haunte, leaves rustled a plaintive forest hymn. The *chirrup* of countless cicadas lent the song a natural rhythm, while the babble of the Bijou offered up the melody of the land. On such an evening, the threat of the Haunte seemed many leagues away.

In the purple gloaming, Mustapha lay in the long grass beside Will. Two more days gone, since the revelation of the White Queen and the vision of Lhestra. Since that time, they had been inseparable.

Their flight from the Haunte cost much of their strength. Now, with the oppression and witchery of the Wilden Realm behind them, the company sought an evening of respite. They found a place close to an ancient stone expanse, a bridge which led back across the Bijou into forest, on the Petrichor bank. Before them lay the rolling verdure of upper Nurtenan.

Harold and Leith stretched their wings, suggesting a

reconnaissance flight. Meadow and Dique, proud of their emerging skills as hunters, claimed supper duty. Torr Yosef made the short trek to the riverbank, expressing a desire to pray and attempt to commune with his brethren, in far-off Warnom Bore. That left the gourd farmer and the strangeling in each other's company, beneath the waxing light of Anato, along with a smattering of early-rising stars.

'Hey, did you notice ...?' said Will.

'Mm?' came the languorous reply.

'It stopped raining.'

'I did notice. I wonder if it had anything to do with the April Lady's transformation.'

'Do you think so?'

Mustapha turned towards Will, rising on an elbow. With a delicate fingertip, he traced the rugged contours of his lover's face. Will's eyes, the colour of burnt honey, complimented broad cheeks and a square jaw. Tousled hair the colour of straw set off the picture, in a wholesome way that Mustapha found most appealing.

'Perhaps,' the strangeling said. 'This storm ... I feel it is beyond mundane. Yosef said something similar. It appeared on the horizon, at about the time Lord Rogar must have died. The rain started after Oberon and Titania fell. Now, in the aftermath of Lhestra's appearance, it has abated.

'Conflict rages ... not only here on Rhye, but in the firmament.'

'I suspect we haven't seen the last of it. Those thunderheads in the north-west still threaten.'

'That is the direction Leith and Harold took. I hope they turn back before the foul weather returns.'

Will studied Mustapha's countenance. Solemnity was etched there, but no fear — he gave the impression of being able to confront a storm all by himself. His face carried a look both alluring and terrifying, just as the sorcerous argent fire had been.

'Mustapha ... what happened to you?'

The strangeling smiled. An open smile that reached his eyes, showing his pearlescent teeth. A smile he only gave in candid moments.

'I honestly don't know!' he laughed. He let the laugh dissolve in a kiss, which he planted on Will's lips. 'One minute, we were talking with Lily about the Song of the Prophet, casting some rather terrible theories about. The next thing I recall, I was falling.'

'Falling? In a dream?'

'No, silly man! Really, truly, falling. I fell from the tower. It was the strangest thing, though. Everything seemed to happen in extreme slow motion.

'At first, my entire body felt like molasses. Each breath, the passing of an Age. In between breaths, I knew nothing ... nothing but the sound of Lady Maybeth's voice. She sang to me.

'Her voice entered every fibre of my body, speaking not only to my ears, but to my heart, lungs, stomach and everything in between.'

'Did she speak to your hair?'

'Well, I don't know, maybe —'

'Did she speak to your left foot?'

'Probably not —'

'Did she speak to your ...'

'Hey! Get your grabby hands off me. Will, darling: listen. She sang of a *hero*. She sang of a lost love. I just know it — she sang of the King of Rhye. The one who can save the land.

'Her words spoke of a cold place and a forbidden love — someone she left behind shortly before she disappeared.

'So, tell me. Who do we know, who lives where it's cold? Who might have made a valid suitor to Lady Maybeth Giltenan, if only their cultures condoned it?'

'Hmm,' Will frowned.

'Let me help you.' Mustapha feigned a taciturn scowl.

'Sinotar!'

'Exactly.' The scowl became a proud smile.

'Do you think that might be why he's grumpy all the time? I mean ... I'd be upset too, if I fell in love with someone I could never be with.'

Mustapha replied with another kiss. The fleeting brush of lips electrified Will. As their faces came apart, he saw a glint in his lover's eyes that he had never noticed before.

Will's own crooked smile appeared. 'Are you telling me, hand on heart, that this revelation came to you as you were falling?'

'I am telling you just that! It was the most unbelievable thing. Lady Maybeth opened her mind to me. I saw the whole world in a teacup ... or perhaps, all of history in a moment. My path is clear. I must go to find Sinotar, in Wintergard. I need to confront him with this truth: that his lost love survived and is now the White Queen. That he is the King of Rhye!

'I suspect he has known all along. The way he acts strangely when the Song of the Prophet is being discussed ... it's all so apparent now. He doesn't want to deal with it.'

Will sat up, scratching his head. 'In fairness, the Song also speaks of the old Lords crumbling to nothing,' he said. 'The General Prime is the Sylphic Lord, in all but title. He may be feeling vulnerable.'

'"Vulnerable" is not a word I would use to describe Bastian Sinotar.' In the throes of contemplation, Mustapha pulled the pistol from his sash and began twirling it, his finger through the trigger guard. 'Besides — if he has a monumental role to play, it is hardly the time for vulnerability.'

Will's eyes settled on the gun. In the deepening light of dusk, the etched metal plating gleamed with a sinister aura. The weapon looked at once ancient and modern, righteous, and evil. 'Where did you get that?' he asked.

Mustapha aimed skywards. To wield the gun by the moonlight reminded him of when he had last held it — preparing to blast the Sylphic General Prime in the chest.

To think, I almost killed the King of Rhye.

'Belladonna gave it to me,' he said, his tone absent, almost dismissive. 'She only said I might need it one day. I have no idea where she came across it. Perhaps part of her gypsy loot.'

Will had seen such weaponry before: in the armamentarium of Figaro, the Ploughman.

He changed the subject.

'Mustapha, my heart swells to see you alive, so hale,' he said. 'The White Queen changed you. She brought you back from the brink somehow. What did it feel like?'

Mustapha stopped twirling the pistol. 'I feel the poison still,' he answered, 'though it is not the same. A fundamental shift has occurred ... my blood is no longer blood. The cinnabar is transformed. In its place is something altogether new.

'If I was alive before, it was a borrowed, diluted kind of life. Now both of my eyes can see. Both of my ears can hear. My limbs feel imbued with a virtuous strength. My heart has a boundless energy, to beat and to love.'

The words filled Will with joy. To see his companion bristling with such vitality swelled his chest with awe. Overhead, the light of Anato shone silver, a beam of glitter upon the burbling waters nearby.

'Tell me then, strange and beautiful creature,' said Will, 'with the River Bijou as your witness: Though the world may break and the heavens be torn asunder, would you be mine for all time?'

The pair came together, taking each other's hands. At their backs, the dark, creaking eaves of Banwah Haunte receded into nothingness.

'We two are for now and always,' replied Mustapha, a breath above a whisper. 'Though the winds may blow from the west or the east; though the land may be consumed in fire and flood, this moment is forever.

'You are mine and I am yours. Nothing truly matters but you and me, for the rest of our lives.'

Will exhaled. 'I love you, Mustapha.'

They embraced. For several heartbeats, the world stopped.

Mustapha wore a contented smile, though he said nothing.

'Come on, don't leave me yearning!' said Will, with an affable laugh. 'Don't you love me too, if even a little bit?'

Mustapha's smile drooped by a fraction. His eyes darted from side to side, searching the wagoner's.

'Mustapha?'

'Will please, I —'

Will's brow furrowed. 'I'm sorry. A step too far, I see. I can have your "forever", but not your heart.'

'No, that's not it, I promise …' the embrace slackened.

Mustapha's chest pounded. His face fell. His head swam with visions of stark and horrific dreams.

Lub-dup … lub-dup … lub-dup …

A momentous crash and the roar of the ocean, the splitting crack of thunder over the waves.

The frigid depths, a watery tomb known only to fish.

There, once again, he saw the face of Anuvin — that harsh laugh, followed by words of condemnation. A challenge, to set his soul on ice.

"Kill the one you love. Then you will find us there, waiting. At the end of the earth."

Mustapha clenched his teeth and shook his head to dislodge the memory. He looked up to find Will's eyes rimmed with sadness and concern, still only inches from his own.

'Are you alright, Mustapha?' His voice soft, conceding.

'Will, I ... no. No, I don't love you.'

The two came apart.

For what seemed like an hour, each could only stare at the grasses, swaying gently by their feet.

Will broke the silence. 'I understand. No,' he corrected, 'in truth, I understand so very little. I understand how to plough the earth and harvest a crop. Now, I also understand how to master a blade and slay a redcap, or two.

'I understand that you are on a journey I cannot follow. There are places you have been in recent days that I know I cannot go. The workings of your mind are, likewise, a world unto themselves.

'I do have your words. They tell me all I need to understand. So, too, do you have mine — I have no intention of drawing them back.'

Mustapha's body slumped. He looked midway between failure and loss. 'Will ... if only I could tell you what is in my heart to say, I would. But there's something you ...'

He paused, leaving his thoughts unfinished. The whir and swoop of wings interrupted his words. The returning figures of Harold and Leith greeted the pair.

Will unleashed a sigh of relief.

The aerial duo alighted, re-joining their companions. They both moved and spoke in animated fashion, affected by what they had seen. Oblivious to the tension hanging in the air, Harold cut right through it.

'Trouble in the east,' explained the dragonfly, while explaining nothing.

'Storms?' asked Will.

'Yes, but worse than that. Far east of here, the sky grows black with a massive pall of dark cloud. Think Petrichor, only that one was chicken feed. Within this cloud, scarlet lightning breaks, spearing towards the ground. The whole monstrosity seems to come from a place beyond the north-eastern horizon.'

'The moors of Fenmarck Haunte, perhaps?' probed Mustapha.

'Further. Maybe even beyond the Peaks of Obelis.'

They all looked at each other in knowing dread.

'Nevermore,' murmured the strangeling.

'What a time to be alive,' said Will. He turned to the sylph. 'Have you better news, Leith?'

Leith Lourden shook her head, eyes afire with the ill she had seen. 'Trouble in the west as well, I'm afraid.' She and Harold separated on their reconnaissance, risking security to cover more territory.

She elaborated. 'My flight path took me along the northern boundary of Petrichor, where the Bijou meanders in and out of view beneath the forest canopy. I travelled far enough to see, some leagues hence, the confluence of the Bijou with Berthelot Stream and the bridge beyond. This was sufficient for me to behold the distant horror.

'An ominous host marches on some kind of pilgrimage. They come from the Southern Realm in clusters and small formations, by road and wagon-track. Their number consists of the strangest creatures I have seen in many a mission. They appear as cherubs, though there is something very wrong about them. Noxious things, a bilious green glow beneath the moon.'

'Their origin can be guessed at. I recall seeing a similar, foul ichor upon the roadway to the Halls of the Wilden Lord.'

'It explains the vats of effluent we found in the vaults below his lair,' said Mustapha.

'I noticed it on the roadway, too,' said Will. 'Though if these creatures were birthed in Ponerog's stronghold, how are they now appearing in the south of Rhye?'

Mustapha struggled to let his eyes meet Will's. He had the answer. A youth spent exploring the far reaches of the Mother Forest had given him an intimate knowledge of her secret byways.

Gazing at his boots, he answered. 'There are many forgotten ways through the eastern wilds of Petrichor. Dryad habitation is thin and road maintenance is non-existent. It would not be too difficult for a force to move through that region undetected, provided they did not molest any trees and trigger the awareness of Oberon's Yew.

'Deep in the wilderness, an ancient bridge crosses the Bijou, into the Haunte. Traffic is almost nil. I'll wager this cherub army travelled by those ways, crossing into Sontenan near the Sour Milk Sea.'

Will's gut turned. The company missed encountering the dire creatures by a matter of days.

Leith continued her chilling report. 'The cherubs move across the land like a plague. In the heart of Nurtenan, civilians flee north from them — refugees in their own Realm. Humans and sylphs in heavy numbers travel the roads. They may be only a day's march from here, judging by their pace.'

'We need a plan,' said Will.

The safest — and simplest — manoeuvre would be to take the great bridge at their backs, crossing the Bijou into the relative sanctuary of northern Petrichor. Here, they would be able to conceal themselves and wait out the coming calamity.

None of them considered this option.

To the north, three strongholds of vast power remained, untested. In the unfathomable pit of Warnom Bore, the race of golems represented enormous might. Wintergard, high in the Vultan Range, homed the Vrendari, Sylphic warriors and mountaineers of the highest pedigree. Then, there was Aerglo ...

distant, yet perhaps the most formidable of all. Since the Council of Rhye, the coven of Adept had fallen silent, an unknowable entity.

'We will confer a northward route with Yosef when he returns,' said Leith.

<*Yosef returns,*> grated the familiar mechanical voice. The group turned to see the golem striding towards them from the riverbank.

'What news, Yosef?' called Will.

<*Nil positive, to my regret. I bring grave tidings from the land of my brethren.*>

The others stood in mute dismay. As an automaton, Yosef was not expected to display genuine emotion. Across the breadth of their travels, however, the golem had been a consistent surprise. The spark that animated him imbued a special kind of magic.

Now he stood, shoulders and head downcast. His voice came to them as a low whine, empty of verve.

<*Anuvin approaches the mainland. War will make landfall at the Immortal Cliffs before tomorrow afternoon. Lord Enoch knows he is at the door. It remains to be seen how he will achieve the Peaks of Light, or the Bore itself. The Torrs make what preparations they can, should he choose to enter our demesne.*

<*If Anuvin can reach the North Wolds and the Corridor, little will waylay him. I anticipate his goal will be to scale the Peaks of Obelis, making an attempt at Nevermore.*>

'To reunite with Valendyne,' said Leith.

It was as they all had feared. Without doubt, this would be the doom foretold in the Song of the Prophet. None knew how Valendyne might be liberated from his prison, though War would surely have his plans.

The Fae Ring had already sustained some arcane assault, or so it seemed.

Into this glum ambience, there erupted the sound of rattled

shrubbery. From nearby bushes exploded the oblivious forms of Meadow and Dique, laden with game.

'Rabbit stew, anyone?' said Meadow with a grin.

The faces that met him stopped he and Dique in their tracks.

They ate a joyless supper. The coming days promised challenge and hardship. Despite diminished appetites, the company filled their bellies in a mechanical torpor.

Afterwards, each found a sheltered niche to gain some rest. The gravity of events deterred most.

Will's inner voice refused to be silenced. In his mind, he replayed his interlude with Mustapha dozens of times. Every time, it became a warped, surreal version of events, wherein Mustapha would requite his love ... only for some calamity to befall them, keeping them apart for all time.

At length, exhausted, Will found refuge in a broken sleep.

With the coming of morning, the companions discussed the next step of their journey.

For most, the goals of their quest had become ill-defined. While they all aimed to stay ahead of the impending crisis, none knew how that could be best achieved.

Given the circumstances of his people, Yosef felt the pull to return to Warnom Bore. His difficulty lay in the very existence of the Vultan Range, which blocked him. To travel around it, by the Greenway or upper Nurtenan, would cost him many days. Instead, he reasoned, he might encounter other travellers on his journey north; if he met with sylphic refugees, they might know of a pass through the mountains.

If such a pass did exist, it was a secret beyond Leith Lourden.

'You'll never make it, Torr Yosef,' she said, worry creasing her graceful features. 'Whichever way you take, the journey is too far. You will never arrive ahead of Anuvin. Please don't walk into a trap — you will be destroyed.'

Dique murmured to Meadow, 'If he were anyone else, you'd say he was thinking with his heart, not his head.'

'Most peculiar,' agreed Meadow.

The golem sat down on a rock, staring towards the distant ranges, saying nothing more.

Leith suggested heading to Wintergard, as an alternative. There they would find the relative protection of her people, who were preparing for war under the eye of the General Prime.

'That's where I'm going,' announced Mustapha.

Leith, Harold, and the pixies all turned to the strangeling. By this time, they had grown accustomed to his unexpected revelations.

'You sound sure of yourself,' said Meadow.

Mustapha explained his theory, as he had done for Will, the night before.

'Instinct tells me that Bastian Sinotar is somehow the key to all of this,' he concluded.

'It does make some sense … and we've nothing to lose,' said Dique.

There were no other dissenters.

'It is decided,' said Leith. 'Yosef, I do hope you will see fit to join us. Such a journey will be safest in numbers. Certainly, your singular talents will give us the greatest chance of success.'

<Then it is my humble pleasure to serve,> replied the golem, without turning his head.

'Perhaps you'll let me take a look at that horn of yours on the way, Harold,' offered Dique. 'I might have a few tricks in my tool belt.'

'Harold is coming with me, this time,' said Mustapha. The dragonfly shrugged.

Meadow shot Mustapha a quizzical look. 'Aren't we all going together?'

'I'm sorry, dear friends. I'm in a bit of a hurry this time. I'll be going on ahead.'

'It's too far for me to carry you, if that's what you're thinking,' said Harold.

'You don't need to. I'm going to run.'

Meadow scoffed. 'Run! Just a little jog across the Greenway, if you like! Never mind that it's three days' walk from here to the foothills of the Vultans, or thereabouts. Forget for a second that it's now treacherous country — threats to your left and right, with not a skerrick of cover to hide yourself in. Not a problem if you just run, am I right?'

'I feel like Mustapha has another surprise for us,' said Dique, seeing a flash in the strangeling's eyes.

'Fair enough,' said Harold. 'You head along on foot and I'll — ah — try to keep up?'

Mustapha nodded. He approached Will, who stood apart from the others.

'I imagine you're thinking of going home now, too.'

Will pursed his lips. He waved his empty hands in a vague gesture.

'I've hurt you and I'm sorry,' continued Mustapha. 'Come to think of it, this whole jaunt seems to be about me leading people on a wild goose chase, then apologising for it.'

'You're a wild goose, right enough,' answered Will. They shared a moment of meek laughter.

'I hope one day you will forgive me.'

'Mustapha … I can't lie to you. You've hurt me. Now you're running away, in a literal sense. All I can dream is that one day, you'll come back, because you remember what I told you. I love you for all of time.

'Perhaps, when this madness has all blown over, I can grow old by your side.

'Go now — do whatever it is you need to do. I'll be there when you need me.' He leaned forward, kissing Mustapha on the brow.

With the cinnabar transmogrified in his blood, Mustapha's sinews crackled, muscles like coiled springs, ready to explode. Lightning laced his veins. The stored energy chewed at him, straining his limbs for release.

His white, winged boots crunched in the dirt by the foot of the stone bridge. He would travel due north, across the plains and along the alpine verge of the Greenway, in the shade of the gargantuan Vultan Range.

One by one, he embraced his friends. Nobody knew where or when they might meet up again. To his surprise, Leith squeezed him hardest and longest. 'Vrendari don't get to hug much,' she said.

As Harold lifted into the air, the strangeling turned for a last look at his companions. Such a disparate band they made, yet without them, he would certainly be dead. He waved with a flourish.

Then, like quicksilver, he ran.

Easy, bounding steps he took, out across the wild grasses of Nurtenan. Five yards to a pace, up and over hills without the slightest exertion. Faster, ever faster he moved, letting out a screaming whoop and shouting to Harold to catch him. The wind rippled his hair and took his breath away as he ran.

His companions stood at the bridge and watched. The vast plain rolled out before them. They could see him, a bolt of white energy, dust trailing in the aftermath of his passage. Their eyes followed as he shrank from them, the dragonfly over his shoulder.

'Easy come, easy go,' said Will, with a sigh.

CHAPTER 16

ROCK OF AGES

Despite the sweltering heat, Sorcerer Faymorgan felt the chill of trepidation in her bones. Her blood ran cold as she stared into the pool at her feet. At the same time, sweat ran in silvered trails down her grimy face. She pushed back the Deep Blue cowl of her cloak, revealing tense, aquiline features.

'The cobalt deposit was a gift of Fortune,' she said, 'but I can only guess at its efficacy.'

<*Oska be praised.*>

The imposing face of Lord Enoch stared back at her, a giant skull of iron, glinting in the pale lamplight. His lambent eyes conveyed nothing, though apprehension radiated from his entire exoskeleton.

<*The will of the Gods is at play here now,*> he said. <*We golems remain both pawns and diligent disciples of the Pantheon, as has been our lot since our Creation. What sorcery does the blue mineral bring, that it might subvert our destinies at this late time?*>

His telepathy conveyed simultaneous desire and doubt.

Faymorgan quavered. The creature's emotion exceeded anything his immutable features could portray. The Lord of Golems — like all his subjects — regarded the Pantheon with fervour — to challenge the destiny of his race, in his mind, represented sacrilege. Still, the spark of his existence clung to the desire to survive, to live ... whatever that meant for a golem.

In his words, she heard it: He feared to hope.

The two were not alone. A coven of Deep-Blue Wearers stood in a wide circle — beneath every cowl, a Sorcerer. No fewer than thirty Adept ringed the black pool, a stone's throw across. In the flickering shadows beyond them, a multitude of hulking forms with lantern eyes also faced the pool, expressionless.

'Our efforts with bismuth and dolomite bore no fruit,' answered Faymorgan. Her voice dripped with frustration, for the hours and days lost in vain endeavour. The hourglass contained precious few grains, for the crisis of war came ever nearer. 'In excavating the vein of cobalt, your drillers have presented us with a much more encouraging prospect.

'The cobalt, powdered and suspended as a film over the pool, will freely conduct our ardent magic. The resultant rays of energy carry force enough to destroy living tissue.

'If we can ensnare Anuvin in a net of ensorcelled cobalt ... then perchance, we might dismantle his physical form. We cannot destroy his essence — for war is his unassailable nature — but he will be forced to return to the Pantheon, to face divine judgement. His path across Rhye can be interrupted here.'

Lord Enoch gave a contemplative nod. Since the Council of Rhye, the drillers' energies focussed on veins and schists of ore that the Sorcerers felt held promise. During their harried toil, the eerie *THOOM* coming from the marrow of the earth ceased. Certainly, then, the sound did not originate in work conducted within the Bore.

Only the preceding day was the chilling riddle solved. The answer arrived upon a prodigious telepathic wave, from missing Emissary Torr Yosef. Displaying unfathomable strength, Yosef reached out to every golem within the scope of his percipience. With this most urgent wave rode a dire warning.

<PREPARE. WAR MAKES LANDFALL TOMORROW.>

The revelation struck with the force of a blast.

Mighty though they were, the golems did not prepare for battle. To challenge Anuvin in combat was, in their eyes, folly; to do so in their own home would welcome devastation. Instead, they entered a kind of solemn trance — a communion with each other and with Marnis, to whom they attributed their existence.

Marnis remained silent.

Lord Enoch studied the pool. A deep rumble, almost beyond perception, caused the surface to ripple and distort.

The Sorcerers noted the disturbance as well. Faymorgan stepped forward, an urn of cobalt powder cradled in her arms.

Nearby, Torr Methuselah stood amidst his brethren.

<Lord?>

A concerned inflection tilted his single word. The Torr did not question his Sovereign, a veteran nearing the completion of his two-hundred-year Lordship. Instead, his enquiry was ever more profound: He doubted the lore of his people.

<Every scripture, every Song, every augury utters the same truth,> replied Enoch with calm authority. *<The Creator guides our fate. At the time of crisis, we shall learn his designs for us.>*

The rumble grew. It could be felt beneath the feet of all, golem and Adept. Above the Stygian cavern, an entire mountain bore down, undeniable witness to destiny. Throughout the vast, cylindrical shaft of Warnom Bore, every golem stood ready to countenance the God of War.

With deliberate care, Faymorgan poured a film of blue-black powder onto the rippling pool. Below the surface, from a place deeper than the eye could see, an eerie glow emanated.

The malign ambience bloomed brighter, an inexorable terror.

Around the rocky brim, the Adept commenced a chant. Low, archaic words echoed across the pool and around the cavern. The spell harmonised with the rumble from beneath the earth, which swelled and rose towards them.

The Sorcerers began gesticulating, as one; an intricate hand movement, like spiders weaving silk.

<*Marnis, hear our prayer,*> intoned Lord Enoch.

<*Marnis, hear our prayer,*> replied hundreds of golems in unison. A full circle of lamplight eyes cast a hopeful radiance down upon the scene.

The rumble grew to a roar. The pool swirled and ruptured with innumerable bubbles, like a giant, frothing cauldron.

The chant of the Adept rose in pitch, evolving into a frantic wail — a spellbinding fever of voices. Over the troubled surface of the water, a web of blue sorcery snapped and sparkled. Arcs of electric power zapped from rim to opposite rim. A metallic odour permeated the entire subterranean vault.

A frenzy of turbulence and magic surged within the pool. Beneath the waters, a terrible light still came, punching up through the darkness. The shadows of the Bore shrank into deep crevices.

The water churned, a violent maelstrom.

The Sorcerers shrieked. A shower of sparks blasted from the pool as their chorus reached a crescendo.

'There!' cried Faymorgan.

A figure sprang from the pool, landing upon the brim of stone with a crash.

Light and power wreathed the body of Anuvin. His yowl rang out above the clamour as he fought with the mystical cobalt snare. His muscular form writhed, grappling and straining. The remnant of his ancient loin cloth burned away, unable to withstand the extremes of sorcery.

All around, the Wearers of Deep Blue leaned forward, faces anxious, gleaming with sweat. None could tear their eyes from the sight of the God, convulsing in the sorcerous tangle. His fearsome cries epitomised torture and pain.

With an impassioned bellow, he overcame the trap. Skeins of magic fell from him in tatters.

The glow of ensorcelled cobalt darkened and was snuffed upon the rock.

Seeming pleased to find his feet on solid ground, he turned a slow circle, facing his tormentors. He stood naked, gleaming with water, cloaked in only antagonism. In his fist he held a long-shafted weapon, with which he brushed the crackling net of sorcery from his limbs and torso. The Sorcerer's foil he cast aside, with nonchalant disdain. Steam rose from his reddened skin.

The Adept slumped to the ground, their efforts shattered like broken bones.

'This is not the welcome I hoped for, after so long on accursed ground,' said the God of War. He spoke through the grin of a fiend. The light of sputtering magic cast his features in garish relief. His molten voice boomed in the cavernous heart of the Bore.

Many golems twitched, uneasy. Here stood a God, amongst the denizens of Rhye. Maleficent strength pulsed from him. A paralysing quandary faced them: to kneel in obeisance, or to defy and assault a divine intruder?

Lord Enoch stepped forward, obliterating doubt.

<Mighty Anuvin, it is not your presence we fortify against, but rather,

your intent.>

Anuvin's smile remained. 'My intent is to be free, Lord of Golems,' he replied, 'yet you affront me with bitter magic. An interesting tactic.' He cast an eye around at the Wearers of Deep Blue, tremulous and uncertain on the brink of shadows. 'I suppose you imagined these paltry tricks would undo me.'

The golem did not answer directly. <*Your freedom is foretold as a harbinger of doom.*>

Lord Enoch towered over War and looked capable of raining deathly blows upon him. To do so in this place would risk bringing down the entire mountain. He remained still.

Enoch continued. <*Already, we see that your freedom may have visited doom upon our allies.*> He inclined his iron head, indicating the weapon Anuvin carried. <*Neptune would not have relinquished that without a fight.*>

The Trident glowed red hot, issuing tendrils of steam. Anuvin held it in sinister triumph. He used it to light his way through the hellish fissure, linking the undersea vent to the chambers at the root of Warnom Bore.

'Every Warlord needs a standard,' said Anuvin. 'My last one was lost on the field of battle. The Mer-Lord obliged, in offering me his. Already, I have drawn upon its power, summoning the steed I shall ride into battle.'

The grind of protesting metal came from within the ranks of stunned onlookers. <*We will not bow and be slaughtered,*> grated Torr Jasher, advancing on Anuvin. <*The death of valiant Neptune must be avenged.*>

With a casual movement, the God of War raised the dripping, red Trident. An air of boredom crossed his visage as he executed a simple gesture with the weapon.

The hideous shriek of crumpling iron rent the air. Jasher's

skull collapsed, his body crushed, as if pulled within itself by an invisible hand. His scrapped form toppled to the ground, sending several Adept diving out of harm's way.

In a moment, Jasher's eyes blinked into darkness.

Without a word, Anuvin spread his Herculean arms. His expression invited any further challengers.

None were forthcoming.

Lord Enoch stood his ground. For a moment, he did not speak. Perhaps he communicated with only some of the assembled minds.

The Adept huddled away from Anuvin, sidling towards the corners farthest from him. He ignored their obvious retreat.

With the impassivity of stone, Enoch again addressed the God of War. His words gave little indication he even acknowledged the fall of Torr Jasher.

<Most potent Anuvin. Be you incarcerated, or be you free to roam, the fact of war is inevitable here in Rhye. Your brethren have placed upon this land seven Realms, brimming with higher forms of life. Each has its own lore, customs, and aspirations. Conflict is, then, as inescapable as the turn of the seasons, or the Grand Dance itself.

<I ask of you now: Why are you here? Why do you darken our door? You defy the quartz entrapments of Marnis and scorn the very Peaks of Light, simply burrowing beneath them in your bid to gain land. Why?>

Though Enoch already felt the answer deep in his integument, he asked anyway. Anuvin would not resist answering. The golem eyed the Adept over War's shoulder, conversing in hushed tones.

The teeth of Anuvin gleamed, a sardonic smile glued to his face. 'I see no need to obscure my cause from you. Shortly, your awareness will not matter.

'I come in this moment to restore the balance of power. For too long an age, have Death and War stood castrate. Across millennia, Valendyne has borne the weight of humiliation at the hands of the

Pantheon; as have I, for seeking to aid him. The time has arrived for us to be unshackled — to realise the vision of Valendyne, remaking Rhye as a world of conflict and shade. Though previous attempts failed, on this occasion, it is we, who will rise as victors.'

Enoch hunkered down. <*You will not hold dominion over my people. Peace is our edict, and our vital spark is sacrosanct. We will never again be possessed. You will destroy us first.*>

'I do not come with the intent to destroy the Golem race,' said Anuvin, with a devious grin. 'Your demise, Lord Enoch, is unavoidable — a necessary part of the plan to dismantle the Fae Ring. The rest of your people simply represent collateral damage, in my eyes.'

The Adept wrung their hands. The instinct to somehow wield the Sorcerer's Art to subvert impending tragedy collided with their sense of self-preservation. The God of War shrugged off their initial attempt at offence. His callous regard for life might not brook any further efforts to forestall him.

War not only thrived on conflict — he required it.

The Golem Lord did not flinch at the promise of his own doom. Instead, he leaned forward, looming over Anuvin.

<*In the name of Torr Jasher, first amongst martyrs, I say this to you: We respect you, as we respect every God and Goddess. We do not fear you, for fear and respect are two very different things. In this place we will stand against everything you represent. Well may you assail the race of Golems, for we shall be avenged.*>

Anuvin still grinned. Of a will to attack, he showed no sign. Perhaps he, too, felt the gargantuan weight of the Peaks of Light above him. In the deepest well of the Bore — the *sanctum sanctorum* of golem life — even his earthly form could be irretrievably crushed by a show of celestial might.

'None of you dare stand against me,' he said. 'You claim the strike of vengeance, Golem Lord, were I to wipe you from the face of Rhye. Yet who will visit this retribution upon me, if none step forward as champion?'

<You speak only to provoke. I will not be fooled into striking you. You know golem lore and the writings of prophets as well as I. We are guided and protected by our Creator. Should you bring my people to harm, you shall encounter the wrath of Marnis, with Lhestra to mete out Justice befitting your crime.>

Emboldened, dozens of golems edged toward the pool and the rock upon which Anuvin stood. Torr Methuselah turned his head, his lamplight falling upon the God of War.

Anuvin glared at Lord Enoch. His gaze traversed the expanse of time, weighing the Golem Sovereign against every instance of his people since the dawn of Rhye.

With a gesture that shattered the gravid air, he threw back his head and exploded in cruel laughter.

'Marnis? Marnis! In the name of all that is sacred! My ears might fall off, for hearing such a mockery of the truth.' He raised a finger, levelling it at Enoch. 'Am I to deduce that you perceive Marnis to be your Creator? Is that how you interpret your lore?'

Enoch stood silent, assimilating the words of Anuvin, seeking the trap or deceit that might be there.

He found none. Behind Anuvin's glee shone a wicked earnestness.

The God of War uttered the devastating confirmation in a whisper.

'You are mistaken. Your beloved Marnis laughed — much as I do now — as your race was birthed from the mantle of the world. You are the progeny of none other than Valendyne, whom Marnis ridiculed for having such an audacious vision.

'Do you see it, then? Golems are the antithesis of every other pallid being that roams the land. While they suffer life, you are the pure embodiment of what lies beyond! Do you see now, how your years are limitless? How you inhabit Rhye without a soul? Souls and mortality are shackles of the living. The *living*' — he said the word with disgust — 'are your inferiors.

'Now that your eyes are open, may they descry that possession is not your destiny. You are already perfect — true scions of Valendyne.

'See also, that you have a choice. Your people can follow me in my campaign to see your true Creator liberated from Nevermore. In his glory will Golemkind bask, an eternal existence as his favoured. Your sacrifice, Lord Enoch, will be enshrined in remembrance of this moment.

'The alternative is that my campaign proceeds, heedless of your resistance. Your shattered remains — along with all your people — will be strewn throughout the ruined cloak of this mountain. Your memory will fade with the passing of each miserable mortal generation.

'Answer, then. Will the golems march with me?'

Lord Enoch did not reply. Not because he cowed from Anuvin's proposition, but because either road would see him destroyed. He would not accept, as his legacy, a decision that could commit his people to torment for all of time. Instead, he gave a tacit nod to Torr Methuselah.

Methuselah did not hesitate. The immensity of golem lore flashed through his consciousness in an instant. Every trial and tribulation, every struggle and triumph. His percipience flowed throughout the cavern where his kin stood united, up the dizzying spiral of the Bore — the monument to their toil, first burrowed by the hand of Valendyne. There he found the minds of many thousands more, all sharing his decision.

<No. We do not march with you,> answered Torr Methuselah.

In the aftermath of this pronouncement, frenzied responses erupted in rapid succession.

In a dim corner, where a wide stair rose into the main shaft of the Bore, the Adept uttered a brief incantation. Their figures shimmered and blurred, on the edge of solid reality. Then, in a swirling, bursting conflagration, they vanished. Their translocation left the scent of sorcery in the air — cinnamon and burnt amber.

Following the escape of the Adept, the golem host locked minds. Faced with the reality that no divine intervention would protect them — and a commitment to oppose Anuvin from their surrogate leader — the iron colossi saw little recourse but to close ranks, preparing for dread conflict. Even before the Adept departed, Anuvin found himself confronted across the pool by a wall of mechanised defiance. The sound of golems stamping their feet and pounding their fists shook the bedrock around them. Pebbles and dust rained from the ceiling.

STOMP-STOMP-MASH ... STOMP-STOMP-MASH ...

'The children of Valendyne welcome their own doom!' cried Anuvin with wild laughter. Lord Enoch lurched towards him with great hands clenched, ready to engage.

Anuvin held the Trident aloft, his voice a searing blaze above the tumult:

Ealing Sea, harken to my call!
The Mer-Lord's Trident now casts its thrall.
Gather hence your wrathful might;
The Warnom Bore, your waters smite.

He brought down the Trident's heel upon the rock, creating a thunderous sound.

<*You will not escape,*> declared Lord Enoch. <*Your body will perish,*

here in this tomb of your own making.> Reaching Anuvin, he lunged. War ducked under the golem's massive swing, driving upwards with the vicious prongs of the Trident. It caught Enoch in the midsection, piercing his iron shell with ease.

Though he stood skewered, the Lord of Golems still fought, attempting to mash Anuvin with furious blows. Anuvin dodged and weaved, forcing his weapon deeper into Enoch's abdomen, until it passed out the far side. Then, as swift and powerful as a hurricane, he tore off the golem's arms, one at a time.

'You only defer the inevitable,' said Anuvin. The waning husk of his adversary offered no reply.

The golem host closed in on the combatants. Their intended counter strike soon unravelled, as the ground beneath them began to quake. A sudden upheaval tossed many to the ground. An ominous roar filled the room and the black pool churned.

With prodigious strength, Anuvin grasped the haft of the Trident and kicked the body of Lord Enoch from it. Enoch's remains fell heavily into the water, which rose and spilled out into the cavern. The Lord of Golems disappeared from view.

'May you all follow your Sovereign into oblivion,' cried the God of War, clearing the pool in a single great leap. He hurled himself into the throng of Torrs, crashing from one hulking creature to the next, wrecking and dismembering as he went. His path cleared, he raced up the stone stair.

As Anuvin vanished into the shaft of Warnom Bore, the floor of the cavern began to crack and tear apart. The roar grew deafening as the Sea broke through, sweeping everything away in its path.

A tectonic earthquake shook the land.

With Warnom Bore at its epicentre, the foundations of Rhye trembled, sending shockwaves through the Peaks of Light. Rumbles from below triggered a chain of avalanches, hurling tremendous slews of rock and ice down into many a jagged crevasse.

Untold volumes of seawater and compressed steam blasted from within the Bore, stripping gigantic fragments of rock from the core as it came. The eruption carried the sound of an awakening leviathan, a *boom* that could be heard hundreds of leagues away. A great geyser shot from the midst of the mountain range, spewing water and cloud towards the heavens. Enormous stones flew a great distance into the sky, raining down in a lethal tempest upon the north-western plains of The Corridor.

With the hail of rock came a shower of iron debris. The shattered remains of countless golems fell, a catastrophic deluge of scrap. Many more were obliterated within the Bore itself, smashed to pieces against the walls of the shaft by the unstoppable surge.

No golem survived the devastation.

Trident clenched in a vice-like grip, Anuvin rode the giant column of water, right from the very basement of Warnom Bore. He hurtled upwards at sickening speed. Above, the tremendous pressure tore a gaping hole in the mountainside, where once the proud entrance to the Bore stood. Anuvin vaulted like a catapult shot into the brooding, grey sky, along with huge boulders and vast quantities of scree. Higher and higher he soared, gaining momentary vision of all the northern region of Rhye. At his apogee, he beheld the destruction he wrought — a gargantuan hole was blown in the side of the range. Afar, he saw his goal: the black spume of power above Nevermore, where Valendyne began to emerge from the tree of his incarceration.

After a serene pause, the God of War fell to earth.

Far below, the Ealing Sea flooded from the Peaks of Light out upon the plain. The landscape would be forever altered. A new inland swamp appeared, the water surging forth in a tidal wave.

Wind whistled in his long, auburn hair, whipping it behind and above him. Guided by his own divine will, his trajectory brought him down close to the leading edge of the water.

By the time his feet splashed down on muddy soil, the surge of water slowed to a languid gush. He had travelled many leagues out over The Corridor, once known for its lush and fertile agricultural land. To the north, forested worlds homed denizens of Nurtenan, who knew little of the land's imminent crisis. So isolated were the rural sylphic and human folk, they would be too late to escape the closing snare.

Anuvin straightened, evaluating his flesh for non-existent damage. The turbulent passage from Warnom Bore tore beings of iron to pieces, yet he emerged unscathed.

He chuckled to himself and surveyed the land. Rain fell, pattering on his bare skin. The light of Adatar barely penetrated the bleak, marbled canvas above.

'I'm back, Father,' he murmured, with vehemence.

Finding his bearings, he studied the horizon. In the south-west, through the mist, he spied movement, within a spray of water. The spray grew larger, as a dark speck raced towards him.

'My warhorse arrives,' he cried, 'and here am I, unprepared! I cannot ride into battle without armour.'

On mere suggestion, plates, scales, and spines burst from his naked body, growing from inside him. The armour gleamed a dark red-black, gnarling and hardening like thorns of chitin. In a few heartbeats, the God of War was clad from helm to sabatons.

All the while, the spray billowed larger. The speck emerged as a great beast, charging across the diluvian plain towards Anuvin. With an intense gaze, he watched the beast materialise, closing the distance at an alarming pace. Galloping on meaty paws, the animal bellowed — a chilling sound like the blare of a trumpet.

At last, it arrived, wreathed in the spray clouds of its travel. It came, at the sound of Anuvin's command, from far in the south — the fiery Dunes of Sordd.

The massive face resembled man, rather than beast. Only a maw full of razor-sharp teeth and eyes the colour of vivid blue distinguished it from Humankind. About its countenance bloomed a rippling, fire-red mane, in keeping with its enormous, leonine body. It bore a tawny hide, similar in shade to the sand of the earth it trod. At its back, two huge wings, like those of a bat or wyvern, were folded away.

The manticore: wild and potent, complete but for its tail, missing since the elder days of the Mer-Lords.

The manticore recaptured its breath, huffing deep blasts of steam from mouth and nostrils. Its great thorax heaved. A forepaw splashed the tepid saltwater in which it stood, scarcely an inch deep. Blue eyes, threatening instant death, appraised the God of War and the Trident he bore.

Anuvin spoke. 'Yes, I have something of yours. To regain it, you must convey me into battle. We march upon Fenmarck Haunte.'

'We? What of a warlord's army? Or do you ride alone?'

Anuvin whirled around. Neither God nor beast had spoken. The voice of a woman called to him, from overhead.

He looked skyward.

Against a backdrop of thunderheads and the billowing eruption swooped a pterippus, as black as midnight. It circled them — once, twice, three times, appraising the man and beast below. The manticore rustled its leathery wings with vitriol, though it made no attempt to leave the ground. It remained focused on the bristling form of Anuvin.

'Declare yourself or die,' shouted Anuvin to the winged horse, as it entered a gradual descent.

'Predictable, brutish behaviour from the God of War,' replied the pterippus, using a feminine voice that oozed with sophistication and a taste for control.

The creature alighted nearby, before executing a flawless transformation. In a shimmering swirl of bespangled black smoke, the pterippus became a tall, elegant woman.

Raising an eyebrow, Anuvin noted that she stood bedecked in the ancient garb of a Necromancer.

'You bear the likeness of Valendyne's acolytes,' he said, 'though by my reckoning, it has been nearly three and a half millennia since the Seer banished the last of the Necromancers from Rhye. Speak and show just cause for your appearance.'

'The Seer, weak and righteous as she was, failed in her task. I stand before you as the last Necromancer — she who has risen from obscurity to prominence, to return the lost Wearers of Black from oblivion.

'You may call me the Black Queen.'

The manticore snorted and issued a snarl, like grinding bones.

The woman's smile was not beautiful, in the way of fairy tale princesses. Her features were somehow twisted, affected by the taint of her Art. Yet she held a lustrous magnetism in her gleaming eye and smirking lips. Opulent black robes draped about her figure in pleasing curves and folds, cinched at her waist with a sash, emblazoned with myriad runes in a near-forgotten text. Her nails — talons, tapered to a stylish point — were also black. She wielded them like claws as she spoke.

Gone was Belladonna, gypsy paramour and consort to Lord Rogar. Through her dark evolution, the Black Queen regained her ancient splendour. Her power swelled to that of a demigod.

Anuvin sensed this and stayed his wrath.

He decided to find out what she knew.

'Who are our allies?'

'For now, you are *my* ally.' Her confidence disarmed him. 'I bring the knowledge that will aid us both. Rhye is not the place you knew at the end of the Godsryche. There are newer alliances. Higher beings mount defences against our cause. There are — complications — that warrant a considered approach.'

Anuvin's gaze burned like a furnace. He said nothing.

'I, like you, have spent an Age simply trying to survive,' the Black Queen said, 'with hopes of this moment being the very oxygen I breathed. I have spent many long years eroding the wards of the Fae Ring. Now, I also reunite the forsaken Adept — ready to claim this land at the turning tide.'

Even as the words left her lips, Anuvin looked beyond her and saw that she spoke truth. Through the mist and settling dust from the mountain, he spied them: Dark figures, spectres emerging from a dream. The longer he watched, the more appeared — first there were dozens, then hundreds. Multitudes of Black-robed Adept, drifting silently into view. Voluminous cowls concealed their faces.

Raising the banished Necromancers had cost the Black Queen every shred of her own soul.

Anuvin nodded, acknowledging her masterwork with a single, curt gesture. His ire dimmed.

'What is the situation?' he asked.

'With the demise of each Sovereign, Valendyne's power grows. This is manifest in storms and flooding. All the lowlands in Rhye are now submerged.

'Plague seeps through Sontenan and lower Nurtenan, courtesy of the Wilden Lord, who is now perished. People flee their homes. Protective bunkers, thrown open by the human pretender, are overfull. Hapless beings who manage to evade the plague are on a forced march through Nurtenan. Much of the human population now wanders into a trap. They wander somewhat knowingly, though they have little choice. If we march now, we will corral them in the Haunte, beneath the Peaks of Obelis. There, they will be at the whim of ravenous moorland wights, as well as their own dead who are resurrected in their wake.

'In Fenmarck Haunte, the old Lords will be vanquished and Valendyne freed, to assert his new reign.'

'His subjects will scarcely be willing,' chuckled Anuvin.

'His subjects will be either dead, undead, or enslaved.'

'Who are we aligned against?'

The Black Queen counted off their foes on pointed fingertips. 'The humans will mount an offensive, though their forces are severely depleted. Likewise, Petrichor is weakened. The Sylphic General Prime remains a threat, with the Vrendari host behind him. We will pass through that gauntlet on our way to the Haunte. Lastly, there is the Archimage, Benjulius. Perhaps he intends an ambush. Perhaps he considers his Adept beyond the tribulations of other higher beings. Whatever the reason, he remains silent.'

Anuvin stroked his jaw. 'Some fire remains in the belly of our enemy.'

'We have the God of War.'

'We also shall have an army.'

'What of the golems?' asked the Black Queen, eyeing the ruinous collapse on the western horizon.

'They failed to accept my offer. It is of no consequence. In their stead, I shall bring the mountains themselves as my army.' He leapt astride the waiting manticore, using his Trident to angle the terrifying creature towards the east.

'Lead the march, O Black Queen,' he said.

At their backs, the debris of a shattered mountain littered the plain.

Rubble, boulders, and rocky shards the size of houses lay scattered, like a giant's playthings. As the floodwater from the Ealing Sea receded, the monoliths sat exposed.

They might have remained, a mute testament to catastrophe, for all time. Instead, the words of Anuvin called to them.

Across leagues of devastation, enormous hunks of stone started to quiver and move.

CHAPTER 17

ALL THE WRETCHES RUN

'There! Did you hear it this time?' inquired Meadow.

'Yes! I did, just now. The sound of drums, as you said.' Leith Lourden sat beside him, head swivelling, pointed ears pricked to catch the elusive sound.

'What do you make of it?'

'I can't be sure ... I only hope it isn't more redcaps. I'm all redcapped out, for the time being.'

Meadow stared into the distance. 'It reminds me of parades my folks would take me to see, through the streets of Flaxae. Titania always loved throwing a parade. No excuses necessary.'

Leith smiled. After a time, anyone would exchange the thrills and spoils of adventure for familiar comforts. She understood the sentiment very well.

Any hope of familiar comforts faded over distant horizons.

The pair sat on the same spot where Harold and Mustapha left them. A short distance away, Dique tinkered, plying his skills with several strange tools upon Torr Yosef's inner workings. Since holding communion with his fellow golems, Yosef had changed in a fundamental way. Dique offered to make sure the rust wasn't setting in, 'what with all the unnatural rain and such.' They both knew rust would not trouble the golem, but Yosef let him poke around in there just the same. Will observed their endeavour, happily distracted by the opportunity to learn about golem mechanics.

Meanwhile, a parade of a very different kind began traipsing past the companions' place of respite.

A giant serpent of miserable Sontenan refugees trudged past, half a mile from the forest verge. An interminable mass of humans, sylphs and other creatures formed a slow-moving caravan, heading north-east towards Fenmarck Haunte.

As Leith predicted, the flood of refugees appeared within hours of Mustapha and Harold's departure. The remaining companions initially intended to follow in their wake. Only the arrival of un-homed thousands, bearing piteous faces, prompted an amended plan.

'How best to help a torrent of the helpless?' wondered Leith. A pitiful few Vian knights and Vrendari travelled with the caravan. The territory harboured abrupt danger at the best of times. Now, with flooded marshlands and the looming threat of wights and banshees, the pilgrimage wandered from frying pan into fire.

'I don't think Dique and I can catch enough game to feed everyone,' said Meadow.

'Hunger is only one of their concerns, whether they know it or not.' Leith wore a glum expression. 'The path they follow is a dead end — pardon the term — unless sanctuary can be found in Mages Pass or the —'

She stopped. It came again: the hollow resonance of drums. Clattering refugees raised a modest din, but above that came the nearer sound of many feet, large and small.

The others heard it, too. Dique ceased his mechanical exploration and the three re-joined Leith and Meadow, with questioning faces.

'It comes from behind us,' noted the sylph.

They spun to their backs, where the dark wall of forest — the convergence of Banwah Haunte and Petrichor — stared them down. The great stone bridge stood resolute, oblivious to any occurrence, as the Bijou swirled beneath it.

A gentle wind ruffled lesser boughs and branches, but soon, the trees were shaken by a more substantial force. The steady tramp of feet and splintering of undergrowth could not be mistaken. At the canopy, trees not only shook in a frenzy ... they moved.

<*An army.*> Yosef spoke the thoughts of all.

On instinct, the companions sought cover. The nearby terrain provided ample protection, with plentiful outcroppings and overhangs of rock. They concealed themselves in a place that gave good vantage of the bridge and roadway.

The clamour of an approaching force drowned out the pilgrimage passing behind them. Trees crashed and split as the forest itself came alive. The rhythmic drums and marching feet marked the beat of battle.

At last, an army emerged from the eaves of Petrichor. A liveried swarm of green tunics and gold-plated armour, with an array of ornate and deadly weaponry.

'The Fae!' cried Meadow.

He spoke truly, for the ranks of warriors to first appear were a vanguard of Fae infantry. They bore a proud standard known to all across the land — a stylised icon of Oberon's Yew in gold, on a green background. Their weapons gleamed and their faces bore valour and determination.

With unwavering purpose, they reached the bridge and marched across.

The stream of pixie warriors grew and grew. Beyond the vanguard came knights and archers. Great, docile forest beasts — manubani — hauled covered wagons, plodding on giant feet behind the forward regiment.

Enthralled, Meadow rose from cover.

'Wait!' said Leith, hand on his shoulder. 'Look.'

She pointed, beyond the vanguard, the beasts, and the bridge, to the tree line.

The trees themselves lumbered forward.

From within the shadows of Banwah Haunte, joining with the Fae army, broke a horde of towering forest trolls. Free from their shackles, abandoned by the foul elements of the Haunte and liberated by the death of Lord Ponerog, the trolls showed their true allegiance to the Mother Forest. Massive, misshapen bodies, borne on trunk-like limbs, advanced from the shadows.

'The vengeance of trees,' uttered Will.

<No doubt their passion is fierce,> said Yosef.

The trolls bristled with ferocity.

By this time, the caravan of refugees had also spied the Fae army. A fatigued cheer arose from the masses. Many paused to watch the approaching spectacle, greeting the oncoming force with an outburst of joy and filthy tears.

Beyond the trolls, still more infantry appeared. The sheer size of the Fae resistance buoyed the companions' spirits.

The next sight to greet them caused their hearts to skip.

A noble formation of pterippi, five abreast and ten rows deep, marched into view, gaining the foot of the bridge. Each bore a rider — an armoured Fae Commander. Amongst their ranks were

Halliwell, Dartmoor and Puck.

At their fore, astride a mighty creature of glorious marigold, sat Trixel Tate.

The fixie shone with resplendence in a cloak of fern and heather, beneath which showed the glint of emerald mail. Above her brow, like a pronged shout of retribution, she wore the antlered crown.

Meadow gasped. No longer to be held back, he sprang from cover, with Dique on his heels. The others, too, emerged from hiding.

In a headlong rush, the pixies dashed for the formation of winged horses. On open ground, the marching infantry spotted them and unsheathed glistening blades. A cursory analysis found that the newcomers posed no threat. The infantry stayed their attack.

'Halt!' cried Commander Halliwell, as the pixies barrelled towards the mounted Fae. Knights relayed the order along the line and the huge column ground to a stop. Trixel's beast stood at the crest of the bridge, snorting and pawing stone. When the fixie spied the companions, she unleashed an impish grin.

'You didn't think you were leaving us behind?' she said.

For Meadow, the five days since leaving Petrichor felt like five weeks. 'You're a sight for sore eyes ... my Lady,' he said, glancing at the crown and executing a bow.

Dique followed. 'A change of mind, Miss Tate?'

Introspection showed in her eyes. Despite her unbridled past life, Trixel bore the antlered crown with a majesty that elevated her.

'I'm no Oberon or Titania,' she replied, 'nor could I ever be. But the Fae Folk call out for leadership. They long to give answer to the needs of the land.

'The dryads strive to renew the scorched forest. Though the recovery of Petrichor will take some time, they have the spirit of every forest creature to aid their task. Little remains for us to do but commit our energy to the defence of Rhye.' With a gesture, she indicated the vast, snaking column of civilians beyond.

'It is an honour to have you with us, my Lady,' said Leith Lourden, reaching the bridge. 'You lead your forces well, to catch us up so quickly.'

Trixel's face lit up. 'I needed to ensure you had these vagabonds under control. As for this exodus,' she said, indicating the caravan with a wave, 'what is your analysis?'

Leith raised empty hands. 'The civilians will need a bolstered escort and enriched resources if they are to seek safety with minimal casualties. The mountains of the north, with deep caves and sheltering passes, hold greatest promise ... though they are still a few days' travel away. We also sense a trap, waiting to be sprung upon the old battleground of the Haunte.'

Trixel nodded, only half listening. A brief head count revealed that two of the 'vagabonds' were absent.

'Mustapha ...?' she said, features drawn in sorrow.

Will spoke. 'Mustapha lives. Much more than that, he has evolved. Such a wonder you must behold for yourself. You must have seen the new light that reshapes the darkness of Banwah Haunte?'

'I have,' confirmed the fixie. 'From that light came this procession of forest trolls, lush in the resurgence of their freedom. Warmth flows from that place, which has known evil for so long. The shadows shrink away, from some kind of magic.'

'It is more than magic,' said Will. 'It is the grace of Lhestra. The spirit of Maybeth Giltenan dwells in that tower, as the White Queen. She visited her power upon Mustapha, who not only thrives, but shows unprecedented vigour. Even now, he races for Wintergard, with Harold in his wake. They seek an audience with the General Prime.'

Trixel Tate fell silent. Her eyes ranged over the destitute masses, trudging into uncertainty, then towards the distant range. She appeared lost in contemplation, staring into the bleak distance.

'How would a dragonfly and a strangeling ...'

Recollection flashed in her mind. The hovel of Lily, the Seer. Once, in a past century; and again, in much more recent times. She saw the Seer counsel Oberon. She heard the prophecy, the wailing of a rescued child and the plaintive questions of a motherless son.

'By the love of Ophynea,' she whispered. 'How did I miss it?'

'My Lady?' said Leith Lourden.

'Never mind. Come — we waste precious time, standing on this bridge swapping pleasantries. A million restless souls wander into danger. We must do what is needed to help them.'

'Our lives for the good of Rhye,' said Meadow.

'You, young pixies, are now official Fae knights,' said Trixel Tate. 'There are no spare mounts, so you will have to saddle up with us.' She held out a hand, hoisting Meadow onto the golden pterippus behind her. The back of the beast easily accommodated them both. Meadow blushed at his sudden promotion. Will lifted Dique onto the mount of Commander Dartmoor.

'What will be my orders?' asked Meadow eagerly, thoughts of home forgotten.

'For now, you can help keep the rhythm of the march,' Trixel said.

In response, an infantryman at the rear produced a burnished, pigskin drum.

'You are now responsible for marching us onto the plains,' said Commander Halliwell.

Meadow gawped.

Dique grinned. 'Don't just stare at it — give us something we can move to!'

The refugee caravan moved at a crawl. In only a short time,

the Fae army intercepted it. Promptly, Trixel's Commanders set about evaluating the relative wellbeing of those who evacuated the Southern Realm, as well as liaising with the soldiers and Vrendari amongst them.

Desperation and misery consumed the civilians. Their column shuffled with barely enough pace to stay ahead of the advancing Pox, half a league behind the last stragglers. Cruel fate saw the weak and infirm fall behind, despite the efforts of others to usher them onwards. Dropping with exhaustion, frail humans could do little to fend off the viscid, creeping foe. A brace of Vrendari remained with the tail end, though they were stretched too thin to protect everyone.

Along the caravan's length, inanition and hunger were threats as great as the Pox. Manubani and other beasts of burden were slain for food, but nobody lingered long enough to eat their fill. Half-devoured carcasses littered the terrain behind the refugees, who now struggled to carry enough food or water for coming days.

Leith Lourden flew here and there, amongst the miserable multitudes, attempting to quell fears and buoy spirits. Close by, the Bijou still flowed pure; Leith recruited other Vrendari to help convey skins of fresh water. To the masses, it came as a small gesture. To individuals, it brought vital sustenance.

In her task, the sylph met countless faces, stained by oppression and grit. Hope shone through the weariness for many, while terror gnawed at many more.

'What became of Sontenan?' she asked, walking alongside a middle-aged peasant and his wife.

'Tragedy,' he said, through sunken cheeks. 'Everywhere we turned, floodwater cut us off. Many of Lord Rogar's shelters were too perilous to reach. Some folk gave up their lives in the attempt. We left it too late to seek shelter.'

The woman by his side said nothing, her face haunted.

A young tailor also shared his tale. 'By the time we arrived at a bunker, there was no room left for us! We knocked on the door for all our lives, but they wouldn't let us in.'

Amidst the commoners, there were also noble folk. A wealthy landowner, from outside the city walls, opined his loss. 'All is in ruin. My neighbour and his family were overcome by the dread ill. I was attacked by the ghouls that arose where they fell! I have my life and the clothes I wear, but nothing else.'

Other witnesses, to the darkest of horror, were rendered speechless. A lone woman ambled, clutching a scrap of material: a fragment of a young girl's dress.

The bloated column wandered onwards, into the fringe of Fenmarck Haunte.

The following day, the rain grew heavier.

Storm clouds mingled with an ominous threat in the distant east. Without voluntary thought, the column veered north. Trepidation steered the wandering populace away from the blanket of black mammatus clouds, with their forked lightning and sulphurous air. Across the vast fens, through a curtain of mist, the Peaks of Obelis stood in looming silhouette.

The mountains spelled uncertain refuge.

Will marched alongside Torr Yosef. In the past day, the golem had withdrawn into himself, sharing little. Occasionally the creature would glance back, giving an indication as to the proximity of the Pox. The cherubic monsters maintained their pursuit upon reaching the Haunte, as did the throng of undead that followed like a ghastly mirage.

The wagoner attempted to lure out his friend. 'Is there a worthy prayer, for a time such as this?'

The huge, iron visage turned towards him. <*What would you value most, to pray for?*>

'My hopes still rest with Mustapha. In some small way, I believe his mission holds great importance.'

<*I also sense the weight of destiny upon his shoulders. Well may he find the strength to accomplish his task.*>

'You seem distracted, Torr Yosef. What troubles you?'

<*War has come, young wagoner.*> The golem did not speak in allegory. Will realised that Yosef could see the very real horror of Anuvin, through the eyes of his peers. <*He who is also called The Rival. He comes in the name of conflict and waste. He takes no sides but works towards chaos for the sake of chaos. He stands amongst my people, threatening the demise of Lord Enoch. His greater purpose, within the glade of Nevermore, is confirmed: He declares that War and Death shall rule in a new Age of the land.*>

Will's face fell. 'Can the golems stand against him?'

<*They shall not. Nor do they bow down to him. They defy him, refusing possession.*>

'May Marnis protect them.' The human strode on, boots squelching on terrain that gripped him with every step. Somewhere beyond the haze, the strangled cry of a beast rang out, drawing alarm from timorous folk as they marched.

'My parents always warned that a banshee wail could drive a person mad ... that it was a herald of the Two-Legged Death,' said Will.

There came no response.

'Yosef?'

Will turned. He walked alone.

The golem stood, motionless, a dozen paces behind. He may well have been a statue, immobile since Creation. The dreary column skirted about him, as did wisps of enshrouding fog. Grey rain struck his shell with a gentle *tink-tink-tink*.

'Yosef, are you in there?'

The golem moved at last, grasping his head in massive hands. He collapsed to his knees, sinking into the peat bog. Those who passed by stopped, in curious apprehension.

The dam ruptured, releasing a flood of torment. Torr Yosef threw his face to the wretched heavens, releasing an anguished cry that rattled the minds of all around him.

~

Battered and bleeding, the Fairy Feller limped through the snow. A strip of torn cloak, dark and wet, staunched a wound on his thigh. His left arm hung at a strange angle from the shoulder. It throbbed, the numbing cold a small mercy. The ichor of numerous assailants stained the long-handled axe, slung at his back.

He shuddered, teeth chattering. The brutal chill was a foe beyond his axe. He drew a cloak of wight's hide, freshly obtained, tighter around him.

Of his entire journey, the Peaks of Obelis proved the most dangerous. It wasn't so much the steep trails, littered with rubble and scree, or even the merciless cold. Unpredictable threats emerged: the predatory mountain creatures, dwelling in icy warrens, preying on unwary wanderers for food or sport. A cave wight found him, back along the way a day and a half. With a brutal swipe of scythe-like claws, it opened his leg and sent him flying into an edifice of stone. Only the dogged will to survive — and a vicious, single-handed axe blow — saved the Feller from being mauled to death.

Other things, more dreadful than wights, also haunted the trails. Winged skeletons — revenants of slain Vrendari — patrolled the slopes. A clatter of bones, armour and weaponry heralded the approach of the ghoulish warriors. It was all the Feller could do to conceal himself — they were more than a match for him.

Every step of the way, the words of the Fairy King were a colossal yoke about the Feller's shoulders. In a few softly spoken moments, a great weight had passed from Lord to liegeman. The Fairy Feller bore profound expectation, all the way from the dappled woods of Petrichor, across the expanse of Nurtenan and the knolls of the Greenway, to this place where the land met the heavens.

The peril of his journey sapped the very last of his reserves.

Every step grew leaden, the ground a blanket of frigid molasses beneath him. Each footfall took an effort of will.

Ahead, he saw a figure. A shadow on the brink of imagination, yet real enough. Through skirling snowflakes came the suggestion of a brown robe, cowl upturned.

Only twenty yards separated him from the figure. It held up a hand — perhaps a gesture of welcome.

Twenty yards may well have been twenty leagues.

The Fairy Feller teetered, his field of view swimming in and out of focus. His world began to spin. He lurched forward, planting face-first in the snow.

For a time, he knew nothing.

Then, in his mind's eye, he saw it: a tremendous monastery, nestled in the crook of the mountain peaks, bedded in cloud like eiderdown.

The hulking cluster of buildings appeared ancient. It clung to the mountains, huddling in a high plateau, just as a nest of giant eggs. Whitewashed walls, dotted with countless tiny windows, were topped with domes and steeples of many different sizes. An imposing gatehouse fronted the complex.

The Fairy Feller drifted — carried? — towards double oaken

doors, thrown open by more brown-robed figures. As the monastery swallowed him, his vision grew dim.

His awareness snuffed out.

A huddle of green vultures flocked over him.

Scuttling, clamouring over his corpse.

No, not yet a corpse. These were not vultures, for they spoke. Here and there, he heard familiar words. For the most part, an unfamiliar tongue met his ears. Ruffling green robes, moving with haste. Desperate hands, administering ointments. Poultices. The heat of spell-fire lanced his skin. He did not burn.

With a murmur of hushed voices, they left him.

He could not move, though he knew he was hale. He felt no pain. He tried to speak, moving his mouth, but heard nothing. Curiously, this did not bring a sense of alarm.

In a dreamlike state, he drifted once more, under an unknown compulsion. Deeper he moved into this monastic place.

The sacred demesne of the Adept.

Aerglo.

His drift carried him along sheltered walks, lined with brickwork and stone; past cloistered gardens, where gnarled olive trees froze in twisted beauty. Beside an open concourse sat a neat row of chapter houses, each flaunting banners and flags of a different colour. A squat greenhouse, stuffed with exotic herbs and creeping plants, brought vivid scents to his subconscious nose. Other buildings, on the periphery of his awareness, could only be guessed at. A refectory? A reliquary? A library? Mere glimpses revealed little.

With every blink of his mind's eye, the Fairy Feller found bursts of vibrancy. The monumental sanctuary, itself an edifice of cheerless grey-white, bustled with a rich palette of clothing and decoration. There came yellow in abundance — swathes of buttercup and sunshine. Likewise, the browns of chocolate and charred cedar met him at every turn, parting for him as he came. Here and there, he saw the flash of crimson and a pop of azure and green. The Adept swarmed like technicolour bees in his vision. They watched him — not in a foreboding way, but in the manner of observing an uncommon guest.

Try as he might, the Feller could not engage them.

Adrift, uncoupled from any voluntary act, he was drawn onwards.

A magnificent building, capped with a gleaming spire and bristling with white flags, swallowed him via a gaping doorway. He noted the seven-pointed Star of Rhye, hewn in stone, above the portal as he entered.

Within, thin daylight barely penetrated a cavernous interior. The plume of swaying censers cast a mysterious pall about the space. As the smoke lifted — and the Fairy Feller's eyes adjusted to the subdued light within — surprise took him.

On a low dais waited the Wearer of White, Benjulius the Archimage.

The Lord of the Adept offered a stern expression, peering at the Feller over his neat, white beard. It reminded the Feller of a common Fae jest: that Benjulius was born frowning, disappointed in his own mother. In reality, the Archimage possessed a sharp wit, warmth and generosity. Only the need to protect the lore of the Adept brought about his aloof affect … and subsequent reputation.

White robes, the shade of fresh snowfall on a midwinter's morning, cloaked his tall frame. An overcoat of scale mail and intricate gold filigree set his attire above that of all other Adept. His stance bespoke lore-wise power. Few beings in the land held greater potency than he.

The presence of the Archimage did not cause the Fairy Feller's wonderment.

He rubbed his eyes, fearing their deception. Benjulius was accompanied.

Flanking him were four Wearers of Violet, two to each side.

The Warlocks stood on ceremony. Each wore a coat of lacquered karuta and an armoured skirt, over the distinctive shade of their coven. They gripped swords of violet fire, which flickered in the gloom without making a sound.

By the light of their flaming blades, the Fairy Feller saw the Warlocks' faces watching him with large, luminous eyes.

He drew breath at the startling sight.

They resembled no other Adept he had ever seen. Elongated, bestial visages, imbued with a quiet intelligence, stared out at him. While most Adept could be mistaken for humans in any other clothing, these creatures were a species altogether different.

The hands, which clutched fiery weapons, ended in claws.

The Feller's mind raced.

Perhaps the Warlocks became a people apart from their fellow Adept? A separate evolution, of sorts?

But the Warlocks were all destroyed —

The Archimage spoke, breaking through the Feller's tumultuous thoughts. His voice, like rich butter, defied the perpetual frost of his abode.

'Welcome to Aerglo. Our Astrologers anticipated your arrival for the longest time. We know your path has been fraught with peril — we are glad you appear amongst us whole.'

The Fairy Feller blinked. 'My Lord ... Is this real, or am I dreaming?'

Benjulius smiled. 'All is a matter of perspective.'

Of course. Nothing so simple as a straight answer. As the Feller learned from the Fairy King, the more potent the being, the more oblique its rhetoric. He fought back a wince.

'Lord, I do hope all is real. I feel the balm of your healers. The mountain trails almost ended me ... If I still lie back there, collapsed on the mountainside, I am undone.'

The benign smile remained. 'If you hope it is real, then real it shall be.'

The Archimage gave a brisk gesture. With a brilliant *snap*, white light flashed in the Feller's mind. The sense of dissociation vanished, along with the swirling veil from censers overhead.

His restitution proved true: The Feller carried no injury. Even the integrity of his battered raiment was restored, the axe sharp and glinting at his back.

New surprises waited beyond the curtain of his dream.

They stood in a yawning cathedral. Behind the Archimage, there were not four Warlocks, but closer to four thousand. Row upon Violet row, an army raised from history long past.

Benjulius read incredulity on the Fae axeman's face. 'You behold the preparation of an Age,' he said.

'But ... the Warlocks ...'

'By the grace of the Creator, the Warrior Adept are strong in number once more.'

'But how ...?'

Another flash and the Fairy Feller knew. The buried history of a people, long thought lost to Rhye, illuminated his mind.

The mysteries of a bygone era became known to him, in an instant.

'Oh,' he said. His mouth formed a perfect letter 'O'.

Benjulius held his hands wide. 'You understand now, young Feller, that the Adept have not sat idle, as the rest of Rhye prepared for cataclysm. We recall the Godsryche. We remember the tragedy of loss. This time, we stand in readiness. The host before you embodies our pledge.

'Though the Lords may fall, the last of us will stand united. Upon the moors of Fenmarck Haunte, the armies of sylphs and humans — and yes, even the Fae — will face the forces of Necromancy. War himself marches at their fore. They believe they will conquer, but lo, they will be routed, for the wrath of the Warrior Adept is unsurpassed.

'This is our final bid for a hero, a Song ... and a new King of Rhye.'

The Feller nodded. 'The words of the Prophet are manifest. Lord Oberon feared the breaking of the Fae Ring. He sends me with a message — and a task — to help protect the remaining Sovereigns.'

Condolences flickered in the eyes of Benjulius. 'Your mission to Aerglo shall be the final legacy of the Fairy King — his parting blow to our enemies. Alas, the mighty Oberon is dead. Those of us who live on must redouble our efforts, that his passing shall not be in vain.'

The Fairy Feller's 'O' returned. His head sank and he mumbled a quiet prayer.

'You have not failed him,' continued the Archimage, in a softer tone. 'You arrive at the perfect moment. Moreover — as you know — only you could deliver such a message ... for it is you who are destined to fulfil it.'

The Fairy Feller said nothing. The Archimage already knew the message that Lord Oberon had entrusted to him. Only the task itself remained.

'Will you carry forth the will of your Lord, the Fairy King?'

Another nod. 'I shall, Archimage.'

The Wearer of White gave an approving smile. At his back, thousands of Warlocks raised their arms, hands aflame. In unison, they shouted a battle cry. As the choir of their voices echoed through the cathedral, towers of roaring, purple fire reached for the roof, from every pair of hands.

The show of might was quelled and Benjulius spoke into the ensuing silence. 'Timbrad?'

A vortex of crimson power rose from the floor, between the Archimage and the Fairy Feller. When the churning red magic dissipated, in its place stood a formidable Wearer of Red. Resplendent in vibrant robes, lustrous, dark hair and a capable jaw, the Mage held an aura of great competence.

Timbrad executed a short bow before Benjulius.

'My Lord?'

'Mage Timbrad: Amidst such calamitous tidings as we have recently known, it is a moment for joy. We are joined, today, by the Fairy Feller.'

Timbrad regarded the Feller with a confident eye and a second respectful bow.

'Do I presume the honour of guiding him, my Lord?'

Benjulius confirmed, with a tilt of his head. 'There is no time to waste. Bring him fresh provisions, then direct him to the Way of the Prophet.'

CHAPTER 18

THE AIR YOU BREATHE

Mustapha ran as swift as a typhoon. Distance was no object in his race across Rhye. Quicksilver surged within him, charging every fibre with delectable might. He became, across the expanse of upper Nurtenan, an avatar of incarnate speed.

He felt lighter than the air around him, but for his heart, which carried a new weight. In his wake he left a lie, along with his crestfallen beloved. In hope, he imagined the moment of pain might have spared Will's life. An angry cry ripped from his throat as he cast Anuvin's sinister threat from his mind. Will would be *safe*.

The iota of relief did not prevent tears from streaking down his face as he ran.

Unbridled energy saw him hurtle through Rothgate, a remote *ville* where sylphs and humans alike dwelled on the fringe of the misty moors. The denizens of Rothgate knew little of the peril that lay beyond their valley. They looked up in pure wonder, as the strangeling whipped past with a determined dragonfly in pursuit.

He blasted across the Wracked Plains, where in the Age of Obelis, the armies of Walther Giltenan crossed blades with the sylphic host of General Prime Arnaut Vrendar. After decades of bloody conflict, that same arena would see an alliance forged between man and sylph.

Harold, striving to keep up, gained altitude to remain in sight of his friend.

Next, they came to the Hidden Wolds. Legends sang of secret meetings in those glades, between sylphs and Adept. None knew to what agenda they conspired; only that the Wolds were shaped by the potent theurgy of Mages ... power seldom seen, in latter days.

Mustapha ran with the strength of the divine. He held vague recollections of wanting to ride the great pterippi. Now, he bolted across the land, he himself a creature of God-power.

As he travelled, the storm clouds gathered and the rain fell once more. Mustapha became aware of swollen fens, broken dams, and treacherous low-lying floodwater. Though he swerved and detoured to avoid them, he dared not slacken his gift of speed.

At length, dragonfly and strangeling entered the Greenway, a verge of rolling hills that nudged against the looming Vultan Range. Mustapha climbed the foothills with gleeful strides and leaps, rising above the threat of floods. From this elevation, he saw across the vast moors of Fenmarck Haunte, home to wailing banshees, hostile swamp wights and the doom of many lost expeditions.

On the distant north-east horizon rose the Peaks of Obelis. The jagged fangs of a megalithic beast, reaching for the turbulent sky. Above the range soared the greatest peak in all of Rhye: Two-Way Mirror Mountain. Few other natural landmarks, save for Oberon's Yew, fostered such fervent superstition. To approach the Mountain would tempt the wrath of the Gods; besides, it would bring a hapless wanderer within eyeshot of the fell creatures trapped inside.

Mustapha's vision — made vivid by the same magic that coursed in his veins — alighted not on Two-Way Mirror Mountain, but on the calamity that spewed from beyond it. An immense thunderhead, such as Harold had described, engulfed the sky in a blanket of horror. Dread bolts of lightning danced in the heavens and walked across the land. The storm front issued beyond the Peaks of Obelis and over the far reaches of Fenmarck Haunte, threatening to cast despair all over northern Rhye.

Mustapha strove harder, pushing his limits. The hours passed, league by miraculous league. To his left, the sheer Vultans rose as cliffs — a battlement for giants. In his enlightened mind, he knew the terrain like a seasoned voyager. In the diminishing distance, he sought a mountain pass — one he knew would take him to lofty, wind-blown trails, where only the hardiest would venture.

There lay the irrefutable fortress of Wintergard.

Overhead, Harold matched every twist and turn of the strangeling's journey. As true evening fell, they took a final glimpse at the cataclysm unfolding in the north-east.

The trenchant Vultan Range enveloped them.

General Prime Bastian Sinotar rarely sat idle.

Renowned for operating on little sleep, he often traversed the barracks and passages of Wintergard in the strange hours, even in times of relative peace. Now that a sequence of events threatened the very foundations of Rhye, his activity had ramped to a new level of dynamism.

He swept through the breezeways and barracks-chambers, conferring with his senior officers, evaluating intelligence, and formulating lines of defence and counterstrike.

The true enemy remained concealed, which provided a unique challenge.

Sinotar stalked through the Tarven Wing, eyes forward, mouth set in a customary grim line. The austere lack of ornamentation in the Wing — as throughout most of Wintergard — gave the space a tone of frugal functionality, in keeping with the lives of Vrendari warriors.

Under ordinary circumstances, Sinotar favoured this Wing over all other places in the sylphic stronghold. It featured a landing platform with a giant window, looking out over the dramatic mountain vista. From here, the General Prime could reflect on the lot of his people. Not all sylphs were Vrendari. The lofts of civilians pockmarked the sheer sides of surrounding peaks. Hunters, engineers, artisans, and clerics all dwelled within the honeycombed range, forever under the guardianship of those who donned armour and bore lethal weapons.

Coming days brought peril to them all.

The General Prime did not divert his gaze to the windows as he passed. He headed at pace for the Brumada Map Room, for his second briefing of the morning. His boots sounded a brisk tempo upon the polished stone.

The Map Room bristled with efficiency. Scores of platinum-tressed heads and ruffling sets of wings moved about in ceaseless activity. Subordinate Vrendari arrived from distant sectors, with intelligence for their commanding officers, before leaving again with new instructions. The officers — Majors, Commanders and Brigadiers — swarmed about a huge tablet, illustrating a large topographical view of Rhye. Officers pushed markers all over the map, updating the known movements of allied and opposing entities.

As the General Prime entered, all stood at attention. The Vrendari sensed his crackling energy in the Room.

'Proceed,' he ordered. Activity resumed.

Commander Dexler Roth approached him, presenting the Vrendari salute: hands held over the chest, in a representation of eagle's wings.

Sinotar returned the gesture. 'Give me a sitrep. Western Eyrie,' he said.

Commander Roth delivered a sombre and succinct situation report. Sentries positioned at the Western Eyrie — one of twin lookout posts, each a day's hike from Wintergard — had signalled a bleak update.

'General Prime. In the early hours of this morning, our eyes detected a severe upheaval in the region of Warnom Bore.'

'I was myself privy to it,' replied Sinotar. He had been taking rare respite in his quarters when a distant rumble roused him. 'What more do we know?'

'Sir, the sentries could not detect much at such a distance in the poor light, though later in the morning, appearances were of some great seismic disturbance, or sudden tectonic shift.'

'Hm. The Peaks of Light are not volcanic. The Bore itself, however, is a conduit from the floor of the Ealing Sea. What is the latest intelligence?'

'The Ealing Sea now visits the land, sir.'

'Spell it out for me,' growled Sinotar.

Roth's face was stone grey. 'A blast brought down the side of a neighbouring mountain. The resulting avalanche spilled debris across a square league. Water flooded the pass between the Peaks and the Corridor. The best evaluation is that the water erupted from the Bore itself.'

Sinotar choked down a groan.

As the Lord of a militaristic race, his thoughts flew directly to casualties. He knew little of what may have caused the catastrophe

— his astute mind could certainly speculate — though he held primary concern for the golems.

'Sitrep, Eastern Eyrie,' he said, with a bitter inflection.

'The black pall continues to rise from a place beyond Two-Way Mirror Mountain, sir. Nobody can be certain, but its origin appears to be Nevermore.'

'It is not a storm cloud, then? If even one cast by some dark theurgy?'

'No, General Prime. It is a plume that rises, like steam might, from one of those mining or farming machines ... except that this one is vast beyond compare. It brings a terrible power, like none but the Adept could muster.'

'Range?'

'It spills well south of the Peaks of Obelis, out over Fenmarck Haunte. Range is difficult, sir, as the cloud advances rapidly. It has risen to this from nought in less than three days.'

The beginnings of despondency flickered across Sinotar's face.

'Anything more?' asked the General Prime, staring off over Commander Roth's winged shoulder.

'Yes, sir. From the Eastern Eyrie: You have visitors.'

Sinotar's gaze snapped back to meet Roth's. 'Elaborate.'

'Two beings arrive from the Greenway Pass —'

'Two?'

'Two, sir.'

The twitch of a smile replaced despondency. 'Continue.'

'They appear to have made the journey without aid,' Roth said. 'One is a dragonfly. The other ... we cannot be sure. He has pointed ears, like ours, or perhaps those of the Fae, though he is neither. He may be a Wilden, only he is too forthright —'

A wry grin curled the General Prime's lip at one end. 'Do you not recognise this one? Does he not look familiar?'

'Why no, sir. He is a strange creature, bedecked in garb I do not recognise. Should I know him?'

Sinotar waved the question away. 'Are they armed?'

'Not that we detected, sir. The dragonfly bears some form of musical instrument. We are suspicious it may conceal something, for it does not issue sound.'

For a long while — almost to the point of awkwardness — the General Prime said nothing. An unfathomable look crossed his stern features — softening edges, smoothing creases. A light like realised prophecy burned in his eyes.

Finally, he nodded. 'Bring them into Wintergard.'

'Sir?'

'I have a missive to prepare. I will be in my quarters. Provide for them cured game and *vapir*. I will meet with them presently.'

'Where will you give them audience?'

'The Sacristy.' The General Prime turned away.

Roth stared in dumb shock. 'Sir?'

'Follow your orders, Commander,' barked Sinotar, whirling on him. 'And if you give me one more "Sir", I'll dock your wings with the dullest blade I can find.'

Like a dragonfly trapped, Harold's attention shifted in erratic bursts around the chamber. He worked to regain his breath, still coming in exhausted heaves. At least his teeth had ceased chattering.

'Something is very out of place, here,' he puffed.

Mustapha did not respond immediately. He sipped *vapir* from a goblet in long, slow draughts. The beverage, made from crisp alpine spring water and the fermented juice of mountain berries, acted as a potent restorative. His gleaming brown eyes absorbed their surroundings as he drank.

'I see what you mean. It is decidedly un-sylphic, isn't it?'

Their passage into the sylphs' domain brought many eye-opening moments, with this room perhaps the most astonishing of all.

The indomitable force of the White Queen's gift swept Mustapha to the doorstep of Wintergard. Harold scraped in behind him, using every ounce of his strength just to keep up. A huge, vaulted gate formed the entrance to the sylphic fortress. It stood closed, guarded by armoured Vrendari. Above the gate, a megalithic wall of granite rose towards the clouds. In the sky over the gate and the mountain trail, dark specks zoomed around cathedral-spire peaks: sylphs, on currents of air, using their natural ability to traverse their majestic home.

The two Vrendari on sentry duty could have been clones. Tall males, clad in their distinctive, burnished armour, glistening shades of dusk in the crepuscular air. Both owned long, platinum hair tied back in a severe ponytail. Their faces suggested simultaneous wariness and bafflement. Evaluating the newcomers as little threat, they left their weapons sheathed.

The strangeling stepped forward, intent on directness. 'I am Mustapha. This is Harold, of the Fae. We are allies of your General Prime and wish to speak with him.'

With a doubtful air, one sentry sought their Captain, who appeared and appraised the pair with vague interest.

The Captain conferred with the Vrendari recently returned from the Western Eyrie, before seeking her Major.

The Major peered at the two with an air of genuine intrigue, before going in search of the Brigadier.

The Brigadier simply gawped, wide-eyed, as if seeing a childhood campfire yarn come to life.

He questioned them. 'From whence have you come?'

'Most recently, the Wilden Ream, sir,' answered Harold, shivering and panting tiny clouds of condensation. 'Before that, Petrichor.'

'How did you arrive? You appear alone and unaided.'

'I flew,' said Harold, clearly exhausted.

'I ran,' said Mustapha, seemingly fresh.

The Brigadier frowned. 'Search them,' he ordered the sentries. 'I will confer with Commander Roth.'

Soon, the strangeling and the dragonfly were led through the massive gate. Harold was allowed to keep his horn.

They were guided, not by a sentry, but by a seasoned, battle-hardened sylph of middle age. Mustapha recognised Commander Dexler Roth, having last encountered him at the Council of Rhye. The Commander appeared not to know him, which suited Mustapha well. The Council brought back memories of ignominy and accusation.

A tremendous vault welcomed the travellers. The entryway had a ceiling, soaring high above them. From this vast communal space, myriad passages, openings, and halls branched, at multiple levels. The stronghold stood over twenty storeys high. Deeper within, all facilities and destinations were neatly signed. Surfaces were of clean, polished stone, the walls adorned only by necessary maps, direction markers and panels of scrallin.

The sound of footfalls reverberated through the vast interior of Wintergard. Not just the bootsteps of Roth and his charges, but of many hundreds of sylphs. Everywhere Mustapha and Harold looked, flocks of Vrendari strode or flew, hurrying about their business. Harold watched agape as squadrons of winged warriors marched, in perfect unison, in front of him. The group of two-dozen sylphs emerged from an intersecting corridor. They headed in an arrow-straight line towards another enormous space, hewn from the vault of the mountain, which lay exposed to the frigid world outside by a massive portal.

'Impressive,' gasped Harold.

'That is the Hangar,' explained Roth. 'Launch and retrieval facility for all airborne missions. Not a place for ... civilians.' He delivered this last line with a dubious side-eye to the pair next to him.

As they passed the door to the Hangar, Harold caught an awed glimpse of the Vrendari might on display within. Entire regiments stood in razor-sharp lines, awaiting briefing and dispatch, destined for sorties throughout Nurtenan and beyond.

Roth hurried the lingering dragonfly onwards.

The Commander led Mustapha and Harold further into Wintergard. Training barracks, administration wings, mission planning centres and a huge armoury all interconnected with a central channel, which drove deep into the ancient breast of the mountain. The interior of the stronghold resembled an orderly hive of passages and chambers, centred around the very heart of the Vultans. At every step, minimalist architecture offered them a blank stare. Not a statue, nor an idol, nor a sign of leisure could be seen.

'Not big on recreation?' ventured Mustapha.

'If Vrendari wish for holidays, they are deployed to Via,' replied Roth.

The Commander's response did not clarify whether this was considered reward or punishment. Mustapha recalled his conversation with Leith, in the warmer climes of Kash Valley. For her, deployment represented time away from family.

Ahead of the Commander, sentried doorways opened without question, accompanied by crisp Vrendari salutes. The trio passed through several such portals, leading to less populated zones within the fortress. Soon enough, they were alone in a scrallin-lit corridor. Footsteps echoed with the resonance of a tomb.

Harold tried to remember their route but became horribly lost. Mustapha, fascinated by all he saw, said nothing.

Eventually, Commander Roth showed the pair into a small, unidentified antechamber. They arrived at a simple door, likewise without designation. Roth opened it with a key, drawn from inside his own breastplate.

'The General Prime wishes for you to wait in here,' he said.

The pair baulked on the threshold. Beyond, a warm glow emanated, candlelight upon gold. The room itself thrummed with a sense of occasion, rather than danger.

Commander Roth folded his arms. 'I am not a manservant. Enter and be seated. You will find refreshments. The General Prime has deigned to meet with you — pray spend his time wisely.'

'Pray ...?' said the dragonfly, once he and Mustapha were alone.

'Mhm,' said Mustapha, pulling flesh from a roasted mountain goat haunch with his teeth. His eyes flicked around the room, but the joint of meat dominated his attention.

They perched on a wooden bench, like a pew, adjacent to a low table. These two bland furnishings were the only congruous items, in an otherwise remarkable room.

The immaculate space welcomed them, a cosy invitation to worship. Cedar and teak, inlaid with gold, formed panels lining every wall, of which there were seven. Ornate tapers of ever-present scrallin lit the heptagonal room. The tapers stood as tall as an adult human, their light butter yellow, in welcome contrast to the chill of polished stone throughout the fortress. The glint of gold and encrusted precious stones winked in every corner.

A shrine dominated the room, set against one wall, upon a low stage. It stood the full height of the room — about twelve feet — and immediately enthralled Harold.

The shrine featured a sculpture in pure gold, writhing and undulating with the lifelike forms of intermingled bodies. Eleven gracious figures, frozen in a moment of ecstasy, lay beneath beaming images of the Sun and Moon.

The dragonfly could not mistake the forms of sprightly Oska, rotund Phydeas or waif-like Floe. The third eye of Valendyne glared out at the viewer, issuing a curse immortalised in gold.

'I don't understand,' he said.

The entire Pantheon loomed over them.

Mustapha stood, approaching the shrine to study it more closely. The skill and detail bespoke a phenomenal artistry.

'Not what we thought we'd find in the middle of sylphic territory,' he replied. 'I suppose we are about to find out ... Hey! Look at this, Harold. The item Anuvin is holding —'

The click of an opening door behind them caught him mid-sentence. Harold jumped from the pew. Mustapha whirled around.

Bastian Sinotar stood at the door through which they had entered.

Solemnity replaced the typical storm-front of his visage. In his crystal blue eyes, there shone a light that seemed to come from within a bottomless pool.

In a further surprise, he wore no armour.

A long gown adorned his form, with a sky blue stole about his shoulders. His wings were stowed, composed and unruffled, at his back.

With eyes fixed on the two companions, Sinotar entered the room.

'You survived ... again,' he said to the strangeling.

Mustapha bounded from the stage, striding to meet him.

In recent times, the leonine figure of the General Prime had intimidated him. Now –

'We need some answers,' said Mustapha, adopting a hands-on-hips stance, two feet in front of the sylph.

Sinotar studied him, dressed all in white: from the winged boots and the blanched leggings wrapped around his deer-like lower limbs, to the satin tunic and cropped *chaquetilla* in white brocade. To top it all, the shock of wild, dark hair. The strangeling looked for all the world like a Wilden creature, yet ...

'Yes, you do,' answered Sinotar. He issued a Vrendari salute and held out his forearm in a gesture of offered alliance. 'There's a lot to be said and little time to say it.'

After a moment's hesitation, Mustapha accepted Sinotar's embrace. Both gripped firmly, a meeting of peers. Sinotar lowered his head in a fractional bow, then turned to Harold.

The dragonfly had no words. He stumbled forward and grasped the General Prime's proffered forearm. As he did, Sinotar's eye flickered over the ancient horn, still slung at Harold's back.

All three settled around the table.

'Early this morning, the Peaks of Light sustained a seismic assault,' briefed the General Prime. 'The event brought landslide, ruin and floods to the surrounding region.

'Our best intelligence would suggest that War has made landfall in Rhye.'

Harold grimaced. 'Surely, he would have met staunch resistance amidst the forces of the Mer-Lord?'

Sinotar shook his head. 'It seems beyond likelihood. Anuvin is a God, with inestimable wrath. We must assume that Lord Neptune has met his end.'

The air in the Sacristy grew oppressive.

Mustapha spoke. 'War comes from the west. Storms and

flooding roll in from the east. A creeping sickness un-homes the people of the south. The Prophet's warnings of despair are upon us.

'If the threats of the Song become real, can we dare to hope that a saviour also might be found? The Seer spoke of renewal. Could it be true? The shadows lengthen, but we seem no closer to answering the augury.'

Mustapha prayed that he might draw out the General Prime — that the sylph might be emboldened to reveal himself as the long-awaited King of Rhye.

Bastian Sinotar grappled with Mustapha's question. More than mere consternation knitted his brow — he truly exerted himself. There came the characteristic jaw clench, along with turgid forehead veins that looked set to rupture.

Harold leaned forward. 'Are you okay, General Prime?'

Sinotar spat, the tension broken. 'Lily spoke of sacrifice, as well,' he grated. 'Let us not forget that, in our enthusiasm.'

Rage faded from the sylph's face. Regaining himself, he turned to Harold.

'The instrument you carry. May I see it?'

Bewildered, Harold reached to unclasp the horn, passed to him by Trixel Tate. Sinotar held palpable interest in the mysterious item — his tone morphed from wolfish snarl to near supplication, at the mere notion of it.

'Sure, here it is. Can you tell us about it? I can't muster the slightest sound from it.'

Sinotar held out reverent hands, as if accepting a sacred and fragile relic. He turned it over, studying it, the wisp of a smile parting the clouds of his face.

'Of course, he can tell us about it,' Mustapha interjected, leaping from his seat. He returned to the low stage, stabbing a finger towards the golden shrine. 'The horn is depicted right there.

Perhaps, General Prime, you could explain what this is all about? This shrine. This room. All of it.'

Sinotar nodded. 'That is why I brought you here.'

The sylph prepared to relate his tale. All ire fled from his voice, replaced by a deep, resonant calm.

'I realise that this room challenges your expectations,' he began. 'It is meant to. This is the one place in all Sylphdom that lies behind a great façade, maintained for millennia. None but the highest ranks of my own people have been within these seven walls. It is death for my people to speak of it, amongst any but themselves. This shrine — and all it represents — has waited here, holding the true heart of the Sylphic race, for this very moment.'

'I still don't understand,' said Harold. 'The "true heart of the Sylphic race"? Are you saying that your people are, in truth, devout? This shrine is clearly a place of worship … for whom? Only you?'

'It is indeed a place of worship. A place of absolute communion.' Sinotar bowed his head and continued.

'At the end of the Godsryche, Cornavrian traversed the land, seeking the greatest attributes of every higher race. These he used in securing the Fae Ring, ensnaring Valendyne in Nevermore. This much you know.

'Your schoolbooks probably told you that the sylphic people defied him, choosing a secular life instead. That part of the story was the lie, told to protect one of the most compelling secrets of the Pantheon.'

Sinotar looked up. He held the attention of Mustapha and Harold in a steel vice.

'In truth, Cornavrian encountered the most devoted race of beings in all of Rhye. A people prepared to die for their faith — to pledge their lives in battle against the acolytes of Valendyne.

'In return for that pledge, Cornavrian conferred upon my race a sacred and powerful gift, which would bring to bear the full force of Nature, at a time when such was needed most. To protect this gift, the sylphs assumed an outward culture of militant atheism, shielding the treasure within.'

'What is this gift?' said Mustapha.

'The sylphs were blessed with the power to awaken a relic, left upon the broken battlefield of the Godsryche, within Mages Pass. A relic recovered by the then-young Lord of the Fae. You may recall him, for his name was Oberon.'

Harold glanced at the shrine, glistening in ambient scrallin-light, then back at the instrument in Sinotar's hands.

'Are you telling me ... that this is the Horn of Agonies?'

Sinotar nodded. 'One and the same.'

Mustapha wore a knowing look.

The dragonfly's mind boggled.

Sinotar moved to the shrine, placing the Horn of Agonies on the stage, and instructing the others to kneel, one on either side of him.

'In the days that follow, great realisation will come to you both,' he said. 'This is our reckoning. Though we fall short in the eyes of the Pantheon, may they see our plight and show us the way through this darkness.'

He spoke in a tongue Harold did not recognise. Mustapha, on the other hand, twitched; the ancient prayer evoked in him a sense of the familiar. He squirmed, as if reminded of something uncomfortable.

Of its own accord, the shrine swung on unseen hinges, opening like a door with a whine of protestation.

Sinotar rose from his kneeling and beckoned, ushering the others through. Beyond the portal, a tunnel of rough-hewn rock gaped. From somewhere within, the whistle and howl of a chill wind met their ears.

Mystified, Harold and Mustapha obeyed.

A brief tunnel, primitive in adornment, wound through the mountain. At the far end, the promise of light ensured that they were never truly groping blind. The confident footfalls of Sinotar led them, without faltering, along fifty yards of dim passage. All the while, the yowling winds grew closer, creating an icy draft that swirled around them.

Emerging from the tunnel brought a vertiginous shock to the senses.

The three alighted on a tiny stone balcony. Below, a colossal circular pit sank into the core of the mountain, with no floor in sight. Above, the peaks of the surrounding Vultans peered over the abyss, forming a border to the open sky.

Harold wavered, gripping the low, stone wall that hemmed them in — the only obstacle between them and the yawning crevasse.

Frigid wind blasted from below, forceful enough to tear Harold from the air and dash him against the mountainside, should he attempt to fly. As they stood, watching motes of ice being hurled about, the wind calmed. Peace and silence reigned for several moments, before once again the bluster ripped from the blue-black depths.

Bastian Sinotar waited until he could be heard without shouting. 'This is our sacred gift: the Breath of Cornavrian.'

Harold and Mustapha knelt in awe. The General Prime made a gesture of prayer with his hands — the same they had seen Leith Lourden execute, within the Wilden Realm.

'Once Horn and Breath are united, Harold,' said Sinotar, 'you will be in possession of a tool, lost to Rhye since the God of War himself wielded it.'

With trembling pincers, Harold took the Horn of Agonies back from Sinotar. His heart pounded in his throat and his mouth felt as dry as tinder. He leaned over the edge of the balcony, holding the instrument aloft — an offering to the Elements.

They waited.

The universe stood still.

Flakes of snow fluttered on the becalmed air.

Then, the preternatural howl rose from the pit, bringing with it a torrid rush of air. The gelid blast spliced them to the bone. Harold cried out, a wail of terror. A moment later, the hurricane winds tossed them all to the ground.

CHAPTER 19

UNTIL THE LONELINESS IS GONE

By the wan scrallin-light, Sinotar's face glowed pale, almost spectral. His lower lip hung quivering, on the verge of some revelation.

Mustapha sat, looking back at him in expectation. He had never seen the General Prime so vulnerable.

Mustapha and Harold had spent two further days accommodated in spartan quarters amidst the barracks. With each day — almost with each passing hour — the fervour of preparation escalated. A sense of the inevitable grew, like a chancre. Sinotar paced the gang-walks and cornices of Wintergard at all hours — a slick of sweat beading on his brow, fatigue darkening beneath his eyes.

Then came the late evening knock on Mustapha's door. Hardly the disposition of an imperious Sylphic Lord. Sinotar appeared on the threshold, dressed in a simple tunic and robe. With a bow and a wordless wave, the strangeling bid him to enter. Together, they sat on a thin rug covering the floor.

'The last time I recall a midnight confessional like this, the news wasn't good,' said Mustapha, remembering Lily's fateful predictions.

'You seem to have a knack for shrugging off bad news,' the General Prime replied, his baritone lacking its usual gravel. 'I understand it: Something has changed in you. You almost died. Now, you're fearless.'

'Lily told me that I was going to die. So … there's really only one thing left I fear.'

'What is that?'

'I fear that this won't end the way it's supposed to.'

'Oh? Do you know how it is supposed to end?'

Mustapha slapped his own crossed legs in frustration.

'Oh, come on!' he cried. 'For how much longer will we play this charade, when war is at your doorstep and the world is on the cusp of ruin? I see you, fading away with stress and worry. It's time we came clean with each other. I'll go first.

'I know about Lady Maybeth Giltenan. I know the two of you would meet in secret. I know she did not perish when she disappeared. In fact, in a sense, she lives still. Her life-force, transmuted by Lhestra, occupies the stronghold of the Wilden Lord. The Goddess appeared to her, naming her the "Pillar of Rhye" and the "White Queen".

'Now, the tide can turn back … but it is up to you. You see, your Lady sang a final song. A lament it may have been, but also a song of hope. In it, she sang of you … King of Rhye.'

The silence that followed yawned wide, a crevice in the earth.

The two stared at each other; competing wills, with competing truths. The barrage of Mustapha's words stormed across the gaping space between them — an interminable distance, yet only a couple of feet.

In the half-light, the strangeling saw it: Tears rolled down Bastian Sinotar's weathered face.

He made no sound, as he purged the passion of years in a raw torrent. His body shook. The bitterness of secrets kept was washed away.

Mustapha reached for him, but Sinotar swatted his open hand away.

'No,' growled the sylph, features twisted in grief. 'You think yourself clever — you are not. You have misconstrued the situation in breathtaking fashion. Now, it's time for you to sit and listen, while I set your story straight.'

Shadows crowded at the edges of Sinotar's mien. Mustapha realised the sylph cast his mind back to a time of pain — a time Mustapha understood very little.

'Maybeth Giltenan was an icon of grace amidst Humankind,' said Sinotar. 'A spectacle of love and humility.'

Mustapha sat without speaking. Until that moment, he would not have anticipated hearing the word *love* cross the General Prime's lips.

Sinotar settled into his reverie. 'Lhestra and Floe were the foci of her prayers, which suited her to perfection. Children formed the pillar of her heart. She recognised that, without fostering hope for the new generation, the future would be lost.

'I long believed that the Goddesses had invested power in Maybeth. Perhaps, from what you said of her transformation, it shows that I was right.

'I loved her. With all my energy, I loved her. Born on the same day, in the same year, we were kindred spirits. I watched her build safe houses for orphaned children, with little but her own bare hands. Along with those houses, the fortifications of my heart grew, as well.

'I was forced to watch from afar, of course. It was too difficult to work alongside her and keep my affections inside; but also, it was a time of unrest in Fenmarck Haunte. My attention was with my own people and our campaigns here in the north.

'Still, we found opportunities for escape. I would meet her at Duck House, a retreat overlooking the Imperial Waters. It was far from the prying eyes of Sylphdom and Humankind. A place where our contentious union would be ours alone.'

Mustapha broke in. 'Why do you think this barricade exists? Why cannot sylphs and humans love one another and be together? Fairies and pixies do it all the time. Look at Trixel Tate — she was born of such a union. Blast it, even Maybeth pursued a new liaison with the Wilden Lord. Could this not be seen as legitimate?'

Sinotar gave a brief, low chuckle, though his features winced. 'You make a good point,' he conceded. There seemed to be more for a moment, but he left his thoughts by the wayside. 'It has been the reality since the alliance proposed by Montreux Giltenan. What began as a feudal policy, filtered its way into the culture of both races. Now, it is taken for granted: Never the two shall meet.

'Maybeth and I knew from the start that our liaison was doomed. The representative leaders of both races, in love? It would either revolutionise interracial relations, or shatter the foundations of both societies, fracturing the alliance. Yes, it may have been the courageous act our cultures needed to move forward ... but neither of us wanted to risk the alternative, to meet our own selfish ends.

'It proved Maybeth's strength of spirit when she turned her heart away. Though it tore me in two, I knew our parting to be an inevitable thing.

'Now, as you have pointed out with such eloquence, Maybeth did, in time, journey to seek a union with the Wilden Lord. On the surface, it was a political move. I resigned myself to never knowing if she gave her heart — as well as her allegiance — to Lord Vater. The two of them were certainly creatures of the same ilk. Both were true advocates for their people and voices for the sanctity of the Pantheon. Vater was a devotee of Augustine. He wanted to heal the world, in a literal sense.'

Mustapha leaned forward, ready to interject again. 'The rest I know,' he said. 'Lady Maybeth was entrapped by Lord Ponerog, who had slain his own father. Ponerog abused and tortured your Lady love for many years. But no matter the grief — no matter what she had pledged to Lord Vater — she loved you. She loves you still. It is a love that shines as a beacon of power in a darkened —'

Mustapha halted, for in front of him, Sinotar held up a single finger. In his cloak of dim light and prophetic shadows, the gesture held greater potency than any word.

'You do not know the rest,' said the sylph, with a quiet gravity. 'The one truth of greatest importance is absent from your telling.'

Once again, Sinotar fought a battle with unspoken thoughts. His proud face had, over the passage of days, grown ascetic. A burden gnawed at him. He bared his teeth, railing against it.

In a few moments, he mastered himself. Resolute eyes met with Mustapha, across the intimate space.

'You see,' said Sinotar, 'when Maybeth journeyed to the Wilden Realm … she was already with child.'

Mustapha reeled, rocking back in his place from the General Prime.

The void that followed the sylph's words sank deeper than the pit of Cornavrian's Breath. *With child.* The implications raced in the strangeling's mind like tempest winds.

'No … I don't …' he uttered; his thick tongue unsure of the words it formed. 'Are you saying —'

'You must hear this, Mustapha,' said Sinotar, their eyes now locked. 'It is your story. Only in knowing your past can you hope to understand your destiny.'

Mustapha felt the weight of the mountain fortress pressing down on him. He searched Sinotar's face, looking for the signs he had missed. His tumultuous thoughts still clattered on apace.

'Maybeth Giltenan went to the Wilden Realm with my child in her womb,' said Sinotar, more calmly than the strangeling had ever seen him. 'You ... you are our son.'

Mustapha broke. The flood of excess emotion poured down his face. Was it joy at the revelation? Or anguish, at so many lost years — a misplaced youth? He swayed in his place, unsure whether to embrace his father, or vomit. He brushed hot tears from his cheeks with a sleeve. Through blurry eyes, he looked back at Sinotar.

'Go on,' he said. 'Tell me the rest.'

Now the sylph spoke as one unbridled — as if the telling was a burden relieved. 'The rest is something I myself only learned over a year later. When Maybeth disappeared, I did not know of her pregnancy. I would come to discover the truth from Lord Oberon, who had by chance — or perhaps by prophecy — become involved.'

'By prophecy?'

Sinotar nodded. 'The series of events is as follows.

'As Oberon told it, at some time over two hundred years ago, he sought out the Seer of Kash Valley. With him at the time was the halfling, Trixel Tate. They went in pursuit of augury concerning the Fae Ring, for Oberon had sensed an uneasy tremor in his percipience.

'Apparently — his words, not mine — the Seer told Oberon that the fate of the Fae Ring lay entwined with certain events on the distant horizon.

'The first event would be a union between a sylph and a human, born on the same day. The sylph would be a leader of his race, while the human would be blessed by the Gods themselves.

'Oberon was canny, his memory long. He kept the Seer's counsel in his mind until Maybeth and I were born, fifty-two years ago. He watched us grow — Maybeth rising to the head of her dynastic clan, I climbing the ranks to sylphic Generalship. He must have watched us for all those years, Council by Council, our lives edging closer together. We thought we were so surreptitious ... yet, Oberon knew.

'The second thing the Seer told him was that from our union would be born a child — a unique creature in all of Rhye. The child must be protected at all costs, for its life would be inextricable from the fate of the Fae Ring ... and of the land itself.'

Mustapha swallowed, forcing down a wave of nausea. His fingers and toes were numb, while the back of his neck prickled. The room engulfed him.

'This is the part I don't like,' he said.

Sinotar did not relent. 'Oberon swore to the Seer that he would help protect you — with his own life, if necessary. He convinced Titania of your importance, as well. I can only imagine his despair when Maybeth wandered into oblivion, before giving birth.

'This much I do know: His passion and sense of duty were such that he mounted an offensive into Banwah Haunte, intent on liberating both you and Maybeth. Leaving Trixel Tate at his seat of power in Psithur Grove, he rode into the Wilden Realm with a force of Fae knights. There, heavy conflict ensued. You were saved, though Oberon could not wrest Lady Maybeth away. Lord Ponerog declared that she had vowed to stay with him, for they would be realising a great legacy together. In the name of the late Lord Vater — and with Floe and Augustine as their patrons — the two would unite to create a sanctuary like nothing seen before.

'Oberon harboured doubts, but in the end, he left Banwah Haunte with only the child ... you. By way of a peace treaty, in exchange for your life, he promised not to march unannounced on the Wilden Realm again.

'He never actually saw Lady Maybeth through this entire exchange. He determined this must be her will.'

Mustapha exhaled. 'So that is how I came to live in Petrichor.'

'From your infancy, yes. Oberon sent me a missive, by dragonfly, in the aftermath of your rescue. In it, he told me of your birth and of the Seer's prophecies. Protecting your lineage had now become more than an issue of human-sylphic relations, for it was also linked to the security of the Fae Ring. Oberon promised me that he would watch over you, revealing your past to nobody, until a time came when the hand of destiny interceded and took you away from him.'

'Belladonna,' breathed Mustapha. 'She solicited me to steal sap from Oberon's Yew. I still don't know what she wanted it for ... but that was the trigger for my expulsion from Petrichor. She presented herself as my saviour, lest I be executed for treason.

'I wonder now, knowing it all, whether Oberon and Titania would truly have had me put to death.'

'The question would have brought him tremendous anguish,' replied Sinotar. 'To uphold the law of his own people, or to honour a vow he had made — a vow of great import. The arrival of Belladonna was no doubt a miraculous thing, to him.'

'The hand of destiny,' agreed Mustapha.

A new air hung between them. Certainly, it was fresh — Mustapha was yet to reconcile the General Prime as his true sire — but a sense of earnest camaraderie now prevailed.

Questions still rankled in his mind.

'You're leaving something out,' he said. 'What was the third thing the Seer told Oberon?'

Sinotar ran fingers through his lank hair. 'The third prophecy aligns with what Lily has already told you. Our son would be the one to cross the Seventh Sea … the hero who would find a new Song to save Rhye.'

'Ah,' said Mustapha, expression blank. 'So, I am the sacrifice. That is why she knew I would die.'

Sinotar was grey-faced. 'That is all guesswork and speculation,' he said, a morose note in his voice. 'There is no scripture which says you cannot survive this. We can prepare for it. I have prepared for it.'

'You have?'

'Yes. There was something more Oberon gave me — a piece of augury Lily held that she did not pass on to you. Perhaps she did not quite figure out who you were.

'The origin of the Song is a mystery to me, as it was to Oberon,' he continued. 'But the Seer was able to provide a key to finding it. A key as mysterious as the Song itself. Lily passed it to Oberon. Now, father to son, I am passing it to you.'

Sinotar reached inside his garment, bringing forth a single piece of fresh parchment, folded and sealed.

'Take this letter,' he said to Mustapha. 'Keep it and guard it with all of your strength. Though its contents may be obscure, you will understand it when the time is right.'

Mustapha screwed up his face in dismay, as he took the missive from his father. *Enter a forbidden garden. Cross an uncharted Sea. Find a revelatory Song. Try not to die in the process. Here is a piece of parchment to help you do it.*

The light shone dimly. He would not be able to make out what was written, even if it did make sense to him. Miffed, he slid the missive into his own tunic.

With an imploring look, he engaged Sinotar. 'Why me? I don't feel like I've come much closer to knowing myself. I don't feel ready to be any kind of hero. Or a martyr, what's more. What am I anyway, if part-man, part-sylph?'

Sinotar sighed. He had anticipated the question, though he knew the answer would challenge him.

'In many a lonely hour, I have prayed to Marnis for an answer. You are, after all, his creation ... there are simply no others like you.

'You see, you are indeed part-sylph and part-human ... but you are more than the sum of those parts. The White Queen has passed to you her essence, which contained the alchemic spark of the Pantheon. With it, you are discovering powers beyond the scope of any mortal. Even the Adept might struggle to contend with the likes of you.

'The sacred lore knows of only one outcome when higher beings are paired and granted hallowed power.

'You are a seraph.'

Mustapha frowned, baffled. He dared not question his father deeper, lest he become more confused. He let his mouth form the word. *Seraph.* As he did so, he felt a warmth in his chest and belly, like the heat from a nearby fire. Soon, it faded. He was left with only his bewilderment.

What in the world is a seraph?

The night wore on. They had reached the small hours. Little could be heard in the barracks beyond Mustapha's chamber.

No. I need to ask. I must know.

'General ... Sire. Father. You've had opportunities. Why didn't you tell me all of this before now?'

Sinotar smiled.

It was genuine. A smile of tacit warmth, though pain lanced in his eyes.

'Belladonna,' he answered. Seeing the return of Mustapha's frown, he continued. 'You said she was brewing some sort of elixir, a concoction that would somehow be a Cure for Rhye.

'In truth, she was formulating a hex of silence. I found it when I scoured her chamber in the House of Giltenan. A cauldron of rancid mixture, an icon of my image and the figurine of Valendyne. She was even so bold as to have the necromantic tome open to the appropriate page. I know exactly what she was doing with the sap of Oberon's Yew — procuring my silence.'

Mustapha looked perplexed. 'But … if it was a hex of silence, how are you able to tell me these things now?'

The smile appeared once again. 'It was never intended to keep my mouth physically closed. Belladonna only wanted to threaten me, should I ever open up to you about your lineage, assuming our paths would cross. Every time I've thought about it — every time the subject arose — the hex has threatened me, wracking my brain, turning my stomach, boiling my blood.

'Now, though … now, the hex is triggered. I've revealed to you what she was trying to hide.'

'So, now what?'

'Now, the revelation will cost me my life. I don't know when. I don't know how. But sometime soon, this hex will kill me.'

The following day, Commander Roth showed Harold and Mustapha into the Hangar.

Mustapha strove to conceal the daze of introspection he carried from the night before. If Harold noticed anything, he gave no sign.

There were plenty of other distractions.

As before, Vrendari of every rank moved about the space in a symphony of perfect order. The Hangar featured a massive external gate, which stood open. Into the vast interior flowed freezing gusts of air. They were mere wisps in comparison to the Breath of Cornavrian, but the wind still bit hard on exposed skin.

At intervals came the resonant tolling of a huge bell, suspended near the mouth of the Hangar. The pair soon discovered that this signalled departing missions. With each mighty *bong*, a squadron of winged soldiers lifted off the platform, becoming airborne in close-knit formation.

The atmosphere crackled, for these were missions long foretold. These would be forays into perilous territory, to engage with an enemy beyond hope of estimation.

Many Vrendari would not return once their booted feet left the floor of the Hangar this day.

The presence of four-score Adept took Harold and Mustapha by surprise. The Wearers of Green and Sky Blue were ushered into the ranks of those Vrendari squadrons being briefed on their missions. In their floor-length coloured robes and chasubles, they looked both out of place and somehow utterly congruent. The Adept fastened themselves into odd apparatus that resembled giant slings.

'You engage Apothecaries and Sorcerers on your offensive manoeuvres, too?' Harold asked.

'Certainly,' replied Roth. 'Ever since we learned of the plague creatures marching across Sontenan, we have actively recruited mission-ready Adept. The strategy is for each Apothecary — or Sorcerer — to fly using a special harness, adapted for use between two Vrendari. Together, each trio will form a tactical unit, able to neutralise any deleterious effects cast by the enemy.'

Mustapha's brows were raised. *Deleterious effects*. 'You're going to bombard the sickness-spawn with health potions, from the air.'

'In essence, yes.'

The wild, untested strategy held a fragment of promise.

'Now you just need a zany way to take down the God of War and contain an aberrant weather pattern,' remarked Harold.

Roth grimaced, leading them onwards.

Wintergard prepared to be purged. All frontline Vrendari, briefed for battle, would issue forth into Nurtenan over the coming hours. Harold and Mustapha were assigned to a squadron that would begin on foot, heading back towards Greenway Pass, before cutting east through the foothills towards Fenmarck Haunte.

From the Western Eyrie, the advance of Anuvin could now be witnessed with a spyglass. War sat astride a terrific monster, while at his flank, the Black Queen came in her pterippal form. At their back, a vast cloud of dust soon revealed itself to be a horde of craggy, lumbering creatures. Their movement was slow, but relentless. They would cross the Corridor into Fenmarck Haunte within a couple of days.

Bastian Sinotar's war strategy depended on it.

'Where is the General Prime?' asked Harold.

'Over there,' replied Mustapha, who spied an august and familiar figure, passing by many hundreds of assembled Vrendari.

Sinotar, a formidable presence on even the most mundane of days, commanded the Hangar merely by being within it.

Striding at the fore of half a dozen Commanders and Brigadiers, Sinotar marched as if even the Breath could not blow him away. He shone in full battle raiment. His armour was an intimidating display of sleek blades and protective plates, giving him the appearance of a weaponised armadillo. The suit gleamed, reflecting the astonished faces of his Sovereign warriors.

Commander Roth sucked in a sharp breath. 'He wears the historic regalia of Arnaut Vrendar.'

Harold's eyes boggled. 'Perhaps he wears it to motivate the troops?'

'Well, you're in luck,' said Roth. 'It's your squadron he will be joining on this particular outing.'

Mustapha said nothing, though his chest swelled. He watched as his father marched to a halt, turning to face the glittering ranks of proud Vrendari. Clearing his throat, he addressed them in a booming voice.

'This day counts for all,' he began.

CHAPTER 20

QUEEN OF THE NIGHT

As expected, Lord Rogar's demise offered the most trivial test. Human males were so predictable. Rogar proved no different. Whisper a little something sweet. A little something sultry. Get him horizontal and raise an army of undead skeletons. The rest took care of itself. The Giltenan clan as a whole were proving more bothersome ... but for now, the requirement had been met.

Despite their size, Oberon and Titania presented a weightier challenge. She relished that puzzle as a delectable morsel. In the end, the malleable human mind was her key to success in the Fae Realm, as well; if not sex, then power drove the wheels of manipulation.

Figaro the Ploughman wanted to monopolise. He dabbled in intrigue, with the Mayor of Petrichor. Therein lay the necessary leverage. She gave Figaro clear instructions: build a big machine. Burn down the forest. Destroy the Yew. *In the name of the Black*

Queen, so on and so forth.

Black Queen. She liked that name — her favourite so far.

She did worry, when the winged horses arrived, that the Fae Sovereigns might survive. Yet their own exertions finished the job for her. She made an extra offering of gratitude to Valendyne that night.

The death of Lord Ponerog stood apart, as the pinnacle of her accomplishments. A war of attrition, fought entirely in his mind. The Wilden Lord was not born inherently aligned to the doctrines of Valendyne — Vater had been raising a virtuous child. So, she placed in him an earworm from an early age, making him dependent on her subliminal advice. She taught him greed and a lust for infamy. Only then did the demands begin.

Ponerog killed Lord Vater almost dutifully. He thought he did it of his own initiative.

Next, she asked of him a plague army, subverting the intentions of his slain father. In this, he excelled; she had only to toss the Giltenan bauble his way. She anticipated that Ponerog would dispatch Maybeth. In that one regard, he failed ... but by then, it no longer mattered. His sense of hope eroded to the point of no return.

The Black Queen learned the timing of Anuvin's emancipation through her communion with Valendyne, who remained cognisant of all, despite his incarceration. That Anuvin's freedom coincided with Neptune's departure from Via came down to serendipity. The pair would surely meet, in the deep waters off the coast of Rhye. There, the might of a God proved too great for the redoubtable Neptune.

Or so she assumed.

With each Lord's demise — with each fracturing of the Fae Ring — the Black Queen felt her own power grow in magnitude. No surge in her dark potency followed the death of Neptune. The issue nagged at her, though after a while, she shrugged it from her mind.

The expanse of her own might grew greater by the day.

In the present moment, the God of War marched alongside her. Ancient plans coalesced to perfection. On the event horizon, the liberation of Valendyne became inevitable. Only a few Sovereigns remained — perhaps too few to maintain the Ring's binding.

She would need Anuvin's help to overcome the final obstacles.

War sat astride the dreadful manticore, with an air of malignant pleasure. The creature, having conceded to the God within moments, stalked forth as if it were born to be his chosen mount. Now united with its tail, it channelled all the elements, charged with furious energy.

Over the shoulder of Anuvin lumbered his self-raised army. Footfalls shook the ground with the passage of the host, each as large as a hillock and made entirely of stone. Jagged hunks of blasted rock gave them the shape of the Peaks from which they were split. They had no need for armour, nor had they faces. They went wherever Anuvin bade them, without requirement for senses of their own. The rock titans came in great number — such was the damage caused to the shattered range.

Afore of these titans came a frenzied procession.

A river of forsaken Adept flowed across the meadows of The Corridor, trampling the grasses and pastures to slush. The throng of Necromancers, jubilant in their return from the Seer's incarceration, were oblivious to the rain. They cavorted and sang while they marched, shouting high praise to their redeemer:

Hark! Lo, the Black Queen
Heart of Valendyne
She'll take us to the kingdom come
Her majesty divine
She's our leader!

She who brings our Lord back to Rhye
To join the god of War
(He rides the manticore)
Fear the graceless, taunt the faithless — fie!

Hi-ho, the Black Queen
Wrath and thunder-fire
She riles and defiles and
She'll rule the land entire
You can't beat her!

Valendyne breaks free from the Ring!
His bonds in Nevermore
Can't hold him any more
Reap the farrows, charge the narrows — fly!

While many sang, others rattled necklaces of tooth or knuckle. Still more blew into outlandish horns and flutes, carved from the bleached bones of long-dead creatures. A cacophony rose from iniquitous throats.

At the head of the array, the Black Queen strutted in pterippal form, with a sheen as dark as pitch. By her shoulder prowled the manticore, its strange man-face wearing a hideous smile. Anuvin held aloft the Trident — from its prongs sprang forth an emerald flame. The vile glow broke through the thick, grey curtain all around, leading those who followed across a darkening Nurtenan.

The monstrous parade made steady progress. They were heedless of the hour, for day had become as night. Rarely, Anato allowed her silver countenance to penetrate the blanket of gloom; when she did so, eerie luminescence covered the land.

Adatar seemed banished altogether from the cosmos.

Terror rippled, a deathly aura surrounding the host. Creatures skittered from their homes. Villages, warrens, caves, and hovels were abandoned as the wave surged eastward. Any caught up in the advancing nightmare met a horrible fate — shredded in the fangs of the manticore or crushed beneath the giant feet of rock titans. The Necromancers dispatched many more, with a growing swarm of the deceased joining the ranks of the Black Queen's army.

The horde pillaged empty settlements with ruthless efficiency. Wearers of Black poked amidst the private chattels and piles of belongings, discarded by Nurteneans in their flight. They scavenged for scraps of food, descending upon storehouses, picking clean pantries and tables left in haste. They stole weapons, for many a sylph maintained a small armoury.

Inevitable as Death itself, the bloated host came to a natural ridge — a place where the plateau of The Corridor met with the murky moors of Fenmarck Haunte. To the north, a foreboding riddle of hills marked the way to the Peaks of Light. South, the mountains loomed close; only a handful of leagues distant, sentinels of the Vultan Range speared above the plains, seeming to peer over at all that lay beyond.

The Black Queen's army reached the toppled ruins of Vrendar's Rest, where once the sylphic hero founded a soldiers' outpost. Now, it served as his burial place and memorial. Little remained but a small forest of stone columns, tilting and broken, at the crest of the ridge.

Anuvin rubbed his hands together. More voiceless monoliths to recruit to his cause.

'Let us not be impetuous,' said the Black Queen, by his side. With practised grace, she became once again her two-legged self, the midnight gloss of her hide transforming into a weatherproof cloak. An insidious grin twitched her lips. 'A traveller greets us on the road.'

The entire horde ceased marching and stood in the steaming rain; hulking shapes and cavorting shadows, all staring towards the lone figure ahead.

A rogue lightning bolt, arcing across the sky, revealed the glint of armour. It caught the white of snowy wings, half unfurled in a show of militant grandeur — the unflinching aspect of a true warrior. A short distance behind the figure, also motionless, stood a single squad of Vrendari, as well as a lone dragonfly, far from home.

'Do you feel the slow creep of Death yet, Lord of pigeons?' called the Black Queen through the storm.

Bastian Sinotar made no effort to draw nearer. Nor did he respond to the jibe.

'I do not presume to turn aside the God of War, or the cronies of Death, with any misguided plea,' said the General Prime. 'Rather, out of complaisance for the divinity amongst us, I offer a fair warning.'

The God of War scoffed.

Behind Anuvin rose a great jeering and caterwauling. Necromancers by the thousand laughed with derision, while the ghoulish dead clashed their weapons. Rock titans pounded their fists on the earth. The mighty din rumbled up and down the ridge until, with an upraised hand, the God of War silenced them all.

'I see past you, doomed sylph. I see one million souls — the timid, the meek and the homeless — huddled, shivering, against the foot of Two-Way Mirror Mountain. There are they corralled, with no avenue for escape.

'I see the flesh-starved creatures of the Haunte, along with the cherubs of sickness, closing in from south and east. Commanding the sky above, I see the darkling veil of he who seeps from the tree of his imprisonment. He cuts off their last road to freedom, thus preparing them for serfdom in his eternal domain.'

Bastian Sinotar showed no sign of intimidation. 'What you see are those who flee to survive,' he said. 'Those who yearn to see an end to war. A sad irony that they must stand upon the stage of one final battle, to see their dream come to fruition.'

A tremendous peal of thunder punctuated Anuvin's laughter. 'Is this what you offer by way of battle? That army of pixies — pixies! — will be crushed underfoot. Your Vrendari might provide better sport ... though they must, in the end, founder against these creatures at my command.'

The heavy air stirred with restless murmurs. Necromancers hungered for the inevitable slaughter — death with which to honour their hallowed Lord.

'Hold,' intoned the Black Queen. Something more hid in the black shadows of the Rest. 'The General Prime is joined in parley by another. Who skulks there, clinging to the dark?'

Rain drummed the beat of anticipation upon rocky ground.

With deliberate slowness, Mustapha placed himself in the open. A paltry thread of moonlight, spearing through the purple-black sky and a curtain of precipitation, singled him out.

The Black Queen gave a theatrical gasp. Her eyes flashed with dark fire. 'How wonderful!' she cried. 'I do love a family reunion. Tell me: Have you forgiven him yet, Mustapha? Do you forgive your father for abandoning you, before you were even born? He has forsaken you, through every trial of your fledgling life. Is it possible that you might love him still — this creature who hid so much from you?'

Bastian Sinotar did not twitch a muscle. His face gave no sign that the words of the Black Queen held any impact for him.

'You have a lot to answer for,' returned Mustapha, fists clenched, voice quavering. Wet locks of hair, like dark streaks of anguish, were plastered across his face and down his neck. 'Rogar's murder lies at your feet. So does the desecration of Petrichor. Your trail of misery and deception runs right from Lily's broken bonds to this very spot.'

Anuvin let loose a harsh sound, somewhere between a snarl and a chuckle. 'Who is this pitiful whelp?'

The Black Queen raised a placating hand. As quick as blinking, she closed the gap between opposing parties, materialising right before the place where Mustapha and the General Prime stood.

Some distance behind, the Vrendari squad unsheathed their swords.

'Stand down your foolish minions,' she said to Sinotar. 'May they remember that they are in the presence of War himself.' She turned to Mustapha, regarding him with matriarchal fondness. In a heartbeat, her demeanour flipped, acidic disgust melting away. Honey-gold light flashed in her eyes. When she spoke to the strangeling, her words were spun like spider-silk — delicate, yet binding.

'Dear, lost soul. How you have made me fret! How I despaired when you left my side. I feared you must surely have succumbed to the poison coursing through you. My heart swells to see you now!'

A growl came from Mustapha's side. 'Your heart does not swell. Your heart bloats with the noxious fumes that take the place of your soul.'

The Black Queen turned her head, eyes gleaming. 'Silence, Sinotar … for it is your soul I hold in the palm of my hand.'

Once more, agitated howls broke loose from the restless host.

Mustapha glared at her. Again, she spoke to him. Honey, on the edge of a knife.

'Dear child … hear my counsel, for it is I who have guided you on this treacherous road.

'When the charge of treason hung over you, I stepped forward as your protector. Not only did I spare your life, but I also brought it purpose and direction.

'When doubt assailed you — while Lords and Ladies laughed and reviled you, calling you "liar" — I remained by your side, giving you strength.

'When the simpering allies of Humankind tried to eliminate me, I sought to conceal myself, that I might re-emerge to aid you, in your time of crisis.'

Mustapha's fiery stare dimmed to a quiet glower.

The Black Queen pressed her advantage. 'Never have I lied to you, sweetling. In the midnight hours I laboured, using your fine procurements, striving for the land's cure. In this I did not deceive you, nor from my gracious cause did I stray. You must recognise: The land has ailed terribly, beneath the callous whim of the Gods who would claim your devotion. They do not deserve it.

'Valendyne's ambition saw him create a race like none other. He drew the jeering condemnation of his peers and was forced to set aside his creations. Valendyne conceived the elegant perfection of Death; and it was he who, at the mercy of a self-righteous Pantheon, has endured millennia in torment ... for the crime of retaliation.

'Now — in this time — we have the chance to right the wrongs of the Gods. They, too, are answerable to those whose love and faith they seek. Behold! Anuvin stands among us, for it is in the crucible of War that a new Rhye shall rise. The old Lords will be swept aside, making way for those long lost to place and time.'

Bastian Sinotar again opened his mouth to protest, only to be drowned out by the raucous cry of the Black Queen's army. Atop the roar came the manticore's trumpeting call. Anuvin's gaze lent credence to the Necromancer's words.

He gave his implicit endorsement to this blasphemy.

Mustapha's face reflected an unnatural torpor. Though he

appeared to fight it, his now clouded eyes held no argument to the Black Queen's mastering spell.

'But aren't you …?' he looked at Sinotar.

'Mustapha, no! Do not heed her. Her words are only another form of poison!' The General Prime advanced, sword drawn.

The Black Queen worked a gesture, unleashing a bolt of midnight power. Sinotar raised his shield, but the force of the blast threw him backwards, hurling him bodily into a column of stone. He fell to the ground in a pile of rubble, gasping.

'Where was your sire when you were abandoned, to be raised by filthy forest nymphs?' said she. 'Where was he in your moments of strife and uncertainty? Sitting in his nest, waiting for you to come to him! Then, after so many years — when you finally learned the secret that he kept from you — what did he tell you? That you are destined to spend the essence of your life, for the future of Rhye?

'I promise you no such fate. You have become far too precious to me, honey child. Far greater is your worth than any trinket you brought to me. Through your witless moment' — in his beleaguered mind, Mustapha recalled swallowing the cinnabar — 'you have made of yourself a conduit between Death and Life. A channel, by which Valendyne may at last walk among us. You need only place a bloodied palm against the wizened trunk that contains him. The cruel snare that binds him is already weak — soon to lay in tatters. With your touch, the black storm of his puissance will flow through you.'

Mustapha blinked once, slowly. *Sounds like possession.* He did not reply. His head dropped to his chest.

The Black Queen threw her arms skyward, in unbridled glee. 'Long may the God of the Afterlife reign upon Rhye!'

Bastian Sinotar regained his feet; unbroken, but with a face contorted by dread.

Mustapha now knelt in the mud before the Necromancer, his head bowed.

In an abject monotone, he spoke.

'My Lady, Queen of the Night ... Mama. You speak a truth so profound, a word so enlightening, that it is the act of a fool to gainsay you. Though my life has been short, I have spent it all in search of my roots and the meaning of my being. You have led me, with your unswerving will, to the answers I sought. Now that I have learned the truth, I know that my place is with you.'

The Wearers of Black scarcely breathed, in thrall at the power their Queen held over the strangeling. Even the undead shuffled with restless awe, while behind them, the looming shadows of the rock titans were as still as the mountains of their birth.

Mustapha continued, his fingers ploughing the mud, gouging and kneading the wet earth while uttering his devotion.

'My Lady, may I be guided by your wisdom. May I march to your banner and hereafter be your loving acolyte. Shape my destiny in the name of Valendyne, Lord of Rhye. May his Sovereign power manifest in me, though it may claim my very soul.' His hands clamped fistfuls of the earth with a preternatural strength. Steam arose from the ground in front of him.

The Black Queen gave a satisfied smile, looking down upon the grovelling creature at her feet. 'Good, Mustapha,' she praised. 'Shrug off the artificial Sovereignty of your birth. In pledging your fealty to me, you will be honoured among the host of Valendyne.'

Anuvin, silent throughout this exchange, nodded in approval.

The Black Queen spread her hands wide. 'Now, I —'

'Mama?'

She raised a single, fine eyebrow. 'My dear votary?'

'One further indulgence, if I may. A tribute to the Black Queen.'

She smiled. 'Make your tribute, devoted one.'

Mustapha paused. Then, in a lightning movement he straightened, jerking his hands from the earth.

A great, steaming clod of mud struck the Black Queen in the face.

'You pigheaded crone!' the strangeling guffawed. 'Do you swallow any tripe that you are fed? I am slave to nobody! The White Queen is my true forebear. Through her love, I escaped the maw of Death. May you and your underlings prepare for annihilation!'

The Necromancer screamed, clawing at her face, eyes burning with steaming mud.

The dark host yowled in revolt, a chilling uproar that reverberated around Vrendar's Rest.

Anuvin snarled. 'Miserable stripling! Valendyne has a special place in the fires of the Afterlife set aside for you!' The manticore reared, bellowing. A crack of thunder amplified the call.

Mustapha answered with a seismic cry of his own. A detonation of sound hurled the manticore into the throng of creatures at its back, unseating the God of War.

In the shadows of a granite monolith, Sinotar stood stunned. The passing moments were a maelstrom of horror and wonderment, for which he was utterly unprepared.

Mustapha's insolence enraged the Black Queen, who still had mud and rain, in dark rivulets, streaking her face. Anuvin wore a murderous grin as he clambered from amidst stupefied Wearers of Black.

'An exit strategy is wise,' called Sinotar to the strangeling.

The Black Queen shimmered with seething hate. Her form blurred and contorted. She began to transfigure, in a fit of rage.

'Your legacy is dust!' she screeched at the General Prime. 'All of your dreams of salvation will wither in the hot winds of a wasteland. Songs and prophecies of rebirth will be dashed to nothing. The only sound will be the wailing cries of those you leave behind. From the blasted plains of Rhye shall rise the City of the Afterlife, with Valendyne upon the throne forever.

'Forever!'

With this final word, she left her sapient form behind. Larger and longer grew the nebulous cloud of her being, until it became clear that she had learned a new shape. Mustapha, Sinotar and the squad at their backs retreated, as a serpentine menace uncoiled towards them.

'Fall back!' ordered Sinotar, a desperate cry. Mustapha ran for the darkened ridge. The sylphs and the dragonfly took to the air, with an entire deathly host on their heels.

Dique clung tight to Commander Dartmoor, trying to extract some semblance of warmth from his fellow pixie. Beneath them, the dusk-orange pterippus trod the lumpy ground with confident hooves, somehow oblivious to the terrors of recent days.

'They're coming, aren't they?' asked a timorous Dique.

Dartmoor — Dique had long known him simply as "Dart" — peered into the south. The vast maze of tumbledown stones, moss-clad knolls and treacherous bogs rolled on well beyond the blanket of precipitous mist.

'Yes, they are. Every so often I hear the crack of deadwood underfoot or see a flicker of that acid green and I know they are close by.'

'I've never been so afraid.'

'Me neither.' Liveried duty had aged Dart in a short space of weeks, as it had Halli and Puck. The time of pranks and shenanigans seemed as distant as the cosy treehouses of Reed.

If not for the arrival of Trixel Tate and the Fae army, many more refugees would have perished on the precarious journey. The forest trolls made an excellent rear guard. Many of them endured torturous labour in the cavern of Lord Ponerog, building a resistance to the acrid plague. They swung sturdy limbs and makeshift weapons at the advancing cherubs, slowing the swarm of their progress. In time, the corrosive essence of the Pox did burn and injure the trolls, who were forced to fall back; though in return, they had bought almost a full day's advantage.

Perhaps the inevitable had only been delayed.

Dart guided their noble mount along a snaking defensive line, formed by Fae knights and the remaining trolls. Human soldiers crouched amongst them, having made the perilous exodus from Via. Fires crackled low, while the soldiers triple-checked their pistols and blades. Sentinels stared into the murk, on high alert for the emergence of their foe across the Haunte.

Behind the line, a frightened populace hugged the foot of the Peaks of Obelis. The Peaks rose in an abrupt wall beyond, introduced by only a narrow verge of broken foothills.

There was no place to hide. One million refugees pressed against the unsympathetic mountains, trying to gain shelter. Meagre provisions, scoured and shared by Fae, humans and Vrendari alike, quickly diminished. Soon, the filth of so many concentrated bodies would also defile their place of respite.

The fragile and the forsaken huddled side by side in fear, with those who would protect them.

Towering above them all, Two-Way Mirror Mountain thrust towards a wrathful sky. The summit jabbed the clouds, a gnarled finger accusing the Gods. Far below, at ground level, a ramp of natural stone wound to the fabled place where stood the largest scrallin monolith in all of Rhye.

Nobody alive knew for certain what — if anything — lay behind the enormous slab. The unfolding crisis seemed to indicate that the lore of the devout was, indeed, reality. The faithful sat in groups, or alone, facing the Mountain to pray. A general hubbub of murmurs and sobs arose from the multitude.

The Mountain — with its forbidding stone portal — stood silent as a tomb.

Outside the defensive line, in the wide corridor where the river of refugees had passed, there lay strewn a litter of discarded items. Dique and Dartmoor picked amongst the debris on their mount. The abandoned personal effects told a mournful tale — trampled, forgotten, no longer deemed important in a dwindling future.

Chests of valuables.

Children's toys.

Casks and bottles by the wagonload.

'Wait!' exclaimed Dique, pointing. Dart reined in the pterippus.

Dique leapt from the beast, splashing in a brackish puddle and skipping across the bog, where ten thousand pairs of boots had trod, only hours earlier. He came to an item half buried in the muck. He dragged it free with a wet *plop*, brandishing a filthy, box-like implement. His face suggested a minor victory had been won.

'Tell me that's the solution to all of our problems,' said Dart, with a look of disgust.

'Nope,' replied Dique, though he wore the wistful grin of a child.

'What in Rhye is it? It looks like an instrument. A lute, or something.'

'It's a zither.'

'What, in the name of Phydeas, is a zither?'

'This is! It only needs a minor fix and it'll work like new. A beautiful piece.'

'What is the point of it? Someone left it behind. A valid decision, too: We can't eat it, drink it or fight with it.'

'That's true,' conceded Dique. Still smiling, he turned the item over in his hands, eyes alight, consumed by a delirious reverie of near-forgotten times. 'It may be of no use in battle, but there is no discounting the value of morale ... and a song is good for that.'

'You know how to play it?'

'A little,' answered Dique. 'I'd be rusty, for sure, but you know how the saying goes:

"Whether you're hither or thither and heeding the call,
A well-tuned zither beats no zither at all."

'I've never heard that saying in my life.' Dart looked askance, eyes scanning the moors. An eerie howl rang out in the middle distance, answered by several others.

'Perhaps it's just something my old man told me. He tried teaching me to play when I was a kid back in Reed. You know, when times were slow in the cheese shop —'

'Ah, Dique?' interrupted Dart. He was looking the other way. 'You might dream of serenading a sea of refugees, but I don't think you'll get much time for it.'

The lambent yellow-green line was no longer a figment, beyond sight. The advancing menace of Pox slowly emerged from the mist a stone's throw away.

'The plague babies are here. Hurry!'

Dique yelped. He slung the zither over his shoulder, unable to bring himself to discard it again. Dart leaned down to yank him back astride the pterippus. The creature whinnied and snorted with unease, hooves stamping the wet ground. Broad wings ruffled, threatening to unfurl.

'Easy, girl!' cried Dart, reining his mount back around to face the Fae line. Then, in a commanding tone: 'Ready arms — pass the word!'

The Fae formation tightened, knights in readiness. They, too, had seen the approaching Pox. The order rippled down the way, thousands of warriors preparing for a last stand. The pixies knew that, somewhere beyond the veil, at the foot of Two-Way Mirror Mountain, Lady Trixel Tate made ready for battle.

The pixies anticipated a wave of panic from the mass of frightened civilians, camped behind their thin, green line. Instead, they encountered something altogether different.

A cheer tore from thousands of throats. Up and down the front, as the knights awaited their orders, the sound of exhausted joy erupted. Cries of 'Up there!' and 'Look!' accompanied ecstatic faces, tilted skyward.

The pixies looked to the heavens.

There, they saw hope.

Against a backdrop of rolling thunderheads, lit by the stark flare of lightning bolts, flew a vast flock of Vrendari. Squadron after squadron blanketed the sky, an airborne quilt of fighters in dense and precise formation. At high altitude, almost lost in cloud, many thousands of sylphic warriors flew eastward, across the face of the mountains. Closer to the ground came countless more, who bore projectile weaponry and held a course that thrust deep into the Haunte.

Nearest of all came those Vrendari who hoisted the Adept between them. In a swooping pass they began to bombard the Pox, bringing ever more uproarious cheers from those below.

The Fae held their line as the decimated Pox kept stumbling towards them. The avian fighters maintained a safe distance from the legions of knights and the precious civilian body beyond, lest the explosion of ruptured Pox splash acid upon them. One barrage after another of volatile magic blistered the air, peppering the Pox with coruscations of power.

The Vrendari made several passes along the besieged frontline. Eventually, the march of cherubic ill broke, with scattered Pox remaining to be picked off by armoured Fae as they advanced.

A momentary calm befell the masses. It did not last: With wailing cries, the refugees pointed heavenward once more, for a new vision passed above them. A beast darker than the sunless sky, looming huge and potent, each beat of its mighty wings generating a squall of bitter wind.

The pixies were aghast. Never had a wash of relief been replaced by a lump in the throat with such devastating efficiency.

Dique craned his face to the sky in horror.

The question had to be asked.

'Is that … is that a *dragon*?'

CHAPTER 21

LET TRUMPET CRY

Leith Lourden watched the arriving Vrendari legion with a sanguine bead glistening in her eye. She used the back of her sword arm to wipe it away, as Will gave her a sideways glance.

'Curse this rain!' she grinned, damp cheeks reddening.

Will allowed himself a return smile. He examined a standard-issue pistol, given to him by a heavily armed Giltenan soldier. His trusty machete still hung at his waist, for use in close combat.

'You long to be up there,' he said, pointing skyward.

'I will have my time in the air. Our campaign hinges on the coming battle ... and I doubt it will be over quickly. For now, I stand by the shoulders of my friends, for the good of those at our backs.'

<*The greatest test is upon us,*> remarked Torr Yosef, luminescent eyes fixed on ominous green shapes beyond the mist. <*The first wave, a swarm of Pox, is here. I also sense a tremendous number of the*

undead, headed this way ... as well as a greater evil that approaches from above.>

Since learning of the Golem genocide, Yosef had drawn within himself. He offered only occasional comments on the group's disposition, refusing to discuss the phenomenon of his unprecedented emotional outburst. Two days prior, he offered one last observation to Will, in tones like a wistful dirge: *<The voices of my brethren are gone.>*

At other times, the golem spoke as if to some invisible entity. His words were unintelligible. His companions, knowing not what to make of their troubled friend, watched him without interference.

The companions stood together, amidst the Fae line. As the Vrendari and Adept pummelled the Pox with incendiary magic from overhead, the call to arms swept through the ranks. Out in front of the line, Commander Halliwell sat astride a vermillion pterippus. The elegant beast whinnied and reared. Droplets showered from its vibrant hide.

'Ready arms!' cried Halliwell.

'Engage!'

The slew of staggering Pox wandered, with blind perseverance, beyond the reach of the aerial assault. In a unified wave, the Fae surged forward to destroy them. Over the heads of the Fae blasted a volley of pistol fire, from the soldiers of Via. Pox ruptured in acidic bursts, ahead of the charge. Across the fens the Fae skipped, dodging viscid puddles of disease as they went.

Then, from beyond mist and shadow, lurched the ambush. A chorus of spine-chilling wails and eerie, hooting cries rang out from places hidden by dense fog.

All gangling limbs and dark, bristling manes, the marsh-wights clambered into view from every niche and burrow. Spider-like arms, taught with sinew, swung in wide arcs at the advancing force.

Hooked claws slashed the air, threatening to sever and lacerate. At ground level, gangs of redcaps materialised, ready to catch those who zigzagged between the wights. The nimble Fae advanced on their attackers, their blades keen, eyes sharp for horrors in the gloom.

Leith and Will ran side by side into the melee. Around them thundered pterippi, bearing the bold Fae command into battle. Soon, screams of bestial wrath filled the air.

'More redcaps ... my favourite!' cried Leith, with a flash of gritted teeth. Both hands hefted her broadsword with deadly finesse, cleaving grotesque heads from the shoulders that carried them.

The clash of steel melded with the angry retort of pistols and cries of anguish. Above the clamour arose new sounds, which froze the hearts of the defenders: the beating of monstrous wings and the foul shriek of an airborne calamity.

Leith turned her blood-spattered face to the sky and wailed in alarm.

The Black Queen, in dragon form, soared over the battleground. She appeared as an icon of devastation, pitiless as a raging storm. With incendiary breath, she scorched the corridor below. The blast lit the night and wrought indiscriminate damage. In an instant there leapt a wall of fire, one hundred yards long. Only the rain and floods kept the blaze from spreading unchecked.

With talons of purest black, the creature swooped to grasp warriors from the ground at will, tossing their ragged bodies through the air. She issued a wicked, rasping call that tore the night. The storm answered in kind, with a splitting *crack* of forked lightning.

From the roof of the sky, squadrons of Vrendari fell upon her.

Swirling formations of armoured sylphs encircled the dragon, a spiralling wall of shields and swords. She rose to meet them, dwarfing them all with her immensity. Bat-like wings flared as the dragon roared again, preparing to exhale another torrent of flame.

The Vrendari ruled the air, the way a serpent rules the sea, or a stallion knows the land. With elegant, spinning dives they evaded the dragon's fire, circling around to launch an assault of several dozen pointed blades.

Their swords glanced off the Black Queen's ebony scales.

With a flick of her snaking tail, the dragon swatted a brace of Vrendari from the sky. She rose above them, to a place where she commanded a view of the unfolding battle. A glint of triumph showed in her scarlet, reptilian eyes.

Far in the distant south, beyond the rolling mires of Fenmarck Haunte, the wink of a different light caught the dragon's attention. It shone amidst a sea of impenetrable blackness — the shadowy deep of the Wilden Realm. A glittering ivory cynosure, throwing back the inky cloak of the forest, challenging the very might of Valendyne's storm-front.

A volcanic rumble escaped the dragon's jaws. She saw a thing to be reckoned with. A blight on the dark horizon, perhaps a threat to her supremacy. The illumination bespoke power — a power that stood against the rise of Necromancy and the cloud of Death.

The Black Queen curled her sinuous body, altering her mid-air course. With a lash of tail and a single beat of tremendous wings, she bolted southward at an appalling rate.

Entire squadrons of Vrendari dove in pursuit, flying with all haste in the dragon's wake.

The figure of Leith Lourden rose from the chaos below, chasing close behind on frantic wings.

If anything in nature can approach the speed of light, it is the speed of darkness.

The flood tide of forsaken Adept spilled beyond the ridge into the marshland, a stampeding terror of billowing black robes and scathing war cries. Buoyed by the malign force that drove them, the Necromancers swept across the land with swift and unfaltering fury, their feet barely touching the ground. From an existential limbo they returned, bringing with them the strange energy of unfettered spirits. Alongside them came undead by the thousand — they knew no need for rest and moved like a midnight wind.

At the fore of the charge, Anuvin clung to the rippling mane of the manticore. It bounded across the Haunte with elemental strength, holding aloft its Trident tail, an oriflamme of sickly emerald, to light the way for the Black Queen's army.

Somehow, the strangeling whelp kept ahead of the vast horde, on flying feet. Anuvin recognised the svelte creature for a seraph, at least on instinct. He knew it to be the creature he had taunted in dreams, grooming it in fear, to be the agent of cataclysm.

Yet something was not as it should be. An unexpected ardour stirred in this creature.

No seraph had alighted upon Rhye in thousands of years — not since the Godsryche. This one came alone, unbidden by the Pantheon, seemingly unsure of its destiny ...

It mattered not. The seraph had dealt Anuvin a grave insult. It would be crushed, then dragged to Nevermore to complete the apparent purpose of its miserable birth.

The war host raced through the never-ending night. Across nameless vales and many forgotten leagues, they conquered distance with terrifying ease. A tumult of manic shrieks and laughter marked their passage. The distant mountain chain grew nearer, backlit by the electrified sky.

The seraph had evaded them.

Disappearing amidst the shadows of a snaggletooth terrain, the fleeing creature could no longer be seen. Anuvin dismissed it for the time being. The belligerent thing would surely raise its head at an opportune moment, thus condemning itself. Instead, War focused on the last stretch of this assault, which would bring him, at last, back to the Peaks of Obelis — and closer to another divine being than he had been in an Age.

The Peaks also harboured a piteous crush of souls, ripe for harvest.

A sea of refugees was visible to him now, beyond a frenzied clash of Haunte-spawn and warriors from the southern Realms. Dragon-fire still crackled amidst the fray, casting the desperate fighters in a hellish orange hue.

The manticore hurled him ever closer to battle, across the final leagues. It gave a trumpeting call, answered by the throng of Adept with yammering howls of elation. The undead flowed along behind them in a vast silence borrowed from their graves.

Trixel Tate wheeled on her golden pterippus. She raised her sword, bright where firelight glanced from the blade, dark where the blood of the slain had tainted it. Her keen ears caught the eerie howl above the din, a tremendous sound. A new army appeared — a body great in number. She filled her lungs and gave a commanding shout.

'Fae! Via! Look sharp — a new host is upon us!'

In moments, the line was formed anew; pistols reloaded, swords and halberds at the ready. The remaining wights seemed to stall, leering at the defenders, gleefully watching the flood of evil beings that surged towards them.

Gasps of dismay escaped the weary fighters. They now saw the wild fury of the manticore at full flight, with the God of War sat astride it. The host he led was far too great to overcome. The tide of darkness came with sickening momentum, enough to crush the Fae and engulf the innocents they strove to protect.

'Hold the line!' screamed Trixel Tate.

The horde raced towards them.

Half a league.

A quarter-league.

Hearts pounded in chests. Knuckles whitened.

In a breathless moment, a violet storm cascaded from the west. With cataclysmic force, darkness and might collided on the battlefield.

Mages Pass met the upper reaches of the Haunte as a long, natural stair — a channel of alpine wilderness. It served as the perfect funnel for battalions of Warlocks to enter the conflict.

They needed only patience ... and the perfect moment.

The Warrior Adept waited, concealed within the Pass, for the coming of the Black Queen's army. Astrologers, having foretold the fateful march, aided Benjulius in coordinating the Warlocks, in a manoeuvre designed to entrap the horde. The Archimage believed in the indomitable spirit and feisty mettle of the Fae, as well as the sheer resilience of Humankind in times of war. Provided this frontline held, Benjulius entrusted the Wearers of Violet to deliver a crushing blow to their ancient enemy.

Following the call to arms, the Warlock army swept down the Pass, an incarnation of fury. Amongst them, the formidable Wearers of Red were moments of flame in a dark river. The Adept had spent millennia in grief; the name 'Warlock' synonymous with bitter annihilation, ever since the Godsryche. Now, from that very same killing field stirred the passion of an entire race. The story of the Warrior Adept would be re-written in glory ... for the sake of all Rhye.

The river of Violet surged towards the teeming host of Necromancers. Luminescent projectiles, like balls of Greek fire, were hurled in lofty arcs ahead of the ambush, exploding with violent theurgy amidst the Wearers of Black and their ghoulish followers.

The Necromancers tried to veer away, at a bellowing cry from Anuvin. The evasive move came far too late.

The rival Disciplines collided, a new conflict in a place of ancient conquest. The Warlocks did not baulk at the God of War's return, for time and destiny had steeled them for this encounter. They drew blades of fire, falling upon their foes with the thirst of vengeance.

Benjulius himself entered the clash as a Catherine-wheel of spinning coruscation, arriving amongst the Wearers of Black to deal hammer-blows of retribution all around.

Two hundred yards from the interception, humans and Fae strove against the last of the Haunte-spawn. As marsh-wights toppled and redcaps collapsed in the mud, the defenders re-grouped and once again turned their attention to stormy skies above.

Valendyne's blanket of wrath blocked out the heavens. Not even the silvery face of Anato cast her light upon the land. Flame and theurgy lit the battlefield, as did a ghostly glow from the scrallin monolith by the door of the Mountain.

Lightning brought an occasional flare of brilliance, revealing the aerial dominance of the Vrendari. The sylphic warriors kept a tight formation over the maelstrom below, jockeying airborne Mages into position, to strafe the enemy with vermillion fire. The Necromancers returned volleys of their own deadly power, a vicious ground-to-air counter assault.

Into the skirmish, a bolt from beyond, flew Bastian Sinotar.

The General Prime evoked both admiration and fear, bedecked in the guise of the ancient hero, Vrendar. His antiquated armour shone with sylphic legacy, his shield and sword symbols of ancestral triumph.

The armour enclosed a soul who feared nothing, for he had nothing to lose.

Harold the dragonfly joined Sinotar, following in the sylph's wake as he pursued the dragon and her wicked army across the Haunte. All the while, Harold clutched the strap securing the Horn. The artefact may well have been tethered to his own soul.

As the two streaked towards the perils of battle, neither allowed themselves to be cowed by the horrifying spectacle below. The Prophet had foretold it all: chaos, sickness and tempest, a triumvirate of doom. Only a miracle would subvert the fate of the land.

No time for hesitation remained.

'Over there!' cried Sinotar to Harold, indicating a knurled upthrust of rock. It stood near the scrallin monolith, leaning out over the sea of warring creatures. 'Conceal yourself ... but keep a lookout. You will know when the time has come.'

He swooped away, leaving Harold to zip towards the crag.

Sinotar dove upon the legions of undead, time and again, wreaking havoc with his sword. He cleaved the Necromancers, fending off blasts of dark energy with his shield. His solo blitzkrieg tore a swathe through the Black Queen's army. Commander Roth, weaving through a barrage of lethal spells, directed a unit of Vrendari to support their Lord.

But Sinotar sought no aid. He darted through the chaos, heedless of the bolts that strafed him.

He rocketed towards Anuvin.

War sat proud upon the manticore, atop another rocky knoll, amidst seething warfare. The beast swung talons like butchers' knives at any foes who came near. Its Trident-tipped tail rose in a menacing arc above it, like that of a great scorpion. Winds tore about its natural throne, changing direction with each bellow the manticore gave. It spat balls of fire, peppering the battleground with deadly flame that burst over the combatants.

Sinotar hovered over the knoll, glaring a challenge at Anuvin. 'At Vrendar's Rest, I offered you the respect of a humble mortal,' he called. 'I was a fool to expect the God of War to brook negotiation.'

Anuvin sneered. 'Negotiation? A fool you surely were, enough to challenge me! Now, you set foot in this arena, emboldened by knowing you will not leave it. Is that why you dare to face me? Perchance, your survival only requires you to cower from me, or prostrate yourself at my feet?'

'All the greater incentive to spend my one life in defying you.'

'Ha! Sylph, you may have been born on the field of battle ... but I *am* the battle that forged you! I will grow stronger for our combat. How shall you overcome me?' Anuvin's chest swelled, arms open, welcoming the attempt.

The General Prime shook his head. 'It isn't you I raise my blade against.'

Sinotar dove, like a streak of lightning. With a tremendous sweep of his blade, he slashed the throat of the manticore. The creature's mane and bunched shoulders prevented a clean beheading, but its larynx split open. A river of blood rushed from the muted beast.

Without the manticore's dire energy, the turbulent wind settled. The fireballs ceased.

Both God and monster were incensed.

Though blood flowed from it, the manticore spread its wings

and leapt into the air. Its eerie, blue eyes carried a silent rage.

'You usurp the beast of Cornavrian,' said Sinotar, 'so that the force of his Elements might stoke the fire of battle. Well, hear me: Cornavrian knows of the faith we have concealed behind our swords and shields. His glory shines on those who strive for peace, not the bloodshed of War. He guides my sword as I slay this beast.'

'You live a lie and argue with contradiction, sylph. Stop delaying your inescapable demise. Come and let me silence you, as you have silenced your master's precious pet. Then at last, may you join the soul of your piteous love ... in slavery.'

God and Sylphic Lord waged their battle in a tortured sky. The manticore far outmatched Sinotar in size, its muscular, leonine form an extension of Anuvin himself. It pawed and gnashed at its prey, even as the slashing downpour washed blood from the yawning wound at its throat. Sinotar danced a lethal ballet around the beast, feinting here and slicing there, ever conscious of staying beyond his adversary's grasp.

In time, the manticore weakened. The fire in its eyes grew dim, the ardour of its attacks blunted. It lost height, great wings struggling to beat.

Anuvin grew livid. With a ferocious snarl, he reached behind and tore at the dying creature's tail. He came away with a Trident-shaped shard, while the creature's face spoke of mute agony. Anuvin spurred it to remain in flight, redoubling his assault on the sylph, with borrowed weapon in hand.

At that moment, Sinotar faltered.

He felt no pain. Only a strange, dull paraesthesia. At first, his shield arm slackened. Power left it, as if all nerves and sinews had been cut. The abrupt loss of strength caught him off-guard, though he remained aloft, delivering vicious cuts and thrusts with his sword.

Next to fail were his legs, which became as numb weights, hanging from his torso. In the air, he flew as a rudderless ship upon water — sluggish, awkward, slow to evade.

Anuvin grappled with his own mount, for the manticore finally began to succumb to its haemorrhaging wounds. As it sank towards the earth, the God of War did perceive the General Prime's labours.

'Ah! Do you feel it, dupe of Cornavrian?' he howled. 'Does the Necromancer's hex still your futile efforts at last? Soon, you shall know true despair. May helplessness take you!'

'My task is done,' replied Sinotar. 'Though you may taunt and jeer, a new dawn in Rhye is assured. I may not live to see it, though the blight of War shall also end.' He hoped for this to be true, fixing a mask of cold defiance to his face.

At last, his eagle's wings fluttered once more and went limp, failing to answer him. A creeping chill gnawed at him from the outside in.

Bastian Sinotar rolled once in mid-air and plummeted towards the ground. He held aloft his sword arm, which served him to the last. He angled for the withering manticore below.

The antlered crown triggered a lancing migraine in Trixel's head. She did not need the Yew to know the agony that had beset the Fairy King. The hidden glades of Nevermore — and within, the forsaken tree from lore — were now close enough to shout their disdain directly into her head. With a hoarse rallying cry of her own, she brought knights and soldiers to her side once more. Mounting an extreme effort, the Fae forged deeper southward, across the blood-soaked theatre of battle.

Meadow flanked her, riding his own pterippus. Commander Halliwell had fallen to the fierce battery of a marsh-wight, unseated and lost in the bedlam. The distraught pterippus began to bray, rolling wild eyes. It responded with instant calm when Meadow leapt across from Trixel's mount.

'We have to find Halli!' shouted Meadow, hacking at an undead assailant as it stalked towards him.

'No, we must keep pushing south!' replied Trixel. 'Halli will have the support of his unit. Do not risk your own life. I see how the pterippus responds to you. It is you we need to protect.'

Meadow saw it, too. The winged creature did not simply bear him, as a rider — it sought to guard him, moving deftly through the sea of clashing bodies. Still, the loss of Halli caused Meadow to look about in desperation, searching for familiar faces.

Will battled on nearby, pistol tossed aside in favour of his hefty blade. A gash upon his shoulder coated his arm red, though he appeared not to notice.

A blistering streak of white zigzagged from foe to foe, leaving bodies in its wake — Meadow imagined it to be Mustapha.

Torr Yosef, despite his size, seemed to have disappeared. The hulking shape of the golem, once prominent amidst the turmoil, could not be seen.

Meadow's head spun, eyes darting about. There, at least, he saw Dique in the distance. Dique swatted at a final cluster of redcaps, while his mount lashed out with its hooves, sending fiends in all directions.

Puzzled, Meadow stared at the strange item Dique had slung at his back. As he pondered what looked to be a stringed instrument, a sight beyond caught his breath.

'Ah — Lady Tate?'

'I'm a little busy, Meadow!'

'We're about to be busier.'

Trixel kicked a corpse from the end of her sword and looked up. A moan escaped her lips. 'What, in Cornavrian's name, are those?'

'I'd say they're gigantic rock piles,' answered Meadow. 'Only they're coming this way.'

The rock titans arrived, looming out of the night like sentinels of fate. Fire-glow and flickers of lightning cast garish shadows upon them. Ground-shaking steps brought them closer, a wall of ensorcelled monoliths.

'This isn't Necromancy,' exclaimed Trixel. 'This is the work of Anuvin. May the Pantheon hear our prayers.'

Relentlessly, the titans approached. At the fringe of the battleground, they showed no hesitation. Dozens of gigantic feet, each a boulder the size of an adult manuban, continued to mash the earth as they stomped forward. Sightless faces stared out over the scene. They made no sound, but for the abysmal grinding of their joints as they walked.

Both foes and allies scrambled to escape the path of Anuvin's monsters.

The titans cared not for the scampering warriors about their feet. They were brutal, trampling any who stumbled beneath their footfalls. Despite the frenzy, the Wearers of Black crowed with excitement, for here came a force to swing the battle.

From above, the Vrendari scrambled an offensive strike. A sylphic deluge fell upon the titans, a violent barrage of steel and strength. Airborne Adept rained mystic fire, while Warlocks hurled missiles of power from the ground.

Showers of rubble sprayed from the titans, in the face of a punishing offensive. Yet they brushed away the Vrendari like pestilent gnats. They walked on through the hail of theurgy, protected by the will of a God.

Anuvin's army tramped through mud and carnage, on an unstoppable path to the Peaks of Obelis. Ahead, one million souls quailed in helpless anguish; praying, crying, watching for the spectre of the Two-Legged Death to come for them.

Echoing laughter rolled as peals of mocking thunder across the Haunte.

Harold scurried out from the rock overhang. From his vantage, he had seen it all. He watched as Anuvin chided Bastian Sinotar; then on in slack-jawed wonder as God and sylph clashed, with the storm at their backs. When the combatants fell from the sky, Harold watched still ... until he saw a doom of rock titans, lumbering on colossal legs, from out of the night.

You will know when the time has come.

The time for hiding had passed. Clawing his way atop the crag, Harold stood high above the battle. Rain fell heavily on his upturned face, spattering his helm. Before him, a writhing mass of fighters hacked and blasted their foes. Over his shoulder, the Peaks of Obelis towered, a wall of irrefutable judgement.

With fumbling pincers, Harold unstrapped the Horn of Agonies.

He felt the weight of destiny in his grasp. At the same time, it becalmed his racing heart. For several breaths he held it, sensing the storm and warfare churning around him.

The very next breath he held, bringing the artefact to his lips.

A sound arose that might have come from the throat of the world. A cavernous, resonating note — the voice of exaltation — rang out across the entire Haunte. All who heard it stood in awe, for its sonority had no parallel in Nature. Anuvin flinched in astonishment. He alone had heard it before ... yet he knew not how the Horn had come to be wielded by another.

All turned towards the crag. There, they saw the dragonfly.

The Horn's blare still faded, when there followed a tearing noise like the fissuring of stone. This was no prevarication: A great stone was rent, exploding in a rupture of fragments and a splintering burst of refracted light.

As one, the throng of fighters turned towards Two-Way Mirror Mountain, where the scrallin monolith lay obliterated. Boulders and pebbles tumbled down the natural ramp. A faint, luminescent dust settled beneath the teeming rain. The Two-Way Mirror, now an enormous mouth, opened a gateway to blackness.

In a scurry of terror and uncertainty, all scrambled to clear away from the portico of the Mountain.

All except for the rock titans, who knew no fear and continued their blind advance.

A bellow erupted, which shook the Mountain. An avalanche of scree rolled down the ramp. At the Mountain's foot, the defenceless screamed, for here they witnessed fairy tales, brought to life.

One by one, issuing cries of ancient rage, Ogres spilled from Two-Way Mirror Mountain.

They thundered from the mouth of hell, bare feet on stone, pounding chests and roaring at the heavens. The storm crackled, thunder rumbling in reply; though at that moment, no force could equal the primordial beasts of Marnis.

The Ogres were larger than houses and built like rampaging bulls, each a distinctive monstrosity of misshapen parts. One had four enormous arms and came tossing massive hunks of scrallin. Another was more broad than tall, with a back covered in gnarled armour and a face with one great eye, black as coal. A third resembled a prodigious toad, with a gaping mouth and protuberant belly. On they came, twenty-four such beasts, stampeding down the mountainside with brutal speed.

Ogres met titans as a tsunami might meet an avalanche. Behemoths of flesh and stone collided with pile-driving momentum. The titans, mindless servants of Anuvin, fought to keep their line. Only the God-given compulsion to crush the living and assault the very mountains, drove them onwards.

The Ogres, by contrast, carried a sentience as old as that of any creature on Rhye. They saw the titans as abominations, bereft of the vital essence with which Marnis had blessed every living thing.

Four-Arms-and-One-Eye led a frontal charge, swinging fists in a tornado of blood and rubble. Several others stormed the flanks of the titans' line, tremulous footfalls kicking torrents of water through the air.

The crowd of warriors and Warlocks, defenders and darklings, could do nought but run for their lives.

Meadow clung to his pterippus as it galloped through the tempest. Wind whipped his hair, rain slashing horizontally across his face. Dark shapes on his periphery could be either friend or foe — away from the fires of the battleground, it was impossible to tell which. With grim determination he held on, hoping the pterippus could guide him to safety.

To a place beyond the chaos.

His mount swerved left with a sudden movement, then headed south once again. The colossal shape of an Ogre appeared, locked in titanic combat with a creature of Anuvin. The immense beings, in their death-grip, threatened to topple to the earth. With a moment to spare, Meadow and his mount evaded the crush.

Much too close for comfort.

All around, the pixie sensed a huge number of other beings, flocking southward across the Haunte — a deathly flight in darkness. Some still fought. On occasion, the sound of dancing weaponry met his ears, or the bright flare of magic illuminated the way. The roar of Ogres and the rumble of rock titans never seemed far from him. Screams and howls of unknown beasts cut through the night, from places beyond his vision.

In the distance, a single light beckoned. At intervals, a dazzling beam shot out across the sky, for a fleeting instant, reaching for the heavens. The pterippus galloped on at breakneck speed, drawn towards the light source. The eyes of the beast shone, mirroring an otherworldly glow: a meeting of divine powers.

In a moment of exhilaration, Meadow released one hand from his rollicking mount, pumping the air with his fist and unleashing a whoop of spontaneous delight. In that moment, he felt unstoppable, threading through a maelstrom of terror.

A black shape appeared from nowhere, veering into Meadow's path.

The collision sent him somersaulting from the back of the pterippus, flying like a cartwheel into the mud. The alarmed whickering of not one, but two pterippi, came to him through the driving rain, as did the clatter of spilled and dropped objects.

Meadow collected himself, unhurt. He peered into the blackness, soon realising that he was no longer surrounded by fleeing hordes. A few mysterious shadows flitted through the night, paying him no heed, but in front of him lay the creature he had struck.

A second winged horse clambered from the earth. It astounded Meadow that these animals — so perceptive, so deft of hoof — had collided on the gallop. The conditions were extreme, after all …

He brushed himself off.

Several yards away, a nondescript lump on the ground issued a moan. Not a sinister creature. Perhaps a Fae knight, or a human. Meadow approached it with blade drawn, just in case.

The lump moaned again, shifted position, and sat up, revealing a grubby face and a saturated cloak, over mud-smeared armour.

'Dique!'

Dique shook his head, clearing groggy stars from his eyes. He squinted at Meadow. As realisation dawned, he beamed, a smile bright enough to penetrate the gloom.

'Of all the shady cretins to run into!' he cried.

'A charmed thing, finding you out here,' laughed Meadow, helping his fellow off the ground. The pterippi stood nearby, huffing and pawing, restless.

'We mustn't linger,' warned Dique.

'Right you are. The forces have been scattered — it's long since I last saw Lady Tate. My beast wants to take me south ... so south it is.'

'Agreed. We should try to find higher ground. Or shelter. Or both. Can you give me a hand with my things?'

Dique pottered around in the shadows, poking amongst items lying where they had fallen.

'What have you there, anyway?' asked Meadow.

'Oh, this and that. For some reason, there were things I couldn't bring myself to leave behind.' Dique hoisted one object, which Meadow identified as the strange zither he had seen Dique carrying earlier.

'Wait a minute, Dique. I don't get it. Why are you even carrying this? It will only weigh you — oof!'

Dique found a second item and pushed it towards Meadow, catching him in the belly. 'I really can't say,' he replied. 'But I saw this and figured I'd keep it for you. I thought you might have dropped it.'

It was large and boxy, with steel ribs and animal hide stretched over it.

Meadow looked down to find he was carrying a war drum.

Dique regained his pterippus, securing the zither over his shoulder. 'Come on now, Meadow ... or do you want to be trampled by Ogres?'

Meadow could only shrug. He lashed the instrument to his mount and climbed aboard once more.

The pair rode on together, guided through the vast darkness by the all-knowing pterippi.

Behind them, the Ogres unleashed a fury untold, bringing the might of the Pantheon down upon the rock titans. The battle raged long, with many an earth-shaking cry, until the last of Anuvin's fell host was ground to dust.

Anuvin ground his teeth.

Forces beyond his reckoning drew the conflict into the south. Be it the strange illumination that drew the Black Queen from his side, or the demolishing force of the Ogres … or perhaps even the infuriating will of those winged horses. Whatever the cause, the heat of battle slipped away into the deep of the Haunte.

His head swivelled, looking again into the north. Towards Two-Way Mirror Mountain. He saw an ambling shape, growing small against the immense rock formations. His quarry, the rogue seraph, wandered knowingly into the gullet of despair.

Which way to go? To deliver on a fated promise, goading the strangeling to complete its destiny? Or to follow the chaos, stoking the fires of wrath, to undo the defenders of Rhye?

Even a God must choose.

The beckoning conflict won him over. In the end, the magnitude of his own power required this battle to rage on, into the interminable night. It fed his ego, as much as it did his strength.

He turned and raced into the south, chasing the clash of arms.

Sheets of raindrops fell like a balm of redemption on Bastian Sinotar's face. Alone, immobile, he stared up at the sky. He could almost see the form of Valendyne now, coalescing amidst the vile nebula above.

He forced a bitter grin.

The battle had moved on, rolling southward. The sounds of war still reached him, though they faded into the distance.

The General Prime's breath came in shallow waves. His form lay warped upon a pile of stones, as if the Gods had thrown together a humble cairn for him to fall upon. Nearby lay the manticore — cold and lifeless, a fatal wound upon its breast.

He whispered a fleeting prayer — for Mustapha, for Lady Maybeth and for Rhye. All the while, his eyes drifted back and forth over the ruinous marsh. Searching.

There.

Still a way off, though it would arrive in its own time. Concealed, on occasion, by a pillar of smoke or a mound, covered in trampled reeds. Lingering in the hazy distance, then drawing nearer.

After such monumental threats, Anuvin refused to deliver the killing stroke, preferring to let Sinotar feel the aura of Death creep over him. He had also, with painstaking care, cleared away the nearby litter of discarded weapons. Not that it mattered — Sinotar could no sooner reach for a sword, as fly himself back to Wintergard.

Exposure, then? Starvation? Perhaps the paralysis would at last reach his lungs, as well?

'Father!'

Sinotar started. His head lolled to the right, following the voice.

Mustapha.

The seraph stumbled towards him, covered in grime and gore. Barely a scratch broke his skin. *The gore of others, then.* He wound his way through the detritus of battle, reaching the place where Sinotar had fallen.

'You survive … still,' said the sylph.

'I didn't think I'd find you. Not in that mess.'

'Part of me wishes you hadn't. It is not my finest hour.' Sinotar wheezed, then coughed. Blood spattered against his teeth. 'The letter. Do you still have it?'

Mustapha had almost forgotten the missive his father had given him. Patting his ripped tunic, he felt the reassuring bulge of folded parchment within. He nodded, preparing to bring it out.

'Not now,' said Sinotar. His voice grew low. The seraph knelt by him, to better take in his words.

'My way to the Afterlife lies ahead, just around a near corner,' the sylph said. 'For you, there is another leg to journey. You know what must be done.' His eyes rolled upwards, head tilted, looking beyond his shoulder. Over a scramble of boulders and a shattered ramp, gaped the maw of Two-Way Mirror Mountain.

'I'll get to that,' said Mustapha. 'First, I need to get you to safety. Find you some help.'

Sinotar shook his head. 'This is how it is. I cannot move. You cannot carry me. The legions move south. The battle continues, headed for the Pillar of Rhye. The dragon has drawn the remaining Vrendari in her wake. Leith Lourden commands them now ... it is her destiny.

'This is my place, upon this cairn. Born on one battlefield, dying on another. Here, at least, I can see the light of the White Queen, shining at me across the leagues.'

Mustapha recoiled. 'You can't die! Not here, not now! I have spent my years without you ... not knowing you, not learning from you ... raised by pretenders. It isn't fair!'

'No, it is not,' agreed Sinotar. 'The Gods give us each a soul, with the one flaw that it does not last forever. Ha! The golems, at least, did not suffer such indignity ... though they are all gone now.

'Be not lost, Mustapha. My moments with you have been my

most proud. I have grown more in your presence than in all the years since Maybeth left my side. My own soul has been in a kind of stasis, waiting to grow again. You have done much more than help me grow. You have helped set me free.'

The sylph was pale. Filth and dried blood streaked his face. He rested his head back, staring at the heavens.

For a long time, Mustapha said nothing. He knelt in the mud beside his father. At times, he prayed; for guidance, or for forgiveness, perhaps both. At other times, he looked upon the battered sylph, or into the south, where a steady pulse of white light winked back from the darkness.

'To know you has been an honour, Father,' he said. 'A privilege I never expected.'

'You were in my heart from the moment Oberon told me you were born,' replied the sylph.

The storm rumbled. A cold wind gusted down from the Mountain. All around them, fires burned to embers.

'I must ask you a favour,' said Sinotar.

'Anything.'

A faint smile. 'The Two-Legged Death comes for me. I see it now, picking a way amongst the fens. It lingers too long, keeping me from my peace.

'Anuvin denied me a swift, warrior's death. I pray you — send me across. You must finish this quest, for the sake of Rhye.'

Abject sorrow shaped Mustapha's face. He heaved with bodily sobs, tears flowing free. Though they fell upon Sinotar, no miraculous revival would come.

He knew his father spoke the inevitable truth. There was no other way.

Peace calmed the sylph's face. Gone was the perpetual scowl, the hauteur. Gone was everything but the face of an earnest creature.

A sylph who had loved a human and carried the burden for all his life, bearing consequence for the hope of a new dawn.

'Please.'

Mustapha wailed, a mournful sound.

He moved as if watching somebody else perform a terrible deed. He acted quickly, to be beyond thought, or hope, or regret. With nerveless fingers, he groped at his belt, a twitching hand finding the cold, metal butt of his pistol. Its ornate design appeared both beautiful and horrifying.

His final actions came with a moan of anguish. Mustapha palmed the gun, attempting to steady it with both hands. The slender barrel quavered as he took aim, at point blank range.

His eyes were tight shut as he squeezed the trigger.

Will's bootsteps splashed through low-lying water as he ran. He had almost abandoned the search for his beloved, finding no sign of the seraph amongst the blanket of dead.

The single, sharp retort of a gun, away from the arena of battle, drew his attention.

He ran though his chest heaved and his legs burned like fire. He staggered through slews of bodies, thick upon the countryside.

At one time, he had been Will, the wagoner. A gourd farmer, minding his own business. Now, knee-deep in muck and horror, it seemed like a separate lifetime.

Will ran past groups of refugees, digging hovels or making huddled camps on the lee side of nobbled promontories. They seemed to have found food amongst the devastation. He dared not look at what they might be eating.

'Mustapha!' he called. 'Mustapha!'

There, finally, he saw the seraph. A tiny figure, yet unmistakeable.

Agonising distance separated them.

Will called again. He kept running, forcing himself to move though he knew it was too far. Mustapha worked his way through ruins of stone, winding gradually up the ramp towards Two-Way Mirror Mountain. Once it swallowed him, he would be gone forever.

Will could never reach him in time.

The realisation lay upon him like a leaden shroud. What chance they would both survive a catastrophic battle, only to be separated by such tyranny?

His spirit wilted inside him. 'Mustapha!' he cried once more, with all his might.

The figure did not respond.

Will stopped in place, hands on knees, breath ragged. He never let his gaze leave the diminishing figure, until it crested the ramp and disappeared from sight. His eyes glistened, as he murmured an ode to the hero of his heart.

Fly, my dearest Mustapha, all hope now rests with you.
Remember there's a purpose behind everything you do.
The Prophet spoke of love to save the land and sea and sky,
Love doth abound within your soul — a paragon for Rhye.

The hopes of every precious soul, a vessel fine will be
To buoy you on your gallant way across the Seventh Sea.
To distant shores, to places new, a prophecy foretold,
Keep your spirit bright and true — may fortune grace the bold.

My heart you stole, my life upturned
All through these days, for you I've yearned
I'd follow you to Rhye's new dawn
But now I wait: Return anon.

Go now on your vital quest, on angel wings take flight,
Deliver love, our saving grace, beyond the speed of light.
With every beat my heart does sing, my strength to you I send,
Remember I am there with you, until the very end.

Then he knelt on the ground and allowed himself to cry.

CHAPTER 22

TWO-WAY MIRROR MOUNTAIN

Mustapha wanted to feel numb, more than anything else in the world. He wanted the atrocities of recent hours to fade into a haze of white noise. Instead, his nerves jangled, every muscle ached, and his feet seemed buried in leaden boots.

Climbing the ramp strewn with rockfall felt like ascending the scaffold to his own execution. His remaining task was to meet with his own fate. He forced out any conscious thought, leaving his mind an empty space.

Everything felt too raw.

All the thanks he owed, to those who saved his life. All the goodbyes he had not wished, to his dearest friends. Perhaps he had eschewed a burden too great to bear — how do you bid one final farewell and simply walk away?

So long, everyone. It's time I was facing up to my destiny. I'll see you later ... or not.

Subliminal monsters continued to gnaw at the edges of his consciousness. He tried to cast them out once more. It helped to focus on the physical pain instead.

Still, his cruel imagination taunted him with the voice of Will.

Calling his name.

Surely, Will was dead? So many had been killed — how would a wagoner survive?

He refused to turn around and acknowledge the deceit of his ears. The heartbreak would destroy him.

Mustapha wandered into the mouth of Two-Way Mirror Mountain.

One hundred yards inside the cave mouth, the world turned dark.

In the gullet of the Ogres' den, the air turned cool. A dank smell reached Mustapha's nose, as where water runs in deep places under the rock of the earth. The *drip-drip* of water from stalactites echoed, bouncing off distant corners.

Underfoot, the floor of the cavern was worn smooth. Whether due to the passage of water, or the pounding of giant feet for thousands of years, Mustapha could not know. The passage sloped downwards — not so steep as to be hazardous, but enough to give the impression of descending the throat of the majestic landmark.

Despite his voluntary detachment, a sense of intrusion struck Mustapha. He advanced into a demesne not seen by outsiders in all of Rhye's history.

He picked his way into the Ogres' den with care, for the light in this hidden world was feeble. As his eyes adjusted, Mustapha found he did not wander in pitch blackness. The void retreated, showing a broad tunnel, perhaps some twenty yards to either side of him. On one side, he spied a gigantic vein of scrallin. It wound along the wall like a magnificent, branching serpent, snaking its way through the subterranean gloom. It may well have been the largest single deposit of the enchanted mineral in all the land — much larger than the stone that had secured the Ogres' door. The giant scrallin serpent cast only dim illumination. In this place, there was little light for it to capture. Ghostly silver settled on the surrounding cavern walls ... enough to beckon him onwards.

Mustapha continued his trek through the vault. He wondered what the Ogres ate. Tales from his childhood, shared with him by mischievous pixies — and even, on occasion, by Lord Oberon — told of a hellish cave, piled high with the carcasses of great beasts, upon which the Ogres would chew. Bones stripped bare of flesh would be tossed in a corner, or perhaps wielded as clubs when the Ogres turned upon each other.

No stench of rotting meat permeated the air. The lair of such uncivilised brutes ought to have been cluttered. The more he walked, the more Mustapha pondered the incongruous space around him.

In a contemplative moment, he saw the drawing.

Just visible in the scrallin-shimmer, a pictograph graced the worn rock face. With a few simple but elegant lines, the artist had created the likeness of a misshapen creature. In an image the same height as Mustapha, the creature stood at what appeared to be a wide opening — a window on the world. It looked outwards, with one cyclopean eye.

An Ogre gazed upon Rhye from its mountain prison.

Enchanted by the ancient rendering, Mustapha approached the tunnel wall, reaching out to trace his finger over the faded pigment. It crumbled beneath his touch. In deference, he drew his hand away but continued to study the dimly lit mural.

The watchful figure had company. Alongside it, other shapes materialised, as Mustapha edged along the wall. More Ogres, in an array of shapes and sizes; some a crude smattering of pigment on stone, others drawn with a more refined hand. Occasionally, there appeared an image of alarming realism. Some of the figures stood by themselves. Others appeared in groups. Next came the largest composition Mustapha had yet seen: a gigantic image of twenty-four Ogres, seated in a circle. In fading colours, One-Eye, Four-Arms and Toad-Mouth stared out at him, whilst others he had seen upon the battlefield completed the picture.

Chills danced up and down his spine. The seraph looked back over his shoulder, half expecting the returning Ogres to loom out of the darkness.

Aside from the *drip-drip-drip*, there was silence.

The Ogres of Marnis were fabled as murderous brutes. Certainly, their prowess on the battleground bore out this conception. By contrast, the mural hinted at civility, long hidden from the races that called themselves 'higher beings'.

More pictures followed. Some were embellished in glorious colour, others incomplete. At length, an image stopped Mustapha stone cold. A basic line drawing of a gnarled, hunch-backed creature, who appeared to have two heads. While this Ogre looked familiar to the seraph, the drawing included a second figure — much smaller, yet of much greater significance.

The humanoid figure owned a pair of arms, a pair of legs and only one head, though there the similarity ended. It had strange, elongated jaws and large eyes that portrayed a quiet wisdom. Protruding from the sleeves of a simple tunic, the beast had wide, clawed hands.

With a jolt, Mustapha recalled a memory of faces just like this one. A breathless pursuit, through dense forest under a new moon. A fleeting glimpse, cast over his shoulder. A fateful decision, involving a small fragment of cinnabar.

Mustapha frowned.

That can't be right. Can it?

The image on the cave wall teased him, staring out from Ages past. Challenging him to believe what he saw.

Mustapha followed the wall more closely. The mural flowed on before him, stretching deep into the mountain, a tapestry of unfathomable magnitude. The further he walked, the deeper became the furrows of his brow. Images emerged of tunnelling and carving — these new creatures had arrived from places far beyond the Ogres' ken.

The essence of the story lay beyond refute. Here, buried far beneath Rhye, hid a history kept from the Sovereign races of the land. A history that most had never known.

The seraph pressed on into the depths, uncovering the secret history of the Delves.

The abyssal places of the earth were reserved for the primal and the resilient. Those who were no more terrified of the hellish dark, than by the thoughts that plague an isolated mind.

In such places, the Delves made their abode.

When the Mer-Folk first ventured ashore from the Trident Sea, burrowing amongst the porous cliff faces, the Delves were there to help them create the labyrinthine passages that would one day become known as Artesia.

When the golems settled in the home Valendyne made them, mining ever deeper beneath the Peaks of Light, the Delves met with them, teaching them about all the wondrous ores that Marnis put there.

When Cornavrian bundled the Ogres safely beneath Two-Way Mirror Mountain, they spent an eternity in a state of primitive bewilderment. In the dark, their instinctive fury was quelled, though they were abandoned — forsaken by their Gods, detached from the natural beauty that might have tamed their brutal spirits.

The scrallin window provided their only solace. From there, they could see all of history unfold.

In those times, Fenmarck Haunte blossomed as a sanctuary. A haven of rolling hills and woodlands, where the entire countryside would change colour with the seasons. Not until the Godsryche would devastation scorch the region, destroying all splendour; save for a narrow verge, known much later as the Greenway.

With the blight of unholy conflict, the world became bleak. Ruin stretched as far as the Ogres could see from within their confinement. They retreated into the earth, shunning the atrocity outside.

There came a day when the Ogres discovered that they were not alone, in the depths of the world. They happened upon a tribe of much smaller creatures, who appeared at ease in the claustrophobic caverns. These creatures showed neither fear, nor hostility. With open-handed gestures they indicated each other, making the same sound, over and over.

'Delves.'

The Ogres determined this to be what the dauntless creatures named themselves.

Despite their size, the Delves displayed a mastery of digging and burrowing in the earth — greater even than the Ogres, with their prodigious strength. To declare their alliance, the Delves created for the Ogres a vast underground network of caves and tunnels, into which they could expand their hidden demesne.

The Ogres knew gratitude, though they knew not how to express it. They knew nothing of compassion, or generosity ... or communication.

The Delves attempted to teach their gargantuan companions.

Though the Ogres never truly learned how to speak for themselves, they came to understand much of what the Delves said to them.

The Ogres did learn, with astonishing proficiency, the skill of creating pictographs, on the endless rock that surrounded them.

Using clays and ground minerals, they produced art. They drew everything: Their thoughts, their hopes, their existential questions all came to life in drawing. This revelation enabled the Delves to teach them about greater things — about the land beyond the cave and about the Gods who had made them. The Ogres learned of Adatar and Anato, who danced across the sky; of Marnis the Creator and Cornavrian, who shaped Nature. They also learned of Valendyne, who by that time was imprisoned in the garden of Nevermore.

The Ogres developed conscience, virtue, and a righteous passion, which they longed to direct against those who brought ruin to the land beyond their window.

In time, the Delves discovered ways to the surface, on the far side of the Mountain. They told the Ogres of the garden, Nevermore, rich with glorious beauty. Within the garden, said the Delves, were fruits, wildflowers, cascading waterfalls, and a wide tract of verdant forest, stretching all the way to the shore of the Seventh Sea. In the centre of the garden there grew a lone tree — black and twisted, a hideous thing — that cast a stain upon the grasses around it.

The Ogres wanted nothing of this garden, marred by the vestige of evil.

In their bestial tongue, the Delves explained that they had also found a way to the roof of the mountain range.

Upon a high peak, draped in a white veil, they found a monastery. It must be a construction of the Gods, the Delves insisted, for winged creatures were building it. They were of proud countenance, bearing resemblance to the sacred warriors of Lhestra.

These angels were not the only creatures the Delves encountered atop the mountains. They also met with a race that appeared human, though these people practised mystic arts, unknown to Humankind. They cloaked themselves in vibrant shades.

The Ogres had not seen bright colours of any kind for millennia, though they recalled the beauty of the changing seasons. These creatures, said the Delves, were arrayed in all the hues of Nature.

The Ogres pondered this. Surely, these mystic beings must be the kinfolk of Cornavrian.

The Delves began sharing their time between the deep caverns and the misty peaks. Over a long period, they channelled many passages through the heart of the mountains. These were clandestine byways that only the Delves used, for the Adept — as they came to be known — refused to venture into the sinister caverns or go anywhere near the glade of Nevermore. The Ogres, for their part, chose to avoid the light of Adatar, therefore remaining in a world of entombed darkness and silence.

Thus did their reputation grow.

On one occasion, a traveller from distant Rhye did use the secret tunnels. The Ogres watched from shadow as a lone human, escorted by the Delves, made his way through the chasmal demesne. Never did they learn the reason for the human's passing. One moment he was amongst them, the next he was gone, without a word of explanation.

Many more years passed.

The Delves spent less and less time in the dark with the Ogres. The Adept, they explained, were grieving. Many of their number had been lost in a great conflict, wrought by the Gods. The Adept were now acclimatised to their high niche, which they called Aerglo ... only they were a fledgling community, struggling with the loss of their warrior kindred. The Delves resolved to help them. In return, the Adept imparted on the Delves much of their sacred lore.

For a time, the world went quiet. The Ogres were alone again, with no word from above. Then, after many seasons, the Delves descended, to visit their friends one final time.

Mustapha stared at the wall.

He had walked for what felt like leagues, forgetting the rumbling of his stomach, or the ache of his muscles. Captivated was he, by the tale of the Delves.

Many a revelation had stayed locked beneath these mountains since the Age of Higher Beings.

He stood in front of one final image. A small pictograph, created by a modest hand. Depicted were the Ogres, again in their primal enclave. Beside them were drawn a great number of figures that were, beyond doubt, representations of the Delves.

They were clad, one and all, in Violet.

Mustapha exhaled, nodding slowly to himself in the dark.

The Ogres waited millennia to demonstrate fealty to their Creator and the God of Nature. They had carved out a humble community, all the while pondering their existence; anticipating that moment when they could vie against the forces of Valendyne, who cast a blight upon the world beyond their window.

Now, that moment had passed. *Did the Ogres gain retribution? Did it make a difference to Rhye — so tight in the clutch of despair, so far beyond hope?* Mustapha felt unsure whether it had, in the grand scheme, truly mattered.

Whether anything truly mattered.

Near to the final drawing, Mustapha found a long, wide stair, hewn from rock. He began climbing. Far above, he sensed that a light shone — not the mineral ambience of scrallin, but the light of the world outside.

CHAPTER 23

RAIN STOPPED FALLING

A chill breeze whistled through alpine climes. Now and again arose a grim rumble, in the wake of a vivid lightning flicker. No other sound marred the glacial night air.

Atop the stair, a broad portal, carved by delvish hands, opened on the north face of Two-Way Mirror Mountain.

Mustapha emerged from the doorway. Fresh, crisp air filled his lungs, at once both jarring and rejuvenating. He found himself upon a gravelled trail, a path that led in winding switchbacks to the valley below.

It took the seraph a few moments to realise that rain no longer fell. From a low mountain scarp, the twinkle of stars dotted the north sky. Even the gleaming face of Anato cast her argent glow over the nightscape — a lustrous blanket, thrown across the land by the Goddess herself.

Before Mustapha lay the vista of Nevermore. It held him in

terrified awe. In an instant, he forgot every tale ever told to him, for the vision to greet his eyes made a mockery of them all, to the last word.

A stark wasteland stretched, as a wide bowl, from the rocky slope to the distant Sea. A forest of leafless trees reached their pallid, ivory limbs to the stars. Their twisted forms speared like shrieks of supplication from the blackened ground.

In the centre of the glade — a little over half a league from where Mustapha gazed in wonder — a denuded patch of blasted earth drew his eye. There stood alone a single tree, brooding and dominant, above all.

The tree of Valendyne lorded over the forest, a towering bastion of misery in a place that spoke of sorrow and loss. From the vast reach of its branches issued a dense plume of black cloud, pouring skyward. The plume streamed into the heavens, as if belched forth from a volcano. Overhead it thickened, swirling, carried on a fell wind over the Peaks of Obelis.

The strangeling had reached the source of the maleficent storm that rolled across the land. Just as a bottle, once unsealed, may begin to leak, so did the arbour prison hiss with the escaping God of the Afterlife.

Without utterance, Mustapha absorbed the horror of Nevermore. The desolation chilled his bones. A single, silver streak ran down his face.

This is where I die. In a glade of withered trees, with nothing but my own remorse and the awakening of Rhye's damnation.

The words of Anuvin glowered in his mind. Indeed, he had killed, leaving love on the battlefield. Of the God of War, he saw no sign, but what did it matter? Anuvin had already manoeuvred the seraph to the exact place he needed to be.

At the end of the earth.

Little remained to be done.

Mustapha started on the path, leading down the mountainside into Nevermore. From this elevation, he could easily see out across the graveyard of trunks and branches, to the mesmerising expanse of the Seventh Sea beyond. The dark waters shimmered beneath the light of Anato, beckoning him with glistening allure.

The Tree, or the Sea? The future held Death, whichever path he chose.

As his boots trod in the pebbles and dust of the path, Mustapha spied footprints that ran alongside — and ahead of — his own. With a fleeting consternation he considered them. In the end, it faded into irrelevance.

The bleached white boughs of countless trees reached out, drawing him into the hellscape. Within the valley, not a bloom, nor a single green blade of grass, nor orphan leaf, met his eye. Decay reigned. Nothing could thrive in the toxic presence of Valendyne, be he imprisoned or free. The place where the Gods crafted their greatest natural wonder would never again contain such lush providence.

Wind moaned through the skeletal remains of Nevermore. Gravel crunched underfoot. A whispered susurrus swirled from all around, the phantom sound of a sacred breath through long-dead foliage. Above the steady murmur of the night, one other sound could be heard: an intermittent *thunk, thunk, thunk*, which Mustapha could not place. It came from somewhere in front of him.

He hurried, winding deeper into the valley, chasing the rhythmic knock.

Oblivious to the thing on the prowl behind him.

With sinister patience, it crept from the delvish portal, out into the night. Every movement flowed with malevolent intent, as the being clicked along the ancient path on limbs like a giant mantis.

The Two-Legged Death came swift and silent into Nevermore; at times looming large over the trees, at others slinking between them. Its form was both bloated and emaciated, as if its very essence grew and shrank with the pulse of darkness. Clawed hands reached before it, displaying a spidery poise and menace. Fathomless, black eyes leered in the direction of its victim. Twisted antlers burst from its crown, gleaming under the moonlight.

The creature came relentlessly in Mustapha's wake. It headed for the central tree, eager for the emancipation of its true Lord.

Thunk. Thunk. Thunk.

The sound grew more insistent. More urgent.

Mustapha dared not use his gift of speed, lest he run headlong into some peril wrought by Valendyne; though now he moved with greater haste, threading through the eerie wasteland. Ahead, Valendyne's prison towered, a horrific parody of Oberon's Yew. The blackened tree thrust palsied boughs upward, warding off the blessed illumination of Anato, whom once he had adored.

At this proximity, the billowing column of cloud emitted an ominous rumble as it spiralled into the sky. Splintered bark and other dark debris rained down from the plume.

Mustapha crept forward, using each interceding tree as cover, wondering if the God of the Afterlife could sense his approach.

'Ark! Ark!'

The eruption of sound sent him diving behind the nearest trunk. A raven, fluttering and cawing, rose from an overhead bough. With a final, stark cry, it winged away.

Only a few yards further and Mustapha could no longer hide.

He came upon a clearing of scorched earth, gently sloping, with a northerly aspect towards the Seventh Sea. Within that glade did the prison of Valendyne rise, from sprawling roots, through an elephantine trunk to the myriad warped branches, far above. So black its boughs that moonlight barely reflected from them. The tree met the eye as a void, a place where it almost hurt to look for too long.

Upon the ground, in broken hoops and shards of polished metal, lay the fragmented remains of six massive bands.

A seventh, final band, clenched the trunk of the tree. One last refrain of the binding promise between Gods and Sovereigns, made at the end of the Godsryche. The Fae Ring would soon fail, for even this last band was fractured, ebbing meek lambency from innumerable cracks.

Mustapha near swallowed his tongue in shock. The vision that greeted him was far from what he expected.

An athletic figure stood, feet wide, at the foot of the hideous tree, hewing upon it with desperate blows from a long-handled axe.

Thunk. Thunk. Thunk.

The Fairy Feller did not look away from his labour. A fever of sweat shone upon his forehead. A rictus of pain and wild determination fixed his features. With every strike, a gaping split in the tree trunk grew. The tree itself creaked and groaned in response.

From lofty Aerglo had the Feller come, through ancient delvish tunnels, now known only to the Adept. In the footsteps of the Prophet he walked, bearing the final edict of the Fairy King.

Go to Aerglo. Speak with Benjulius — he will lead you to the Way of the Prophet. Fear neither darkness nor Death. You must cut down the tree ... at all costs.

Mustapha could not tear his eyes away. The Feller chopped with a herculean effort, his stage a barren wilderness, far from the bosom of the Mother Forest. Unaware of the seraph's presence, he worked without hope of honour or admiration. His audience may well have been the Gods alone.

A snaking tendril broke from the vast column of rising cloud.

Seeking, probing, the black tentacle wandered downwards, searching for the threat below. The creeping evil homed in on the Feller, who toiled oblivious to the lurking danger.

It inched closer, moving to envelop him.

'Feller!' cried Mustapha, expelling the word from the vice of his throat. The axeman spun around, startled; not just for the surprise of finding another soul in the wasteland, but also for the profound timbre of the seraph's voice. The air trembled, dead trees rattling. For a moment, the tendril of Valendyne's malice wavered, sensing the presence of opposing might.

Then, in a vicious swirl, the black cloud ensnared its victim.

The Feller's weapon clattered to the ground. Wide-eyed, he stood clenched in a coil of wrath.

'Whoever you are — flee, or be ruined!' he shrieked to Mustapha, who froze to the spot, entranced by the terrible fascination of the Feller's doom.

A creature of shadow burst into the clearing, shattering the seraph's trance. Bounding on bestial limbs and issuing a chilling scream, it appeared at the foot of the tree. Clenching and unclenching clawed hands, it fixed the two interlopers with a bottomless stare.

The Two-Legged Death descended on the Fairy Feller.

'No!' shouted Mustapha, as if he could halt the inevitable. Nearby lay the Feller's axe, his task incomplete. In a selfless instant, Mustapha wondered if he had the strength to fell the tree, subverting Valendyne's liberation.

The Fairy Feller thrashed his legs in valiant defiance. His efforts proved futile: The Two-Legged Death yawned wide its noisome mouth — a maw large enough to devour the Feller whole. Death engulfed the axeman in a single motion. His final cry was extinguished so completely, he may well have never been.

Mustapha gawped in horror.

Then, realisation struck.

I can see the Two-Legged Death, too.

The Tree, or the Sea. This one choice, he could make. To try and topple the tree, but in doing so, to touch it and open the door for Valendyne incarnate. Alternatively, to run for the Seventh Sea, leaving his fate to its deadly embrace.

The Two-Legged Death swivelled towards him, the stench of blood and decay on its breath.

Mustapha ran.

He abandoned all caution as he sprinted for the far side of the clearing. With blinding speed, he dashed into a maze of haunting, white boles. Beyond, he reached a long avenue of trees, with arcing branches that intertwined overhead. Never once did he stop for rest or breath, or to cast a glance over his shoulder. If the creature pursued him, it did so in darkness and silence.

Nevermore sprawled about him, like a vast cathedral sprung from the Afterlife. Ahead, the sparkling Sea winked at him through the trees, a welcome to oblivion. The valley funnelled him towards it — the final leg of his journey across the land.

The low roar of rolling waves upon shore reached his ears. In his mind, he could already feel the water's gelid shroud. He readied himself for it.

Should I try to swim?

Am I destined simply to drown, in the attempt?

Would the creature of Valendyne pursue me, even beyond the shores of Rhye?

The questions fled from him, unanswered. He had arrived.

The whirlwind of his legs kicked up a shower of black sand as he exploded onto the beach. There, at last, he stopped.

Mustapha found himself in a moonlit cove. A wide crescent

of tumbled stone, against which the waves hurled themselves in perpetual cycles. Far in the west, the Peaks of Obelis bordered the cove, a jagged line rising to meet a star-filled sky. To the east, there rose a lesser wall, still trenchant and forbidding.

The sandy verge stretched only a short distance to either side of him. The beach offered a slice of stark beauty, hemmed by a picket fence of bone-white trees and by silvery froth, surging and retreating upon a midnight shore.

The Two-Legged Death had not caught up to him.

As Mustapha looked about, his heart thrummed in his chest. His lungs burned with the cold air. He cast around, unsure as to what he should do, when the shrill pity of a lament drifted to him on the lilting wind.

His eyes darted left.

At the western fringe of the beach, where sand met rock worn smooth by the Sea, huddled a group of figures. Anato's light caught their pallor — the glimpse of white veils and ashen flesh.

Again came the sound of women, keening and crying.

Mustapha jogged towards them. Some of their number saw him approach. The group loosened, revealing the focus of their lament.

Amidst the huddle, a stately body lay upon the stone. Drawing closer, the seraph knew it to be Lord Neptune. His lifeless form lay supine on the natural plinth, the swell lapping at his bare legs. A grievous wound — a dark, purple concavity, evidence of a fatal strike — deformed his imposing chest. Still, he wore a majestic dignity upon his face.

The women mourning him were undines. Amphibious and scaled, beautiful in the same way that a whale song, or an ocean tempest, can be considered beautiful. They crouched and sat upon the rocks surrounding Lord Neptune, poring over him in their grief. Salt spray settled on them, a mist of bereavement.

Most prominent amongst them was Salacia.

The Mer-Lord's consort spied Mustapha with a wail in her voice, but as the seraph neared the undines, her bitter keening transformed. A joyous inflection pierced her misery. She threw up her arms, offering gratitude to the cosmos.

'By the grace of Cornavrian, he is come!' she cried. 'There is yet hope.'

Mustapha slowed, approaching with caution. He knew of Salacia, from the Council of Rhye. Many spoke of her as pure of heart and dedicated to the land's need. Her see-sawing passion made him wary, should she be in the grip of some fell curse.

'My destiny is fresh out of hope,' he demurred. 'I come to this beach to fulfil my own fate. My sacrifice is prophesied.' He crossed the sand, drawing nearer, eyes on the fallen Neptune.

Confirmed ... now, only Benjulius survives.

'Your appearance is, on the contrary, a sign that we are not yet forsaken. The Gods promise truly.' Salacia now smiled through her tears.

'The Gods promise ...? What do they promise?'

In total, eight undines clung to the rocky shoreline. Their bodies were swathed in white mantles, as delicate as the mist that drifted over dancing waves. All of them, having appraised the seraph, now smiled, their distress quelled.

'The events of these past hours would keep a bard singing for many moons. As time is not in our favour, I shall recount that which causes us such joy at your arrival.' As Salacia spoke, her gaze darted from Mustapha to a place far behind him, then back again. Such was her wandering glance that the seraph turned to check over his own shoulder. Seeing nothing, he waited to hear Salacia's story.

'The God of War brought my beloved to this place to die,' the undine began. 'Anuvin declared that my Lord would be in perfect position to witness the demise of all hope on Rhye. He claimed that the Seas would all become great lakes of fire, ushering an end to all marine life.

'By the force of his own will, Lord Neptune survived his heinous injury for many days. This is how we came to find him here, after scouring the coasts for signs that War had indeed made landfall.

'Weakened in body, but not in spirit, my Lord entreated us to sing and pray. Though it hurt him so to fill his lungs, he whispered his praise; to Anato above, to the Creator and to Cornavrian.

'May we be forever thankful for that time spent in prayer and contemplation. The time that passed might have been the length of a day, or perhaps two, though the sky has not changed. Lo, when we felt sure the time had come for Neptune to leave us, our vigil was answered.'

Mustapha found himself leaning forward, clinging to Salacia's words.

'From high upon the air, arrived a being of pure wonder,' she continued. 'He bore wings of flawless white, upon which he descended to the sand. His perfect form seemed chiselled from the solid rock of the earth. The exceptions were his eyes — the blue of purest water — and his glorious head of hair, which glowed and flickered upon his crown like flame.'

The seraph's brows were raised. Any who considered themselves devout knew the being that Salacia described. Mustapha's thoughts raced back to his humble shrine, tucked away in the annexe at the House of Giltenan.

'The being named himself Cornavrian,' the undine confirmed. 'He gave to us his benediction, for we are spirits of the natural world and are, therefore, shaped by his hand. He spoke with mercy of Lord Neptune, who dedicated his life to the service of the Seven Seas of Rhye.

'Cornavrian assured us that the Pantheon can see our plight and know of our suffering. The resolution of War and Death is a matter between mortals and those two unshackled Gods. It is not for one God to directly intervene in the work of another. So, whilst the remaining Pantheon cannot subvert the destiny of our land, they may play a part in shaping it.

'Nature could not save Lord Neptune as he lay dying, any more than Augustine may foster Love, or Phydeas may turn the wheel of Time. Instead, he did offer to grant one boon to the ailing Mer-Lord. One favour which, if chosen with diligence, might alter the fate of Rhye.'

Mustapha's brow creased. He dared not hope for what Salacia might say next. At the same time, he dreaded the re-appearance of Valendyne's beast. The hairs prickled upon his neck. He spun around, searching the stark forest of Nevermore.

A shadow moved there, between the trees — making its way slowly down the valley, towards the beach. A shade of immense size. Though Mustapha peered at it, the delicate beams of moonlight were insufficient to reveal the creature in darkness.

A warm smile entered Salacia's voice. 'You see him ... don't you?'

'I ... I do. Wait — do you see him, also?' The seraph spun back to her in alarm.

'Why yes, I do! He is Mher. He is the boon — the dying wish granted to Lord Neptune, by Cornavrian.'

Flummoxed, Mustapha said: 'I don't know what you mean. Is that not the Two-Legged Death coming down the path behind me?'

'By all that is sacred, no!' Salacia laughed, reaching elation now. All about her, the other undines watched the dead forest — and the form within it — in rapture.

'Then who, or what is Mher?'

'Mher is an Ogre,' replied Salacia. 'A creature of Marnis, cherished and nurtured by Cornavrian. He comes now, in answer to our call.'

Mustapha turned back once more, scanning the gloom between trees. There, he again saw the enormous creature, moving with a ponderous gait, toppling trees to left and right as it came.

The seraph marvelled. *This is not the Two-Legged Death. That foul being must lurk somewhere still, within Nevermore.*

'The Ogres have names?' he asked.

Salacia nodded. 'Cornavrian graced us with this knowledge. The Ogres — so long relegated to myth — are far from uncultured heathens. They may harbour an ancient rage, but they are also with soul and conscience. They have names and also gifts, bequeathed by the God of Nature.'

'Of course, they do,' said Mustapha. He watched the gargantuan Mher emerge from the tree line, near to where he had also arrived on the beach. The rotund, corpulent Mher had great webbed hands and feet. Upon his face, a cavernous mouth stretched wide.

Mustapha recognised the creature as the Ogre he dubbed Toad-Mouth.

The Ogres return home then, from battle? Are they victors?

Salacia still spoke. '… there is Byorndrazil, who can summon lightning, and Thalalladon who can turn fire to ice and back again. There is Goron, who can craft food from clay —'

'I understand,' said Mustapha absently. He watched Mher now, lumbering down the black sand, his pebbled skin glistening. He glanced for a brief moment in the direction of Mustapha and the undines, before fixing coal-black eyes on the place where the waves rushed ashore.

Salacia grinned. 'Lord Neptune beseeched Cornavrian to summon Mher here, to aid the hero who would come to fulfil the prophecy. Mher is here to help you, seraph.'

'But how? What can Mher do?'

'He can swallow up the Sea.'

Mustapha stared, dumbfounded, as Mher waded into the shallows. He wallowed in the swell, where waves lapped his belly. Then, crouching forward, Mher opened his mouth like a giant grotto.

Dipping low into the water, he began to drink.

The vacuous sound of Mher's quaffing was akin to draining the world dry. Mustapha knew that he witnessed something beyond the conceivable. A churning whirlpool developed around the enormous, squat form of the Ogre, a green-grey vortex of foam and seawater. With a voracious energy Mher drank, until, by increments, the tide fell.

The seraph mumbled an incoherent oath.

All around him, the undines gasped, praising Lord Neptune's final wish.

Mher continued to draw in the Seventh Sea. The water kept flowing towards him, unable to escape the preternatural force of his gift. The Ogre distended, not to the volume he had drunk, but enough to stretch his wrinkled hide as taut as a drum.

In time, the seabed lay exposed. Its bed was not deep with trenches and chasms, but gently undulating, like the myriad dunes of Sordd. Countless natural treasures of the marine floor lay high and dry: litters of coral, starfish and conch, the occasional wrecked vessel. Those who had tried to cross the Seventh Sea by sailing invariably failed.

With a final, resounding *shlurp*, Mher imbibed the last of the Sea. He stood, a great balloon, staring out across the alien landscape he had uncovered. His tremendous mouth was clamped tightly shut, though trickles of water seeped from the corners.

Mustapha only stared.

Salacia nudged him. 'Mher can't hold on forever,' she said in a gentle tone. 'He grants us this favour, at the behest of Cornavrian — but it is for us to use wisely.'

Mustapha nodded. For a solemn moment, he gazed upon the body of Neptune. The Mer-Lord was one of many Sovereigns who had faced Death, so that a hero might salvage the future of the land. He thought upon the toils of the Fairy King. The diligence of Lord Rogar.

He thought upon his father.

So many ghosts.

Collecting himself, Mustapha bid goodbye to the undines. For victory or for failure, they would be the last mortal creatures to whom he spoke. Glory or Death awaited him on the far shores of the Seventh Sea.

In the shadow of the swollen Ogre, Mustapha looked out upon the vast seabed. He could not make out the opposite side.

One deep breath, to the furthest recesses of his chest.

In, then out.

Once more, Mustapha began to run.

He moved like a frigid blast, whipping across the frozen northern tundra. The seabed was a blur beneath his boots. Once, twice, he snatched glances back towards the shore. Was that a second, dark shape standing on the sand? Did Death pursue him, even now? It mattered not, as he raced to the edge of charted territory. Incontestable speed whipped his hair in a dark pennant, behind him.

With a *boom* he vanished, beyond the speed of sound. The black shore receded behind him.

Mher continued to clench his broad, rubbery lips. Within him strained the astronomical pressure of the Seventh Sea. The pain he held inside, stoic in his obeisance to Cornavrian. Calm, black eyes roved the horizon, though the strange being who bolted from the beach was no longer visible.

Eddies and currents swirled within his gargantuan belly. Crashing waves surged, a test of the Ogre's immense fortitude.

Still he held on, gaze focused on a point in the bleak distance.

A single bead of sweat ran down his face.

League after eerie league, Mustapha plunged ever deeper into the unknown. He hurtled through places never seen before, hidden beneath waters best known in fable. The undulating seabed cast strange shapes in his path, littered with those mysterious things that lie at great depth. Blind to all of it, he wanted only to cover more distance.

Distance, his only enemy. The inestimable tyrant, taunting him with every leap and bound.

He ran, for those he left behind.

For the hopes of those who lived for tomorrow.

He ran and did not stop, though an ethereal fog draped the leagues that lay ahead of him.

Mher's whole body tremored and quaked.

Slushing rivers of seawater now escaped the corners of his mouth, spilling out where the pressure became too great. The Ogre's face contorted in agony, streaked with the tracks of strain. The Seventh Sea welled up inside him — raging, protesting for release. Though he fought with titanic strength, the indomitable waters threatened to burst free.

Tears streamed from his eyes as he stared into oblivion.

Mustapha ran beyond Rhye.

He ran beyond time and place, beyond thew and blood and bone.

He ran beyond himself.

In the end, Nature finds restitution.

It comes full circle, defying containment and control.

Mher crumpled under the pressure of the Seventh Sea. With a

gushing roar that reverberated from distant mountain slopes, he opened his mouth and allowed the waters to flood out. The surge sent an unstoppable deluge over the seabed — frothing, roiling, overwhelming everything in its path.

The devastating power of the Sea consumed all.

CHAPTER 24

MESSENGER FROM SEVEN SEAS

In this way did Khashoggi's tale reach an abrupt end.

The old hermit sat back in his seat, wearing a faint, satisfied grin. He held his bony hands wide, palms facing upwards — a gesture that said, "Voila!"

There you are.

For a long time, I could only look at him. Something about Khashoggi — those mesmeric eyes as they twinkled back at me, or the cadence of his voice, like a caravel upon the Seas of Rhye — held me entranced. I found myself chewing every word as he fed it to me, waiting for the next morsel. Though it was but a fairy tale, I hankered to hear the final act.

Yet Khashoggi had stopped, mid-stream, offering nothing more than an enigmatic smile. Gleaming teeth showed behind a well-coiffed beard.

'Go on then, man!' I said to him. 'What happened next? You keep me in such suspense!'

At first, he said nothing. The palms remained raised and his shoulders rose, almost imperceptibly.

'You — you don't know?'

It seemed absurd to me. The world of this man's psychosis was so vivid — so visceral, so vital — yet he knew not how to conclude his story. I tore my eyes away from him.

Then, my senses reeled.

Nothing appeared as I recalled it, when Khashoggi's tale began. Was that two hours ago? Two days? Where once there had been a derelict ship, we were now surrounded by opulence. We sat aboard a splendid vessel, as seaworthy as any I had ever encountered. The deck gleamed, polished to a high shine beneath our feet. Crisp, white paint glistened upon the bulkheads. Brass gauges and fittings invited the hand of an able seaman. We sat together in a stateroom, appointed for a captain of the highest calibre.

As for Khashoggi — surely, my eyes deceived me! The man who occupied the facing chair, legs crossed and fingertips pressed together, personified the debonair pilgrim. A collared shirt lay open at his neck, over which lay a dapper, pin-striped waistcoat. A bright kerchief bloomed at his breast. Dark pantaloons ended in Balmoral boots — well worn, but spotless. His visage spoke of elegance and worldliness. His beard, long and pointed, looked groomed with care.

Not a skerrick remained of the unkempt man I had known.

'The ending is yet to be told,' he said in a calm tone, as if he spoke to a fellow only just awoken. To him, my face must have been as white as driven snow.

'I know that you are just now seeing the world, for the first time in a long time,' he continued. 'You may think this is not the same ship you boarded. You may even think that I am not the same man who began this narrative to you. I ask you now to set aside any preconceptions, for the truth can challenge a closed mind.

'The world appeared as you chose to see it. Society moved on; festive colours became blanched, the music faded. Yet there you stayed, frozen at the last moment that made sense to you. Pray, tell me, Fahrenheit: What became of you?'

I stared at nothing, biting my lip. Khashoggi looked straight into my soul. I knew exactly the moment he referred to. I remained silent for a time anyway, letting flashbacks filter through my brain.

A kaleidoscope of images tumbled by.

Arriving on the shores of Dover, armed with my clavinet and my naïve optimism.

Bouncing along the rutted roads in an old cart, trying to scrawl new songs, while crammed in the back amidst my friends.

Meeting Jenny for the first time — that fateful Bank Holiday, at the Sea-Father Inn. She bested me in a beer sculling contest.

Tossing coins over our shoulder into the fountain, making wishes for a prosperous future.

Huddling together in the poorer times, rationing our food through debt, frost, and famine.

The first time Jenny coughed blood.

'Jenny was the coat on my back and the sunshine on my face ... as real to me as my own heartbeat,' I answered at last. 'But since her passing ...'

'... You've lived on the fringe of a dream?'

I nodded.

The old man made to comfort me. 'Do not fret, for you are not lost. This land you have known — this place, Brighton-Upon-Sea — it has existed. You have lived here and dwelled in the warmth of your sweet lady's arms; cradling her, in return, as she lay dying. Yet, you must hear me when I say: All you knew has long since been left behind.

'I have watched you, month on month, year on year, diligently attend to your shop. Your clientele dwindled. Then one day, the last of the troubadours left town. You continued to work your trade, for no-one. Time and again, I called to you ... though you were not prepared to listen. Not ready to wake from your grief, to hear an old man tell a story about another dying world. One that you could help to save.'

Help to save? My eyes widened.

'Why me?' I asked him. 'In my mind's eye, you were a wizened hermit, as dilapidated as the ship you stood upon. As I passed you by — oblivious to your need, as I was to my own plight — you called me, by name. Why?'

Khashoggi's steepled fingers brushed his lips. He smiled. He had been waiting for me to reach this question. 'I ask of you now, as I asked of you then: You work with musical instruments, do you not?'

'I do. I mean ... I did. I think I did.' I no longer knew what I thought.

The smile grew broader. 'I see my story has not given you a stronger sense of yourself, Fahrenheit. Rest assured, your place of business remains — along the promenade, over by the village square. We shall visit it now, if you are prepared?'

My brow furrowed. I looked about for a porthole or window. The stateroom offered only a view of the sea — the colour of slate beneath a dreary afternoon sky. Now? Surely the day had been lost?

Khashoggi anticipated my confusion. 'Rhye is in need of a Song, Fahrenheit. In that regard, you have all of the necessary tools.'

'You expect me to craft an answer to your land's crisis?'

'Not at all. To the contrary, I believe we shall find the songsmith already in residence.'

My frown became a look of wonder. *Could it be?*

'Mustapha ...?'

The old man nodded. 'He is there, toiling inside your shop as we speak.'

My mind boggled. I fought to assimilate this fairy tale become truth. 'How do you know?'

'Ah,' said Khashoggi. 'The seraph is an extraordinary creature. Wittingly or otherwise, he carries a profound aura. Within moments of his arrival, I became aware not only of his nature, but of every tribulation Rhye has faced since he was born. In a way, he told me everything, by simply being here. It was an elementary matter to impart the tale to you.'

'But … you say he simply "arrived" here?' My astonishment bloomed. 'When did this happen?'

'For an Age, I have anticipated that a saviour might reach this place from Rhye. I left a few breadcrumbs, as it were, in the form of my own Song. Nothing was certain, until Mustapha surfaced in my consciousness, only this morning.'

My own Song.

'You're the Prophet …!'

Khashoggi's silence served as an admission.

I leapt to my feet. 'You called to me from the deck of this vessel earlier today?'

'I did,' replied Khashoggi, uncrossing his long legs and rising to meet me. 'I thought you may want a warning, before stumbling upon a strange urchin in your shop.'

'We must go at once!' said I.

'There is no better moment. Come!' Khashoggi beckoned and swept from the room, stopping for neither hat nor coat. I bustled along behind him — down ladders, along passageways and across decks. The interior of the ship, both whimsical and utilitarian, bespoke a splendid sense of adventure. The glow of electric lamps lit our way, while portals with ornate brass latches separated numerous compartments. Gauges displayed all manner of data — temperature, humidity, light levels, and tilt. There were no clocks to be seen anywhere.

On a lower deck, we came to a door marked 'Exit'. With one hand on the opening lever, Khashoggi said, 'Outside of this door lies the gangway, the dock and the world you once knew. You will recognise it, though much has changed.'

He threw open the door.

I was quick to appreciate his warning. I knew the settlement well: from the crumbling dockyard to the esplanade, and the patchwork of gables and chimneys beyond. Without doubt, I surveyed Brighton-Upon-Sea. Yet a fundamental change had occurred — whether to my vision, or to the township itself, I could not be sure.

Khashoggi gave me little chance to reconcile the altered world that I saw. He urged me down the gangway. His manner suggested that the only respite for my dismay would be immersion in its cause. We reached the dock and my dashing host set off at a brisk stride.

Brighton-Upon-Sea had become a ghost town.

Aside from ourselves, not a single soul walked along the foreshore. All gaiety was drained from the promenade, now bleak and foreboding. Litter scurried across the stones, tossed about by bitter gusts of wind. I spied a poster, advertising the latest famed troupe arriving in town. Another called for sightings of a beloved, missing pet. No welcoming lights shone from doorways or windows. The Sea-Father Inn, a reliable source of revelry, sat abandoned.

At the end of the promenade, the urge to stop and look back took hold. Though my addled mind had a sense of what I might see, the demand for validation compelled me.

Looking over my shoulder evinced the splendour of Khashoggi's ship. What a marvel! A vessel of unbridled magnificence rocked to a gentle rhythm in the dock. It gleamed from bow to stern, an ivory hull supporting an enclosed superstructure, like a great, white cigar. It flaunted no masts or sails, instead bristling with an array of funnels, chimneys, and other nautical paraphernalia. As I anticipated from within, the ship looked to be powered by steam, or perhaps even electromagnetics ... the finest of modern propulsive technology.

To my reckoning, the ship had been a hulking eyesore by the shore of my pristine seaside idyll. Khashoggi presented me with a starkly differing picture. His vessel thrummed with vitality, while it was Brighton-Upon-Sea that rotted into ruin.

I aired my vexation with Khashoggi. 'How can it be,' I asked, 'that your ship is now sea-ready, while my town is a faded husk? By your own admission, you began your story to me only this morning. At that hour, your craft was a shell in a glorious harbour.'

He halted his march and turned back to me. 'I have also said to you, Fahrenheit — perhaps you have forgotten? — that time is nought but the space between places. You have not travelled through time to reach me here. You have travelled from fantasy to reality.'

My head spun, pondering the implications behind his words. 'The life I knew was real to me,' I said. 'I still see it clearly in my mind.'

Khashoggi showed remarkable patience. 'Trust not your senses. The mind does not always perceive reality — any inebriant, any hallucinogen will demonstrate that! Instead, trust your heart. It alone holds the key to truth.'

My companion set off again. I wanted to protest my sobriety but remained wordless. I contemplated the profound impact of Jenny's loss on my perceptions.

We reached the town square. Absent were the birds, chirruping and diving from clock tower and church spire. Boarded windows stared blindly back at me from every direction. The buildings themselves decayed, unloved by a carpenter, or a lick of paint, in what seemed like many a year.

One lone shop front offered illumination, a welcoming beacon in a township grown cold.

My signage, cracked and faded, remained legible. The Good Company Ltd., it read. In smaller lettering beneath, Wares & Repairs for Troubadours: A.J. Fahrenheit, Proprietor. Though the windows were opaque with grime, warm light spilled from them onto the square. Apprehension pricked at my skin, to hear a racket emanating from within.

We crossed the cobblestones, heading for the portico.

Brass bells gave a hearty *tinkle-tinkle* as we pushed the door open. Mine was only a small shop: a service counter and a clutter of instruments, some new (in a past life), some in the process of refurbishment. It took Khashoggi and I only a moment to absorb the scene.

Every item sat in a state of disrepair. Several lutes and lyres were strewn about the room. Maybe they had fallen from shelves at some time in the past, or maybe tossed there more recently. Sheet music lay scattered like autumn leaves. One kettle-shaped timpani lay, upturned, on the floor.

At the eye of the storm, a bedraggled creature sat at the piano. Wild black hair, a frenzied mane, fell to his shoulders. Strange attire clothed his lithe, almost ascetic form — a white tunic and leggings, tattered and worn, hung from his frame. He sat hunched over the instrument, dark eyes locked with feverish intent upon the keys. He pounded the ivories in a most indelicate fashion, with his wrists bent, now and again reaching for the higher notes with his left hand, crossing over his right.

I shuddered. My own piano teacher would have writhed in her grave.

Mustapha looked exactly as Khashoggi described him. A stripling — shorter than either Khashoggi or I, yet somehow magnified by the force of his very presence. He ignored the sound of bells as we entered. A maelstrom of sound erupted from the piano. The chords he created were baffling, given that the piano was long out of tune. Despite this — and his catastrophic technique — the music held an eerie majesty.

'Mustapha,' interrupted Khashoggi.

The seraph did not look up. 'Can't you see I'm busy?'

Khashoggi edged nearer, as a lion tamer might approach a beast. 'Mustapha. We are here to help you. We know of your task ... to find a new Song for Rhye.'

The cacophonous pounding stopped.

When the seraph looked up, the sheer earnestness in his gaze startled me. This creature had lost everything and faced Death, only to find himself in this alien world. Hopelessness hung about him like a cloak.

'I don't know where I am,' he lamented, doe eyed.

Khashoggi spoke to the seraph as he had first spoken to me, at my awakening. 'You made it, Mustapha. You crossed the Seventh Sea.'

Mustapha nodded, absently. The achievement registered as a bare flicker of his features. 'You have strange instruments here,' he remarked, tapping Middle C with a *plink*. 'I don't like this place. It has all the despair of the place I left, but none of the things I loved. Nice to have met you, though. Funny that you already know me. Were you expecting me? Am I dead? Who are you, anyway —?'

Mustapha's ramblings trailed off. He had appraised me in

an instant, finding nothing of great interest. As he looked at my companion, however, his face took on an expression of wonderment.

'From love estranged does new love grow,' he said, with reverence.

Khashoggi smiled. 'Across the Seas, the answer found.'

'Fly and find and thence return ...'

'To peace and fortune, all around. We've got some work to do, Mustapha.'

Watching this exchange humbled me. Here, the ancient history of Rhye collided with its endangered present. Khashoggi had been in my world barely more than fifty years, yet an Age had passed in the world of his birth.

Time was, at once, everything and nothing.

Mustapha returned his attention to the piano. He began a new melody, this one imbued with fragility. A paean to bereavement. He sang nonsense words, yet still my heart ached to hear the sound.

Khashoggi moved about, examining the sheets of music that the seraph had discarded, in a flurry of frustration. They were all classics of the modern era — Brahms, Liszt, Debussy — torn from manuscripts I kept on display. Khashoggi moved past them, showing little interest. Instead, his eyes alighted on a single page, folded, resting atop the piano.

I had noticed this document as well. Not the cheap copy paper I regularly used to produce compendia of songs, but a much finer parchment. As Mustapha continued to play, Khashoggi reached across and picked it up.

'You can keep that old scrap,' announced Mustapha, breaking off his song. 'Utterly useless. It made no sense to me at all.'

The seraph's indifference only served to pique my curiosity. I sidled over beside Khashoggi, who unfolded the parchment with a careful hand.

Water-stains marked the document. There were dark flecks upon it, which appeared to be dried blood. The creases were well worn, giving the impression of having been folded and unfolded again, many times.

Khashoggi opened it. The text was deliberate and unhurried, consisting of a single word in the centre of the page.

Bismillah

The old man mouthed the word, a mystified look crossing his face.

I stared over his shoulder at the parchment, my own mind a swirl of memories. In fleeting vignettes, I recalled my travels through Prussia, the Slavic states and beyond. As a younger man, before heading to the English Isles, I wandered as far south as Macedonia and east to Constantinople. There, at the great crossroads of our world, I encountered gypsies, traders, caravans, and errant missionaries; a cultural melange, merging the myriad customs of East and West.

I knew this word. It came from the homeland of mullahs and sheiks. A word spoken with frequency, for it held daily relevance to the people of Allah.

'It means, "In the name of God",' I said.

'A word of your world. How interesting,' remarked Khashoggi.

'My father wrote this,' said Mustapha. His dismissive tone evaporated. His head sank. Perhaps he relived those precious final days, in which Sinotar became part of his life, at last. 'When he gave it to me, he said that it was a piece of augury. A key of some kind. I never got more instruction than that.'

We all fell silent. With Bastian Sinotar's death, the enigmatic parchment held more questions than answers.

'I still don't know what to do with this word ... *Bismillah*,' said Mustapha.

I had an idea. 'He may have intended it to be part of a new Song?'

Khashoggi shrugged, in tacit agreement.

There was nothing to be lost in trying.

Mustapha sang the word in a soft voice, as if feeling it roll over his tongue. '*Bismillah*.' He sang it once more.

'*Bismillah*! No. Let me try that again.

'*Bismillah*! ... No.

'*Bismillah*! No, no, no!'

He played about now, tickling the piano keys, giving the word a new intonation with each recital. First it came forth as a sweet lilt, then a bestial growl, then a falsetto. Though he derided his own efforts, his enthusiasm grew.

At last, mashing a strident piano chord, Mustapha unleashed The Voice — the sound that tantalised me through Khashoggi's narrative. A wall of vocal splendour washed over me. The creature's single larynx seemed capable of producing a choir of harmonised voices. It reminded me of bronze bells, the burble of a forest stream and the drum of rain on a shingled roof, all at once.

'*BISMILLAH!*'

With the flare of an explosion, the room filled with brilliance, the colour of a flowering cherry.

Accompanying this radiance came a new voice, this one female, complimenting Mustapha's tone to perfection.

I first thought that the heavens had opened, ready to receive us. Perhaps I had indeed perished. I soon discarded this notion, for I had not felt so alive since the day I met my beloved.

All three of us were dazzled by the light, each using an arm to shield our eyes. Though Mustapha had ceased his singing, the angelic hymn persisted. After several moments, I determined that this pink-hued illumination did not originate in the shop, but rather, it shone through the front windows from outside.

'The square!' I called to the others.

We made our way to the door. The bright light began to dim, and the glorious chorale faded. We stepped outside, still squinting, adjusting to the banishment of shadow.

In times past, the fountain dominated the square. Now, it stood as a forlorn monument, filled with windblown leaves and devoid of water's laughter. The fountain paled to insignificance, alongside the figure that drifted to earth before it. A woman, bearing wondrous butterfly wings, the red of a vivid sunset. The cherry blossom glow limned her dark olive skin, while her hair fell in dense tresses to caress her voluptuous, nude form. Her eyes gave a white luminescence, having neither iris nor pupil.

A shaft of light poured from the granite sky to pool on the cobblestones. Her bare feet touched down where the light reached the ground, a landing as graceful as the being's song.

I mused that Brighton-Upon-Sea had never seen such a circus of bizarre events, in short succession, even in its heyday.

I alone failed to recognise the being who appeared to us. Both of my companions had prayed at her altar throughout their lives. Almost in unison, they responded in a breath of wonder.

'Ophynea.'

In the presence of the Goddess of Love, I knew the fervour that drove my companions to their knees. Though I considered myself a Christian, my attendance at Mass was an embarrassment. My excuse — a terrible one, at that — had always been that my God felt more distant than the most remote star. Never had I striven to look for that higher plane within myself.

Here stood a deity who could be felt both inside and out. She inspired an adoration that welled in my chest, rising to flush my cheeks against the cold.

She spoke. Her voice did not carry an iota of threat or pretension. Her aura evoked languid power, a sensuousness that enveloped the listener.

'Hail, favoured of the Pantheon of Rhye,' she said. 'Do not quake or flee before me, for I appear to you in the name of Love.'

'Praised be Ophynea,' responded Mustapha and Khashoggi. I remained silent, facing a momentary dilemma of faith.

Ophynea smiled, turning her countenance to me. Her indirect gaze angled towards something that lay beside or behind me. Then, I realised: As far as human perceptions were concerned, Ophynea was blind.

'The strength of your heart speaks to me, human,' she said. 'The Good Company has been your passion in life; now, it is good company you keep.'

With each heartbeat, I felt a golden warmth flow through my veins, washing away all doubt.

The Goddess turned back to my companions. 'Rise, Mustapha, son of Bastian Sinotar. Rise, Khashoggi, esteemed Prophet. I bring tidings from the land of the Seven Seas. A prophecy unfolds — it is time to determine the fate of Rhye.'

Khashoggi bowed his head. Mustapha's eyes glistened, remaining fixed on Ophynea.

'Benjulius has fallen,' announced the Goddess. 'War claimed his courageous soul. Now, the Age of Sovereigns is at a close. The Fae Ring has disintegrated, ending the promise between mortals and the Pantheon. Valendyne walks free upon the land, no longer desirous of a portal to step from his prison. He prepares to shape Rhye to his own designs.'

The message struck my companions as a physical blow. Even I, having only heard of the Archimage through Khashoggi's narrative, felt his loss as a visceral cramp.

'Then is Rhye lost?' The question tumbled from my lips.

'That is not my vision,' said Khashoggi, his voice firm. The lines of his face were stark in the ethereal light of the Goddess, like testament carved upon stone. His bright eyes held a memory of the Song he had penned.

Ophynea waited, letting the Prophet speak.

'The land's redemption has few conditions,' he said. '*Love is key to kingdom come*. The time is now, blessed Ophynea, whilst you are in our presence.

'The *sacred ore* is also within our ken. Once still, locked within a fragment of cinnabar, it now flows within your veins, Mustapha. It has borne you, swift as a dream, across the Seventh Sea.

'What I saw only in my imaginings, is now as clear to me as the land's need. The King stands in our midst, bearing sacred gifts. It is in his coronation that we shall know the new Song of Rhye.'

The Goddess nodded, content.

In that moment, Mustapha seemed pale and small. All eyes rested on him.

'Dear seraph,' said Ophynea, her words a gentle embrace, 'do not be afraid. Let your heart be filled with the fire of joy, for Love is indeed the key.

'I have watched from on high as you grew in devotion; to me and to your blessed companion. You grew beyond the false love of the accursed Lady, who led you from the truth. You cast aside the Mustapha of your youth, prepared to risk the lives of those who meant most to you. In time, your love instead became a shining sword, protecting the fellow of your heart. Though it hurt you both, it spared his life. Let it not be in vain.

'Mustapha: The prayers of your mother and the legacy of your father live on inside of you. Blessed are you, who carry both noble bloodline and the essence of Mother Love. Without you, the throne of Rhye is lost to War and Death. You alone may unlock the power of Song; and with your sacred weapon, vanquish the shades of despair.

'Step forward now and be anointed. Awaken in fire and celebrate your destiny, O King of Rhye.'

Trepidation paralysed Mustapha's face. I felt for him, having known his journey, from carefree urchin to voyager between worlds. The mantle that awaited him promised a burden to daunt even the hardiest of souls.

Despite his fear, he took a chary step forward.

'I am no King,' he said, in a clear, quiet voice, 'though I am much indebted to the people and the land that I have loved. Goddess, you embolden me, as does the memory of my mother and father. My heart is glad, for having known them.

'I understand my destiny — that I must die, for the King of Rhye to be born. I have known of my fate since my counsel with the great Seer, Lily. I also understand that from death comes rebirth, just as from love can new love grow.

'Goddess, I place my humble spirit in your hands. I accept the coronation of fire.'

He knelt once more.

I remained silent, sensing that any utterance would shatter such a sublime moment. Beside me, Khashoggi's eyes were wide.

Ophynea cast open her butterfly wings.

From within those membranes fluttered a multitude of creatures, crimson and luminescent. Like tiny progeny of the Goddess, they flitted on the evening air. After blooming outwards for a moment, a loose cloud of diminutive wings, the swarm drifted towards the seraph.

One by one, the vibrant, red butterflies settled on him — upon his skin, his clothes, his hair. When each creature alighted, it disintegrated in a mote of bright, white flame.

At first, these flames were few. Wicks, like tiny spirits, rested on the kneeling figure. As more of Ophynea's progeny landed, the winking motes coalesced. They lined his body in gleaming puissance.

Soon, a whorl of flickering power cloaked him.

'Mustapha!' I gasped. Consumed in flame! An unimaginable horror.

The fire billowed higher — crackling, roaring. Within the white blaze, Mustapha turned to me, a serene half-smile on his face.

'I feel no pain,' he said. Nothing more.

A moment later, the blaze engulfed him.

The force of the conflagration drove us back. Heat radiated outwards — enough, it seemed, to melt flesh. Barely an outline of the seraph could be seen.

Swallowed by fire.

My stunned fascination, morbid though it was, kept me from turning away. The pyre continued to roar, spiralling into the sky.

'He receives the blessing of the Gods, just as his mother did,' murmured the Prophet. He, too, was spellbound by the scene unfolding before us. We agreed, in a tacit way, to remain by Mustapha's side until the fire burned down.

The evening deepened. We each offered prayers, of a kind. We stood alone, for the Goddess Ophynea had vanished.

A long silence followed.

At some interval — the moon had since risen — I was jerked from my mist-eyed torpor.

'Look!' I cried, stabbing a quivering finger. I had seen movement within the flames. A shape moved — a deliberate shifting of posture, rather than the agonised writhing of a tortured soul.

The shape rose from its knees as the fire began to subside. Leaping white tongues shrank back from the heavens. The roar became a crackle. In the end, only delicate tongues of flame licked the figure who stood facing us.

Stood.

Facing us.

Alive.

The cleansing fire sputtered and died.

We gazed upon a creature who was — yet was not — Mustapha. Recognisable were the dark, sparkling eyes, the straight, almost Grecian nose, the pointed ears, and those lips, perpetually on the verge of mirth. He had become something more than the whippet strangeling I had met. He wore a bold countenance, confident chin held high, as if the fire had burned away every apprehension.

His slender form stood poised, in an unassailable way. Clad was he, head to foot in white, as before; now embellished with articles of gold-trimmed armour. He reminded me of sylphic warriors and of that messenger god from Roman myth — Mercury. Upon his head he bore a circlet of gold, with a wing motif above each ear. Lustrous, black curls poured from his crown to his noble shoulders.

From between his shoulder blades sprouted glorious, snowy wings. They were six in total — one vast, primary pair, beneath which were tucked two more pairs. Never have I seen a finer apparatus — not upon hawk, nor crane, nor albatross.

In his grasp, he bore a sceptre of gold, nearly as tall as himself.

'Hail, King of Rhye,' said Khashoggi, taking a knee.

Almost forgetting myself, I quickly joined him.

'Do not kneel before me!' the seraph laughed. There rang that bell-like sound, the hand coming up to cover his mouth. The Mustapha I knew. 'Not yet, at least. Let me get to the throne first!' He reached down, an arm to each of us, dragging us to our feet.

Khashoggi and I exchanged an incredulous glance.

'I hope that there is still a throne for you to claim,' said I.

He nodded. 'While there is breath, a voice and a Song, there may be victory.'

Khashoggi asked the question I dared not. 'The Song ...?'

Mustapha tapped his temple with two fingers. 'It was within me the entire time. A refrain from the Gods themselves, catalysed by the flames of Love.'

'Then we must return to Rhye, forthwith,' said Khashoggi. After an Age upon the dock of Brighton-Upon-Sea, at last the Prophet could journey home. I prayed that a home still waited for him. 'Your contrivance awaits, my King,' said he.

Mustapha had half-turned to leave the square when he wheeled to face me. 'What of you, Mr Fahrenheit? Will you join us?'

I looked all around me. Everywhere I turned, the dismal grey bid me farewell. Nothing remained in this life for me now — my reality had all but ended with Jenny. I took a final glance back at The Good Company, Ltd.

'I've no reason to stay,' I said. What future might await me, I knew not; but in that moment, adventure stirred my spirit.

'Come on, then!' cried Khashoggi, with a disarming smile and a gleam in his eye. 'Let me take you across the Seventh Sea to Rhye!'

With all haste, we made our way back along the promenade.

A whistling wind skirled through the old square. Dead leaves danced on invisible strings as the township returned to its bitter grave.

Within moments, the township fell silent, our existence forgotten.

CHAPTER 25

THE KING OF RHYE

Constellations wheeled through the sky. Clouds of cosmic dust spanned the heavens, a celestial veil. Far from any civilised world, these nebulous clouds shone with the illumination of a false dawn. True dawn may have been minutes, hours, or weeks away, but one fact could not be escaped: Dawn would come.

Onik's passage through the great void transcended all other forces. Immutable as the tumbling of droplets down a waterfall, or the ageing of trees in the forest. The God of Time knew no interruption.

In his endless travel, Onik was everywhere and nowhere. In some places, he existed as a leviathan, dragging the fabric of reality in his wake. In other places, as a tremendous swarm of invincible gnats; swirling, colliding, hurrying onward from one instance to the next.

Under a vast cosmos, the fleeting lives of mortals came and went. At the same time, tomorrow threatened to never arrive.

The Sea stretched to a far horizon. A vast, undulating plain of purple and grey. The sound of lapping water could be heard but not seen, beneath a dense cloak of mist.

Khashoggi's ship emerged, a pale spirit from the depths of the night. The Seventh Sea rippled whisper-quiet before her prow, the ancient waters parting as butter beneath a whetted knife. The swift vessel needed neither current nor wind, which was fortunate, for the air lay still.

Three figures peered out from the foredeck.

'Do I cross from a nightmare to a new kind of hell?' said Ackley Fahrenheit.

'We venture into a dark unknown,' replied Khashoggi. 'Here, at least, you may fight for your own soul. In Rhye, you do not slip between the cracks of life's experience. Every sweet inhalation is a well-deserved gift. That pounding of your heart is the steady reminder of life's sanctity. Never did I feel it in your world, the way I feel it here.'

'The stars cast familiar shapes, at least.' Fahrenheit pointed. 'There is the belt of Orion, known as the Hunter. Over there — more to the east — is Pegasus. In this place, he might be better known as Pterippus, I suppose.'

The Prophet smiled. 'Ah, the map of the Gods! It is indeed something we share. In a past Age, the Wearers of Midnight Blue learned to read it. They taught us to find our way in darkness. To navigate the Seas.'

Fahrenheit looked over at Mustapha. The seraph grasped the rail, feet planted wide, nose turned to the sky. Sometimes he stared at the millions of twinkling lights overhead. At other times, he closed his eyes, drawing deep breaths, taking in the night air. With each inspiration, the ship surged forward. As he searched the stars, he clenched tight, leaning ever so slightly to one side or the other.

The ship responded, veering to port or starboard through the mist and shrouded water below.

'Remarkable,' whispered Fahrenheit.

'Even now, he guides us safely home,' said the Prophet.

Mustapha glanced over his shoulder. 'The Gods showed me how to read the heavens. There is a clear path, which will take us back to Rhye.' He raised an instructive finger to the sky. 'Above us lies Cancer — you can see its body, with pincers splayed outward. There, that's it. Further to the east, you can make out proud Leo. Last then, far toward the east horizon — a little lower, yes — that is Virgo. Beyond Virgo will we find the shores of Rhye. From that horizon, may the glory of Adatar shine on us once more.'

A bank of cloud hung low, in the direction Mustapha indicated, marring the otherwise pristine sky. Sheet lightning flashed, illuminating a deep, crimson brume.

'Are you sure that is our bearing?' asked Fahrenheit, rubbing his eyes and taking another look.

'Quite sure.'

'Absolutely sure?'

Mustapha turned from the rail. 'You remind me of a dragonfly I know.'

'I pray your friends are alive and have found a safe retreat,' said Fahrenheit.

'In my bones, I know they are alive. As Dique might say, "we've been in tougher scrapes." He would struggle to remember when, though.' The seraph's gaze ranged across the leagues. He unleashed a sigh.

'What can we expect from Valendyne?'

'It won't be pretty,' said Mustapha, returning to the moment. 'You are right to be afraid. An Age of incarceration. Humiliation. He will not be taking any prisoners.

'Any who have survived the battle at the Mountain will be struggling for survival. Then, there are all of those who found sanctuary in the bunkers of Sontenan, the Vultan Range or Petrichor. Only a perfect operation could preserve all those souls.'

The distant flare of a storm lit Khashoggi's visage as he stared into the east. Beyond the billowing pall of cloud, a sprawling shadow suggested mountains.

'I see land,' said the Prophet. 'Do you have a plan?'

'Of course, dear fellow! Much of it relies on happenstance, of course. With luck on our side, we'll get where we need to be.'

'What is our approach?'

'First, I will need to relinquish control of this magnificent vessel to you, its rightful Captain. As for our approach: On our current bearing, there is a chance we will miss our objective. Twenty degrees to port should do it. Stay aligned with Virgo. That will lead you to the shore of Nevermore, beyond that bank of mist.

'Once you're there, I'd recommend staying with the ship. If you simply must explore, keep an eye out for Ogres, Death and a tree spewing deadly cloud.'

Fahrenheit and Khashoggi exchanged grimaces.

'I recall the sacred texts of my own world,' said Fahrenheit. 'In the words of another King: "I am but a stranger in a strange land." This is the fate I have chosen — may I discover this place with my innocent eyes, danger and all. I yearn, just once, to lay eyes upon the Pillar of Rhye.'

Mustapha nodded, his mouth a firm line. 'That is my destination. I cannot be sure how much time has elapsed here since I left … but there is none to waste. I must go!'

'Godspeed,' said Khashoggi. 'May Oska guide you. May Lhestra deliver your decree to the enemies of peace.'

Mustapha raised an arm skyward, as if he could snatch a star from the heavens. His wings unfurled, a broad span, throwing forth a bright display of argent and gold. A single beat of his feathered array and he became airborne, a vision in white armour and celestial fire.

The seraph gave a final wave to his companions. He rose into the air, buoyed by a chorus of sound. Voices swelled in the night, surging with his ascent.

He turned to the south. Phantom mountain peaks lay curtained behind a crimson storm.

Another instant and he winged away, nought but a streak of light and a lingering chorale as proof of his passage.

'This is about the best I can come up with,' said Dique, sitting with his back against the wall. In trembling hands, he held three dried sticks in the shape of a Y, while lashing them together using one of Will's bootlaces.

In the grit by his side, a zither and a war drum sat, neglected.

Will stood nearby, leaning on a parapet of white stone. He turned and knelt beside Dique, one hand on the pixie's shoulder.

'That's a fine slingshot, Dique,' he said. 'I'm sure you could take down a dragon with that. It's a shame that we ran out of shot, several days ago.'

'Truly?'

'I'm afraid so. Some of the Mages — and a couple of Sorcerers — gathered all the loose stones so they could create some more loaves for us.'

Dique bunched his face. 'No wonder the bread tastes so stale! We've been eating rocks!' He cast the makeshift weapon from him, where it dashed against the flags, clattering to pieces.

The pixie slumped against the wall. 'Will?'

'Yes, Dique?'

'Where is Torr Yosef?'

'I don't know. He disappeared a long time ago. Perhaps he fell to the rock titans. Or got caught in the skirmish of the Adept. I can't be certain ... but he's gone.'

'Will?'

'Yes, Dique?'

'Are the titans still about?'

'No, they're gone, too. The Ogres destroyed them all. I can still see a lot of Necromancers though ... and there's the Black Queen out there, somewhere.'

The dragon, an intermittent terror, appeared at intervals to rain torment on the fighters within the Pillar. Swarms of humans, Vrendari and Fae — many of them civilians, flocking from the Forest Realms — were huddled inside. Others sought shelter in the ruin of the Wilden stronghold.

'Will?'

'Yes, Dique?'

'Are they getting nearer?'

'They ...?'

'The Necromancers.' Dique looked at the zither through glossy eyes.

'Ah ... no. The Pillar is well defended. Warlocks keep a firm perimeter, at the verge of the White Queen's influence. No Necromancers have yet been able to penetrate the line.'

'It's only a matter of time,' said Meadow, sitting upon the parapet, tossing a pebble into the air and catching it. His legs dangled over the edge.

'Those aren't the words of a Fae Commander,' said Will. He gazed into a swarm of ant-like figures, far below and away in the distance. In a vast arc around the Pillar of Rhye, Warlocks and Mages effected a cordon of lethal energy. Outside it waited a horde of the Black Queen's faithful — rancorous, antagonistic, yet also patient without end. In the shadows, Anuvin stood, arms folded, anticipating the moment when battle would flare.

He could wait for eternity.

'Even at the Godsryche, the Warlocks only held out for a month,' said Meadow. 'It feels like it's been that long already. We can't hold out forever. People will starve. Or lose the plot. Look at poor old Dique.'

'You'd best get down from there,' replied Will. 'Our shift is almost over. It would be miserable luck to slip and fall when a change of the guard is so close.'

Meadow threw the pebble up in the air and caught it. Once. Twice. Three times. Then he tossed it out into space and watched it fall. It dropped past gleaming white stones, chiselled balconies, and dozens of windows. Eventually, it bounced on enchanted ground, the colour of crisp snow. Meadow did not hear the impact.

'To slip and fall,' he said. 'Would it be so bad?'

Will turned to the pixie. 'Do not fret. Salvation will come.'

'Seeing is believing,' said Dique in a moment of lucidity, pointing into the west. Beyond the scorched leagues once known as Banwah Haunte, above the Sontenean horizon, came a swirling formation of flying shapes. Each carried a staff, tipped with scrallin. Points of illumination bobbed in the night.

An orange bloom of fire lit the sky.

'Vrendari,' said Will. 'And they have a fight on their hands.'

Harold floundered, rolling aside as a molten blast of dragon's breath seared the air. The heat still reached his whirring wings, fraying them at the tip.

He zoomed in a tight arc, dropping altitude. Looking about, he saw the scattered forms of Vrendari, against the black and crimson sky. The nightmare shape of their foe soared near the clouds, then dove once more. It taunted the Vrendari, visiting havoc upon them.

'I don't know if I can keep this up!' cried the dragonfly.

Leith Lourden swooped beside him, her armour and face spattered with black ichor. 'You must try, Harold! Our swords alone cannot end this. We need your help — it's in the palm of our hands this time!'

Peals of laughter boomed. Lightning flared, casting the dreadful, winged shape in silhouette. In her calamitous form, the Black Queen proved near invincible. Astride her serpentine back, her rider imbued the dragon with power beyond reckoning.

The figure had a face of flawless proportions, marred by the guile that snarled his lips. Perfect skin of ashen grey couched his features. A third eye, upon his forehead, stared towards the end of all things.

'Only Death awaits those who defy the Black Queen, monarch of a new Age,' said Valendyne, his declaration clear above the rumble of thunder. Clenching his fist, he summoned a ball of ebony flame and launched it at a brace of sylphic warriors. The projectile clipped two Vrendari on its fateful course. Lifeless, they fell to the ruined woodlands below.

Harold gasped, darting out of harm's way. He whipped the Horn of Agonies to his lips, using a moment's safety to trigger a new attack.

The Horn's blare arose from the throat of the Gods. It drew upon the spirit of its wielder and spoke to the heart of the listener, for good or for ill.

Valendyne writhed in anguish. The Black Queen shuddered in flight, bellowing and coughing out flame.

The God of Death remained astride her.

'Stay brave, Harold!' called Leith. 'The White Queen lights the way ahead. Draw our foes to her brilliance.'

Valendyne whispered, his words sharp as daggers in the ears of those around him. 'Heed my words, insect: You will be crushed. Pillar will become pyre, before your desperate eyes. Just as I lay this land to waste, so will I reduce your monument to rubble.'

'I ruin your plans with utmost respect!' cried Harold. Pulse pounding, he zipped towards the beckoning shelter of ravaged forest.

Petrichor was in splinters. Felled timber, like kindling tossed in a pile, stretched for leagues to east and south. Lumber smouldered, falling to rot and decay beneath the wrathful power of Valendyne. At low altitude, the forest became a perilous maze of giant spears, rising from the ruin beneath. Harold weaved as he flew, staying beyond the grasp of the Black Queen and her rider.

Death and dragon-fire rained from above. Harold darted left and right through familiar gullies, reduced to nothing but scorched landmarks. Innumerable dead lay beneath the charred wreckage.

Harold blinked mist from his eyes as he left Dragonfly Hollow behind.

Without turning to look, he knew the Vrendari had his back. The dragon thrashed and roared in his wake, contending with the relentless sylphic distraction.

Harold rose above the forest, in need of a bearing. In Psithur Grove, away to the south-west, the fabled Yew still stood.

Harold's chest swelled with hope. The lore of the Fae lived on, in Trixel Tate.

Ahead flowed the Bijou — not as the Milk of Petrichor, but as molten fire. The bridges burned, crumbling into magma, leaving thousands of Fae stranded in the remains of their Realm.

Death reshaped the land to his own designs.

The clouds hung low, pregnant with dread. Far to the north,

beyond Nevermore, stars still winked in a peerless sky; calling from a place of respite, which lay beyond reach.

A final beacon stood, a defiant light in a sea of devastation. The Pillar of Rhye rose tall above Banwah Haunte — pristine, shimmering against the black of Rhye's longest night.

A barrage of dark magic and dragon attacks had long since destroyed the shingled roof atop the tower. Only the shell of Lady Maybeth's keep remained — a bare platform, open to the sky, surrounded by a low wall of crenellated stone. A spiral stair disappeared into the core of the tower — the same stair down which Lord Ponerog fled, to his doom.

Harold closed the distance, at the limits of his energy. He saw tiny figures swarming over the platform, the glint of armour and the knocking of flaming arrows. Hints of green and crimson showed amongst the livery — both Fae and Humankind shared the Pillar's defence. Below, Warlocks held their ground against the surge of Necromancy.

Volleys of deadly magic shot skyward as the Black Queen's army fired upon the returning Vrendari. Several sylphic bodies fell to earth, silenced.

Harold gripped the Horn, making a final bolt to the Pillar.

Lady Trixel Tate emerged atop the stair, ahead of a small company of Fae knights. At the change of the guard, she took a moment to survey the landscape and obtain a situation report from her Commanders.

She heard the great beast before she saw it. A volcanic roar filled the air, from a creature threatening to incinerate anything in its path.

Too close. Much closer than ever before.

Trixel charged across to the warriors by the battlement. 'Heads down! This is no place to be with the dragon upon us. Fae! Take cover. Dique! Dique, what are you doing?'

Humans and Fae fell to their bellies, while the incoming guard rushed back towards the stair. A column of fire tore across the platform, followed by the Black Queen's monstrous bulk. She passed over in a rush of hot wind, with determined Vrendari still in pursuit. A slew of arrows, fired in haste, flew after her. None struck the target.

Dique danced upon the parapet, strumming his zither with a flourish. 'Don't you feel it?' he cried. 'The Pillar knows the Black Queen is here!'

With manic glee, he made the instrument sing.

Trixel, crouched low in a corner, had no time to ask questions. Fae knights huddled around her. Beneath them, the Pillar rumbled. Quaking stone sent trickles of dust from every crevice. The entire structure moaned. Then –

WHOOM.

A beam of pure energy blasted across the sky. As a great lamp might illuminate the sea at midnight, so did the beam, from a high window, cut a swathe over Rhye.

The beam collided with the Black Queen in her flight path. She tumbled in the air, almost dislodging Valendyne from her back.

Will flinched. 'What in the name —'

'She's circling around!' shouted Trixel. 'Dique, keep playing!'

Dique shrugged. He moved in a trance, his fingers capering over the strings. From one window, then another, then another, bolts of radiance shot in arrow-straight bands across the sky. Soon, a flare of spokes, like a cartwheel, pursued the dragon and her malevolent rider.

WHOOM. WHOOM. WHOOM.

'Where is this coming from?' said Will. 'This is not the work of Warlocks. Some embodiment of the White Queen, do you think?'

'Who gives a damn?' answered Meadow. 'Our old Lady is fighting back! I guess she must be a fan of music, even if it's Dique's!' He scrambled to the war drum, still lying nearby.

Covered by the White Queen's puissant fire, Harold and the surviving Vrendari regained the Pillar.

Trixel muscled free of her protective huddle and raced across to the returning combatants. She threw her arms around Leith Lourden, the moment the sylph landed. 'I thought you were about to be fried chicken!'

Leith's face flushed. She returned the squeeze. 'Not a chance. I'm sticking around to see how this show ends.'

The dragon pitched and somersaulted in the air, tracked all the while by luminescent shafts of magic. On the ground, her forces grew frenzied, hurling their own dark vitriol against the defensive wave of Adept.

Warlocks responded, unravelling great whips of Violet enchantment. Far-reaching thongs of iridescent power coiled above the Warlocks' heads, before lashing the Necromancers with explosive cracks. At first, the deadly scourge thinned enemy ranks. The vanquished were soon replaced, with Wearers of Black stumbling forward over the bodies of the fallen.

Anuvin stepped forward, wearing a manic grin.

Will gripped the parapet, fixed on the conflict. Trixel and Leith were by his side. 'If Valendyne conquers the Pillar,' he said, 'all of our lives are his for the taking. I hope you've said your prayers —'

The words caught in his throat, for a new vision appeared overhead.

Trixel and Leith stared skyward, mouths agape.

All around, the tumult became still.

The warring Adept fell silent.

Dique stopped playing.

Even the White Queen and the Black ceased their clash, with the dragon alighting on a hillside, encircled by her army.

A meteor seared through the northern sky. In unison, all heads turned to watch.

A rent appeared in the fabric of darkness, even brighter than the White Queen's essence. Lightning flashed as the object streaked through the heavens. It arced towards the Pillar, hurtling on a wave of glorious sound.

The sound of a celestial choir.

Clouds parted, coaxing moonlight through the rift. As the meteor neared, it did not accelerate. Instead, it slowed, banking towards the field of battle. Illumination dimmed. The flying shape became a transcendent figure, floating on brilliant wings. It drifted down atop the Pillar.

Will's mouth formed one word, though no sound issued from his lips.

'Mustapha.'

Speechless warriors, both Fae and human, huddled close to the battlements. Mustapha touched down upon the cleared platform, wings ruffling and folding. Skeins of gold, like shimmering dust, cascaded from his gilded armour.

He offered a gentle smile to the knot of beleaguered fighters. Will and the pixies fought the urge to crowd him; a potent aura swirled about his form. They kept their distance.

The seraph turned to face Valendyne, Anuvin and the Black Queen's host.

The God of War shouldered through the rabid crush, sending Wearers of Black tumbling, and kicking the dead from his path. He advanced until he was toe-to-toe with the Warlocks, who turned their unflinching, delvish faces towards him.

Anuvin peered at Mustapha. 'I see the miserable whelp found a new costume.'

'Hold your tongue, War.' Nobody saw Valendyne dismount from the dragon. One moment, he sat astride her; the next, he appeared beside Anuvin. This time, the Warlocks did flinch, though they held their line, at the verge of the White Queen's territory.

In the light of the Pillar, Valendyne's simple black tunic and leggings shimmered, like finest silk. He stood tall, sinuous, as seductive as his brother was Herculean. He crossed his arms over his chest, in the attitude of a body in repose. Each gloved finger ended in a claw, which sparkled like a gem.

'This creature confounds me,' he said, absorbing the vision of the seraph with all three of his eyes. 'He bears the hallmarks of one who has been — *caressed* — by my sister. Yet something is awry. He comes now as a messenger from the Pantheon.'

Mustapha remained silent.

'For two thousand, seven hundred and thirty-nine years, I have been bound within a cell of the Creator's design,' said Valendyne. 'During those years, my own creation, with great agency, has collected the souls of the dead — devouring them, sending them to the Afterlife. Not a single mortal soul has beheld the Two-Legged Death and lived to tell of it. Not one ... except for you.

'Explain yourself, messenger.'

Mustapha clenched his sceptre with both hands, steadying them. 'My death did not come at the jaws of your beast,' he answered, 'but at the hand of she who had the power to give life back to me.

'It is written in the lore of our land: *From love does new love grow.* In this way are rebirth and renewal part of the natural order.

'Ophynea granted me this honour — to be a part of that natural order. To break free of this descent into darkness. Just as a phoenix rises from flame, so have I witnessed the miracle of death and rebirth. You may rule over the inevitable End, Valendyne … but in life, the End is followed by the Beginning again.'

Anuvin rubbed his hands together. 'Then you will fight! Do tell me — what weapon do you bring, little phoenix, which can overcome the host you see before you? Neptune gave me his Trident. Benjulius relinquished the deepest knowledge of the Adept. What tool can I possibly pry from your cold, lifeless hands?'

Upon the hill, the Black Queen issued a menacing rumble.

Mustapha set aside his sceptre, open palms on display. 'I bring no weapon,' — jeering burst from the sea of forsaken Adept — 'for neither blade, nor gun, nor incendiary device may put an end to War. Weapons, in fighters' hands, promote only Death. They do not staunch its flow.

'I bring against you the sacred power of Song, unifying the people of Rhye under one King. With joyous music, we welcome a new dawn to the land.'

Away in the east, the clouds of Valendyne parted. Blood-red light split the horizon. Luminescence seeped over distant hills, creeping across desolate terrain.

Upon the platform, open to the war-torn sky, Mustapha began to sing.

Can a season change
Without the fall of autumn leaves?
Can a baby, born asleep
Know how her mother grieves?

'No, no, no, no, no!' cried Anuvin, thrusting forward, pushing through the line of Warlocks. Their protective ward crackled, an explosion of sparks. The God of War shrugged it off, storming towards the portal at the base of the Pillar.

Mustapha drew breath to continue his Song. As he did so, the delicate strum of a zither accompanied him. To one side, Dique stood by the parapet, instrument in hand. He picked out a series of notes, filled with longing. All around him drew breath in wonder.

The seraph sang:

And so it goes.
We live in hope both day and night
We pray in darkness and in light
That the wonders of our world may be renewed.

The tune of the zither grew strident, inviting the words that cascaded over it.

In another moment came the stolid beat of a drum. Will and Trixel spun around. Meadow, reclaiming his instrument, gave Mustapha and Dique the pulse of a gallant march.

With each step towards the Pillar, Anuvin shrank. He hurried, striving for the Pillar. It loomed higher, the distance to it further, the more urgent his efforts became.

Soon, he stood no taller than the Fae.

Then, knee-high to a human.

Then, the size of vermin.

His arms and legs strained, trying to cross an ever-increasing expanse of mystical ground.

In the same moment, beams of orange-gold light reached across the land from the slim crescent of a rising sun. The song continued.

Does tomorrow weep
When we choose sides and go to war?

Black or white, it's in our veins
What do we do it for?
Nobody knows
Love your father, bless your mother
Without love, there is no lover
Tomorrow's legacy, it rests with you.

The Black Queen beat her giant wings and struggled into the air. The first rays of sunlight spilled over her scales, burning her, sending wisps of smoke into the air from scorched flesh. She wheezed, a feeble jet of flame escaping her nostrils. With gnashing teeth and reaching claws, she wafted towards the Pillar. Lashing out with desperate talons, she smashed at the enchanted stone, seeking to demolish her adversary. Immediately, she realised her mistake, for the contact brought acrid burns to her flesh.

Horror and fascination collided on Valendyne's face. Unwilling to move, unable to escape, he watched as the mighty Adatar rose in splendour over Rhye.

Sunlight struck glistening white stone. Reflected beams danced over the awestruck multitudes. Necromancers screamed and cried, while for the first time, the defenders of Rhye dared to imagine victory.

Beseech the Sun, entreat the Moon
Embrace the stars above
A prophecy made real today
This gift is born of love.
I make my wish, a dream come true
I name the Gods on high
The miracle within my heart –
To save the land of Rhye.

Dazzling rays flooded across marshlands, mountains, and desecrated forest. Clouds scattered, revealing splashes of azure beyond.

As Adatar crested the horizon, the soaring note of a Horn arose in a magnificent crescendo. Harold took his place beside Mustapha, delivering a wondrous fanfare.

Beams of hallowed light tore the Black Queen apart. Unable to withstand the forces arrayed against her, she disintegrated, a cloud of shredded black hide and leather wings, drifting to earth atop her terrified minions.

Valendyne stood riveted, to the last. No cry of anguish did he give — he simply began to fade, his power diminished by the outpouring of spirit before him.

The melody soared on major chords. It swooned and surged, a song of triumph. Mustapha, Harold, Meadow and Dique played as one, while the arrival of dawn swept the Black Queen's army into oblivion.

Now the pall of Death
Is cast aside with choral prayer.
Ophynea did anoint my brow
With fire's cleansing flare
Her glory shows.
In blessed skies a mystery
The grandest dance in history
A new day dawns and Rhye is born anew!

Fae, humans, Adept and Vrendari spilled forth from the Pillar of Rhye. Many wept with joy, or with relief; embracing, falling to their knees to praise the light of their deliverance.

Soon, a chorus rose from the throng of survivors. They raised arms towards the majestic figure above, flanked by his dear friends.

With joyous hearts we will sing along:
Long Live the King! Long Live the King!
We praise your name with our voices strong;
Long Live the King! We sing Long Live the King!

With joyous hearts we will sing along:
Long Live the King, Long Live the King!
And may your reign be forever long;
Long Live the King! We sing Long Live the King!

In the distant north, two figures stepped from the mouth of Two-Way Mirror Mountain. Boots crunched upon shattered scrallin as the men gained a vantage point high above Fenmarck Haunte. From this place, they could survey the once-accursed waste, upon which a tranquil calm had fallen.

Khashoggi and Fahrenheit squinted, adjusting to the blossoming light of day. They looked beyond the Haunte, to the faraway south, where glory shone almost as bright as the sun.

A tear welled in the eye of Ackley James Fahrenheit, for he witnessed a miracle beyond his estimation.

The light swelled, intensifying, reaching across the land from east to west. Every corner of Rhye basked in the wonder of a day free from War and Death. Brighter it became, banishing the darkness, vanquishing shadow.

At last, all turned to white.

EPILOGUE

JOYFUL THE SOUND

Mustapha drifted in a world of illumination.

He could see nothing but an expanse of white. At first, it dazzled his eyes, causing him to squint against the brightness. After a few moments, he grew accustomed to the change.

Gone were the clouds and the sky. Gone were the distant mountains, scarred plains, and the apocalyptic disarray of Banwah Haunte. The Pillar, the armies and the Gods had vanished.

All that existed was a sublime harmony, carrying him through the void.

His body felt weightless, but so too, his spirit. He laughed, wild and without care, free of any burden. He longed to share his joy with his friends, though they were gone as well.

'Hello!' he called, into the nothingness. 'Who is there? Where am I?'

'This is Now,' announced a voice. 'Sit with me, Mustapha.'

The seraph spun around. Where there was nothing only an instant before, there now sat a youth, in vibrant, flowing robes of many colours. His skin was chocolate brown, his dark hair in tight ringlets. His legs were crossed, though no chair or surface supported him.

'I am Marnis,' the youth said. 'Won't you join me?'

Coaxed by intrigue — and with no other place to go — Mustapha drifted towards the Creator.

'My prayer figurine makes you look older,' said the seraph.

Marnis laughed. 'Call it vanity. After all, I create my own appearance. I can age a little, if you prefer?'

'Please, no. You remind me of a better time in my life.'

'You mean to say, there is a better time to be alive than right Now?' Marnis wore a quizzical smile.

'I'm not entirely sure. Where, exactly, is "Now"?'

'Ah — an excellent question.' Marnis grinned, flashing perfect, even teeth. 'Onik has enveloped us — swept us up in his endless flow. We sit together at the instant of Rhye's rebirth.'

Mustapha frowned, looking about. 'So ... where is everything?'

'Where were you, in the moment before your conception?'

'Hm. You make a fair point. Does that mean that the old Rhye is ... gone?'

'Irretrievably.'

The seraph digested this news in silence. The answer was absolute. The Creator still offered the same benign smile, though even this pleasantry did not assuage a chill of dread.

A question festered within him.

'My friends. They were all around me. Are they —' he gulped his apprehension, like a sticky bolus of food. 'Are they gone, too?'

<I can answer that one.>

The seraph jumped. A new voice emerged — the whirring of a

mechanical device in his mind. From the void appeared a golem, crafted of a fine alloy, the colour of stellite.

'Torr Yosef?'

<You look resplendent, Mustapha. Or should I address you as "my King"?>

Mustapha held his head, tugging fistfuls of hair. 'I don't know what you should be saying. Where have you come from? Where were you, in the battle for Rhye? As a matter of fact,' — he swung to face Marnis — 'where were any of you, aside from Ophynea, when we needed you?'

Marnis chuckled. 'Your exasperation is plain. You are anointed by the Gods' blessing, yet you feel forsaken. You have laboured, Mustapha, for the land you love. In return, you deserve to know that the Gods walked beside you, at every step.'

'Nobody came to our aid, at the last.' Mustapha strained to keep his tone humble. 'I only wish to understand. Was that part of the plan?'

'Victory would never be delivered by an angelic host, charging down from the heavens,' said Marnis. 'This we learned from the Godsryche.'

<You already know it, Mustapha,> added Yosef. *<Anuvin would never be bested on the battleground. Valendyne could not be contained by causing more bloodshed. There had to be another way ... and you found it.>*

Marnis resumed the thread. 'Along the road, the Pantheon conspired to help you save Rhye, whether or not you saw it at the time.

'Augustine preserved you, as poison coursed through your veins. He made his presence known, twice: once in Banwah Haunte, guiding your company towards the place of Lady Maybeth's confinement. There, you found your healing unction — her tears.

He also came to you in Nevermore, warning you of Death's presence. Each time, he chose the form of a raven.

'Lhestra you saw, high upon the tower. Through her did Maybeth become Pillar and White Queen, manifestation of all that is righteous and true in the land.

'Cornavrian shepherded the Ogres, whose savage hearts he tempered. He enabled the Two-Way Mirror to be shattered, freeing my children to fulfil their destiny. Cornavrian guided the sword of your father as he slew the manticore. He also sent Mher to honour the final wish of Lord Neptune.

'Ophynea's role you know. She watched you grow in Love, channelling that power to produce a King fit for Rhye.

'Phydeas and Floe worked to protect the innocent. One million souls — most of them women and children — sheltered by the Peaks of Obelis. Millions more found refuge in the strongholds of noble races. Though many were claimed by Death, many more survived, with blessed Providence.'

Mustapha nodded, bowing his head. His cheeks grew hot and silver streaks ran down his face.

He lifted his chin. 'What about Oska?'

'Ha! Oska made you swallow the cinnabar in the first place. He felt mischievous that night. Rest assured, Oska has been present to offer Fortune, whenever you were in need of it.'

'It's true,' conceded Mustapha. 'I'm still here, after all.'

'Now, it is my turn,' said Marnis. 'It is I who denigrated Valendyne at the outset, millennia ago. I also stood by and watched the golem genocide, thinking it just that Anuvin would destroy all Valendyne's creations.

'Lhestra helped me to see the compassion and wisdom of these creatures, who live without a soul. I recognised my mistake — restitution is mine to deliver.

'With great joy did I discover Torr Yosef, lone survivor of tragedy. I made myself known to him, revealing my plan. At the Mountain, the time came when I needed to lift him up, away from the dangers of battle, lest he also be destroyed.'

Yosef interceded. <*I never had the opportunity to apologise to our friends. All they saw in me was an encroaching strangeness, when in fact, I was being presented with the chance to partake in a miracle.*>

'Torr Yosef is the perfect vessel,' said Marnis. 'Imbued with the virtues of the golem race, but without a soul. Thus has Yosef been the receptacle, in which I have preserved the essence of every living being.'

Mustapha's mouth hung open. 'You saved ...?'

'All who lived, at the moment of your triumph, have been saved. They await only the birth of a new Rhye, in which you shall be honoured as King.'

<*With your vision, Mustapha — and the grace of Marnis — we can create something unique. A place unfettered to black or white. A land where unity and diversity can coexist. We will not be ruled by the fear of darkness. Create a place for fresh beginnings and I will send forth its populace.*>

Myriad thoughts flooded Mustapha's mind. His mouth moved, disconnected from the jumble in his brain.

'You ... you want me to recreate Rhye? I don't know where to begin!'

'You brought with you an outsider, did you not? A human from beyond the Seventh Sea?'

'I did, yes. His own world left him behind.'

'Then you have brought with you a font of infinite wonder,' said Marnis. 'Within this man will you find all the wide-eyed energy you will need.' Marnis sat forward, adjusting the technicolour folds of his flowing cloak. He brought out both hands, each balled in a fist, palms facing up. 'You also begin with these.' He unclenched his hands.

In one palm sat two tiny grains of sand. They were both black as obsidian. The other palm contained a single white stone.

'These two dark grains are all that remain of Anuvin and Valendyne,' said Marnis. 'You cannot create a land that is utterly without War and Death. These entities will exist forever, as my brethren and as your responsibility. You must learn to control and live with them. This promise I make: There is time for peace. If you are wise and just, ruling with love, then the grains of sand shall stay buried.

'The white stone is a fragment from the Pillar of Rhye. Upon this stone shall be built your home. Through it, you will be protected and strengthened, by the legacy of your mother.'

Mustapha held out his hands. The Creator passed the grains and the stone to him, with care.

'The rest is up to you. The Pantheon will watch over your progress, with keen hearts and open eyes.'

In the next instant, Marnis vanished.

'We have quite a job ahead of us,' said Mustapha, to his golem friend.

<*The day is upon us. Onik will not keep us from it forever.*>

Dreams of white-capped mountains and bright blue skies, homely woodlands, and sparkling seas, churned in Mustapha's head. He imagined rivers, castles, rolling hillsides and pastoral havens. Most of all, he imagined faces.

A beautiful sylph, with the gleam of honour in her eye.

An intrepid fixie, the inspired product of conflict and levity.

A dragonfly, dependable in the face of peril.

Two pixies, who readily found both trouble and solutions.

Without any of them, this victory lay beyond reach.

One vivid face outshone all others. The affable wagoner, with his rugged features and tousled hair of straw.

Most appealing.

Mustapha grinned, wondrous visions crowding for release. His heart hammered inside him. The music swelled, voices swirling all around in a wheel of joy.

He threw his arms above his head and gave a great shout:

'Hold fast, my darling Will. Keep our friends by your side. Oh, you had better believe it — I'm coming soon!'

THE END

ACKNOWLEDGEMENTS

In creating this work, I must primarily acknowledge the late, great, Freddie Mercury. Without his boundless creativity, Rhye would not exist — in song, in the pages of this book, or in the hearts of his fans the world over.

I acknowledge the incredible talents of Brian May, Roger Taylor, and John Deacon. As Queen, these men wrought incredible soundscapes for us all. Queen music is the soundtrack of my own life and an indelible part of rock history. This book is an homage to them all.

I would like to thank Luc Hudson, for his tireless contributions to this project. From proofreading to artwork and music, Luc saw this vision, as I did, from Day One. Thank you for the encouragement, friend.

I thank with all my heart the Fat Bottomed Boys, Thibaut Sergent and Louis Henry Chambat. These wonderful musicians helped me realise new Songs for Rhye ... and committed them to record.

Last, but certainly not least, I want to thank everyone who contributed, no matter how great or small. Whether it was time to read and critique, sponsorship, or even just leaving your thoughts and comments on my posts, it all helped. You know who you are — thank you.

APPENDIX A

THE AGES OF RHYE

1. **THE GRAND DANCE**

    - The separation of Land and Sky. The birth of the stars and the Seven Seas.
    - The birth of the Primary Gods — Onik and Cornavrian.
    - Rhye is populated with natural spirits — undines, zephyrs, and dryads.
    - The birth of the Secondary Gods — Marnis and Valendyne.

2. **THE AGE OF HIGHER BEINGS**

    - The Ogres are created, then loathed, by Marnis and ushered into Two-Way Mirror Mountain by Cornavrian.
    - Other higher beings are created — Delves, Fae-Folk, Mer-Folk, Humans, Adept and Sylphs.
    - The birth of the Tertiary Gods — Ophynea, Lhestra, Phydeas, Augustine, Oska, Floe and Anuvin.

3. **THE AGE OF IMMORTALITY**

- Higher beings — for a time, immortal — explore and settle the land of Rhye.
- Humans first leave Petrichor, founding Via by the mouth of the Granventide River.
- The Adept develop their Disciplines. Many choose to worship Valendyne and become Necromancers.
    - Valendyne creates Golems.

4. **THE AGE OF OBELIS**

- Marnis creates Obelis as a gift for Valendyne
- Valendyne creates Death and declares himself God of the Afterlife.
- Anato and Adatar disagree, separating in the sky.
- Humans meet and clash with Necromancers in Kash Valley. All except Belladonna are cast out by Lily, the Seer.
- Walther Giltenan and Arnaut Vrendar do battle in the frontier of Nurtenan.
- Two generations later, Montreux Giltenan forges peace between Humankind and the Sylphic race. The truce is cemented by the commissioning of Vrendari.

5. **THE GODSRYCHE**

6. **THE AGE OF SOVEREIGNS**

- The Delves vanish.
- Khashoggi writes the Song of the Prophet and leaves Rhye.
- Lord Oberon and Trixel Tate first visit Lily of the Valley. Soon after, Belladonna escapes.
- **The events of 'The King of Rhye' take place.**

7. THE AGE OF HARMONY

- Mustapha reigns as the King of Rhye.

APPENDIX B

You Want It All?

Queen hides right throughout this book,
Clues a-plenty if you look.
Some are big and some are small ...
Did you recognise them all?

PROLOGUE: AS IT BEGAN

- Title — ref White Queen (As It Began).
- The Narrator's surname, 'Fahrenheit', is lifted from *Don't Stop Me Now* (Jazz, 1978). His middle name, James, enables the nickname 'Jimmy' — to pair with his beloved, Jenny. Ref — *Brighton Rock* (Sheer Heart Attack, 1974).
- '... the court of the Earl,' refers to Earl's Court, an arena in London, England. It is a cultural hub and home to the Troubadour coffee house and the Exhibition Centre, where Queen played, most famously in 1977.

- The locale, Brighton-Upon-Sea, inspires the Victorian era. Ref — *Brighton Rock* (Sheer Heart Attack, 1974).
- Allusions to 'promenades', 'lantern-lit parades' and 'gay and curious souls' reference *Brighton Rock* (Sheer Heart Attack, 1974).
- The hermit's name, Khashoggi, refers to *Khashoggi's Ship* (The Miracle, 1989). The ship in question is also a prominent feature in the Prologue.
- Khashoggi's ship appears here in the year of '89, the same year the Queen track was released. We know this because the Narrator reminisces upon an earlier time, 'Nearly fifty years ago to the day,' — ergo 'back in '39' — when Khashoggi first created a craft for interstellar travel. Ref — '39 (A Night at the Opera, 1975).
- 'Twenty brave individuals,' refers to 'score brave souls inside,' from '39 (A Night at the Opera, 1975).
- The hermit's ramblings to the Narrator can be traced back to Smile, fronted by Tim Staffel in the pre-Queen era. 'Beneath another sun, this dockyard would cease to exist' and 'a crystal sea I now know only in my dreams.' Ref — *Earth* (Smile EP, 1969).
- Khashoggi is desperate to convince Fahrenheit of his tale's importance. Shaking Fahrenheit, he cries 'Do you hear me?' (This could be followed by 'I know that you can hear me …') Ref — *The Prophet's Song* (A Night at the Opera, 1975).
- The motif of a separate, or dual reality, is referenced in Queen, pre-Queen, and solo member recordings. It is present in Smile's *Earth*, here reflected in Khashoggi's surreal reverie, as well as in the first stanza of *Bohemian Rhapsody* (A Night at the Opera, 1975). Brian May also recorded *An-*

other World (Another World, 1998), which featured in the dual-reality romance-drama *Sliding Doors*. It is also a central motif of 'The King of Rhye'.

PART WHITE

CHAPTER 1: NIGHT'S NOON TIME

- Title — ref *The Fairy Feller's Master Stroke* (Queen II, 1974).
- The general premise of this chapter is an homage to *The Fairy Feller's Master Stroke*; the song in turn inspired by the painting of the same name, by artist Richard Dadd (1817–1886). As such, characters within both the chapter and the song, will be annotated by '(*FFMS*)'.
- Here, our heroes are introduced: A tatterdemalion, a junketer, a thief, and a dragonfly trumpeter (*FFMS*).

  * 'Meadow' — ref Roger Meddows Taylor. Depicted as a lover of drink and celebration, from the very first line of the tale.
  * 'Dique' is, phonetically, a contraction of 'Deacon' or 'Deaky', ref — John Deacon. *Dique* is also a Dominican word implying doubt, or uncertain expectations. Keep an eye out for instances of Dique shrugging, at dubious comments from his friends.
  * 'Harold' — ref Brian Harold May, 'the tallest of the group.' Harold bears his beloved trumpet, ref — *Sleeping on the Sidewalk* (News of the World, 1977).
  * 'Mustapha' — refers, of course, to *Mustapha* (Jazz, 1978). An exotic Mercury track, for an exotic, mercurial protagonist.

- 'The Mayor of Petrichor ... an eminent politician.' 'Politician with senatorial pipe, he's a dilly-dally-o ...' (*FFMS*)
- 'It's the Apothecary I'm after.' '... there's a good apothecary man ...' (*FFMS*)
- '... the Ploughman, a wealthy industrialist.' (*FFMS*)
- 'Alongside the Ploughman was his son.' The 'Ploughboy.' (*FFMS*)
- 'Benjulius the Archimage, Lord of the Adept.' '... the arch magician resides / He is the leader ...' (*FFMS*)
- The four Guild representatives. '... soldier, sailor, tinker, tailor ...' (*FFMS*)
- Will the gourd farmer. Ref — 'Wagoner Will' (*FFMS*).
- The Fairy Feller arrives (*FFMS*).
- The Sovereigns of Petrichor finally arrive, to witness the masterstroke. They are Oberon and Titania (*FFMS*), also known as the Fairy King — ref *My Fairy King* (Queen, 1973) — and Queen Mab. In Shakespearean literature, Titania and Mab are two different characters; here, I have used the two names interchangeably, for the Lady Sovereign of the Fae Folk.
- The Sovereign couple are accompanied by a 'squat, old woman with a stern and officious face,' i.e., they are 'watched by a harridan' (*FFMS*).
- The tempo of the ensuing scene intends to capture the sheer mayhem of the Mercury track from Queen II.
- Mustapha's prize — the object of his thievery — is revealed as a 'piece of cinnabar.' Cinnabar, a highly toxic compound, has historical uses in Asia and the Middle East as a sedative and hypnotic ... and might be better recog-

nised as a source ore, for refining elemental mercury.

- Harold rescues Mustapha from pursuit by the Warlocks ('he's my hero'). Ref — *FFMS*.
- The old woman/harridan reappears and is discovered to be a woman of power, named Lady Belladonna. Ref — 'a belladonic haze,' *Keep Yourself Alive* (Queen, 1973).

CHAPTER 2: I HAVE STOLEN

- Title — ref *Liar* (Queen, 1973).
- Here begins the core theme of lineage and parentage; specifically, the concepts of 'motherhood' and maternal love. Freddie Mercury returned to the subject numerous times through Queen songs, notably in *My Fairy King*, *Liar* (both Queen, 1973), *Bohemian Rhapsody* (A Night at the Opera, 1975) and, much later, *Mother Love* (Made in Heaven, 1995). Mustapha experiences very different bonds to the two dominant women in his early life — Titania (Queen Mab) and Lady Belladonna — though neither of them is his biological mother. In both relationships, he feels a debt of servitude. In one case it is given gladly; in the other, there is an element of coercion.
- Mustapha is saved from capital punishment for his crime of theft from the Fairy King ('Sire I have stolen / Stolen many times ... When I know I never should,' ref — *Liar*). Lady Belladonna conspires to rescue him; hence, he is indebted to her ('Mama I'm gonna be your slave / Gonna try behave,' ref — *Liar*). Throughout this passage, it is unclear whether the 'Father' to whom he refers is Lord Oberon ... or his biological father, who he does not know.

- 'As he felt neither pleasure nor pain ...' ref — *Pain is So Close to Pleasure* (A Kind of Magic, 1986).
- *'Am I awake? Or do I dream still?'* The real/surreal diptych once again. 'Is this the real life? Is this just fantasy?' ref — *Bohemian Rhapsody* (A Night at the Opera, 1975).
- The Seven Seas. The first mention of the *Seven Seas of Rhye* (Queen II, 1974).
- 'Flashes of silver shone around him — schools of large salmon swam in nonchalant circles ...' Ref — *Silver Salmon*, a track dating back to the Smile days, played live by Queen a small number of times, but never recorded.
- 'You! You will help me live forever.' Ref — *Who Wants to Live Forever* (A Kind of Magic, 1986).
- The introductory threat from Anuvin, God of War — albeit delivered in a dream — is a riff on the tone and lyrics of *Gimme the Prize (Kurgan's Theme)* (A Kind of Magic, 1986). He may as well be saying, 'I am the master of your destiny / I am the God of Kingdom Come / Give me your kings / Let me squeeze them in my hands ... Your so-called leaders of your lands ...' This pompous villainy personifies Anuvin and the plans he has for Rhye.
- In the dream, Anuvin also issues Mustapha a terrible ultimatum: 'Kill the one you love.' Mustapha is distraught, waking with a scream. 'Who wants to live forever / when love must die?' Ref — *Who Wants to Live Forever* (A Kind of Magic, 1986).
- Mustapha lives with Lady Belladonna, who is identified as being 'fastidious'; in her quarters, everything is in its proper place, or 'precise'. She keeps liquor in a 'sleek cabinet'; she appears in this scene toting a cigarette; she

has seldom kept the same living quarters, living in recent times as a gypsy; she is perfumed, coiffed and speaks like a Baroness ... though, in essence, she is a consort. Ref — *Killer Queen* (Sheer Heart Attack, 1974).

- Assimilating Lady Belladonna with the title 'Killer Queen' is foreshadowing ... to put it mildly.
- *The Prophet's Song* (A Night at the Opera, 1975) is directly referenced for the first time, here named The Song of the Prophet.
- As well as maternal themes, the concept of religion (or, more broadly, faith) is also strong in this chapter. The presence of idols for worship and the mention of 'wrathful Gods' parallels the 'Gods' that are also mentioned in *In the Lap of the Gods* and ... *Revisited* (Sheer Heart Attack, 1974).
- Lady Belladonna is referred to as *Mama*, Mustapha's deferential name for her — a tie-back to the 'mother' theme.

CHAPTER 3: MY FAIRY KING

- Title — ref *My Fairy King* (Queen, 1973)
- '... old man Kensington's market stall.' Ref — Freddie and Roger once ran a fashion stall at the Kensington Market together. Here, Meadow discusses it as if Dique was there. Dique corrects him, saying, 'I wasn't there, actually. That was you and Mustapha.'
- Dique begins humming, 'in a low, melodic voice.' Meadow starts drumming his fist along in time with him. Bass + drums = A sonic volcano, perhaps?
- First mention of the Bijou River. Ref — *Bijou* (Innuendo, 1991).

- In Petrichor, honeycomb can be pilfered straight from the hive — it sounds as if the 'honeybees have lost their stings.' Days are spent chasing parcels of 'fallow deer'. The water is described here as clear, and later as dark as shiraz. Meadow plays about the shores of the Berthelot Stream ('rivers made from wine so clear') and, soon enough, we catch our first glimpse of a pterippus ... or a 'horse born with eagle wings.' Ref — *My Fairy King* (Queen, 1973).
- Mustapha's introduction here is intended to evoke the image of Freddie Mercury, circa 1974.
- Meadow references both the messenger god, Mercury (of Roman mythology), and Freddie's 1975 white, winged-boot ensemble, in a remark about how fleet of foot the strangeling is. This quote is also foreshadowing a costume change, to come much later.
- 'Blag your way right into Psithur?' Ref — *Blag* (Ghost of a Smile, 1969). Roger Taylor is also quoted as describing the way he and Freddie would go 'poncing and ultra-blagging about' in their youthful days, while tending the Kensington Market stall.
- 'This fairy oozed self-assurance. It would serve Meadow to keep good company.' Phrase used to evoke the nostalgic strum of *Good Company* (A Night at the Opera, 1975).
- Dique is re-introduced, as a quiet pixie and a 'fixer'. This is in keeping with the disposition of John Deacon, a private man and electronics enthusiast.
- Drowseberries. Ref — *Drowse* (A Day at the Races, 1976). Dique enjoys his drowseberry wine. The 'delicious haze' and 'blissful stupor' evokes the feeling of the track, reminiscent of the good old days.

- Dique mentions his 'ma and pa's cheese shop'. The cheese shop, or fromagerie, is mentioned several times throughout the book. Ref — Early in Queen's career, John Deacon famously answered a survey question on his favourite food with "Cheese on toast". It is now an internet meme.
- 'No-good bum-sucker's yard!' A quote from Meadow. Ref — *Modern Times Rock 'n' Roll* (Queen, 1973).
- '... black root ... could be ground to a sweet powder' is a reference to 'a little nigger sugar', and is one of the items Mustapha steals for Lady Belladonna. Ref — *March of the Black Queen* (Queen II, 1974).
- '... a pitcher of bayrne oil' is essentially 'a rub-a-dub-a baby oil', also an item procured by Mustapha and named in *March of the Black Queen*.
- Titania infers that the Fairy Feller was earlier 'spooked by a bugle,' i.e., 'bugle blower, let trumpet cry.' Ref — *Ogre Battle* (Queen II, 1974). This is some heavily cloaked foreshadowing.
- The 'Fae Ring', a vital artefact and chief McGuffin, is mentioned for the first time. It is mentioned only once in recorded Queen, being the line 'someone ...has drained the colour from my wings / Broken my fairy circle ring.' Ref — *My Fairy King* (Queen, 1973).
- 'The Seer of Kash' is named after her abode, Kash Valley. 'Kash' is the shortened name Freddie Bulsara gave to his sister Kashmira Bulsara, with whom he shared tales of Rhye as a child.
- One of two progenitors of the gods is mentioned here: Adatar, whom the devout upon Rhye worship as the Sun, or God of the Day. Adatar = ADATR = A Day At The Races.

- The Seer of Kash (Valley) is further introduced — 'she has a name, by the way, it's Lily.' Ref — *Lily of the Valley* (Sheer Heart Attack, 1974).
- 'Night came down.' Dusk becomes night at the end of this chapter, as beautifully evoked in *The Night Comes Down* (Queen, 1973).

CHAPTER 4: PEERS AND PRIVY COUNCILLORS

- Title — ref *Seven Seas of Rhye* (Queen II, 1974).
- '... the Lady who, one golden April afternoon ...' I am preparing to introduce the recent Giltenan ancestor as the *April Lady* (Ghost of a Smile, 1969). She is described in this passage as a 'mentor' and a 'lover of children'; as is the focal Lady in the Smile track, who sounds like a kindergarten or junior-school teacher. In both instances, the loss of the April Lady is being lamented, albeit in whimsical fashion.
- The Council of Rhye is, naturally, attended by 'peers and privy Councillors' ... or perhaps, by 'Lords and Lady preachers'. Ref — *Seven Seas of Rhye* (Queen II, 1974).
- Amongst the Adept retinue is Astrologer Mayhampton. Brian *May* was born in a home in *Hampton* Hill, Twickenham; he also received his education at the *Hampton* (Grammar) School. At the formation of Queen, he had been undertaking his PhD in *Astrophysics*.
- The Lord of the Mer-Folk is Neptune. Ref — 'Neptune of the Seas', *Lily of the Valley* (Sheer Heart Attack, 1974).
- The sylphic race here can be considered a nod to the Hawkmen in the 1980 film, *Flash Gordon*.

- The golem is drawn from 'Frank', the robot appearing on the sleeve of *News of the World* (1977), illustrated by Frank Kelly Freas. Freas essentially adapted a previous science fiction artwork of his own for this album cover, at the request of Roger Taylor.
- 'The Song of the prophet' again becomes pivotal in this chapter. It is a piece of ancient augury, left behind centuries before by a mysterious figure who subsequently vanished from the land. The higher beings of Rhye believe that the Song warns of a precipitous doom, and that this doom is now imminent. This aligns with the general tone — and some specific lines — from *The Prophet's Song* (A Night at the Opera, 1975).
- '... the two-legged shade we know as Death.' A terrifying and maligned spirit that all mortals must face. Ref — *Death on Two Legs (Dedicated to ...* (A Night at the Opera, 1975).
- 'Ibex Trench ...' Ref — Freddie's pre-Queen band, Ibex.
- 'Ealing Sea'. Ref — the Ealing School of Art, where Freddie studied.
- 'Two-Way Mirror Mountain'. The fabled place is mentioned for the first time. Ref — *Ogre Battle* (Queen II, 1974).
- 'The earth will shake ...!' Ref — *The Prophet's Song* (A Night at the Opera, 1975).
- 'If ever there were Ogres ...' The foreshadowing gets deeper. It's almost a promise now, isn't it?
- 'The Song of the Prophet' is produced, in full. Scattered throughout are paraphrases of Brian May's classic original. Such paraphrases are interspersed with plot elements of my story, to tie in and give credence to later events.
- At the Council, Mustapha is accused of thieving a precious

stone during the Ceremony of the Nut and is called 'Liar!' by Apothecary Renfelix. 'Liar / Nobody believes me …' Ref — *Liar* (Queen, 1973).

- 'The honourable Apothecary says I was there, but now I'm here?' Mustapha denies translocation, stirring the image of Freddie seemingly transporting across stage. Ref — *Now I'm Here* (Sheer Heart Attack, 1974).
- 'I am a poor orphan with few personal effects, save those that Lady Belladonna allows me to keep in her apartment.' Mustapha owns very little. He alludes to his relationship with Belladonna in terms of allowance and ownership. This gives a sense that their union is truly one of master/slave, more so than one borne of real affection. Ref — 'I'm just a poor boy nobody loves me / He's just a poor boy from a poor family' — *Bohemian Rhapsody* (A Night at the Opera, 1975).

CHAPTER 5: KILL LIKE KNIVES

- Title — ref *My Fairy King* (Queen, 1973).
- Mustapha, house-bound, retreats as if 'going back' to the womb. The very first paragraph is a tangential nod to the sentiments of *Goin' Back* (B-side to *I Can Hear Music*, Larry Lurex, 1973): 'I think I'm going back / To the things I learned so well in my youth / I think I'm returning to / All those days when I was young enough to know the truth.'
- This opening passage (from 'Following his moment of condemnation at the Council …') also references the fever-dream atmosphere and sense of dependent love in *She Makes Me (Stormtrooper in Stilettos)* (Sheer Heart Attack, 1974). 'She makes me need / She is my love … Who knows who she'll make me / As I lie in her cocoon? / And

the world will surely heal my ills / I'm warm and terrified / She makes me so.'

- The resurrected Giltenan dead advance, weapons drawn, to attack and overcome the living Sovereign. The grander plan, to remove the power of Sovereignty in the land, begins with Lord Rogar. 'Then came man to savage in the night / To run like thieves and to kill like knives / To take away the power from the magic hand / To bring about the ruin to the promised land.' Ref — *My Fairy King* (Queen, 1973).
- As Mustapha moves downstairs, there is a casual reference to *Misfire* (Sheer Heart Attack, 1974).
- The remainder of this chapter moves the narrative forward with an action sequence — not heavy in Queen lore, but perhaps the closing minute of *My Fairy King* captures the tumult of battle, within the House of Giltenan.

CHAPTER 6: THROUGH STORMY SKIES

- Title — ref *Lily of the Valley* (Sheer Heart Attack, 1974).
- A narrative passage begins, with mention made of Adatar (previously discussed, ref — A Day at the Races) and now Anato, Goddess of Night, embodied by the Moon (ANATO = A Night At The Opera). Through this same passage, Lily of the Valley is also given a more direct introduction.
- The motifs of White and Black, Day and Night surface once again. The Wearers of Black are contrasted against the virtuous spirit of the Seer, Lily, who is named after the white flowers of her vale. Later, fleeing from the House of Giltenan, Mustapha reveals he is carrying the alabaster figurine of Valendyne, God of the Afterlife. It has been scorched black, in contrast to the figurines of his shrine, which are white.

- Mustapha battles with the revelation of Belladonna's evil: The woman he knew as Mama, who he looked up to for protection, for guidance and for a kind of love, has been using him. With the shattering of the alabaster figurine, her spell of binding is broken. 'From mother's love is the son estranged.' Ref — *The Prophet's Song* (A Night at the Opera, 1975).
- In this chapter, Mustapha explores 'strangeness' with a new acquaintance, Trixel Tate. While Trixel knows that she is the result of interracial parentage, she is estranged from her parents. Mustapha never knew his and is not even certain of his own racial heritage. By the time Queen were recording their early music, Freddie was clearly exploring his own inner conflicts through music. He came from a Zoroastrian faith, and from parents who perhaps carried certain social and professional expectations of him. Meanwhile, he struggled with a very different, internalised reality. It is reasonable to imagine he endured, at some time, a crisis of identity.

CHAPTER 7: MILK INTO SOUR

- Title — ref *My Fairy King* (Queen, 1973).
- At the end of the previous chapter, the Bijou River is referred to by Torr Yosef as the Milk of Petrichor. This is a colloquial term — correspondingly, the Granventide is sometimes named the Tears of Marnis. Both are terms referencing the bounty of Rhye. In this chapter, we learn that the Bijou has been befouled through evil sorcery, hence turning 'Milk into Sour'.
- We are introduced to Ponerog, Lord of Wilden Folk. He

lives in a dilapidated stronghold in squalor, with filthy beasts as servants and slaves. The place is riddled with vermin. Belladonna, paying him a visit, likens him to a 'king of rats'. Ref — *Great King Rat* (Queen, 1973).

- Lord Ponerog does not hold his murdered father in high esteem. 'I'm baffled by how he managed even to impregnate my hussy of a mother, with such a flaccid prick.' In other words, he was 'the son of a whore'. Ref — *Great King Rat* (Queen, 1973).
- It is revealed that long ago, Lord Ponerog kidnapped the April Lady and has held her hostage in his tower. We are reminded that her identity is Lady Maybeth, elder sibling of Lord Rogar … hence, she is of the noble Giltenan line.
- Through their conversation, Belladonna makes a first reference to Nevermore. This is a sacred garden, known to most only in fables of the Gods. Belladonna's plans — to free Valendyne, the God of Death, from where he is imprisoned — will take her to this place. Ponerog believes it to be imaginary. Ref — *Nevermore* (Queen II, 1974).
- The tainted effluvium of Ponerog's work washes down the Bijou River to the *Sour Milk Sea* — the name of one of Freddie's pre-Queen groups. Fitting, then, that the Milk (of Petrichor) turned sour ends up here.

CHAPTER 8: THE EARTH WILL SHAKE

- Title — ref *The Prophet's Song* (A Night at the Opera, 1975).
- Will, pixies and dryads make a midnight trek through Petrichor, 'across rivulets as dark as flowing shiraz,' or perhaps 'rivers made from wine so clear,' ref — *My Fairy King* (Queen, 1973).

- More discussion of 'mother's love' and maternal estrangement takes place, en route to Psithur Grove.
- In Psithur Grove, discussing the Fairy King: 'Capable of channelling the arcane magic of trees, the crown brought Oberon word from all of Petrichor, as well as from forests the land over.' The Lord of the Fae 'can see things that are not there for you and me / (he) can do right and nothing wrong.' Ref — *My Fairy King* (Queen, 1973). Oberon is later illustrated as having the gift of percipience, reading the fate of trees via his antlered crown and the all-powerful Yew. Principally, he is tasked with watching over one specific tree, in Nevermore. Valendyne is bound within it, courtesy of the Fae Ring.
- Oberon states, to a dryad warrior: 'You will stand down, while I learn of their whys and wherefores.' He then turns to Will. A play on words, evoking a lovely lyric in *March of the Black Queen* (Queen II, 1974): 'Everything you do bears a will and a why and a wherefore.'
- Oberon: 'I did indeed know of the Mayor's dalliance.' Recall — 'A politician with senatorial pipe / he's a dilly-dally-o' — *The Fairy Feller's Master Stroke* (Queen II, 1974).
- A passage exploring the burgeoning terror of guns — a relatively new and frightening technology — is a tangential reference to the anti-gun message of *Put Out the Fire* (Hot Space, 1982). The potential of these new weapons is difficult for the Fae Folk to conceive.
- Realising the predicament of his people, Oberon concludes that the fate of Petrichor rests with the temperaments of Lhestra, goddess of Justice and Anuvin, God of War. In other terms ... they are *In the Lap of the Gods* (Sheer Heart Attack, 1974).

- Oberon has a near-death experience, overcome by a wave of fell power. In his vision, he sees the ground tremble ('the earth will shake,' ref *The Prophet's Song* (A Night at the Opera, 1975)). He name-drops Nevermore, where their nemesis is entrapped; lastly, he has a vision of the Fae Ring breaking. 'Someone ... (has) broken my fairy circle ring.' Ref — *My Fairy King* (Queen, 1973).

CHAPTER 9: A WORD IN YOUR EAR

- Title — ref *Father to Son* (Queen II, 1974).
- In general, this title alludes to the chapter as one shaped by conversation. But for a Queen fan paying closer attention, the title itself is a significant piece of foreshadowing. The key moment in the chapter is a conversation between Mustapha and the Sylphic General Prime, Bastian Sinotar. The title itself is a lyric from *Father to Son* (Queen II, 1974).
- Mustapha declares himself a fool, for not detecting Belladonna's deceit. 'Oh, what a fool I've been!' A blatant reference to *See What a Fool I've Been*, B-Side to *Seven Seas of Rhye* (Queen II, 1974).
- The travellers arrive at the hovel of the Seer, Lily, within Kash Valley. Inspecting the group, she mutters '... Death all around ...' in reference to what she sees of their futures. Ref — *The Prophet's Song* (A Night at the Opera, 1975).

CHAPTER 10: MY KINGDOM FOR A HORSE

- Title — ref *Lily of the Valley* (Sheer Heart Attack, 1974).
- Lily declares that, to save the land, 'Rhye needs a King.'

This quest is the impetus behind the very title of this novel. We know that, at some stage, a King ruled over all Rhye, for he is referenced in *Lily of the Valley.*

- 'The true King of Rhye will emerge, armed with a new Song as a manifestation of holy power, ordained by the Gods themselves.' See 'God give you grace to purge this place / and peace all around shall be your fortune.' Ref — *The Prophet's Song* (A Night at the Opera, 1975).
- '... one by one, the fall of your present Sovereigns ... others will follow ... In darkness then, will all the Realms crumble, for the power of Sovereignty ... is bonded to the Fae Ring.' See 'Soon the cold of night will fall / summoned by your own hand' and 'These kings of beasts now counting their days.' Ref — *The Prophet's Song* (A Night at the Opera, 1975). The old Lords fall, making way for a cataclysmic power shift — an Armageddon, of sorts.
- The Seventh Sea is named directly. Ref — *Seven Seas of Rhye* (Queen II, 1974). It is the last and the least known, thought to be impossible to traverse without forfeiting one's life. Paradoxically, augury tells that a saviour of the land will need to cross it ... ergo, a suicide mission.
- Lily and Mustapha share a pivotal late-night discussion. Lily reveals that she can see very little of either Mustapha's past, or his future. Both are frustrated at the limits of her prescient vision. Ref — 'Lily of the Valley doesn't know,' *Lily of the Valley* (Sheer Heart Attack, 1974).
- The dwindle of Mustapha's strength, as the poison in his blood takes hold, can be compared to the solemnity of the tone and lyrics of *The Show Must Go On* (Innuendo, 1991).
- In the latter part of the chapter, Mustapha is too weak to travel. Torr Yosef, as the largest and strongest of the group,

elects to carry the strangeling. This imagery is reminiscent of the album cover for *News of the World* (1977), where the robot (dubbed 'Frank') holds the bodies of both Brian May and Freddie Mercury.

CHAPTER 11: DEATH ALL AROUND

- Title — ref *The Prophet's Song* (A Night at the Opera, 1975).
- Skeleton warriors march on Petrichor, at the break of dawn — this has been prophesied. Ref — 'He told of death as a bone-white haze,' *The Prophet's Song* (A Night at the Opera, 1975).
- In the heat of battle, Will calls to the pixies, 'just keep yourselves alive!' Phrases relating to keeping or staying alive are also scattered elsewhere throughout the story. Ref — *Keep Yourself Alive* (Queen, 1973).
- The *Black Queen* is referenced for the first time — it is evident that she wields power over the Ploughman, compelling him to wreak havoc without regard to his own survival. It is inferred here that the Black Queen and Lady Belladonna are one and the same. She is, in fact, the very Necromancer long held captive by Lily the Seer. Ref — *March of the Black Queen* (Queen II, 1974).
- The Ploughman has another trick up his sleeve. To his son he cries, 'deploy the parahumanoid.' Ref — *Machines (Or 'Back to Humans')* (The Works, 1984). The terrifying potential of technological advancement is a key unifying element of this scene, as well as the song *Machines*; as with George Orwell's novel, *1984*. A neat thread of connection.
- After the destruction of the pterippi, a storm that has

threatened since early in the tale finally breaks. Blessedly, the rain immediately begins to soothe the forest, ravaged by flames. This is a different, more literal angle on the title of *Put Out the Fire* (Hot Space, 1982). Alternatively, one might imagine that *Rain Must Fall* (The Miracle, 1989).

INTERLUDE: THE LAP OF THE GODS

- Title — ref *In the Lap of the Gods* (Sheer Heart Attack, 1974).
- Anato (The Moon) and Adatar (The Sun) are pivotal figures in this creation story, just as *A Night at the Opera* and *A Day at the Races* were pivotal albums in Queen's career.
- In the religious lore of Rhye, the early moments of Creation are known as the 'Grand Dance'. This was also a name that Brian May initially suggested for the newly formed band.
- Onik, God of Time, is described as 'impetuous', 'impatient' and 'waiting for no direction'. 'Time waits for no one.' Ref — *'Time,'* Freddie Mercury, 1986.
- Marnis creates the Ogres. They are brutal and wild — not at all what Marnis had in mind. Cornavrian helps him, by giving the Ogres a home under a great mountain. The mountain is sealed with a giant shard of the precious mineral, scrallin. Scrallin has the mystical property of storing and refracting light on one face, while being transparent on another. 'The ogre-men are still inside the Two-Way Mirror Mountain ... / You can't see in, but they can see out.' Ref — *Ogre Battle* (Queen II, 1974).
- Anato and Adatar, who begin the Grand Dance together, are eventually estranged, seeking different parts of the heavens in which to dwell. *Opera* and *Races* are considered

by many (including Brian May, once quoted) as being one extended body of work in two parts — a unified phase in Queen's career. Many others, of course, simply see them as two distinct albums.

CHAPTER 12: THE SHAPE OF THINGS

- Title — ref *Funny How Love Is* (Queen II, 1974).
- '*The Lords of old will crumble hence ...*' states Lord Neptune. Later, 'If the Song speaks true, my days may be numbered.' The italicised is a line from the in-story version of The Prophet's Song, which plays upon the lyrical undercurrent of the Queen original. See 'Late, too late, all the wretches run / these kings of beasts now counting their days.' The rulers of the recent age are nearing the end of their dominance. Ref — *The Prophet's Song* (A Night at the Opera, 1975).
- Neptune and Salacia discuss the virtue of succession planning, in times of imminent cataclysm. Neptune says, 'A worthy ruler always plans ahead, Salacia. If not for next year, then for tomorrow.' 'Tomorrow' and 'yesterday' are often used, in modern English, to infer any time in the future, or the past, respectively. This is tangential, but it plays into the lyric 'tomorrow comes, tomorrow brings / tomorrow brings love in the shape of things' from *Funny How Love Is* (Queen II, 1974). It sends a message of optimism in uncertain times. The sentiment also lends itself to the title of the chapter.
- Neptune immerses his trident in the water, immediately gaining knowledge of all Rhye's Seas. New mentions are given to the Melancholy Blue (ref — *My Melancholy Blues* (News of the World, 1977)) and the Clementine Sea (ref

— 'I ask you to be my Clementine,' *Seaside Rendezvous* (A Night at the Opera, 1975)).

- Neptune realises that the return of Anuvin is upon them, declaring, 'The Rival, he comes.' In the central movement of *Great King Rat* (Queen, 1973), the singer warns us, 'Don't listen to what mama says / Not a word, not a word mama says / Or else you'll find yourself being the rival.' In this song, Mama's message is clearly one of temptation, leading the virtuous and the pure on the path to evil. Freddie Mercury's lyrics seem to capture a more Biblical context; but in-story, we know that Mama (Lady Belladonna, aka The Black Queen) has aligned herself with Anuvin in a quest to liberate Valendyne. The inferences are the same. We will be returning to this lyrical passage once again, later in the story.

CHAPTER 13: WAITING FOR THE SUN

- Title — ref *Doing All Right* (Queen, 1973)
- The scene opens to our protagonists facing an uncertain, though likely grim, future. This echoes the sentiment of *Doing All Right* (Queen, 1973). The group have just survived a near-death experience, with a large-scale assault on Petrichor ('Yesterday, my life was in ruin.') Meadow stares out the window, returning his attention to a table of glum and introspective companions ('Looking round to find the words to say / Should be waiting for the skies to clear ...').
- A passing reference is made to *Blurred Vision*, B-Side to *One Vision* (A Kind of Magic, 1986).
- 'Everyone faced unattended bowls of cold soup.' Ref — 'When the soup is cold on your table,' *Ogre Battle* (Queen II, 1974). Just a subtle nudge that the narrative is drawing

our heroes closer to the tale's crescendo ('That is a sign ...').

- 'The barman, a lugubrious butterfly named Sammy ... looked like he'd rather be anywhere else.' A glimpse into the life of Sammy, from the Emerald Bar, in *Spread Your Wings* (News of the World, 1977).
- Lord Oberon and Lady Titania have died. A preternatural storm brews — one that seems born of darkness. 'Someone ... shamed the king in all his pride / Changed the winds and wronged the tides.' Meanwhile, Mustapha is gravely ill, seemingly destined to an early grave. 'Mother Mercury, look what you've done to me / I cannot run, I cannot hide.' Ref — *My Fairy King* (Queen, 1973).
- There follows a brief exchange, playing directly on the title of *Doing All Right* (Queen, 1973).
- Harold recounts his adventure of recent days. He describes zipping through the forest, wondering how best to aid his friends. '*Take heart, my friend. You're not alone*,' are his thoughts, in contemplation of Mustapha, who is currently in the clutches of Lady Belladonna. He follows the guidance of the stars as they wink at him through the treetops. Ref — 'Take heart my friend, we love you / Though it seems like you're alone / A million lights above you / Smile down upon your home' from *Long Away* (A Day at the Races, 1976), by Brian (Harold) May.
- Harold inadvertently encounters The Ploughman, ploughboy, and the Mayor of Petrichor, in the forest. They are returning from the Ceremony of the Nut. In the darkness, Harold can hear them, but only make out their darkened shapes ... or *silhouettes*. 'I see a little silhouetto of a man —' Ref *Bohemian Rhapsody* (A Night at the Opera, 1975).

- The Mayor's name is revealed to be Scaramouch. A little later, Scaramouch calls the Ploughman by name — Figaro. Figaro is outlining his alliance with Belladonna, and the scheme to resurrect Valendyne. A new world order is in the making; the Ploughman wants to know if he can count on the Mayor to remain his ally. 'I ask you then, Scaramouch: Will you dance alongside us?' is, of course, 'Scaramouch, Scaramouch, will you do the fandango?' from *Bohemian Rhapsody* (A Night at the Opera, 1975).
- Scaramouch declines the offer with a sneer. 'Give me your gold, Figaro, but you can keep your special brand of claptrap.' See — 'My money, that's all you want to talk about / I can see what you want me to be / But I'm no fool ...' Ref *In the Lap of the Gods... Revisited* (Sheer Heart Attack, 1974).
- 'Would you like to see?' might conjure up the same line from *Great King Rat* (Queen, 1973), implying that Figaro is also something of a 'dirty old man'.
- Back at the Inn, Harold is still recounting his tale — now to a much larger crowd. A random pixie cries, 'Won't you tell us all about it?' to which the dragonfly responds, 'I shall! Never in your life have you seen anything like it ... It was a journey to heaven and back.' See 'You've never seen nothing like it, no never in your life / Like going up to heaven and then coming back alive / Let me tell you all about it / And the world will so allow it ...' Ref — *March of the Black Queen* (Queen II, 1974).
- Harold recounts what he saw, flying with the pterippi. Amongst his visions, he sees 'undines singing atop glittering lilyponds' ('water babies singing in a lily pool delight'). He also witnesses peril. This includes sighting Mustapha, prostrate in prayer, while held in the thrall of Belladonna.

By way of background: 'Powder monkeys' were youths used essentially as slaves, to run dangerous goods — usually explosive powder on the gun decks of ships — in the Age of Sail. Here, Belladonna uses Mustapha as her slave to run dangerous errands, ferrying her goods from all over the land. He is blue — or depressed and upset — by the knowledge of his own fate, hence his late-night prayer. In summary: we can consider Mustapha a 'blue powder monkey, praying in the dead of night' if we draw a long enough bow. Ref — *March of the Black Queen* (Queen II, 1974).

- We are reminded that the Fairy Feller is out there, somewhere, undertaking his final mission under the Fairy King.
- Meadow offers Leith Lourden some famous 'Rhye' whiskey. 'It'll put stars in your eyes and ants in your pants.' Ref — *Modern Times Rock 'n' Roll* (Queen, 1973).

CHAPTER 14: STARS OF LOVINGNESS

- Title — ref *White Queen (As it Began)* (Queen II, 1974).
- The scourge of the Pox is unleashed on Rhye, forcing the helpless to flee across the land, through an impending storm. 'And two by two my human zoo / They'll be running for to come / Running for to come out of the rain.' Ref — *The Prophet's Song* (A Night at the Opera, 1975).
- Traversing Banwah Haunte, the group find themselves being led by a mysterious raven. It leads them onward, using a charm of destination. This is another subtle narrative nudge: 'And if the black crow flies, to find a new destination / That is a sign.' Ref — *Ogre Battle* (Queen II, 1974).
- Meadow and Torr Yosef discuss mortality. The golem asks, <*Are you afraid of dying?*> to which Meadow replies, 'I sure

as hell don't want to die ... Sometimes, I figure it'd be easier if I'd never been —' This incomplete thought is a spin on 'I don't want to die / I sometimes wish I'd never been born at all,' ref — *Bohemian Rhapsody* (A Night at the Opera, 1975). The sentiment could also be quite fitting for Mustapha ... only he remains comatose, at this point.

- In a trance, Mustapha approaches the Halls of Pox. The night is still, with only the barest ruffle from the leaves of trees. A Lady emerges on the high balcony. She holds incredible beauty and power, while mourning her own destiny. The passage is intended to evoke one of Brian May's most mystical and powerful lyrical passages — the opening verse of *White Queen (As it Began)* (Queen II, 1974). The night air is illuminated in her presence. She carries 'a plethora of pinpoint lights' (or perhaps 'stars of lovingness') in her hair. Surely, these are a sign of blessing from the Gods.
- Mustapha climbs the tower, to be nearer this incredible being. His mouth is dry. He remains spellbound, unable to hail her in his awe. Read on: 'And 'neath her window have I stayed / I loved the footsteps that she made / And when she came / White Queen how my heart did ache / And dry my lips, no word will make.' Ref — *White Queen (As it Began)* (Queen II, 1974).
- The being is confirmed to be the April Lady, or the long-lost Lady Maybeth Giltenan.
- A newly awoken Mustapha re-joins his friends, finding them in the throes of conflict against a throng of lethal redcaps. 'Looks like I'm dead on time ...' he says. Ref — *Dead on Time* (Jazz, 1978).
- 'Look — winged boots!' cries Meadow, referencing the ear-

ly scene, of their meeting in Petrichor. Again, we see the image of Freddie in our heads; either on the 'Opera' Tour of 1975/76, or in the *Bohemian Rhapsody* video.

- Mustapha obliterates the enemy by unfurling his new-found weapon — a seismic voice. It carries the sound of an abbey choir — a reference to Freddie's ability to create perfect harmonies, by overdubbing his own voice.
- At the end of the chapter, Lord Ponerog hurls himself into a vat of the foetid essence of the Pox. He is overcome by his own plague, enduring several hideous afflictions. In essence, within a few moments, he suffers the entire gamut of syphilis. He was probably about the age of forty-four at the time. Ref — *Great King Rat* (Queen, 1973).

CHAPTER 15: BLOOD OF MY VEINS

- Title — ref *My Fairy King* (Queen, 1973).
- Will and Mustapha, together at last, lie together. Will says, 'It stopped raining.' This is foreshadowing for a later chapter, though here the couple discuss the implications of changes in the weather. Ref — *Nevermore* (Queen II, 1974).
- Mustapha describes the way in which the puissance of the White Queen pervaded his body. Her blessed energy crackles in the 'blood of [his] veins.' Ref — *My Fairy King* (Queen, 1973).
- The conversation turns to love. Will seeks commitment, naming the nearby River Bijou his witness. The passage is inspired by *Bijou* (Innuendo, 1991).
- Will declares his love for Mustapha. In a crestfallen moment, Mustapha does not return the sentiment. Inside,

Mustapha's heart cries out to requite his lover, though he recalls the ultimatum of Anuvin. *Kill the one you love.* He hopes to spare Will, by breaking his heart instead. This is also a moment of foreshadowing. Ref — *Nevermore* (Queen II, 1974).

- The reconnaissance team returns, with bad news. Harold reports 'trouble in the east,' while Leith confirms 'trouble in the west,' as well. Ref — *The Hitman* (Innuendo, 1991).
- The following day, the company make new travel plans. They will head for the Vultan Peaks, within to find the sylphic stronghold, Wintergard. The name of the range is a direct nod to Prince Vultan, ruler of the Winged Hawkmen, in *Flash Gordon*.
- Mustapha will use his new gift of speed to go on ahead of his companions. By way of farewell, Will offers him some sentimental lines. They are inspired by *Love of My Life* (A Night at the Opera, 1975).
- As Mustapha disappears in the distance, Will utters, 'Easy come, easy go,' in reference to *Bohemian Rhapsody* (A Night at the Opera, 1975).

CHAPTER 16: ROCK OF AGES

- Title — ref *Brighton Rock* (Sheer Heart Attack, 1974).
- The Golems are pious — subservient to their Gods, who they see as delivering their divine destiny. This maps to the opening lyrics of *In the Lap of the Gods* (Sheer Heart Attack, 1974): 'I live my life for you / Think all my thoughts of you and only you / Everything you ask I do, for you … Leave it in the lap of the gods / What more can I do?' There

is irony, in such powerful beings being hamstrung by their blind faith.

- The frenzy of Anuvin's arrival can be accompanied beautifully by the tumultuous opening of *In the Lap of the Gods* — Roger Taylor's scream, swirling guitars and a rising crescendo. Picture an eruption of light and magic, over a cavernous pool, deep in the earth.
- As Anuvin addresses the Golems, he can be thought of as the voice for the second verse of *Seven Seas of Rhye* (Queen II, 1974): 'Can you hear me, you peers and privy councillors / I stand before you naked to the eyes / I will destroy any man who dares abuse my trust / I swear that you'll be mine …' he comes as conqueror. The first verse belongs, more properly, to the Black Queen; the final two verses, to Mustapha … but we'll come back to that later.
- In the light of revelations, the Golems prepare to defend Warnom Bore. They know they are outmatched, burdened by reluctance to strike at a God. *STOMP-STOMP-MASH* is the sound of stamping feet and pounding fists … an approximation of the beat to *We Will Rock You* (News of the World, 1977).
- After escaping the destruction of Warnom Bore, Anuvin meets with the Black Queen. She appears to him first as a black pterippus, coming from above. Now, her motive becomes more apparent: 'Fear me, you Lords and Lady preachers / I descend upon your earth from the skies / I command your very souls, you unbelievers / Bring before me what is mine / The Seven Seas of Rhye.' Ref — *Seven Seas of Rhye* (Queen II, 1974).

CHAPTER 17: ALL THE WRETCHES RUN

- Title — ref *The Prophet's Song* (A Night at the Opera, 1975).
- Dique tinkers with Torr Yosef, exploring his inner workings — much the way John Deacon was inclined to do, as a student of electronics.
- The refugees pass by in great number, fleeing the plague and floods of the lowlands — 'all the wretches run', ref *The Prophet's Song* (A Night at the Opera, 1975).
- Trixel Tate describes the burgeoning power of the White Queen as 'some kind of magic', ref *A Kind of Magic* (song & album, 1986).
- Dique and Meadow are recruited as Fae knights. Meadow is tasked with leading the drum corps, therefore pacing the march across the Haunte. A nod to our drum hero, Roger Meddows Taylor.

CHAPTER 18: THE AIR YOU BREATHE

- Title — ref *Father to Son* (Queen II, 1974).
- Mustapha and Harold meet in Wintergard with Bastian Sinotar. Here begins a thread of great revelation. The General Prime wants them to know of the great truths that wait to dawn on them both. He urges them to kneel and pray with him. We return to *Great King Rat* (Queen, 1973): 'The great Lord before he died / Knelt sinners by his side / He said, "You're going to realise tomorrow."' This interpretation will be contentious with purists, who see it only as a reference to Jesus Christ, in the Biblical context of Queen's song. In 'The King of Rhye', there are several

figures of sacrifice and martyrdom — Sinotar is certainly amongst them.

- Sinotar brings the pair to witness the Breath of Cornavrian, a sacred gift from the God of Nature. The Horn of Agonies is imbued with the Breath, activating it as not only relic, but devastating weapon. Its potential depends on the hands that wield it. The sylphic race have fought to keep the Breath a secret, locked away until a time of crisis and need. That time is now. The wielder of the Horn is Harold. 'The air you breathe I live to give you,' as it were. Ref — *Father to Son* (Queen II, 1974).

CHAPTER 19: UNTIL THE LONELINESS IS GONE

- Title — ref *Father to Son* (Queen II, 1974).
- Almost all references in this chapter are to this one Queen track, except where noted.
- Sinotar has come to confront Mustapha — to discuss deep truths, to share long-kept secrets. Mustapha believes he knows the situation and confronts the General Prime. To his surprise, he has facts misconstrued. Sinotar abruptly calls for the strangeling to listen — this time, to the truth. 'Funny, you don't hear a single word I say.'
- Sinotar proceeds to explain his past, which gives valid context to the upcoming revelations. 'I fought with you, fought on your side / Long before you were born.'
- Sinotar and Maybeth would meet, away from prying eyes, to conduct their liaison in secret. The place they chose was tucked far in the south of Sontenan — a retreat known as Duck House. This name is shared with a holiday villa in

Montreux, on the shores of Lac Leman in Switzerland. It is known to have been a favoured retreat for Freddie Mercury and appears on the cover of *Made in Heaven* (1995).

- The confirmation finally arrives. Bastian Sinotar is Mustapha's father, while Lady Maybeth — the White Queen — was his mother. This cements the place of *Father to Son* in this tale.
- Loneliness is a recurrent theme shared by several characters, prominently Mustapha and Sinotar. Mustapha has had to disavow his beloved, Will, in a bid to protect him. Sinotar has spent his life apart from Lady Maybeth; initially for political reasons, later due to her disappearance. (Yosef is another, who has just witnessed the genocide of his entire race). *'Until the Loneliness is Gone'* acknowledges that the characters feeling the depths of loneliness long to have it assuaged but cannot.
- Sinotar has prepared a missive, with which to aid Mustapha in his ordained quest … a quest which is prophesied to be a suicide mission. He admits that the letter's contents might be obscure but understanding will come when the time is right. 'Take this letter that I give you / Take it sonny, hold it high / You won't understand a word that's in it / But you'll write it out again before you die.'
- The General Prime reveals he, too, is destined to die — tragically, as a consequence of sharing these enlightenments. Perhaps he sees the letter as a moment shared between himself and his son — something Mustapha can take on his own journey as a tangible item, once Sinotar has died. 'My letter to you will stay by your side / Through the years, till the loneliness is gone.'

CHAPTER 20: QUEEN OF THE NIGHT

- Title — ref *March of the Black Queen* (Queen II, 1974).
- Amidst the war host of the Black Queen are Anuvin's rock titans — creatures birthed from the shattered rubble of the Peaks of Light. These rock titans might represent the huge names in rock who were Queen's contemporaries and inspirations — Hendrix, Cream, David Bowie, Led Zeppelin, and many others. All are on the march to the battlefield, but who will prevail?
- The remainder of the host are Necromancers and the undead, a raucous swarm of creatures who sing and dance wildly as they follow in their leader's wake. They pillage and ruin as they come. 'Here comes the Black Queen, poking in the pile / Fie-fo the Black Queen, marching single file ...' even the sing-song nature of this lyric speaks to the jeering attitude of this evil army. I have attempted to capture some of this sinister playfulness in my own singalong song. The prowess of the Black Queen is undeniable — 'I reign with my left hand, I rule with my right / I'm Lord of all darkness, I'm Queen of the Night / I've got the power / Now do the march of the Black Queen.' Ref — *March of the Black Queen* (Queen II, 1974).
- Anuvin speaks to Bastian Sinotar of the plight of refugees. Sinotar describes those who flee as survivors — 'Those who yearn to see *an end to War.*' A miracle, perhaps? Ref — *The Miracle*, from the album of the same name (1989).
- The Black Queen wields her formidable persuasive powers, attempting to latch on to Mustapha's mind and prey on his previous fealty. At first, her ploy seems to be working. 'My life is in your hands, I'll fo and I'll fie / I'll be what you

make me, I'll do what you like / I'll be a bad boy, I'll be your bad boy ...' et cetera.

- Ultimately, Mustapha proves that he has become master of his own destiny. 'I am slave to nobody!' This is reminiscent of the second verse of *In the Lap of the Gods ... Revisited* (Sheer Heart Attack, 1974): 'You say I (you can do it) / Can't (you can do it) / (You can go and set him free) Set you free from me / But that's not true!'
- The Black Queen ends up with a steaming clod of *mud on her face*. What a big disgrace! Ref — *We Will Rock You* (News of the World, 1977).
- 'Miserable stripling! Valendyne has a special place in the fires of the Afterlife, set aside for you!' is the equivalent of 'Beelzebub has a devil set aside for me!' Ref — *Bohemian Rhapsody* (A Night at the Opera, 1975).
- 'You pigheaded crone!' I had the vitriol from *Death on Two Legs (Dedicated to ...* (A Night at the Opera, 1975) in my head. 'Misguided old mule, with your pigheaded rules ...' Hatred and eloquence combined.
- The Black Queen's final monologue, beginning 'Your legacy is dust!' through to 'Forever!' is a celebration of that glorious extra verse which finishes *March of the Black Queen* (Queen II, 1974).
- Towards the close of the chapter, the Vrendari appear in a bid to counter-strike. Feel free to let *Vultan's Theme (Attack of the Hawk Men)* (Flash Gordon OST, 1980) play in your head here.
- The last laugh shall be the Black Queen's. 'Is that ... is that a dragon?' mutters Dique. Why, naturally. Ref — *Dragon Attack* (The Game, 1980).

CHAPTER 21: LET TRUMPET CRY

- Title — ref *Ogre Battle* (Queen II, 1974).
- The Black Queen, in calamitous form, wreaks havoc over the early stages of the Battle of Rhye. Confirmation of a *Dragon Attack* (The Game, 1980).
- 'Hold the line!' screamed Trixel Tate' — a moment borrowed from *The Show Must Go On* (Innuendo, 1991). Does anybody want to take it anymore?
- To Harold, Bastian Sinotar says, 'Conceal yourself … but keep a lookout.' Those last three words are a nod to *Ogre Battle* (Queen II, 1974). You just know it's coming, don't you?
- Harold wields the Horn of Agonies at last. 'Bugle blower, let trumpet cry.' Ref — *Ogre Battle* (Queen II, 1974).
- The Ogre Battle is on! 'The Ogre-men are coming out / From the Two-Way Mirror Mountain / They're coming up behind and they're running all about / Can't go east 'cause you've gotta go south.' Ref — *Ogre Battle* (Queen II, 1974).
- Several of the Ogres are described, having distinctive features. One has 'one great big eye' with a focus in your direction … Ref — *Ogre Battle* (Queen II, 1974).
- As the Ogres battle the rock titans, the warring armies flee into the south, continuing the fight as they go. The narrative shifts to Meadow, who is speeding through the night on his pterippus. This references *Ride the Wild Wind* (Innuendo, 1991), a Roger (Meddows) Taylor track. The winged horse has eyes that shine, mirroring an otherworldly glow. 'Get your head down baby / We're gonna ride tonight / Your angel eyes are shining bright / I wanna take your hand,

lead you from this place / Gonna leave it all behind, get out of this rat race ... We got freaks to the left / We got jerks to the right ...' et cetera. Meadow's whoop of delight celebrates the exhilaration of the Queen song.

- As the battle moves south, Sinotar is left crippled on the battlefield. Anuvin has left him to the ravages of the Two-Legged Death. Mustapha appears and a long interlude takes place. At the end, Mustapha grants his father's wish for a swift death. He pulls out the Phoenix pistol, which he has carried since leaving Via. 'Mama, just killed a man / Put a gun against his head / Pulled my trigger now he's dead.' Mustapha laments that he barely got to know his father and already, their time has come to a tragic end. 'Mama, life had just begun / But now I've gone and thrown it all away.' Ref — *Bohemian Rhapsody* (A Night at the Opera, 1975).
- Will searches the battleground for Mustapha. He sees him, too far in the distance. He realises that Mustapha goes ahead on his quest and will never be returning. He sings an ode to his lover. This ode draws heavily on the 'quiet' section from *The March of the Black Queen* (Queen II, 1974): 'A voice from behind me reminds me / Spread out your wings you are an angel / Remember to deliver with the speed of light / A little bit of love and joy / Everything you do bears a will and a why and a wherefore / A little bit of love and joy ... Even 'til the end of his life / He'll bring a little love.'

CHAPTER 22: TWO-WAY MIRROR MOUNTAIN

- Title — ref *Ogre Battle* (Queen II, 1974).
- '... his nerves jangled, every muscle ached and his feet seemed buried in leaden boots.' This refers to 'Mama, my

time has come / Sends shivers down my spine / Body's aching all the time' from *Bohemian Rhapsody* (A Night at the Opera, 1975).

- '*So long, everyone. It's time I was facing up to my destiny. I'll see you later ... or not.*' This is a nod to the line 'Goodbye everybody, I've got to go / Got to leave you all behind and face the truth' from *Bohemian Rhapsody* (A Night at the Opera, 1975).
- At the end of the chapter, Mustapha ruminates on whether the long-awaited retribution of the Ogres really makes a difference, if Rhye is still doomed. He wonders 'whether anything truly mattered.' Or perhaps, 'Nothing really matters / Anyone can see / Nothing really matters to me.' Ref — *Bohemian Rhapsody* (A Night at the Opera, 1975).

CHAPTER 23: RAIN STOPPED FALLING

- Title — ref *Nevermore* (Queen II, 1974).
- After emerging from the mountain tunnels, Mustapha sees that the moon and stars are out, and it is not raining. See '... the rain's stopped falling.' Before him lies a gravel trail, or 'the path of Nevermore.' Ref — *Nevermore* (Queen II, 1974).
- It is a cold night on the mountainside, denoted by a 'chill breeze' and 'fresh, crisp air'. The extended night has been referenced here, as with previous chapters; additionally, Salacia notes later that the 'sky has not changed.' This is in reference to 'Soon the cold of night will fall / Summoned by your own hand.' Ref — *The Prophet's Song* (A Night at the Opera, 1975).
- The garden of Nevermore — once known as a beauteous

glade, a natural jewel of the Gods — has been devastated by the presence of Valendyne. All the trees are dead, bleached white, while the earth is scorched black. Likewise, 'Even the valleys below / Where the rays of the sun were so warm and tender / Now haven't anything to grow / Can't you see?' Ref — *Nevermore* (Queen II, 1974).

- *'This is where I die.'* See 'There's no living in my life anymore.' Ref — *Nevermore* (Queen II, 1974).
- 'Oblivious to the thing on the prowl behind him.' A whimsical, entirely random nod to *Man on the Prowl* (The Works, 1984).
- Whilst not a Queen reference per se, a raven makes a sudden appearance as Mustapha wanders deeper into Nevermore. This harks back to the raven's appearance, luring the company, in *Stars of Lovingness* (Chapter 14). Here, it is Mustapha being led against his greater instincts, to the tree of Valendyne. The secondary relevance of this is in reference to Edgar Allan Poe's narrative poem, *The Raven* (1845), in which the titular animal squawks "Nevermore" repeatedly.
- The Two-Legged Death is at last revealed and has its moment of greatest prominence. He may be nothing like the late Norman Sheffield, but he's still a nasty piece of work. Visually, he is at least partially inspired by the creature from the 1997 video game *Queen: The eYe*, by Electronic Arts. Ref — *Death on Two Legs (Dedicated to ...* (A Night at the Opera, 1975).
- One of the Ogres, Mher, emerges from Nevermore, summoned by Cornavrian — a boon granted for the dying Lord Neptune, to assist Rhye's hero. 'Neptune of the Seas / An answer for me please.' Ref — *Lily of the Valley* (Sheer Heart Attack, 1974).

- Mher, like each of the Ogres, harbours a unique natural gift. 'He can swallow up the [ocean].' Ref — *Ogre Battle* (Queen II, 1974).
- Mher drinks the Seventh Sea to dryness, exposing the seabed. 'The Seas have gone dry ...' Ref — *Nevermore* (Queen II, 1974).
- As Mher holds the Seventh Sea within him, the intimation is made that he is ... *Under Pressure* (Hot Space, 1982).
- Mustapha runs with such speed that a boom fills the air, and he runs beyond the sound of his own footfalls. Such is the ability of a supersonic man ... Ref — *Don't Stop Me Now* (Jazz, 1978).

CHAPTER 24: MESSENGER FROM SEVEN SEAS

- Title — ref *Lily of the Valley* (Sheer Heart Attack, 1974).
- A general thread of this chapter is the fantasy/reality theme, most prominently referenced in the opening line of *Bohemian Rhapsody* (A Night at the Opera, 1975).
- In his reverie, 'Jimmy' Fahrenheit meets Jenny one fateful Bank Holiday. This alludes to the first stanza of *Brighton Rock* (Sheer Heart Attack, 1974): 'Happy little day, Jimmy went away / Met his little Jenny on a public holiday.'
- A cheeky, totally unbidden reference to *Sweet Lady* (A Night at the Opera, 1975).
- Fahrenheit and Khashoggi leave the ship. Fahrenheit is confronted by the reality of his hometown for the first time. They make their way across a decaying ghost town — not the bustling hamlet Fahrenheit thought he was living in. He is baffled by everything he sees and is uncer-

tain about what this new reality means for him. There are subtle nods here to *The Show Must Go On* (Innuendo, 1991): 'Empty spaces, what are we living for / Abandoned places, I guess we know the score / On and on, does anybody know what we are looking for?'

- En route, Fahrenheit spies a couple of posters blowing about in the wind. One is calling for sightings of a beloved, missing pet. This is a suggestive reference to Brian May's *All Dead, All Dead* (News of the World, 1977), a song about his cat.
- The pair reach Fahrenheit's business. It is named *The Good Company, Ltd.*, a direct reference to *Good Company* (A Night at the Opera, 1975): 'Reward for all my efforts / My own Limited Company.' It is a place for troubadours — or perhaps entire dixie jazz bands? — to buy and have instruments repaired.
- 'A kettle shaped timpani' lies upturned on the floor of the shop. The timpani formed part of Roger Taylor's drum kit during many of the mid-to-late 1970s tours, up until around 1980.
- A description of Mustapha at the piano follows. It alludes to Freddie Mercury's playing style, with atypical wrist position, striking technique, and hand crossover for playing the opening bars of *Bohemian Rhapsody* (A Night at the Opera, 1975).
- Khashoggi opens the missive that Sinotar gave to Mustapha. Upon it is written one word: *Bismillah*. This word is a well-known lyric from the operatic section of *Bohemian Rhapsody* (A Night at the Opera, 1975).
- As Sinotar predicted, 'You won't understand a word that's

in it,' as sung in *Father to Son* (Queen II, 1974). Mustapha is baffled by the missive's contents. Importantly, there is but a single word on the parchment. This is alluded to numerous times in the track: 'A WORD in your ear / From father to son / Hear THE WORD that I say ... Joyful the sound / THE WORD goes around ... You won't understand A WORD that's in it ... Funny you don't hear A SINGLE WORD I say.' Plainly, it wasn't going to be a very long missive.

- Mustapha practices singing the word *Bismillah*. He is initially unimpressed with his own efforts. 'Bismillah! No, no, no!' echoes the operatic lyrics from *Bohemian Rhapsody* (A Night at the Opera, 1975).
- The Goddess Ophynea appears. She has descended with a message: The seven Sovereigns are all overcome, with the death of Benjulius. The Fae Ring is destroyed and the throne of Rhye will belong to Valendyne unless the fate of the land is otherwise challenged. 'Messenger from Seven Seas has come / To tell the King of Rhye he's lost his throne.' Ref — *Lily of the Valley* (Sheer Heart Attack, 1974). It is this lyric, and this scene, which lend themselves to the title of this entire work.
- Mustapha accepts the holy coronation from Ophynea, who spreads her butterfly wings. Tiny creatures alight upon Mustapha, setting him on fire. Eventually, from the blaze walks the seraph's final incarnation — the King of Rhye. As well as an allusion to the phoenix rising from the ashes, this is also an exploration of that exquisite lyric from *The Show Must Go On* (Innuendo, 1991): 'My soul is painted like the wings of butterflies / Fairy tales of yesterday grow but never die / I can fly, my friends.' The King stands before

his companions, a winged demigod.

- Fahrenheit, in narration, refers to 'that messenger god from Roman myth — Mercury.'
- Mustapha's new golden sceptre is the correlate of Freddie Mercury's sawn-off microphone stand.
- In the end, Fahrenheit decides to join the others in returning to Rhye. Khashoggi's disarming invitation is very much like the final lyrics of *Seven Seas of Rhye* (Queen II, 1974): 'And with a smile / I'll take you to the Seven Seas of Rhye.'

CHAPTER 25: THE KING OF RHYE

- Title — ref *Lily of the Valley* (Sheer Heart Attack, 1974).
- Talk of 'cosmic dust' and 'a false dawn' do not directly reference Queen's work. They are nods to Brian May's long-awaited PhD in Astrophysics: *Radial Velocities in the Zodiacal Dust Cloud.* In fairness, Brian and Roger Taylor's 2008 collaboration with Paul Rogers, *The Cosmos Rocks*, also rates a mention here.
- Further discussion ensues, regarding constellations. The 'Zodiac' theme now crosses over from Brian's PhD to specific formations of stars — Cancer, Leo, and Virgo. Fans might recognise these entities as appearing in Queen's crest, designed by Freddie Mercury — representing the band members' star signs.
- Mustapha appears to have the power to guide Khashoggi's ship by sheer force of will. 'Even now, he guides us safely home,' says Khashoggi. Now we visit the solo works of Freddie Mercury, with *Guide Me Home* (Barcelona, 1988).

- 'Seeing is believing,' says Dique, talking with his companions atop the Pillar. Now it is John Deacon's turn: This is a line from Deacon's track with the Immortals, *No Turning Back* (Biggles: Adventures in Time, 1986).
- Trixel to Leith Lourden: 'I thought you were about to be fried chicken!' references the irreverent closing lyric to *One Vision* (A Kind of Magic, 1986).

EPILOGUE: JOYFUL THE SOUND

- Title — ref *Father to Son* (Queen II, 1974).
- The Epilogue is an homage to the spirit of *One Vision* (A Kind of Magic, 1986). In reading the lyrics of the song, you will see reflected this tale's summation.
- 'You cannot create a land that is utterly without War and Death. These entities will exist forever ...' is closely followed by the promise: 'There is time for peace.' This is a further reference to the lyrics 'Wars will never cease / Is there time enough for peace?' from *Lily of the Valley* (Sheer Heart Attack, 1974).
- With the final two words of the story, we squeeze in one last reference! *Coming Soon* (The Game, 1980).

Was it a worthwhile experience ...?